Robot
Dreams

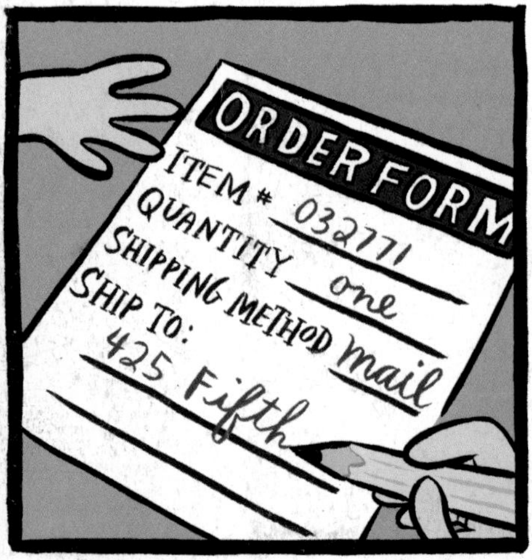
ORDER FORM
ITEM # 032771
QUANTITY one
SHIPPING METHOD mail
SHIP TO:
425 Fifth

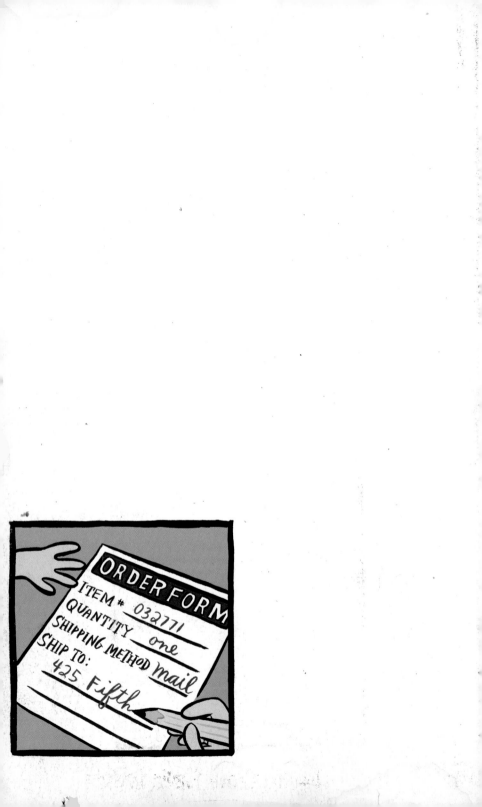

ROBOT DREAMS

Sara Varon

:01
First Second
New York & London

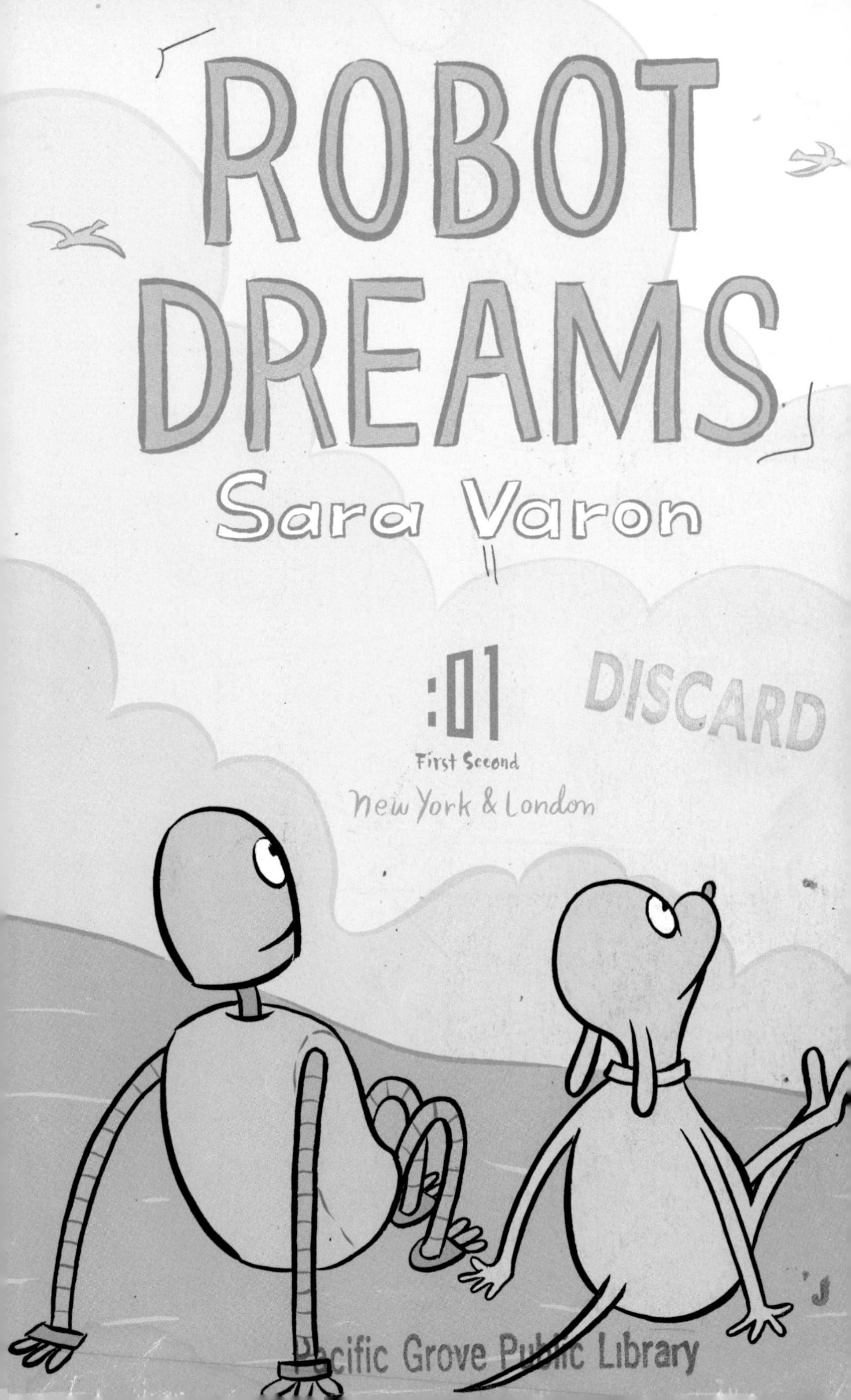

Special thanks to my mom, Maureen Panzera, & Tanya McKinnon

First Second

New York & London

Copyright © 2007 by Sara Varon

Published by First Second
First Second is an imprint of Roaring Brook Press, a division of
   Holtzbrinck Publishing Holdings Limited Partnership
175 Fifth Avenue, New York, NY 10010

Distributed in Canada by H.B. Fenn and Company Ltd.
Distributed in the United Kingdom by Macmillan Children's Books,
   a division of Pan Macmillan.

Cataloging-in-Publication Data is on file at the Library of Congress.

ISBN-13: 978-1-59643-108-9
ISBN-10: 1-59643-108-3

First Second books are available for special promotions and premiums.
For details, contact: Director of Special Markets, Holtzbrinck Publishers.

FIRST EDITION

First Edition
September 2007

Printed in the United States of America

10 9 8 7 6 5 4 3 2

BY ART
WE LIVE

August

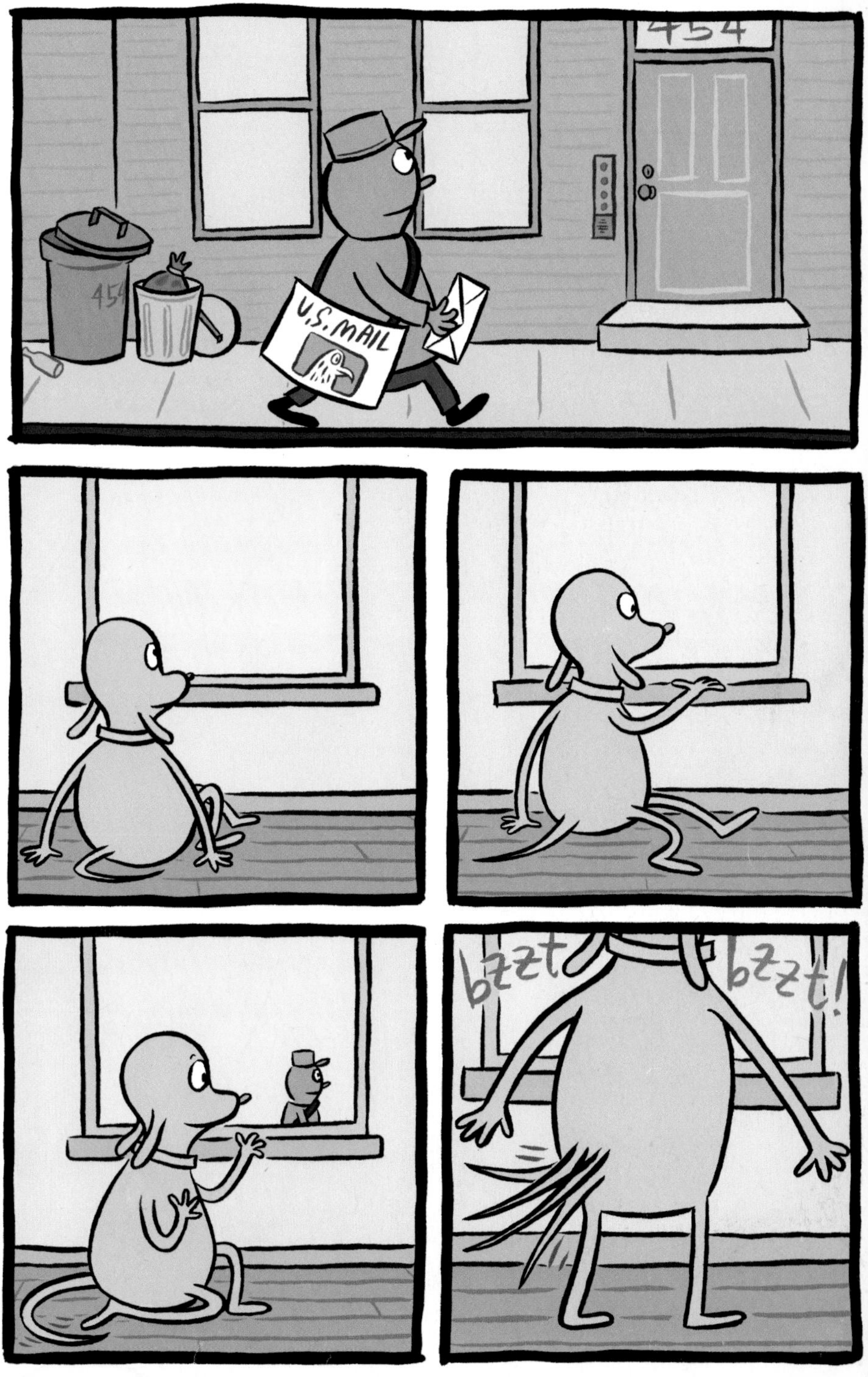
454
454
U.S. MAIL
bzzt
bzzt!

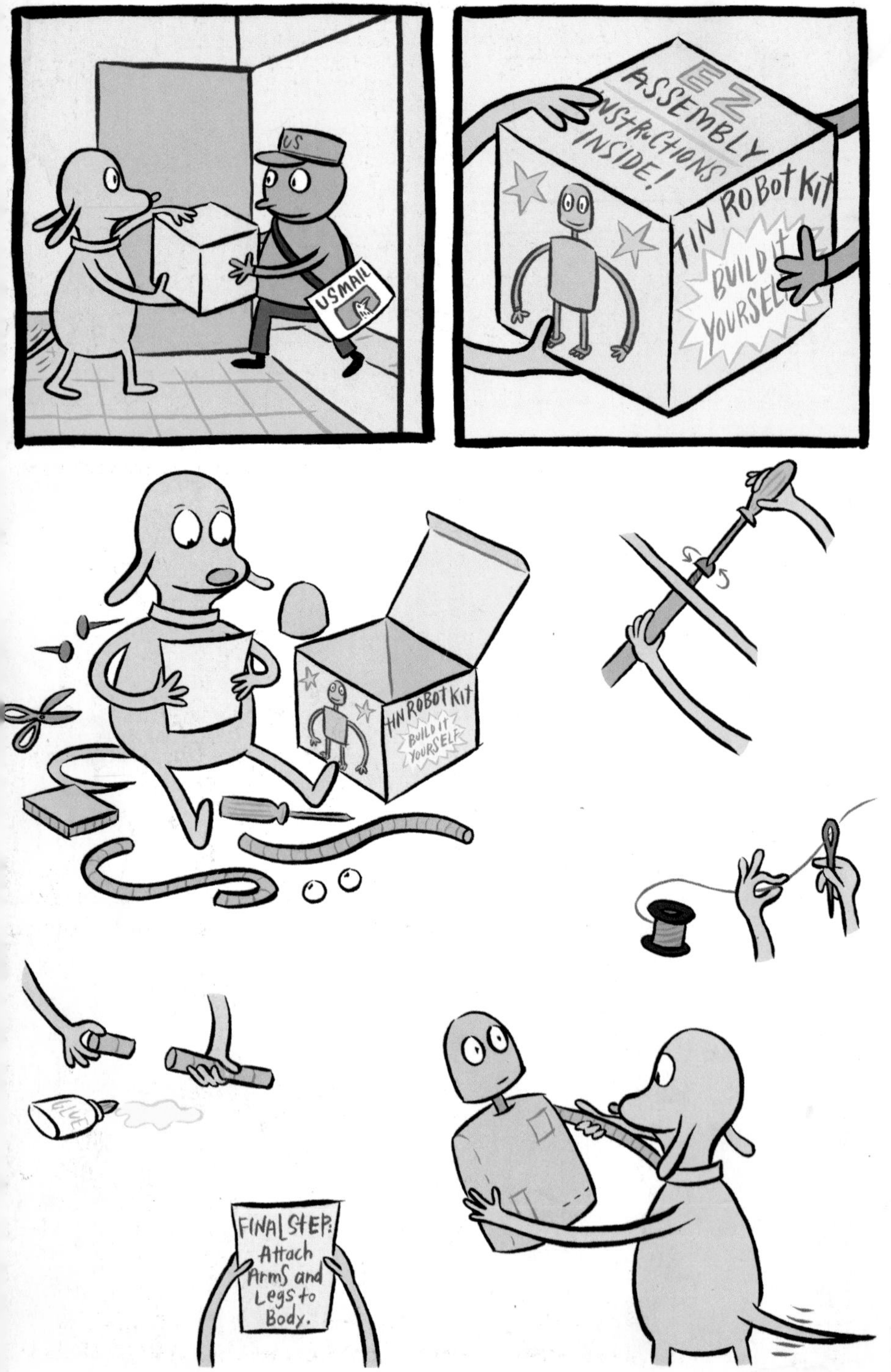
US
US MAIL
EZ ASSEMBLY
INSTRUCTIONS INSIDE!
TIN ROBOT KIT
BUILD IT YOURSELF
TIN ROBOT KIT
BUILD IT YOURSELF
GLUE
FINAL STEP: Attach Arms and Legs to Body.

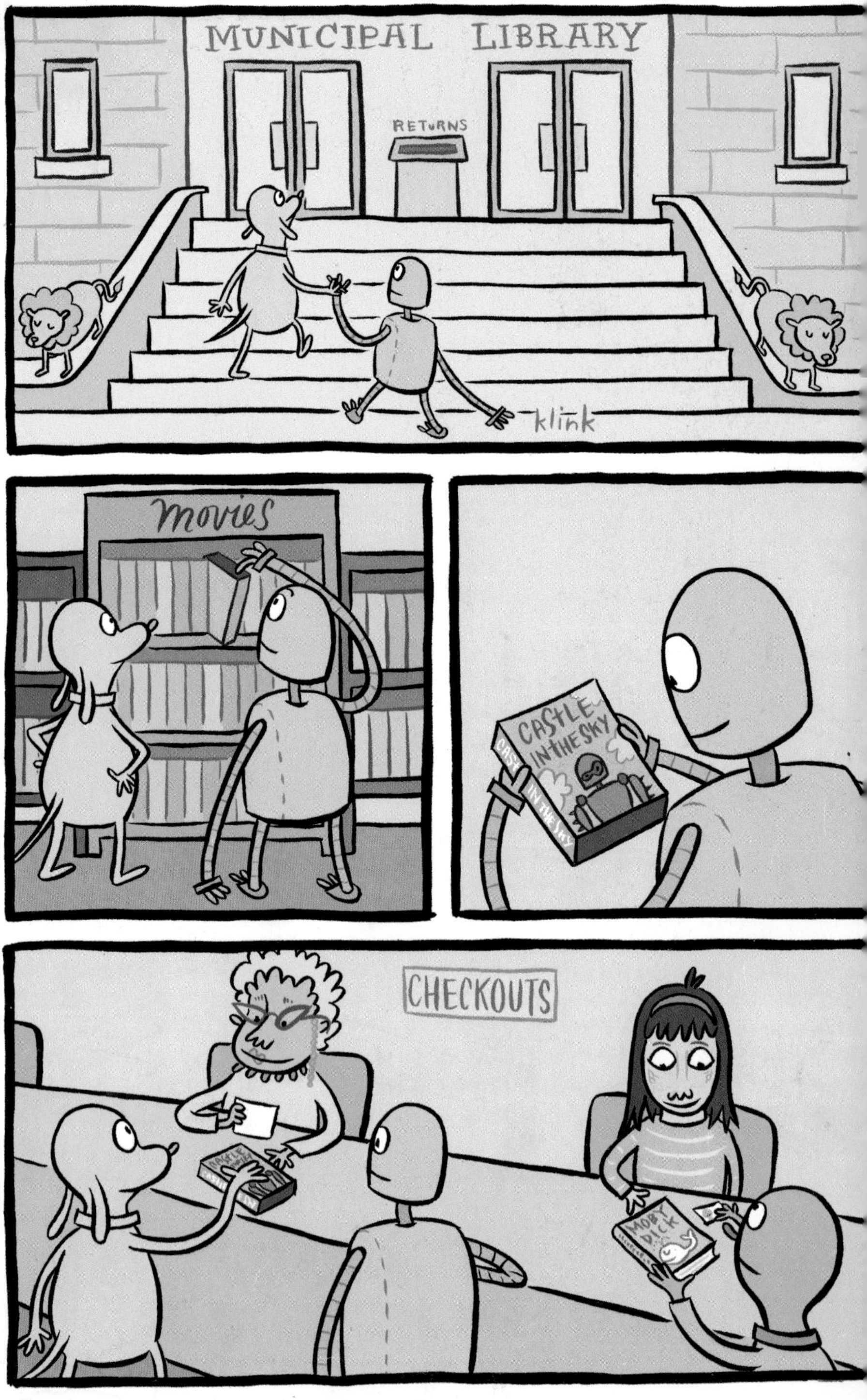
MUNICIPAL LIBRARY
RETURNS
klink
movies
CASTLE IN THE SKY
CHECKOUTS
MOBY DICK

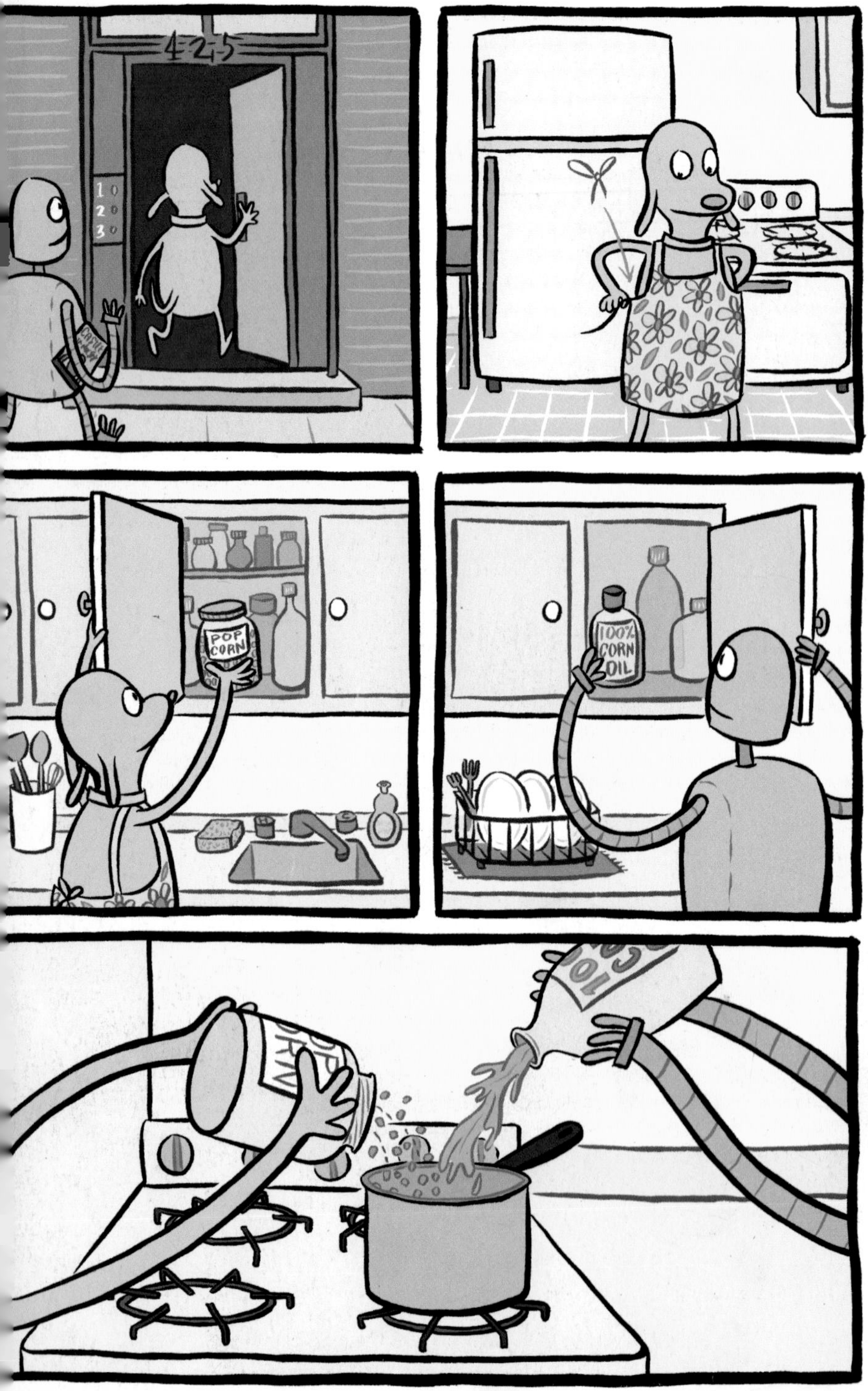
425
1
2
3
POP CORN
100% CORN OIL

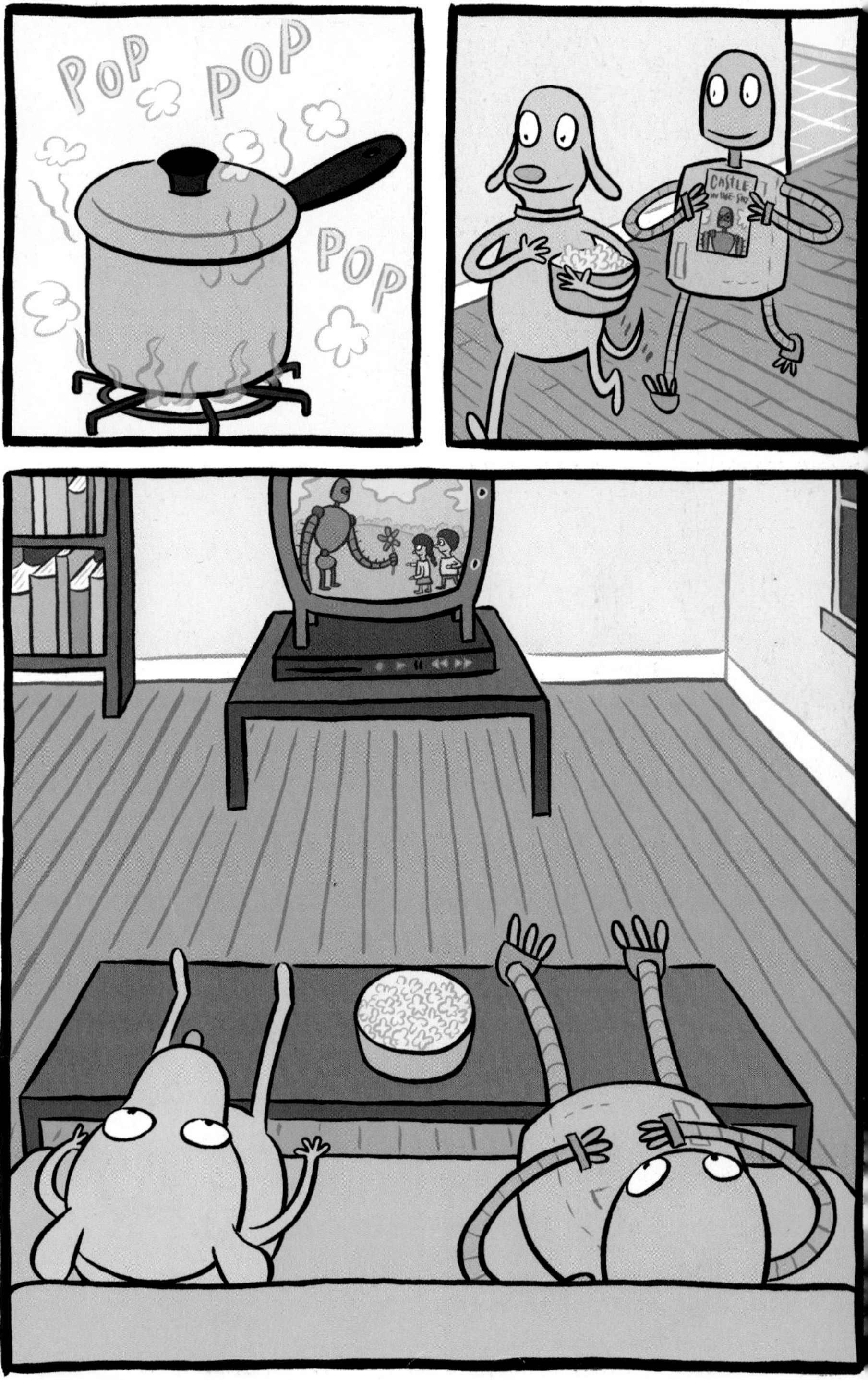
POP POP
POP
CASTLE

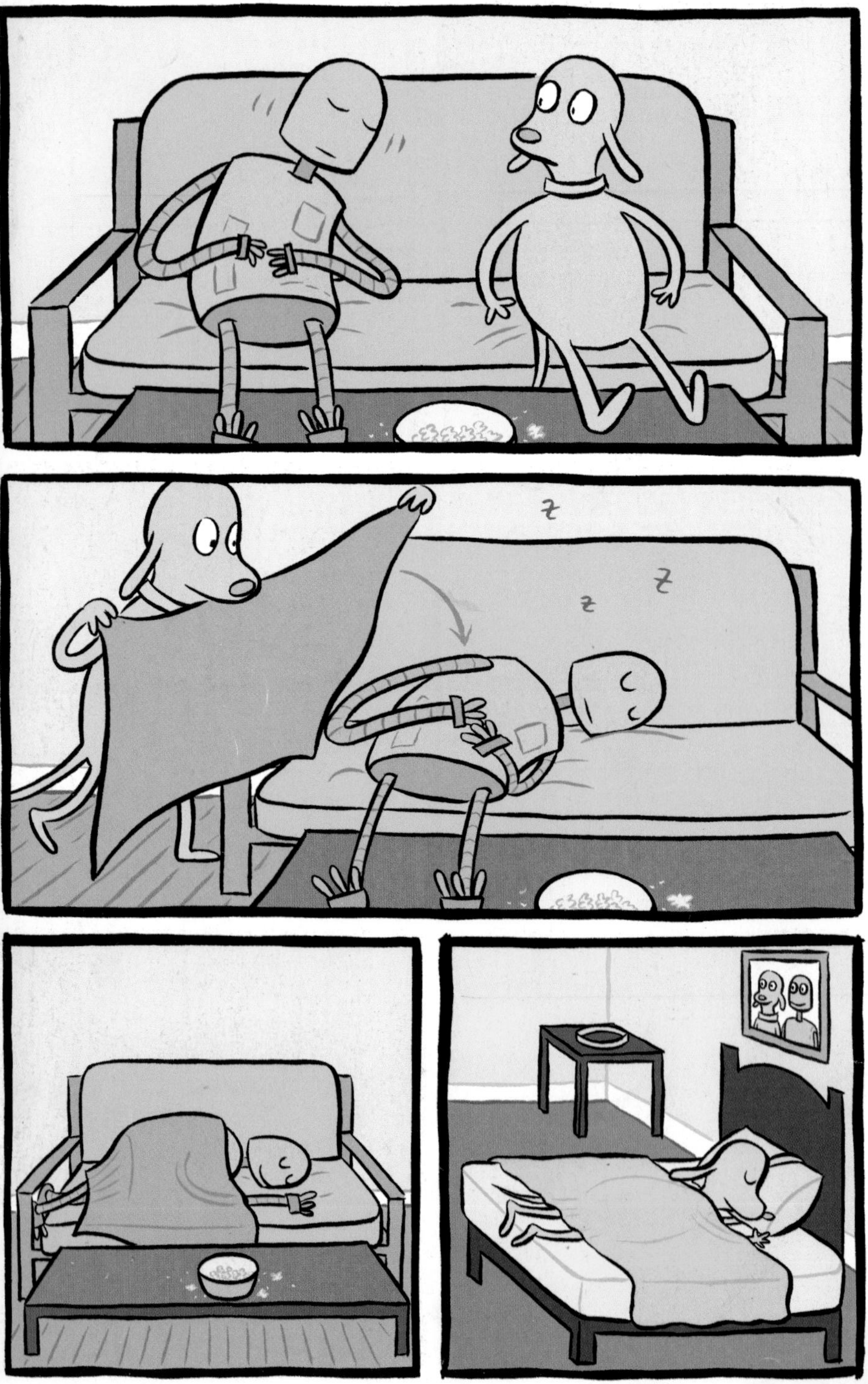
z
z
z

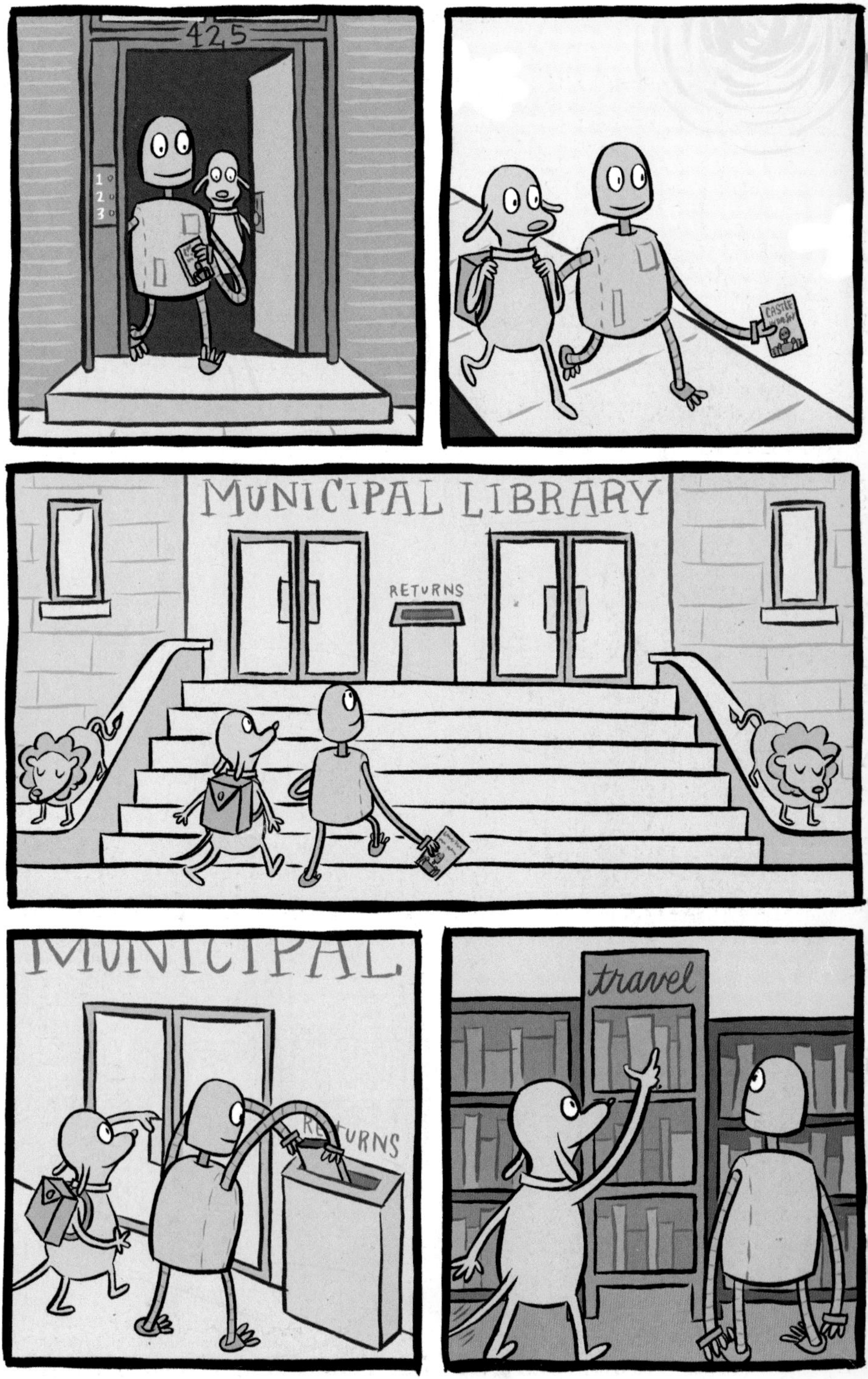
425
1
2
3
CASTLE
MUNICIPAL LIBRARY
RETURNS
MUNICIPAL
RETURNS
travel

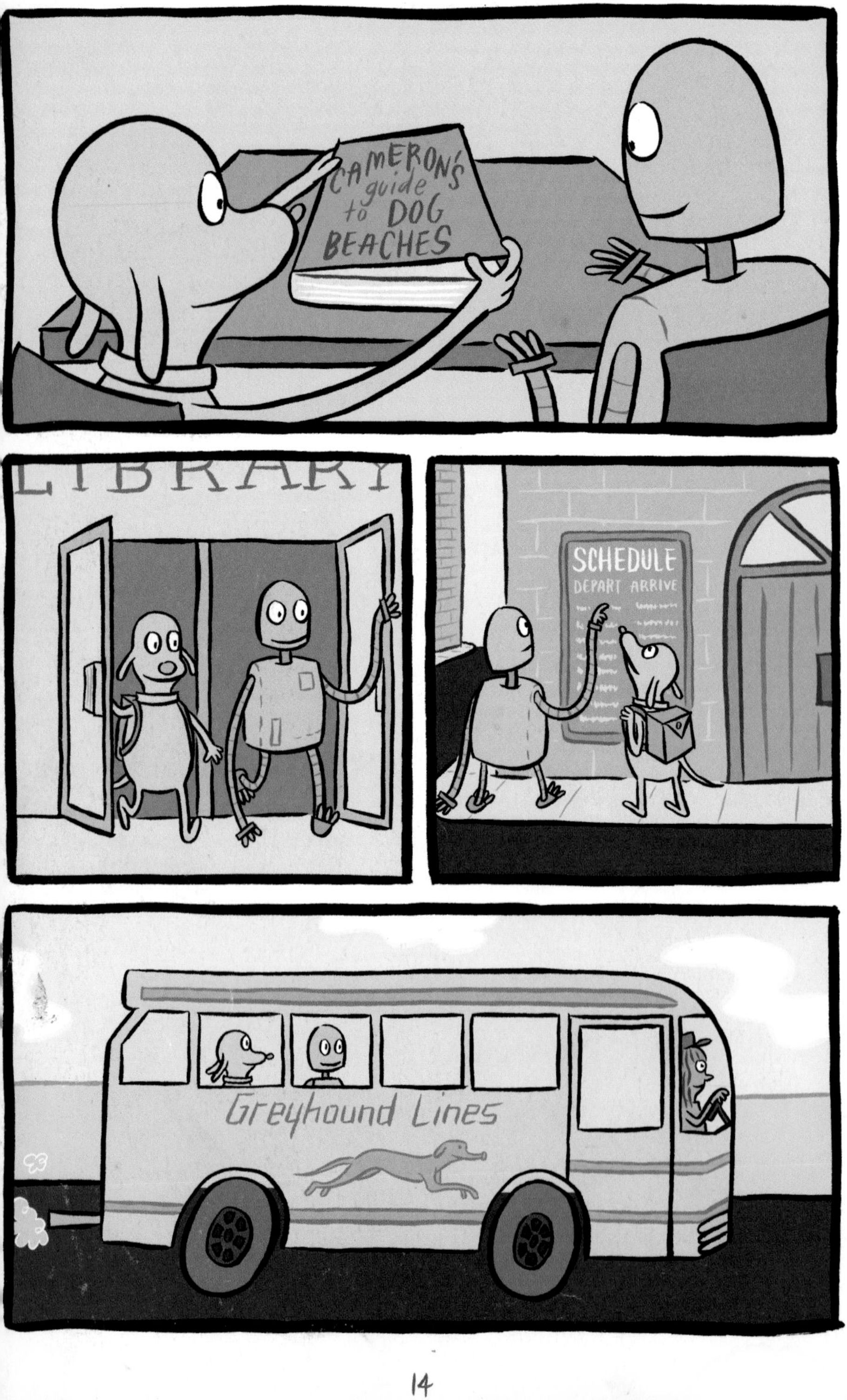
CAMERON'S guide to DOG BEACHES
LIBRARY
SCHEDULE
DEPART ARRIVE
Greyhound Lines

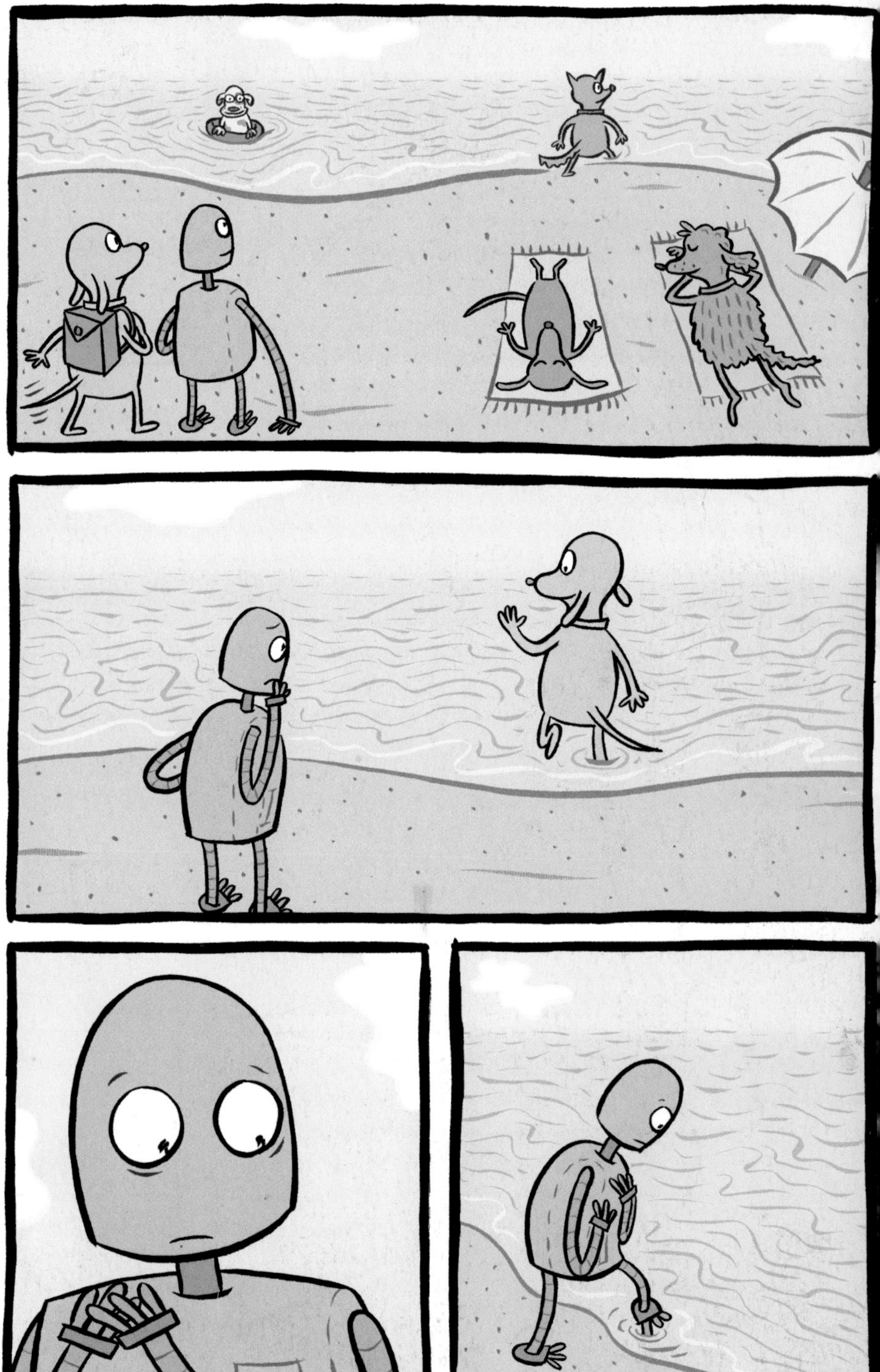

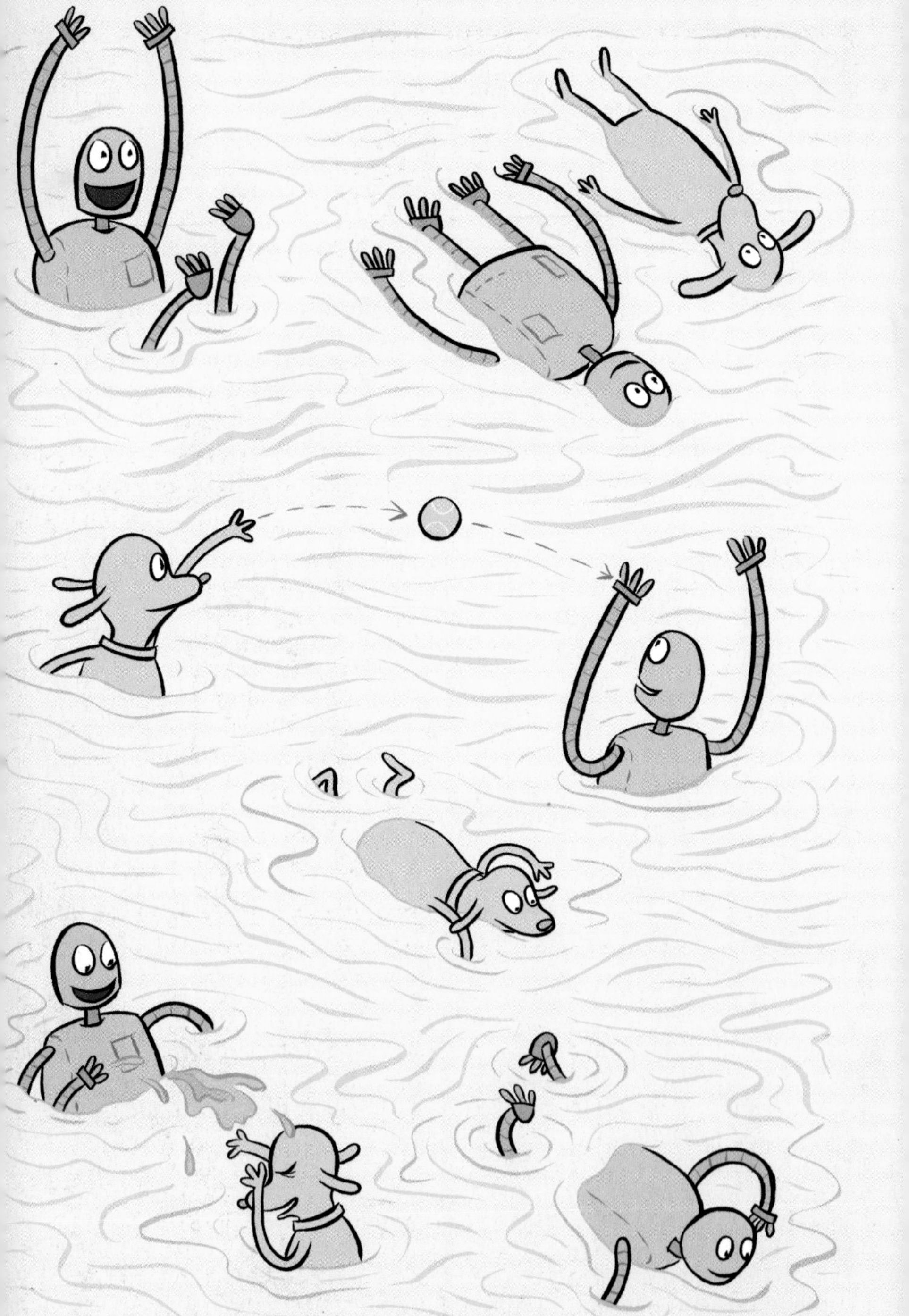

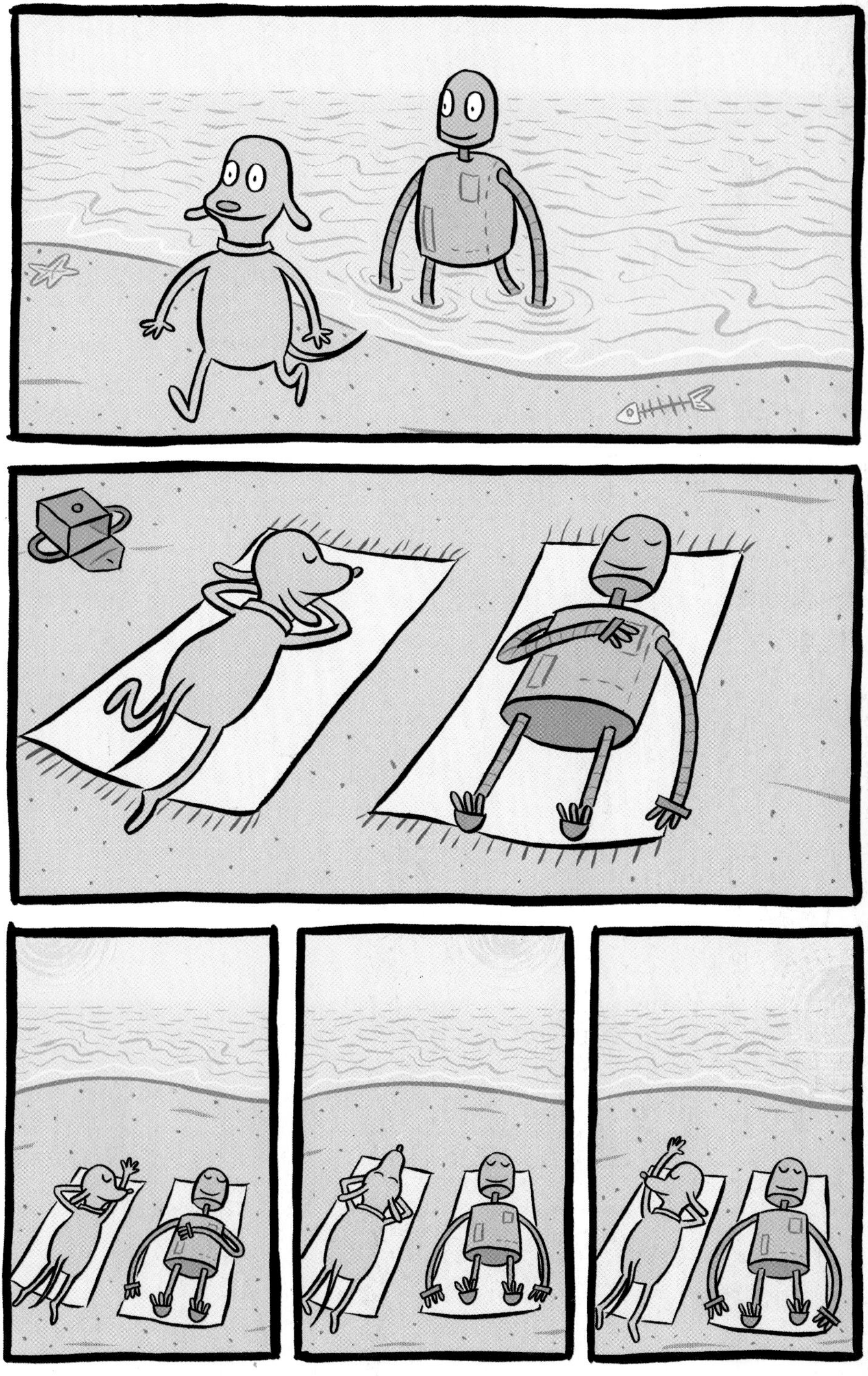

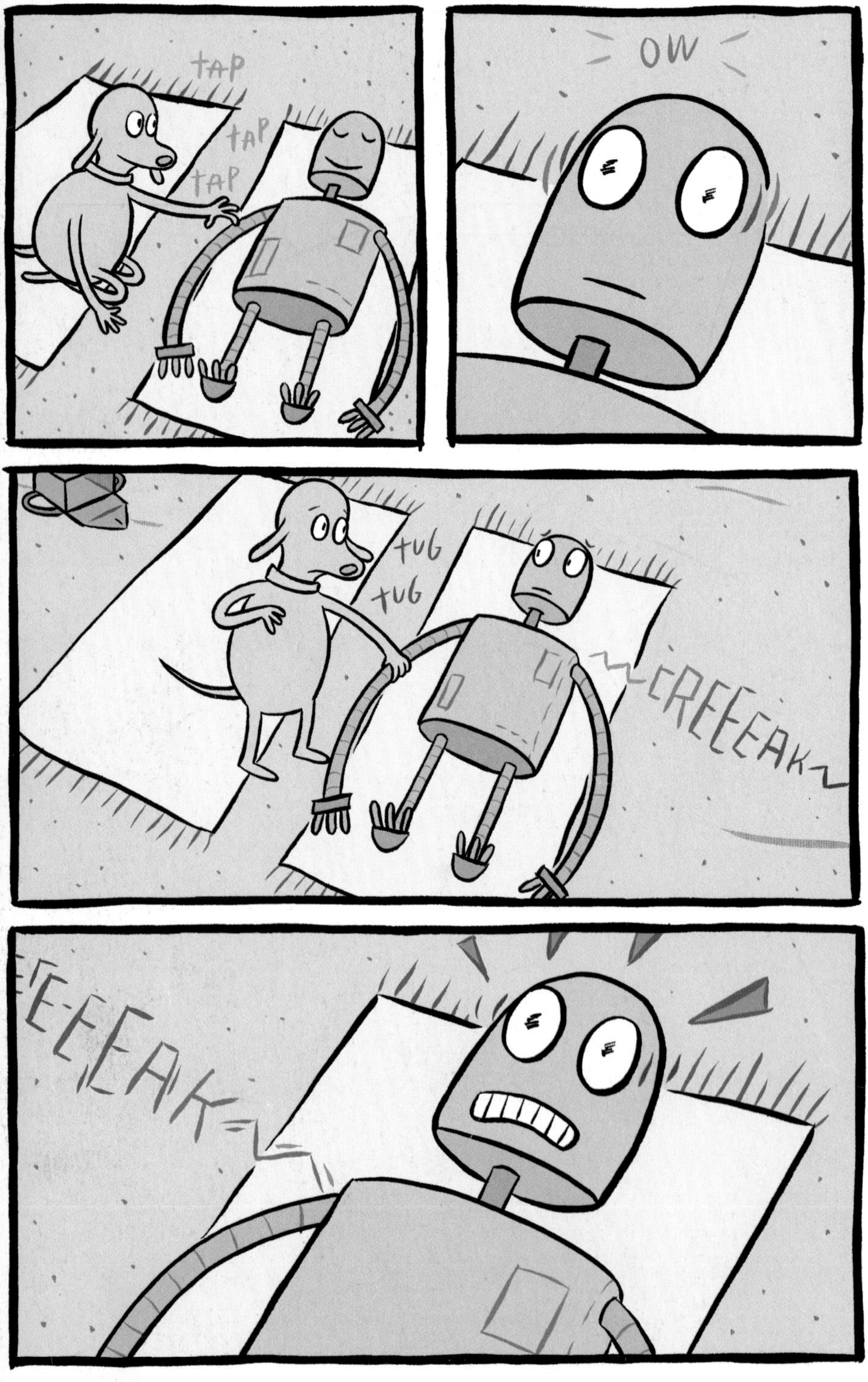
TAP
TAP
TAP
OW
TUG
TUG
CREEEAK
EEEEAK

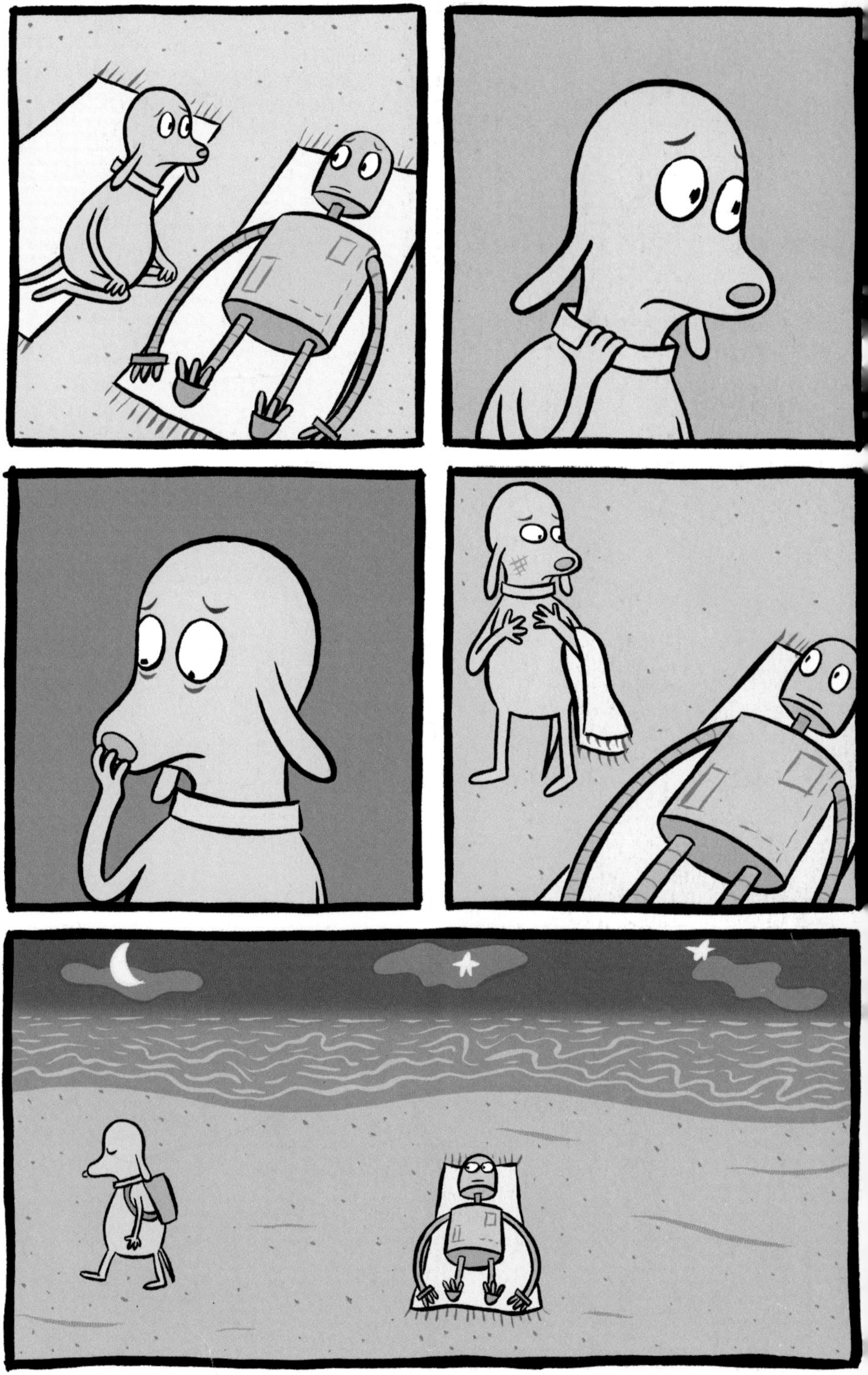

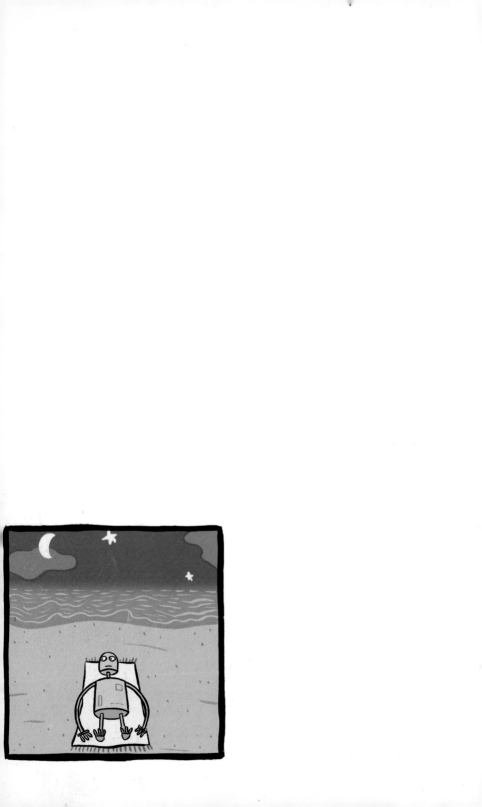

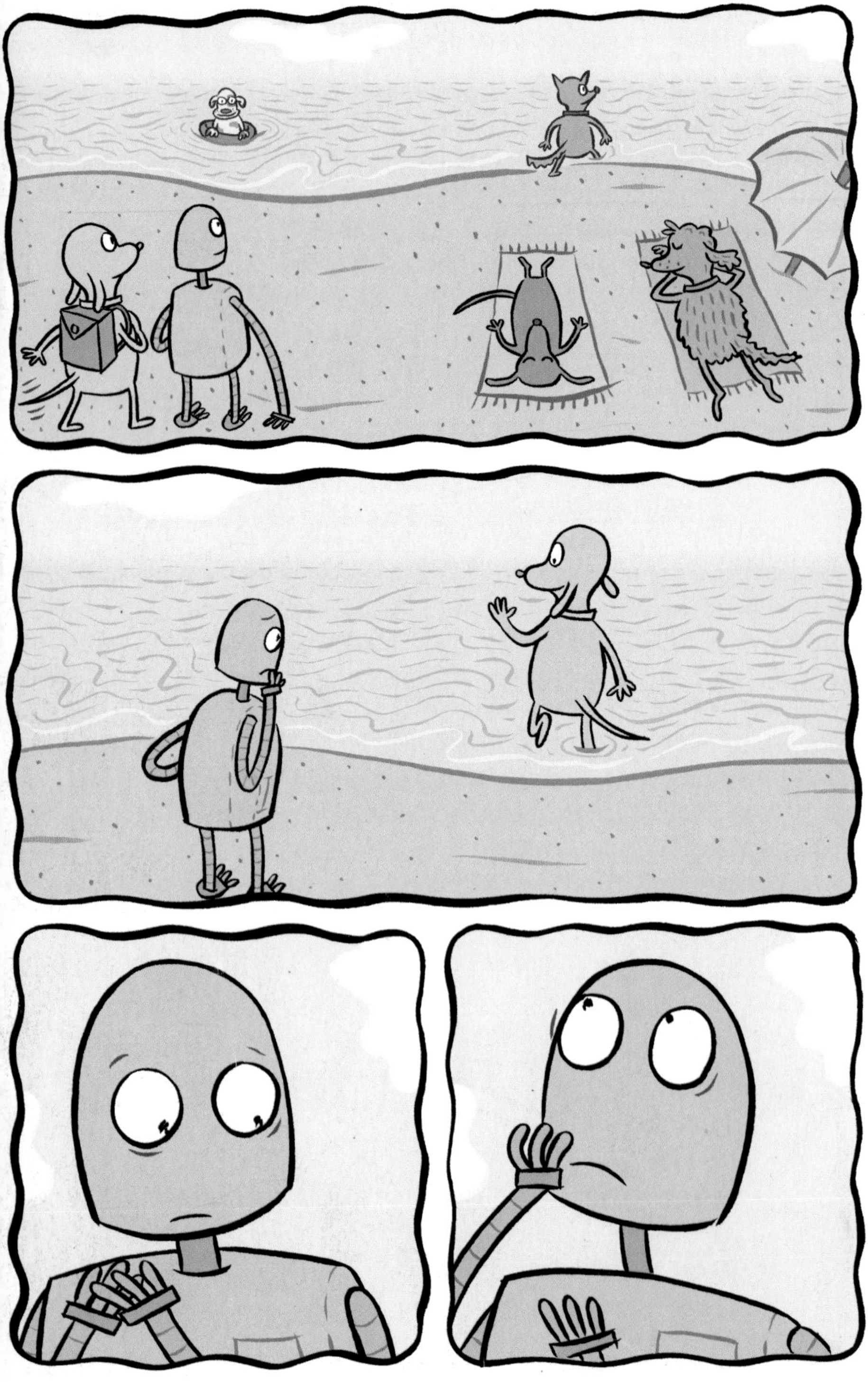

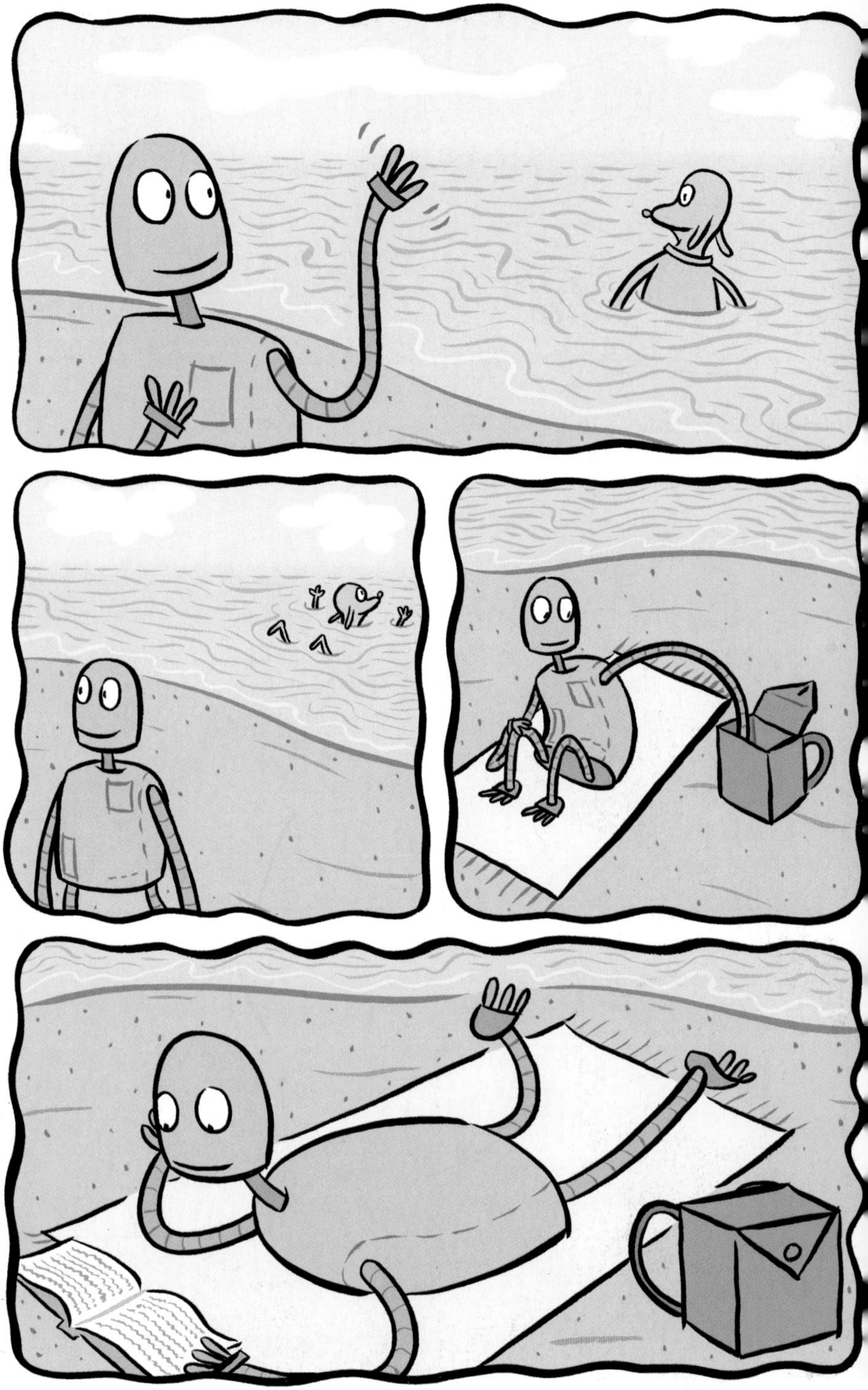

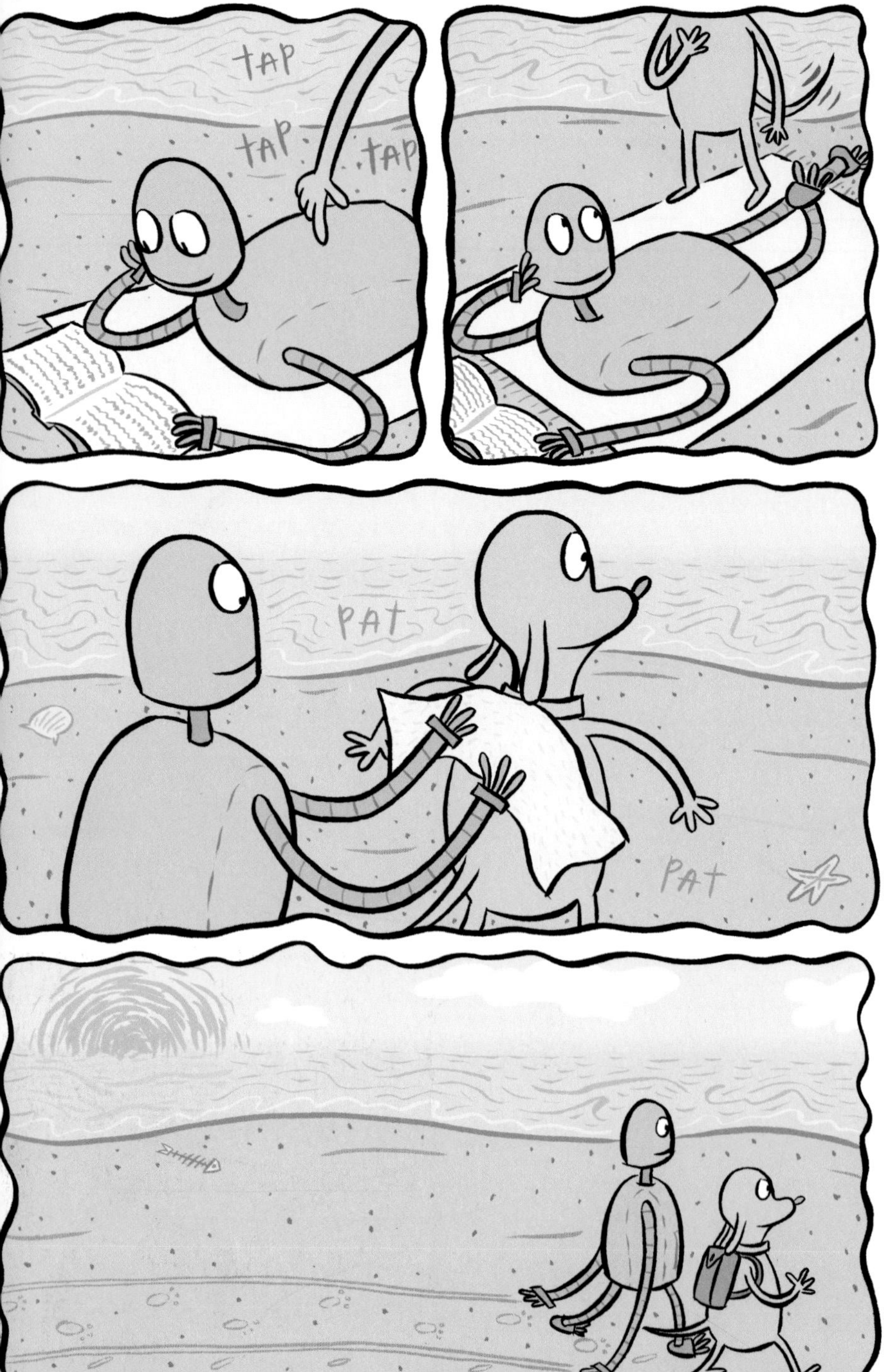
TAP
TAP
TAP
PAT
PAT

September

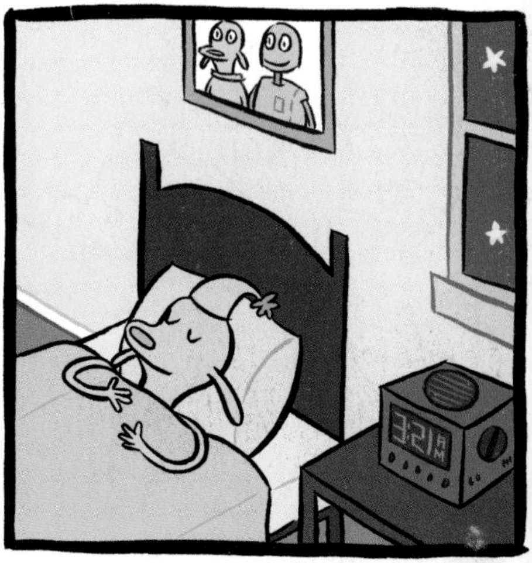
3:21 AM
LO
HI

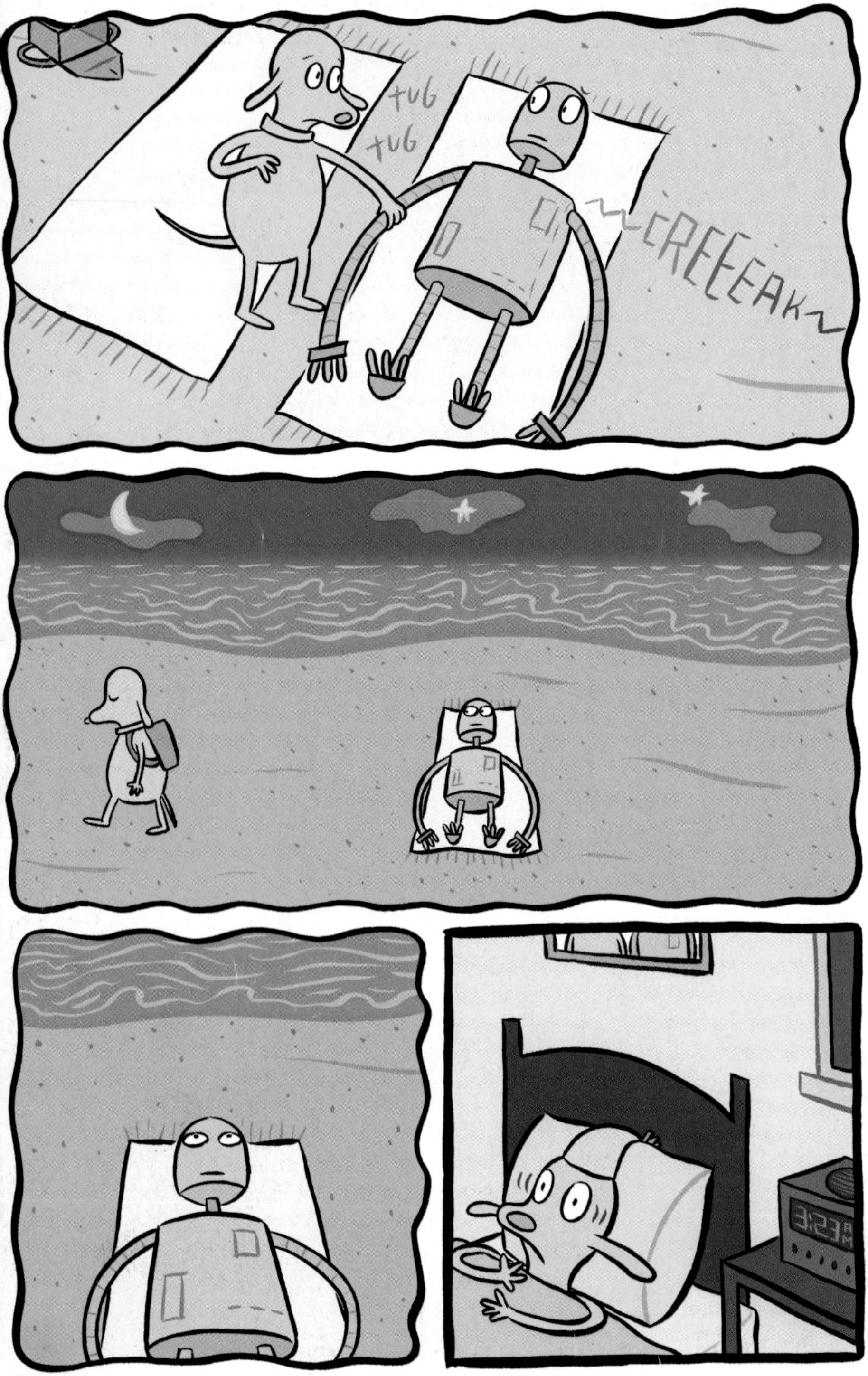
TUG
TUG
CREEEEAK
3:23 AM

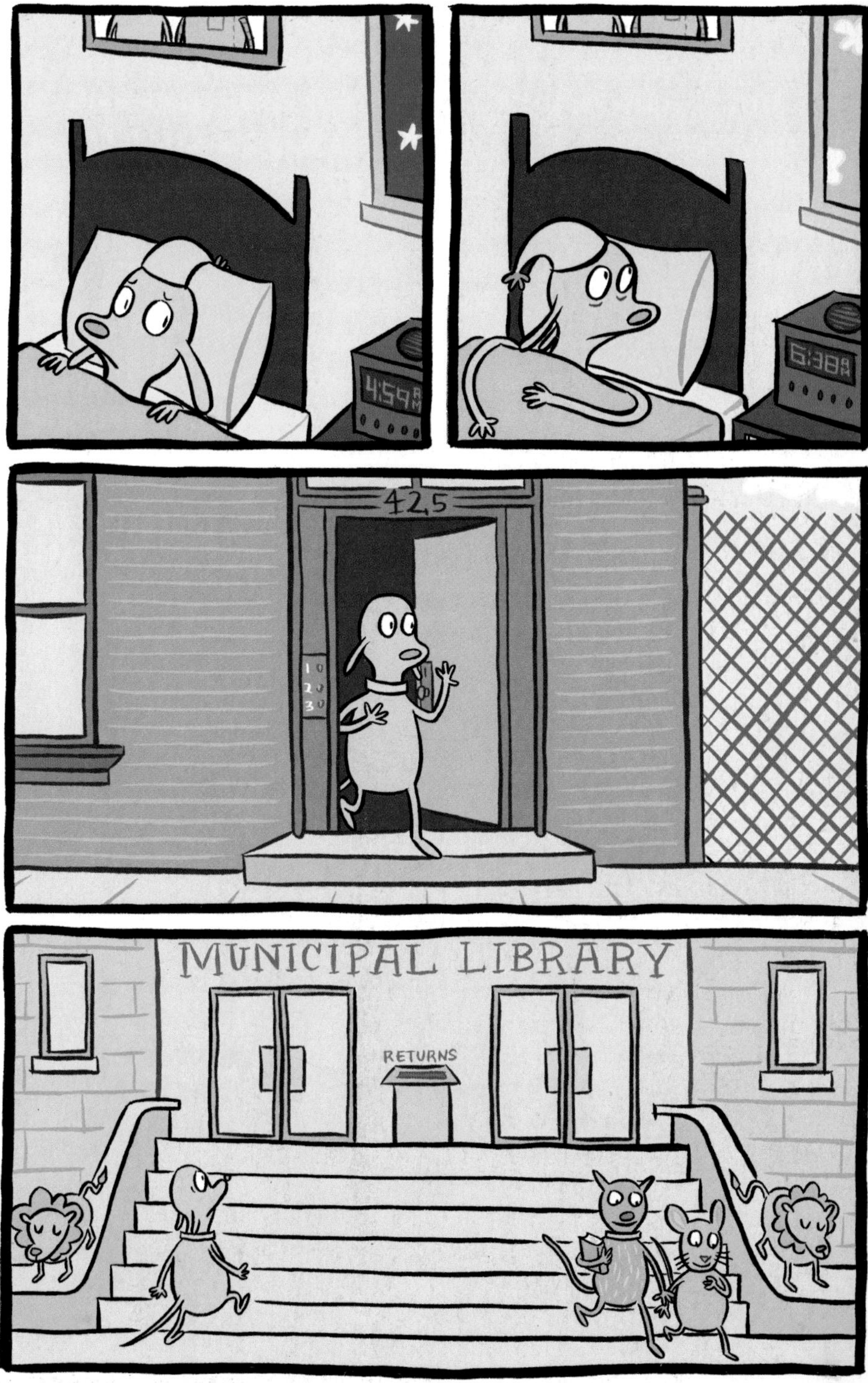
4:59
6:38
425
MUNICIPAL LIBRARY
RETURNS

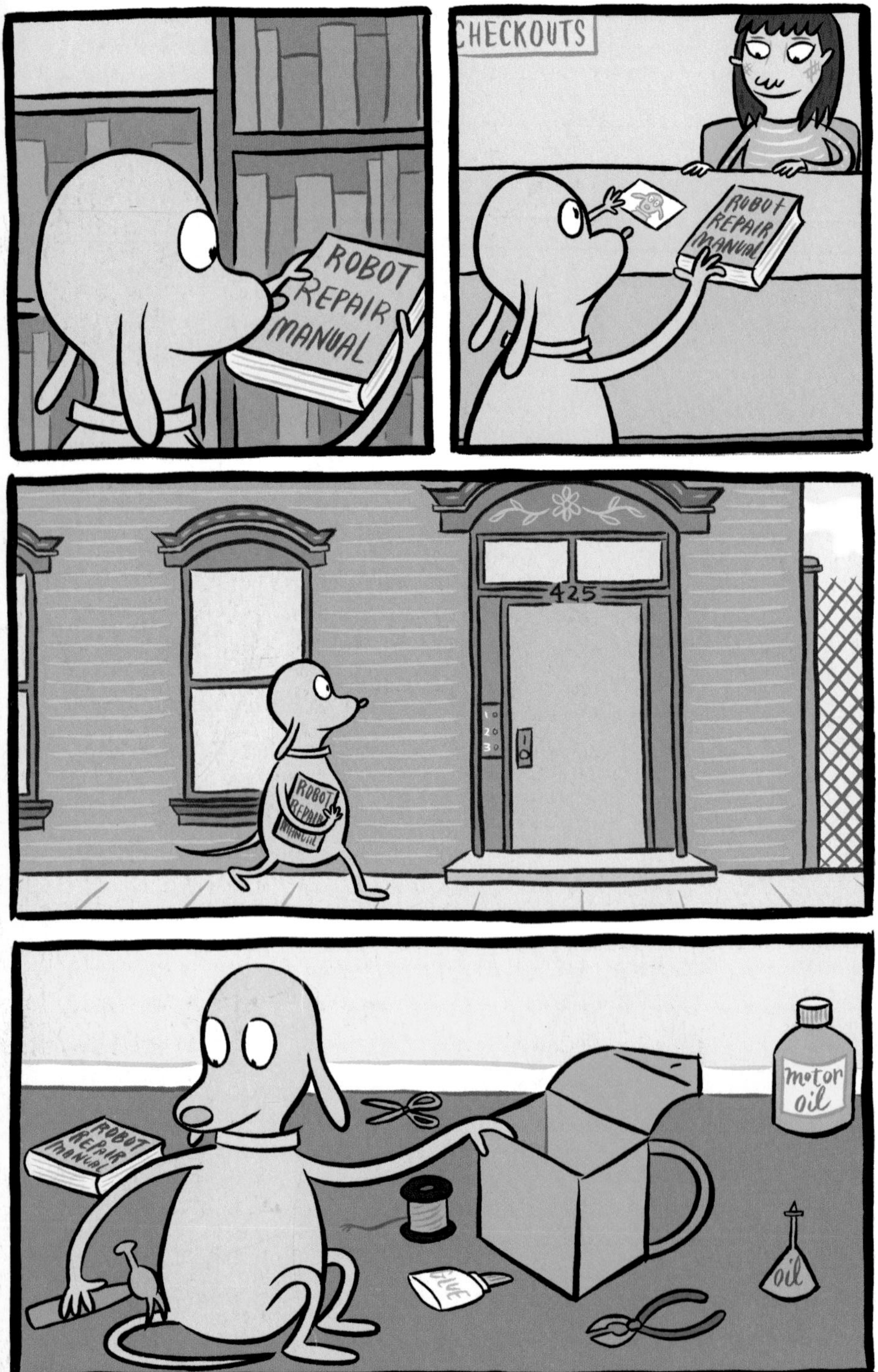
ROBOT REPAIR MANUAL
CHECKOUTS
ROBOT REPAIR MANUAL
ROBOT REPAIR MANUAL
425
1
2
3
ROBOT REPAIR MANUAL
motor oil
GLUE
oil

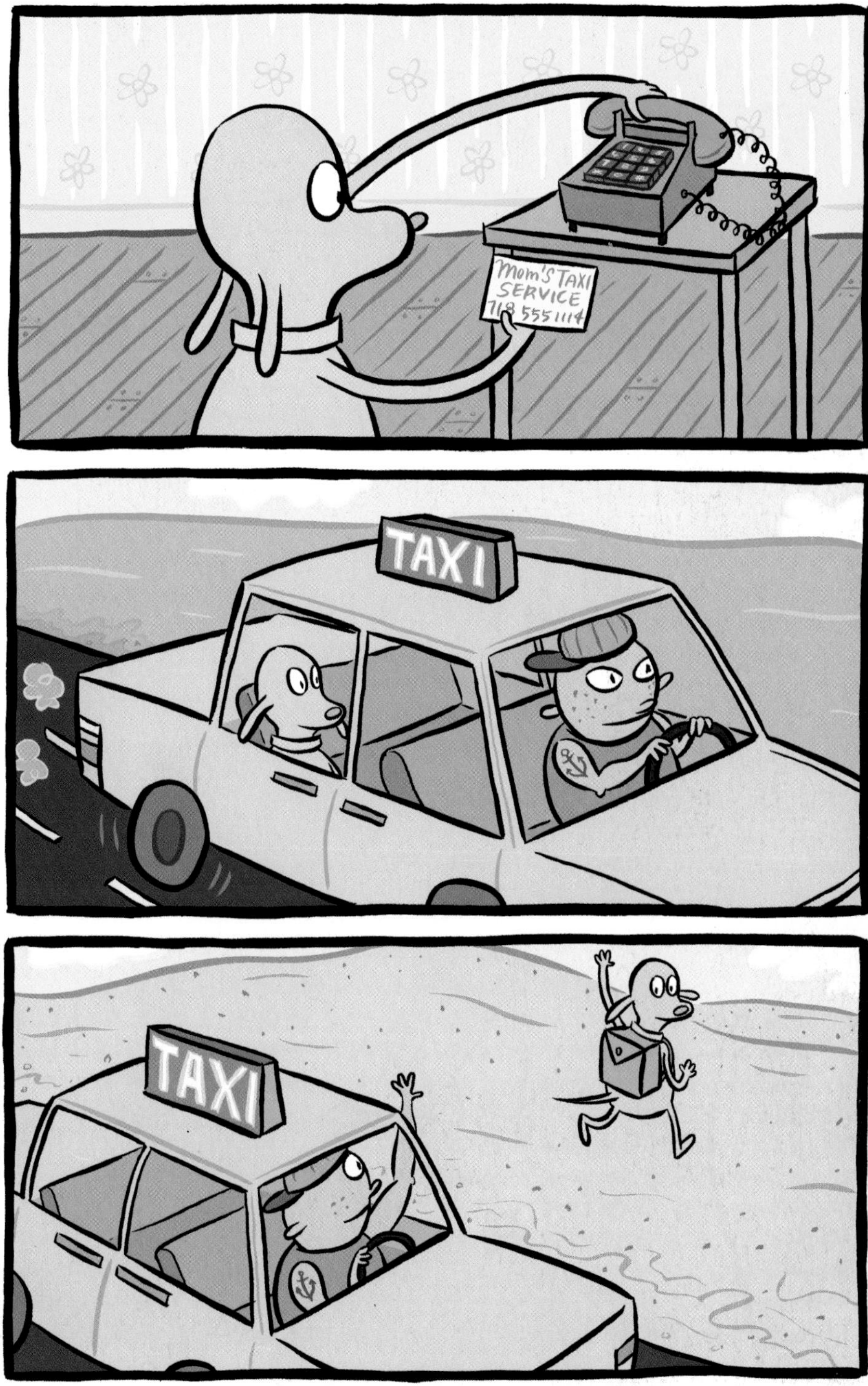
Mom's TAXI
SERVICE
718 555 1114
TAXI
TAXI

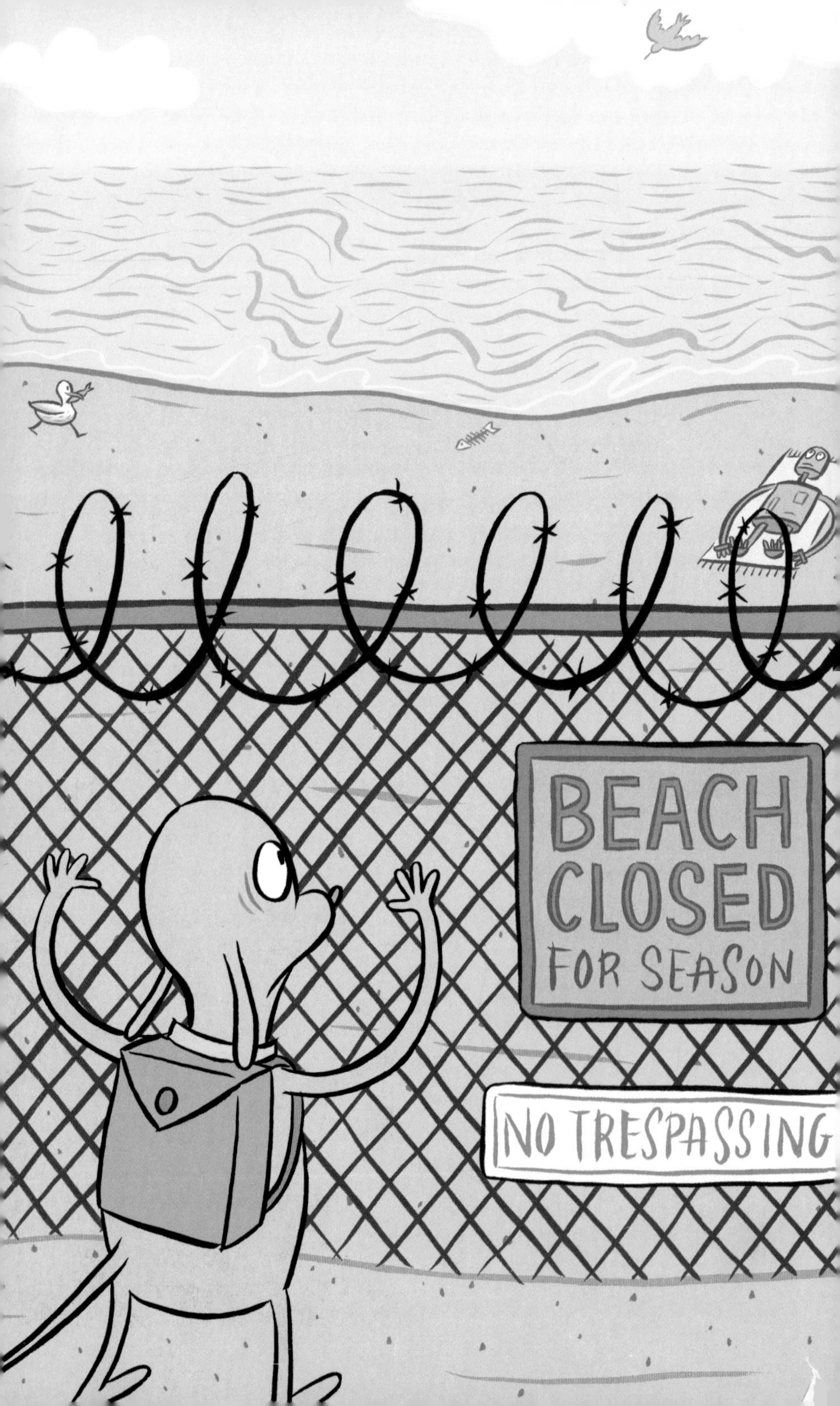
BEACH CLOSED FOR SEASON
NO TRESPASSING

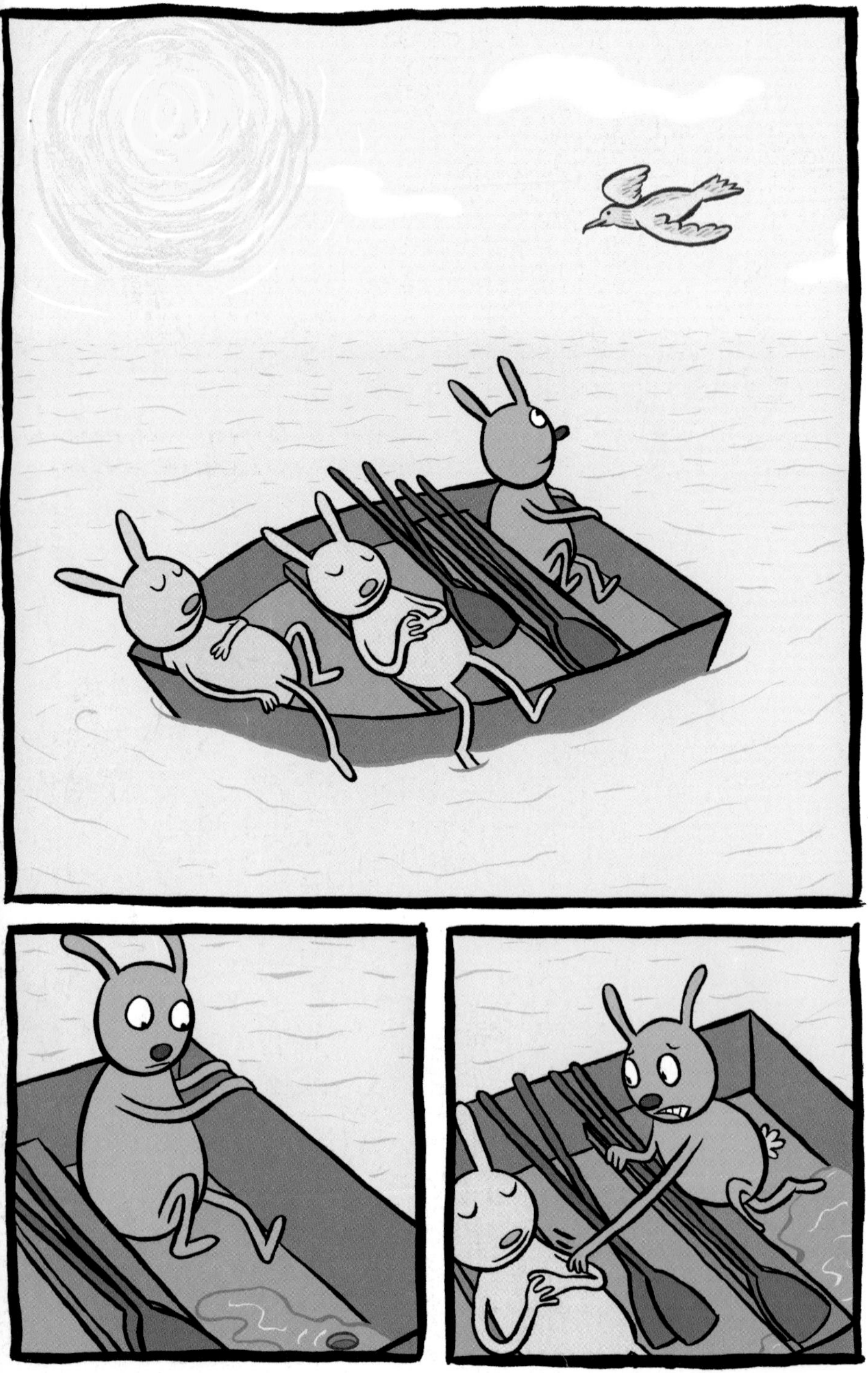

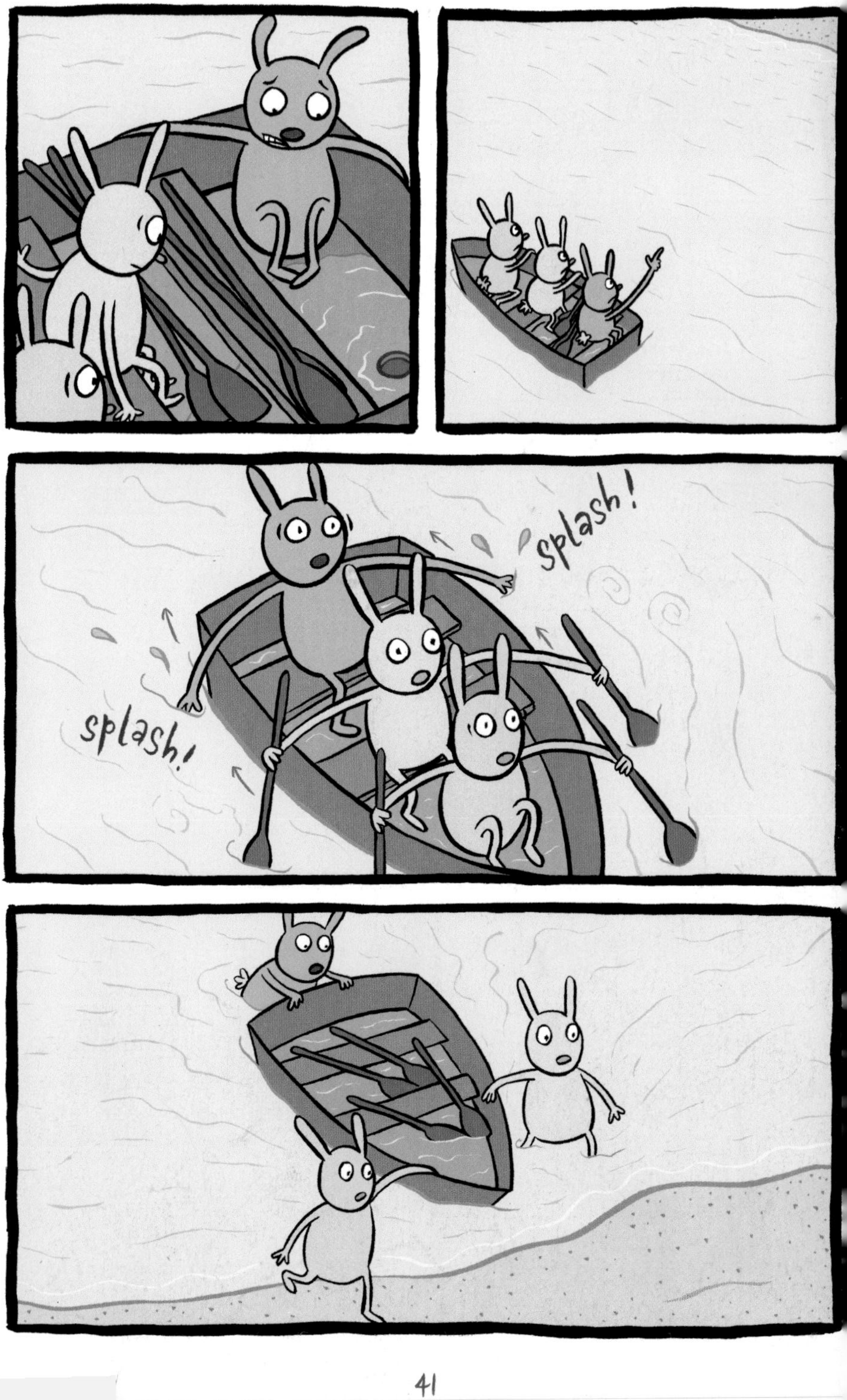
splash!
splash!

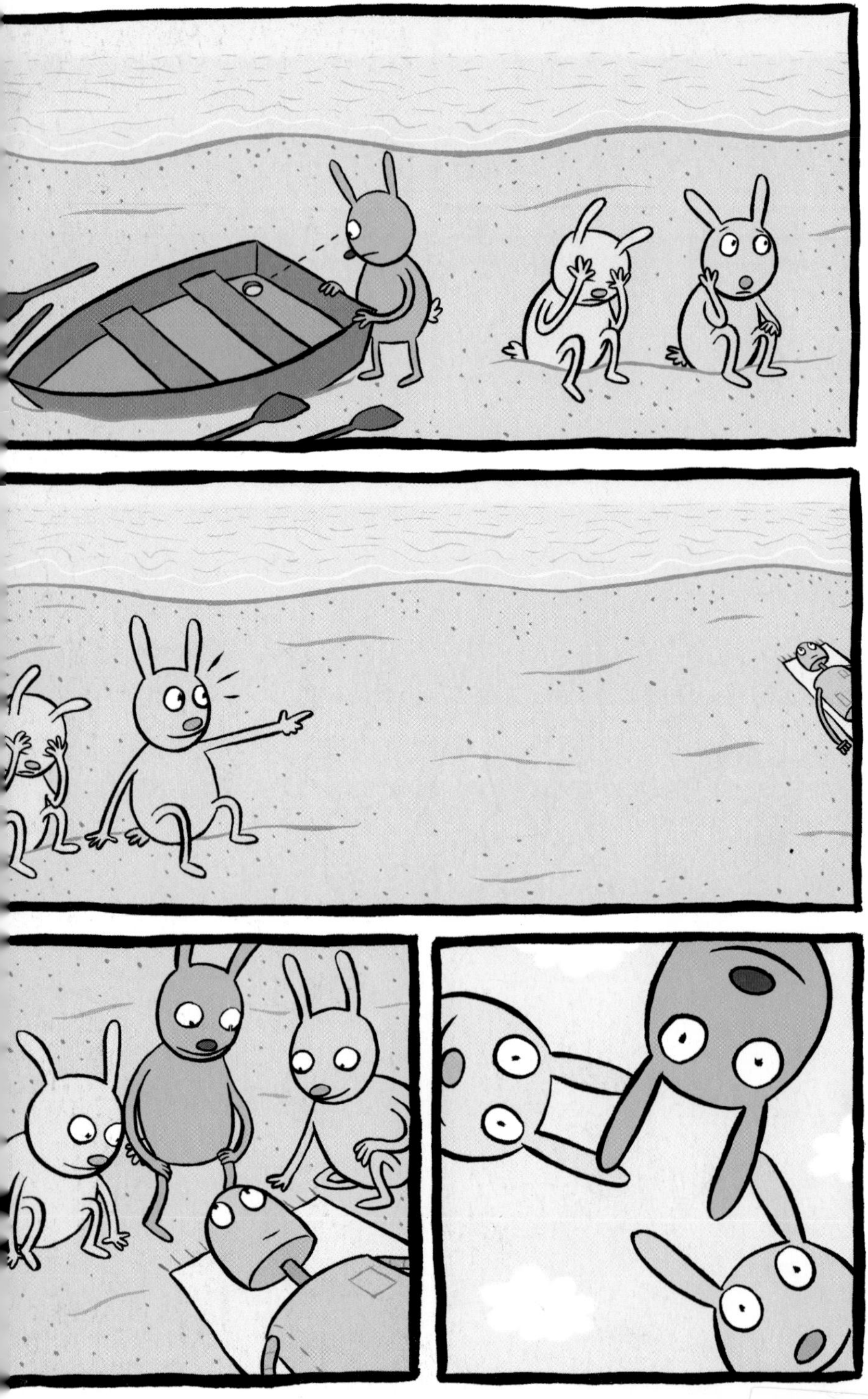

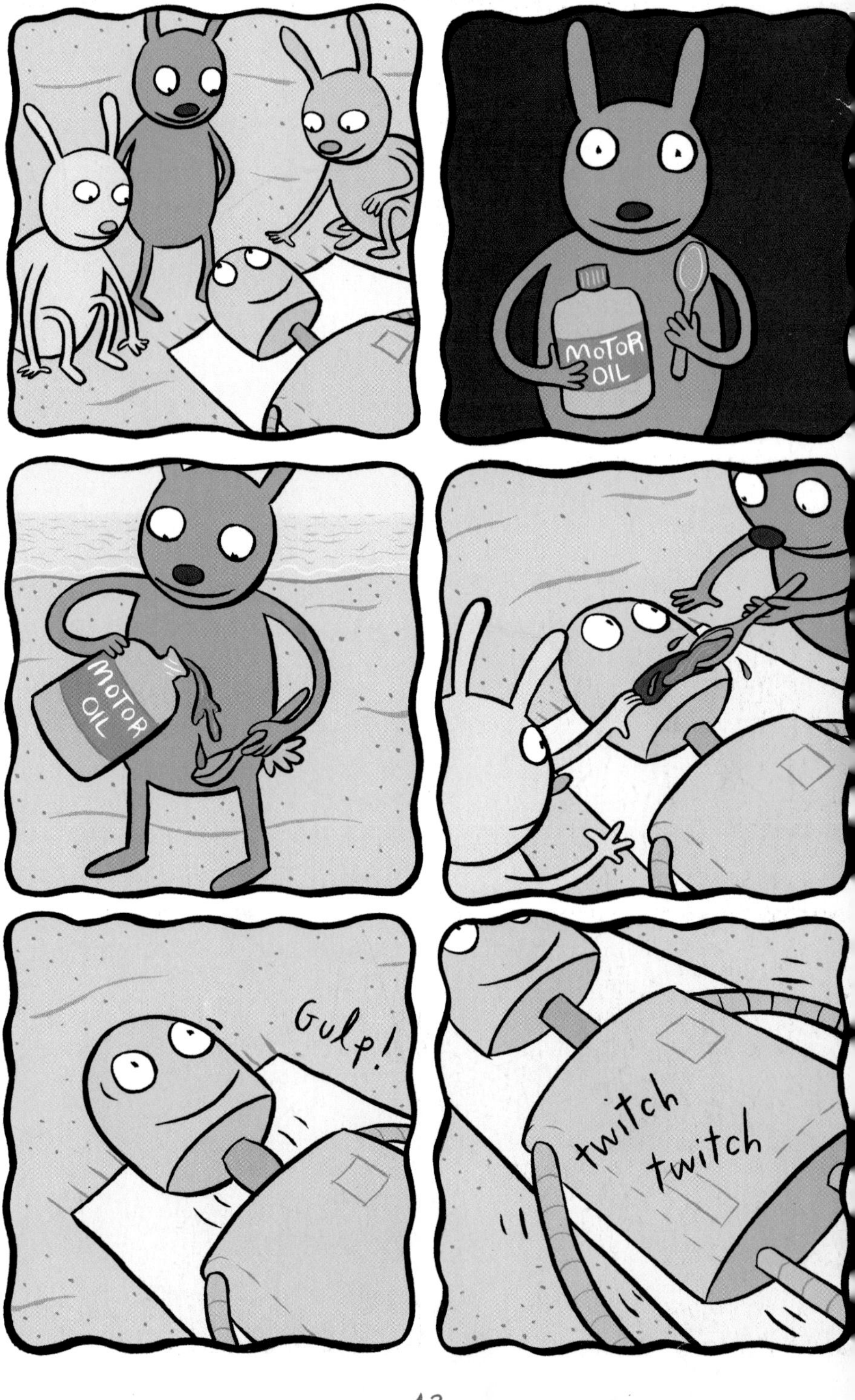
MOTOR OIL
MOTOR OIL
Gulp!
twitch
twitch

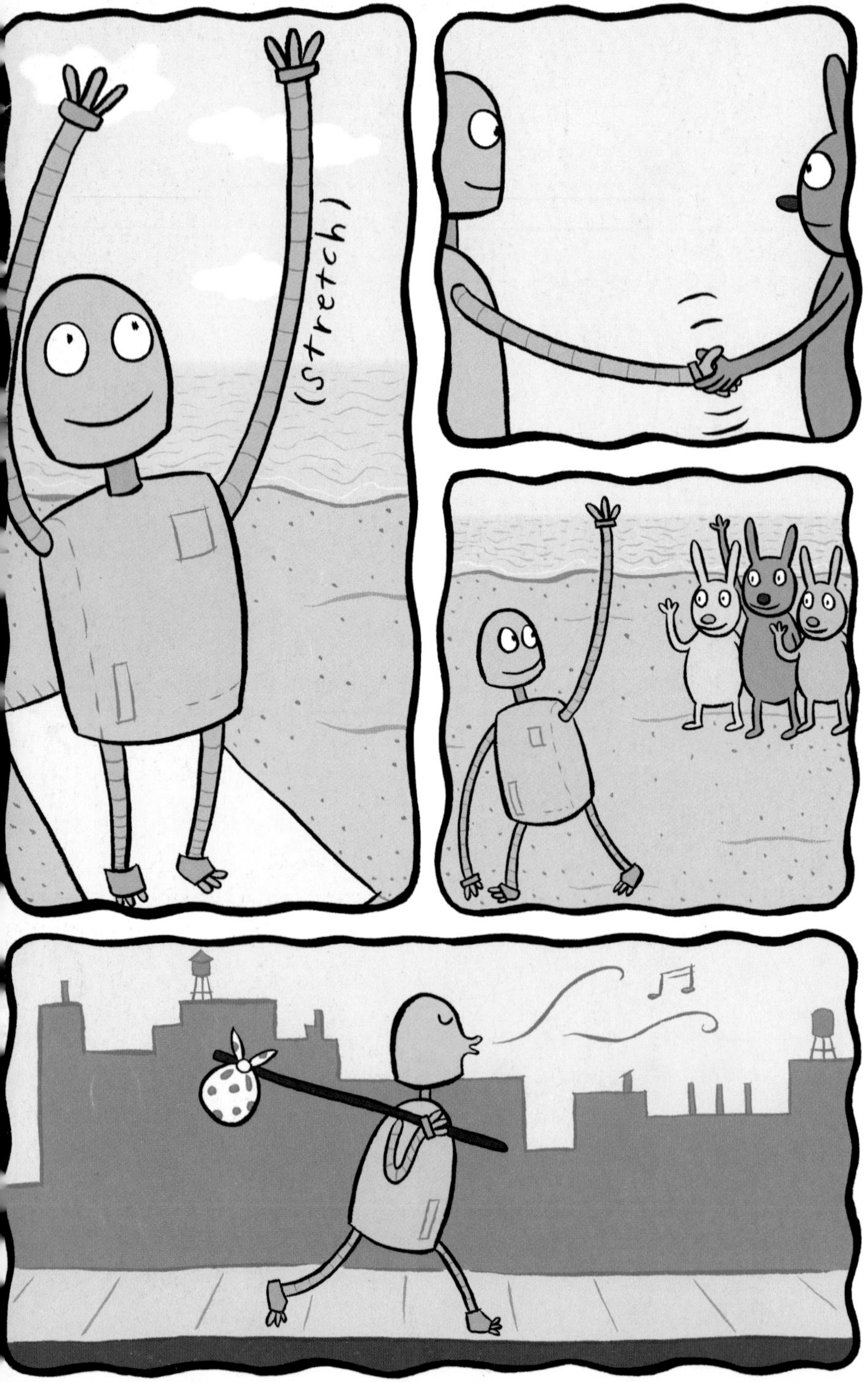
(stretch)

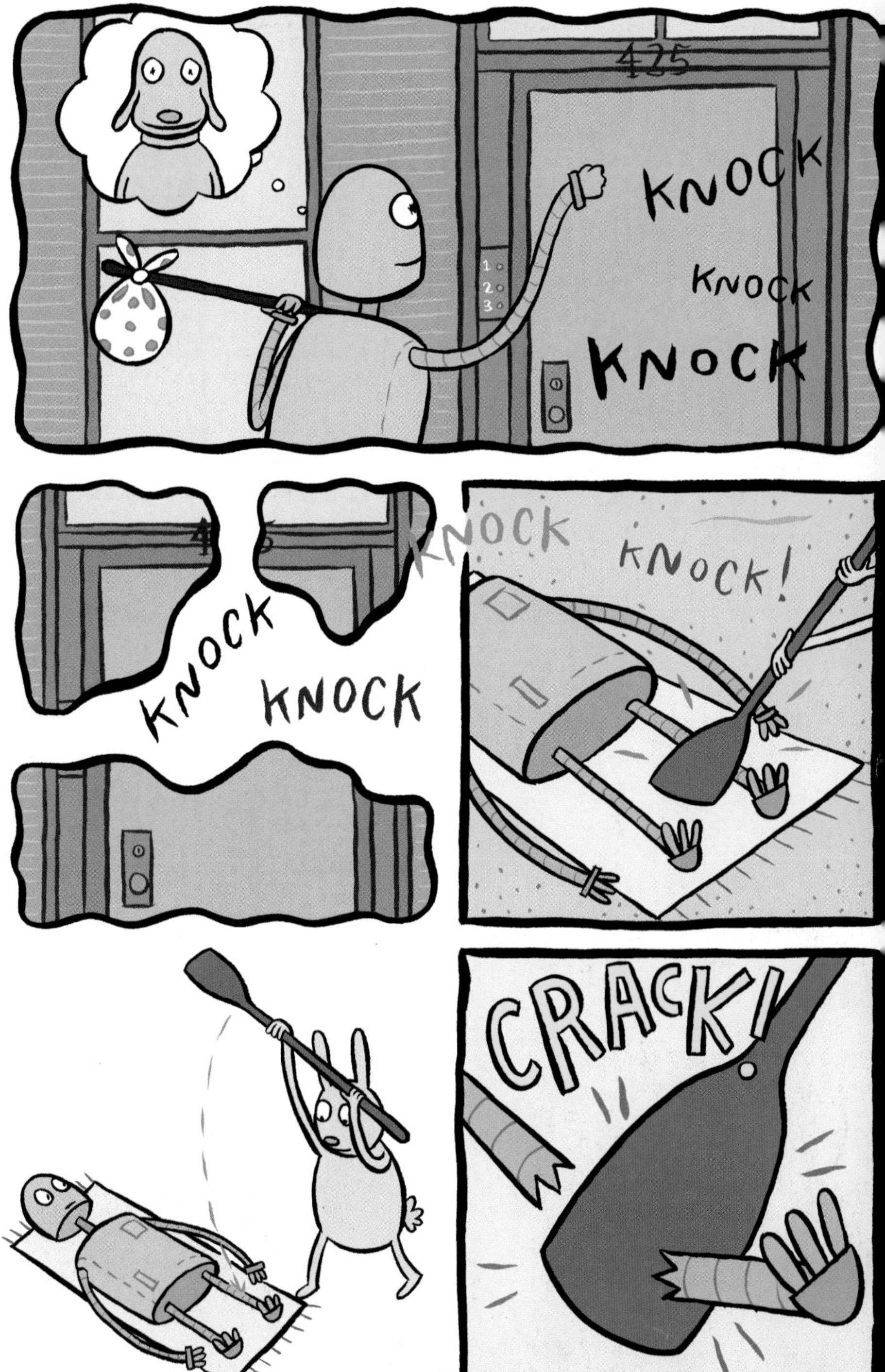
425
KNOCK
KNOCK
KNOCK
KNOCK
KNOCK
KNOCK
KNOCK!
CRACK!

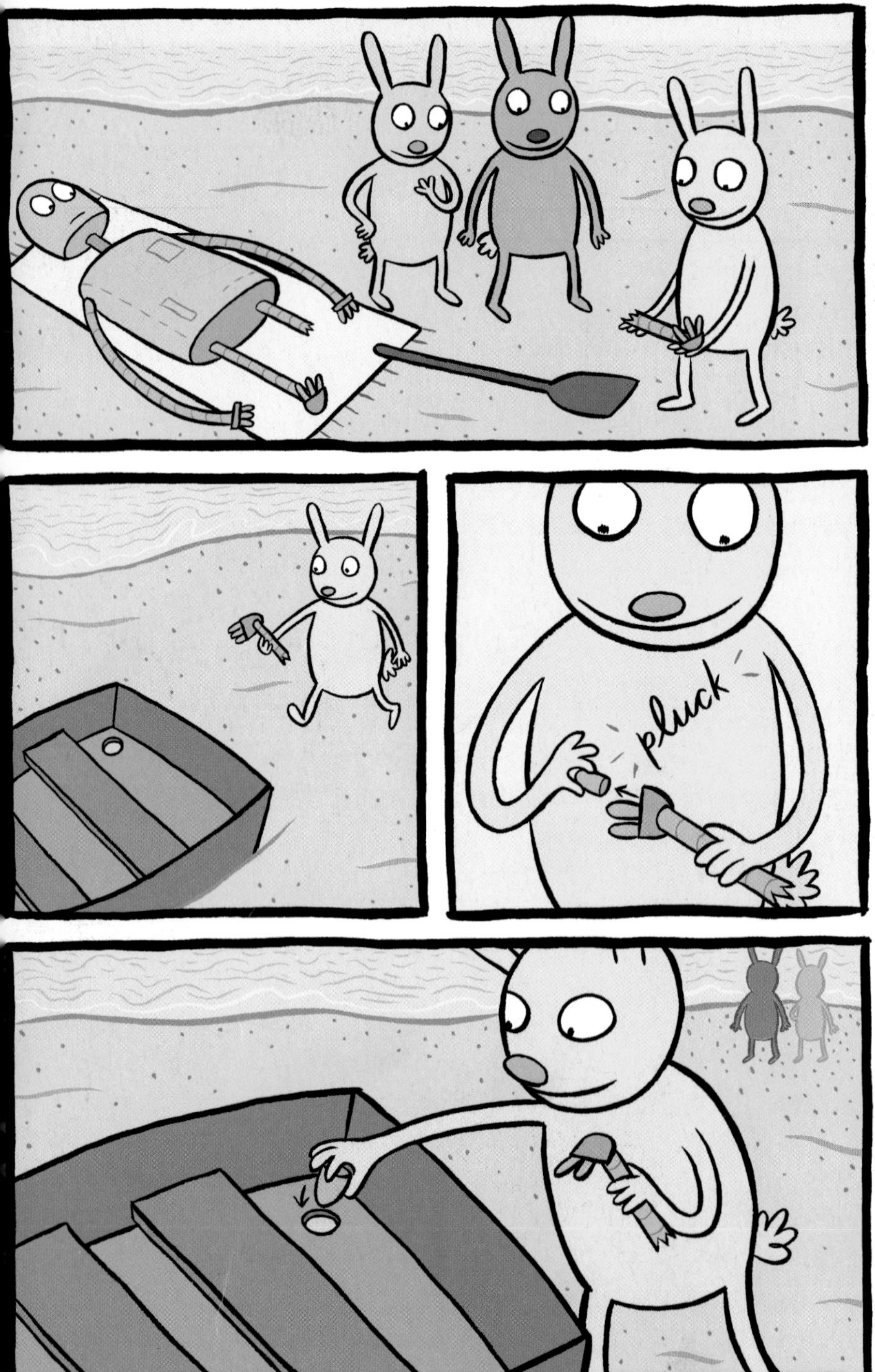
pluck

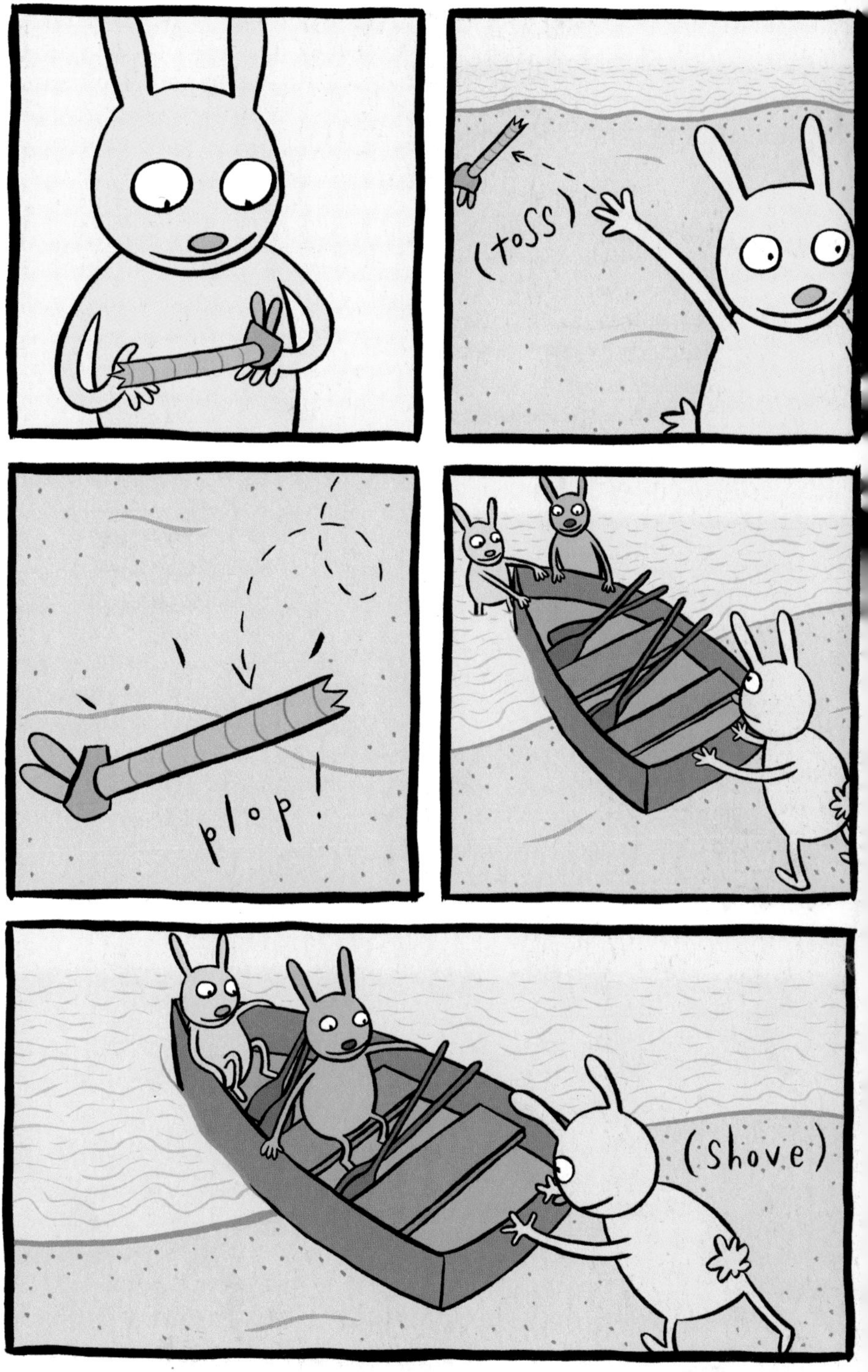
(toss)
plop!
(shove)

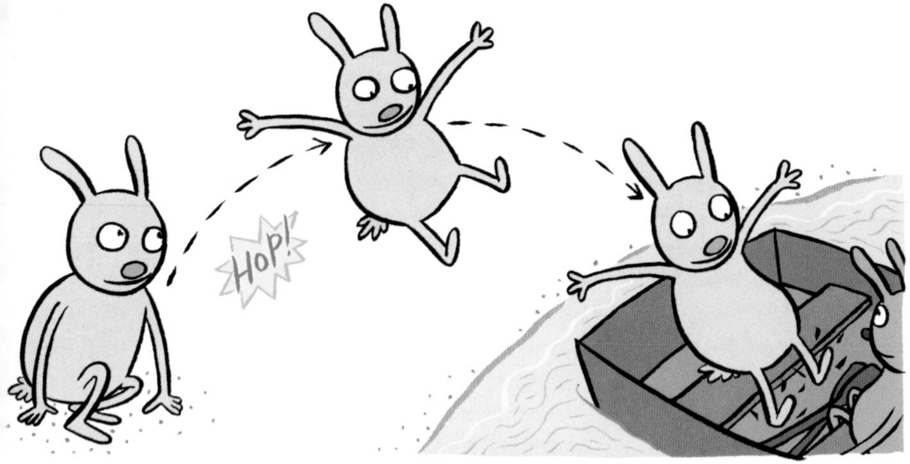
HOP!

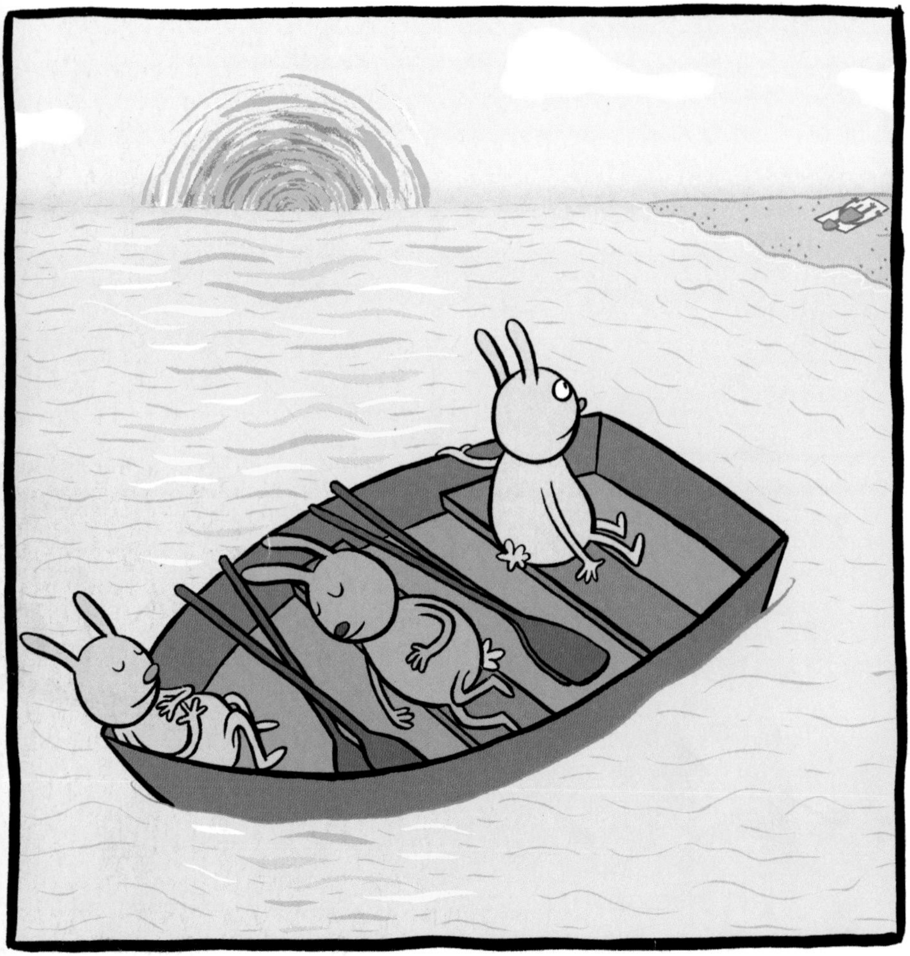

October

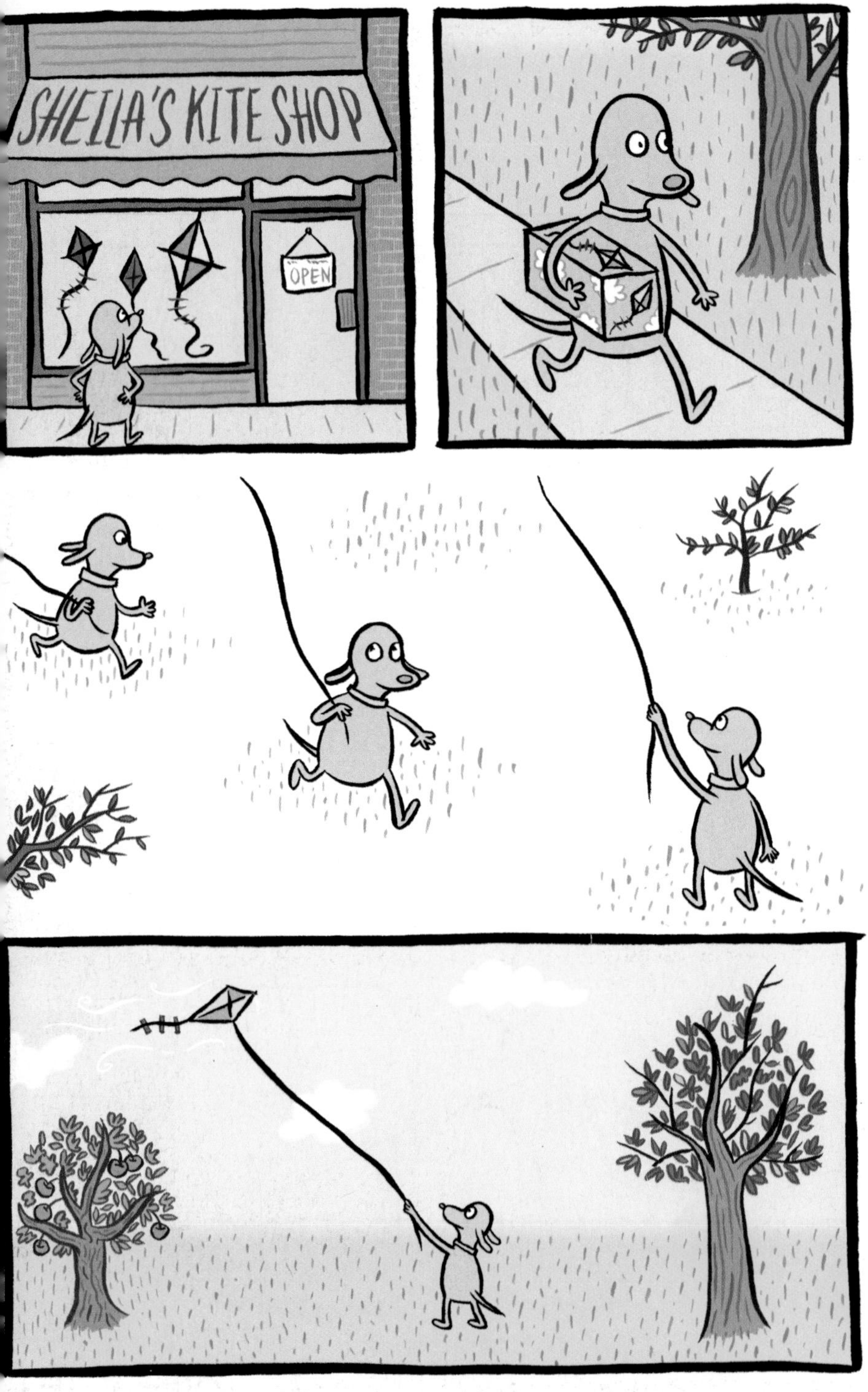

SHEILA'S KITE SHOP
OPEN

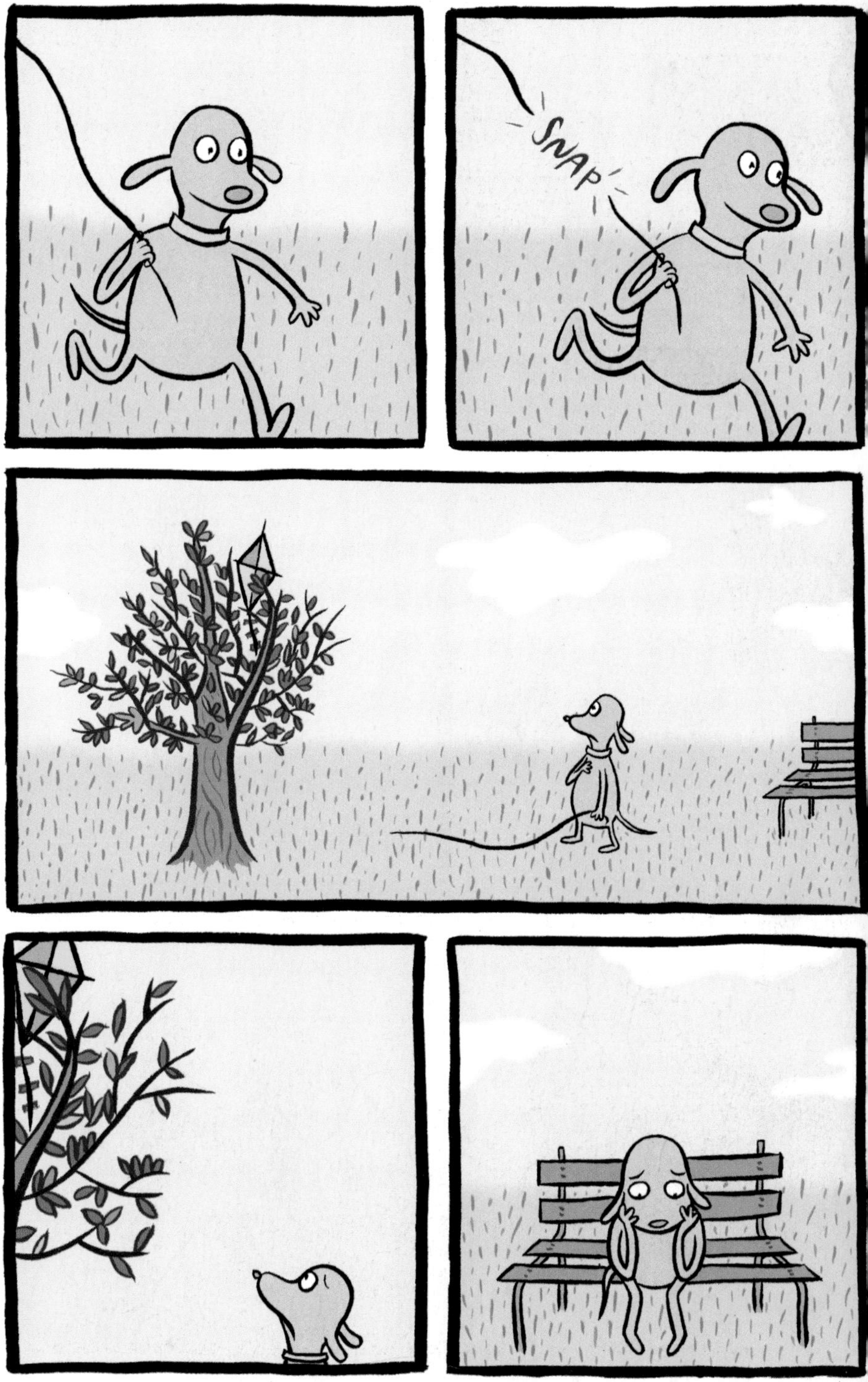
SNAP

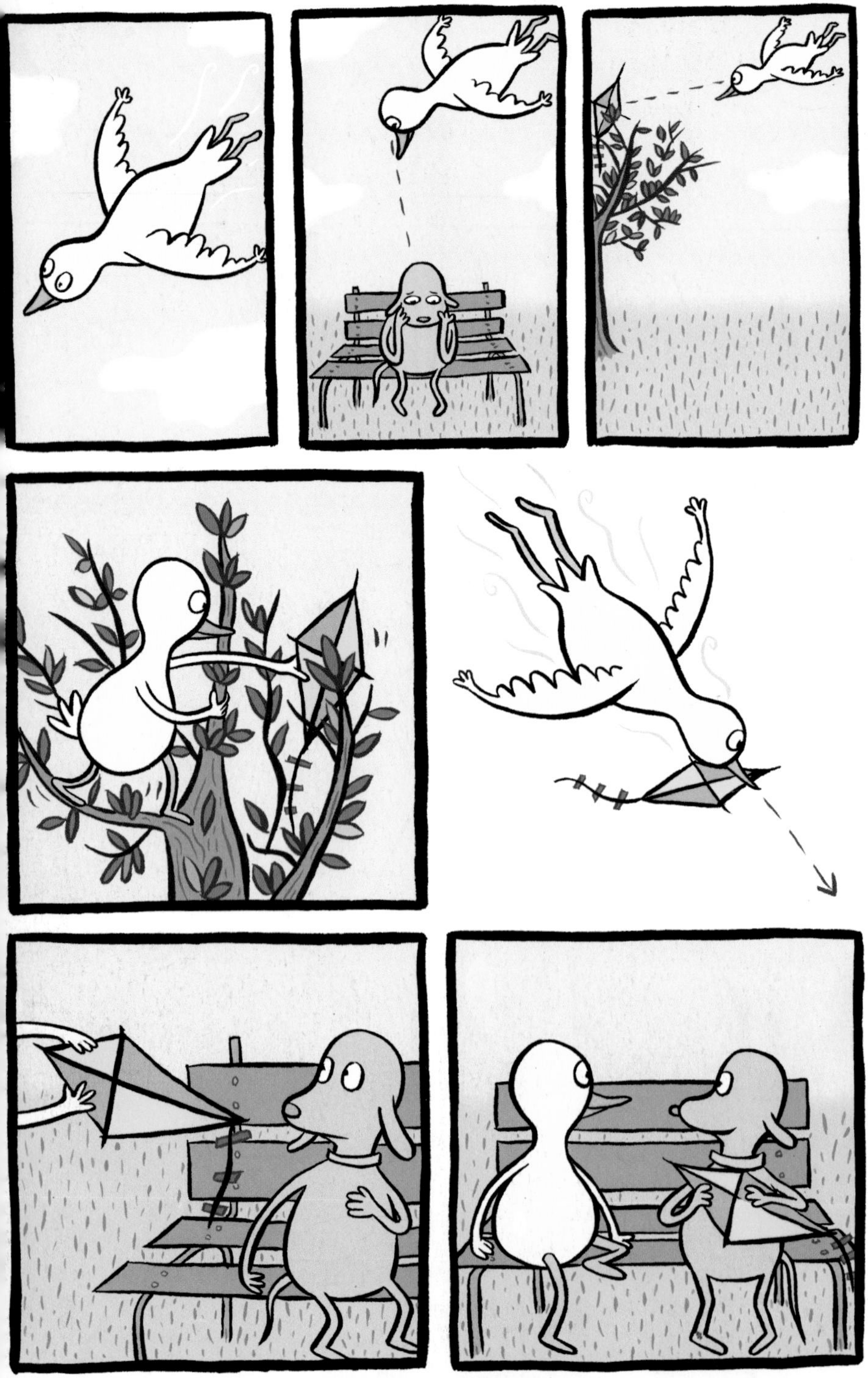

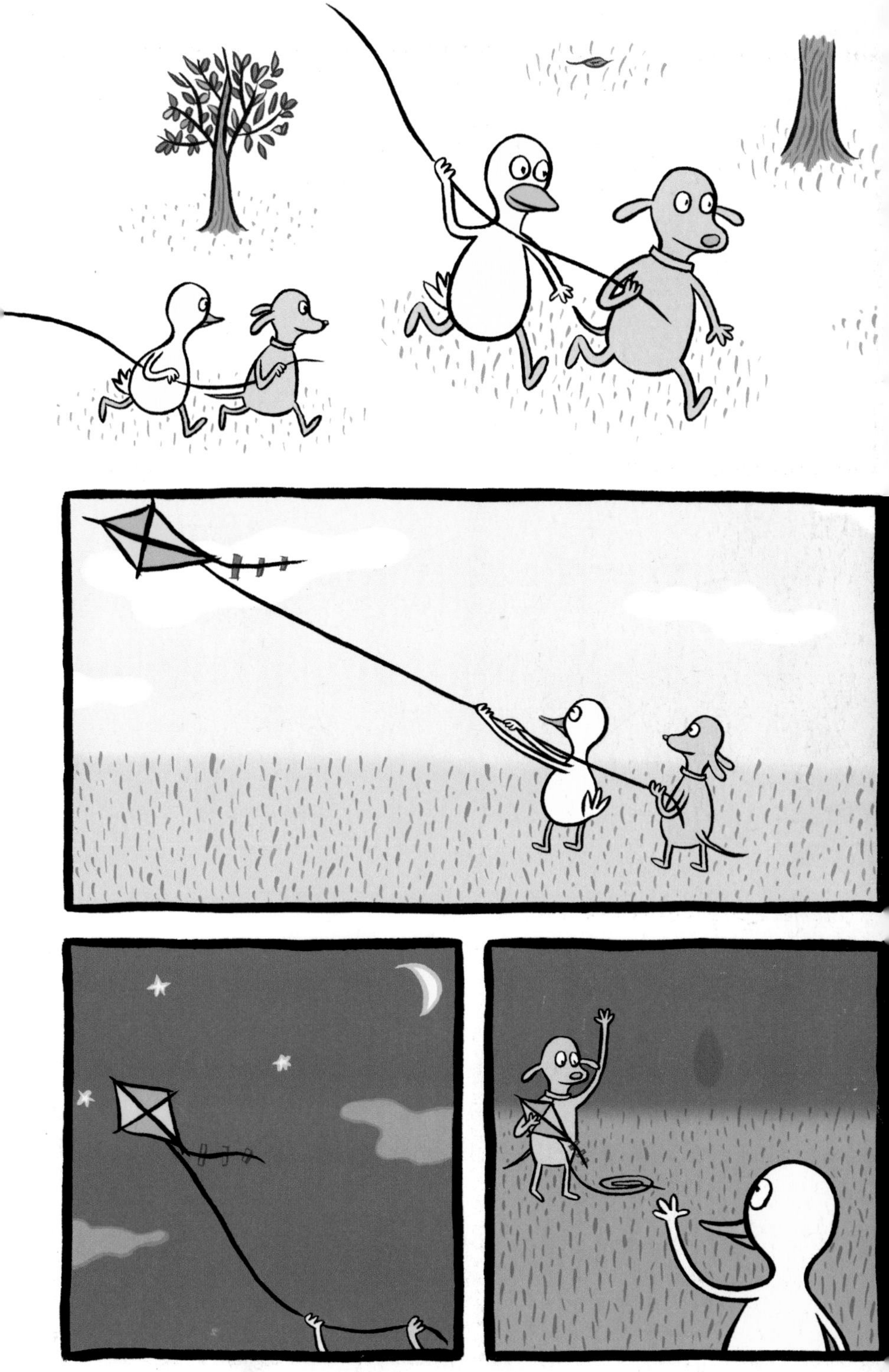

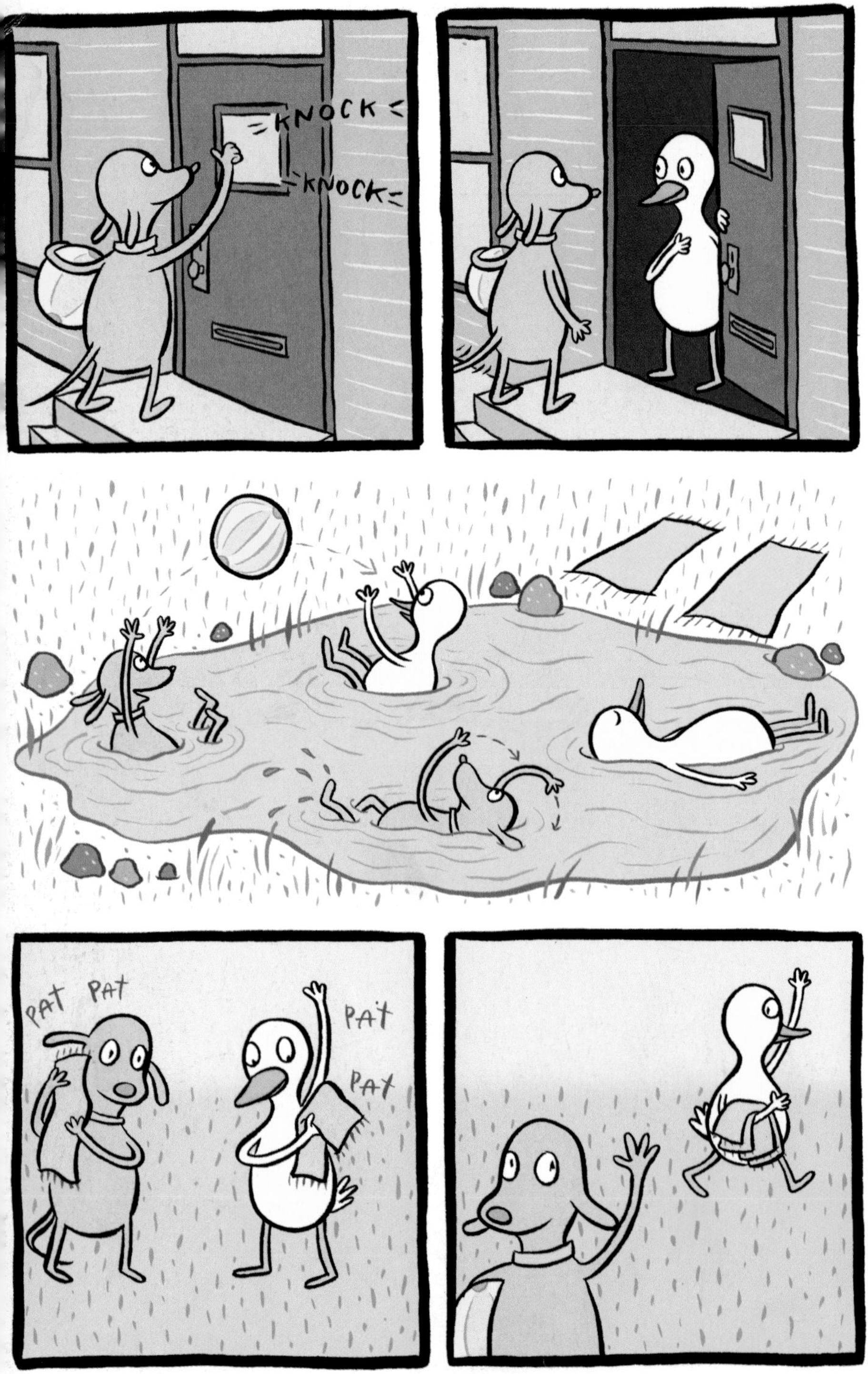
KNOCK
KNOCK
PAT PAT
PAT
PAT

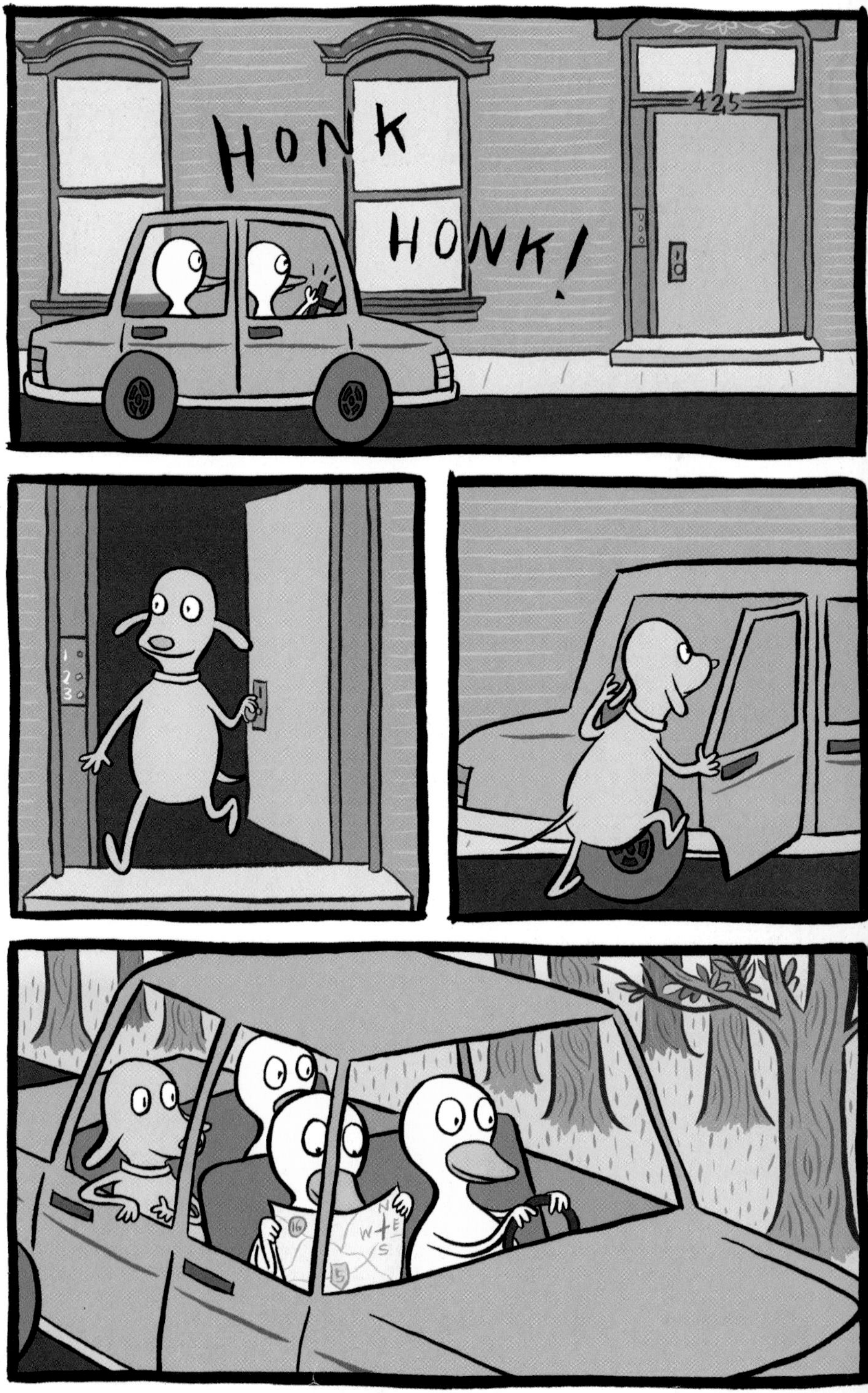
425
HONK
HONK!
1
2
3
N
W E
S
16
5

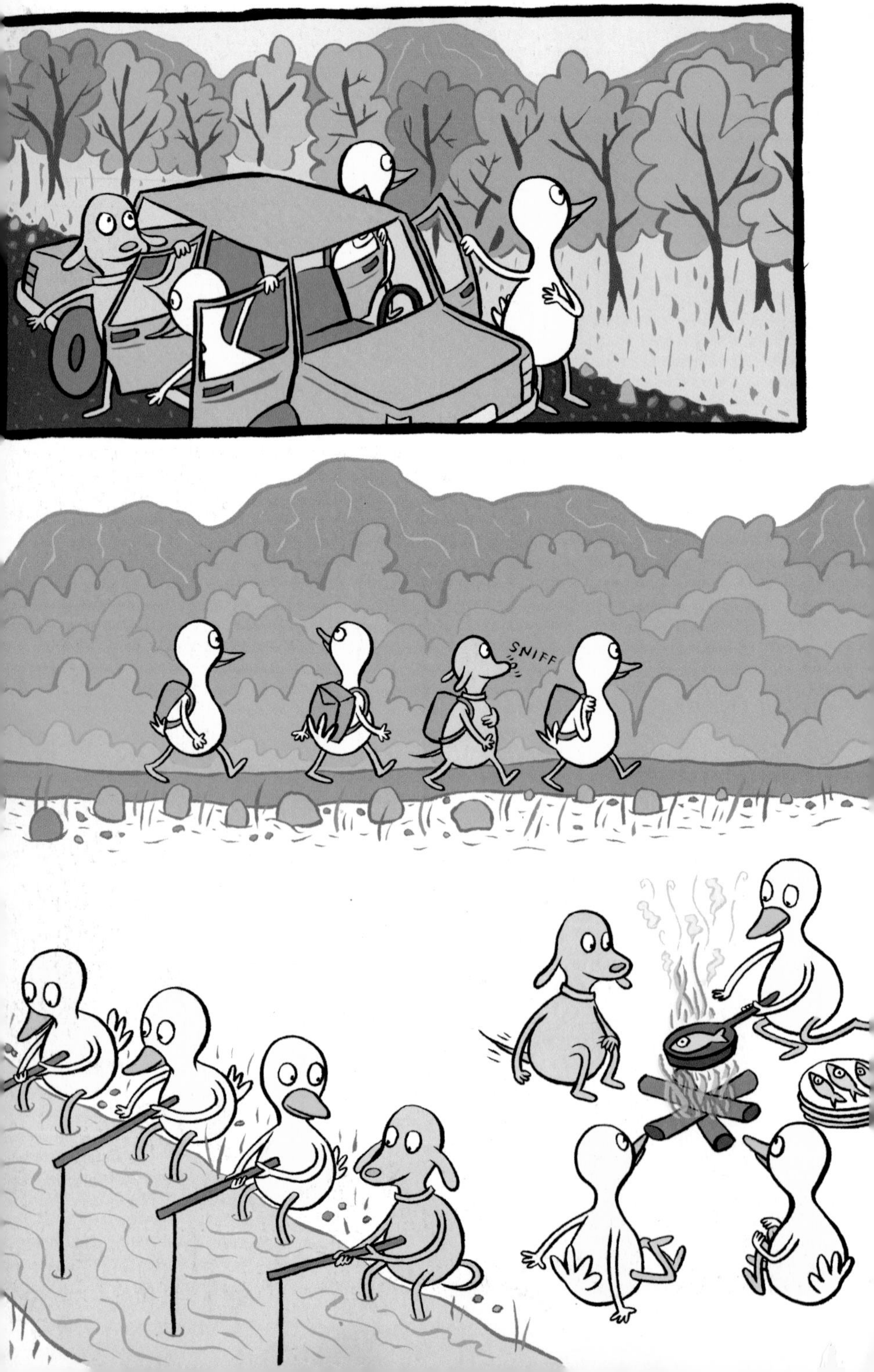
SNIFF

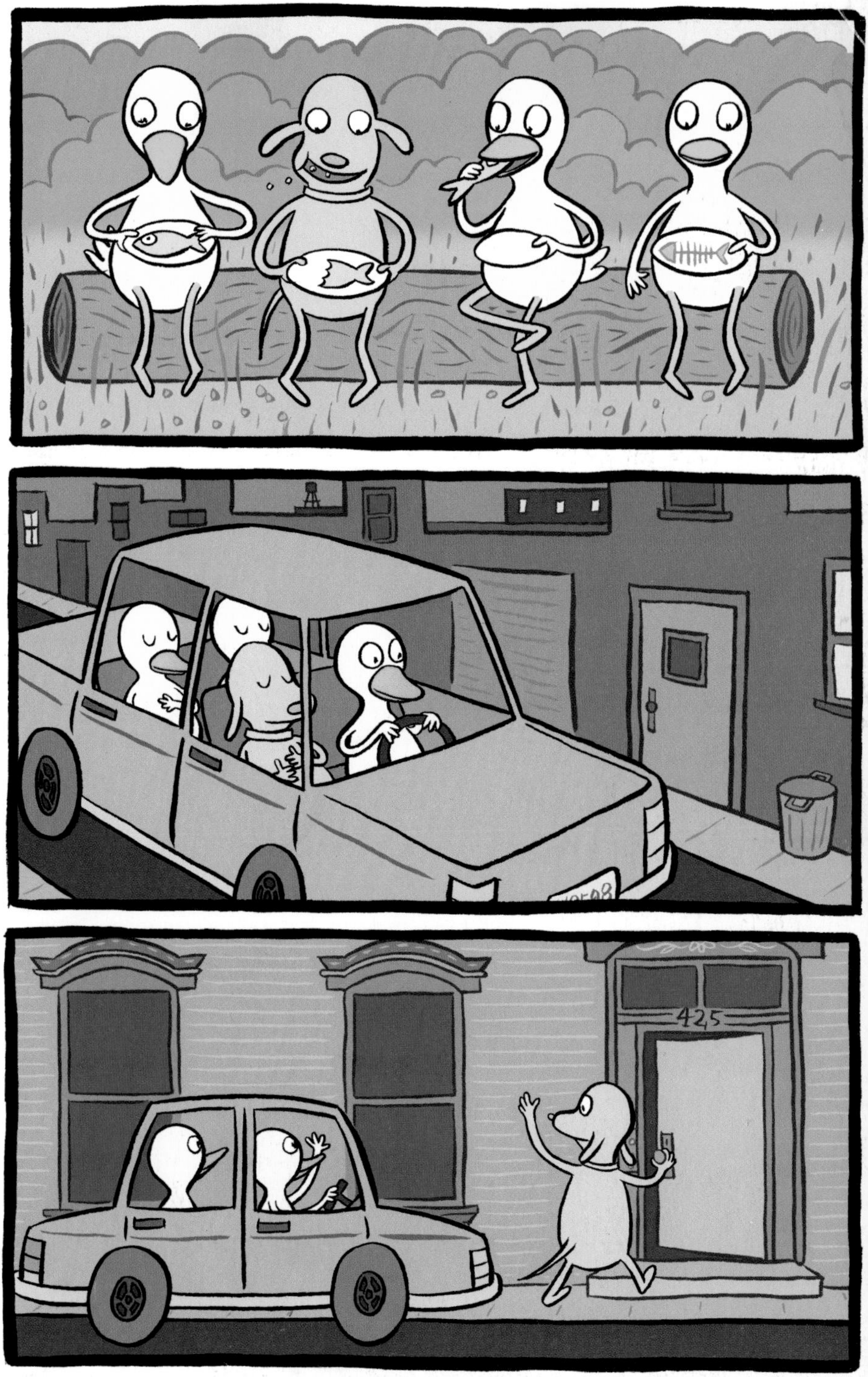
425

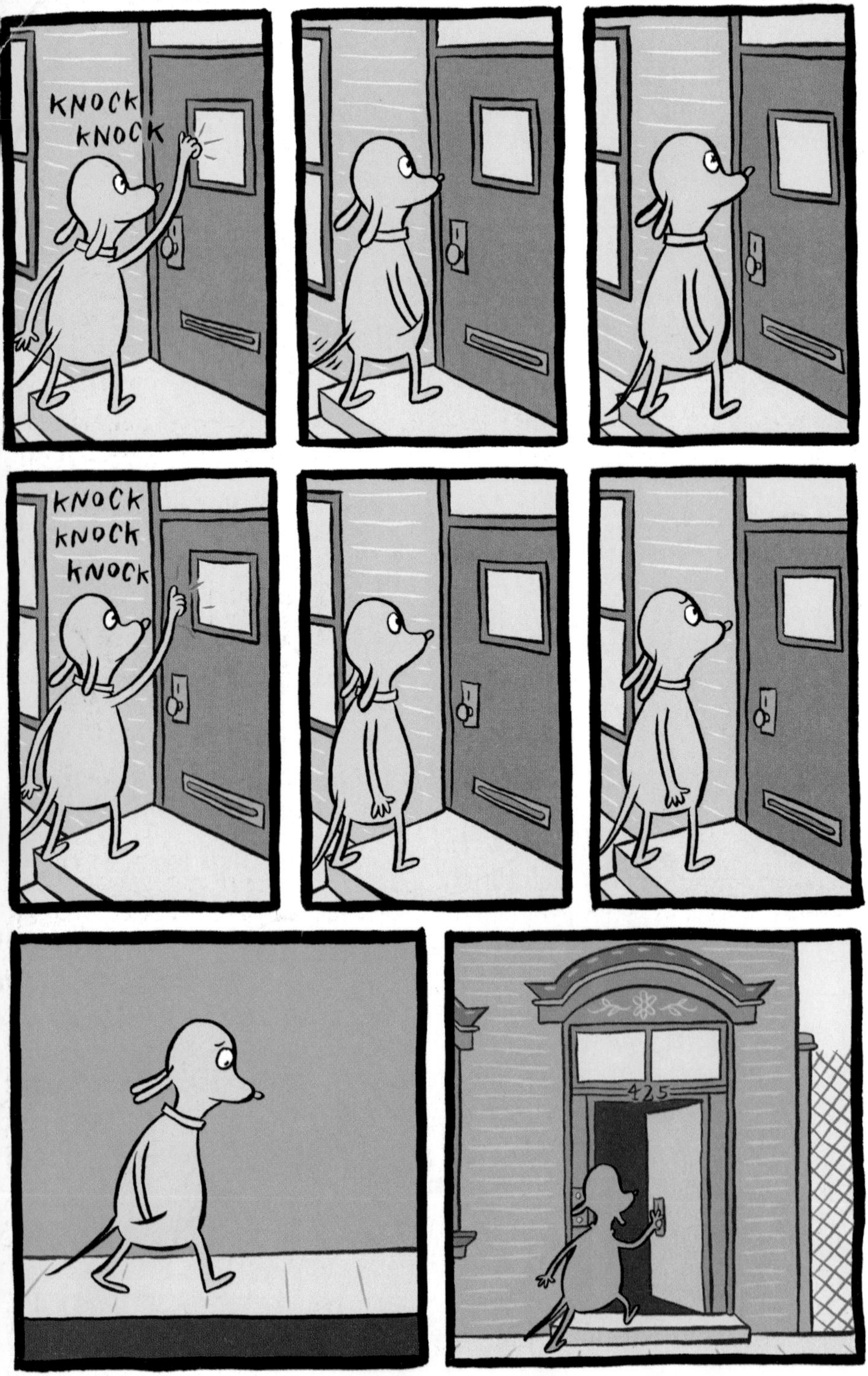
KNOCK KNOCK
KNOCK KNOCK KNOCK
425

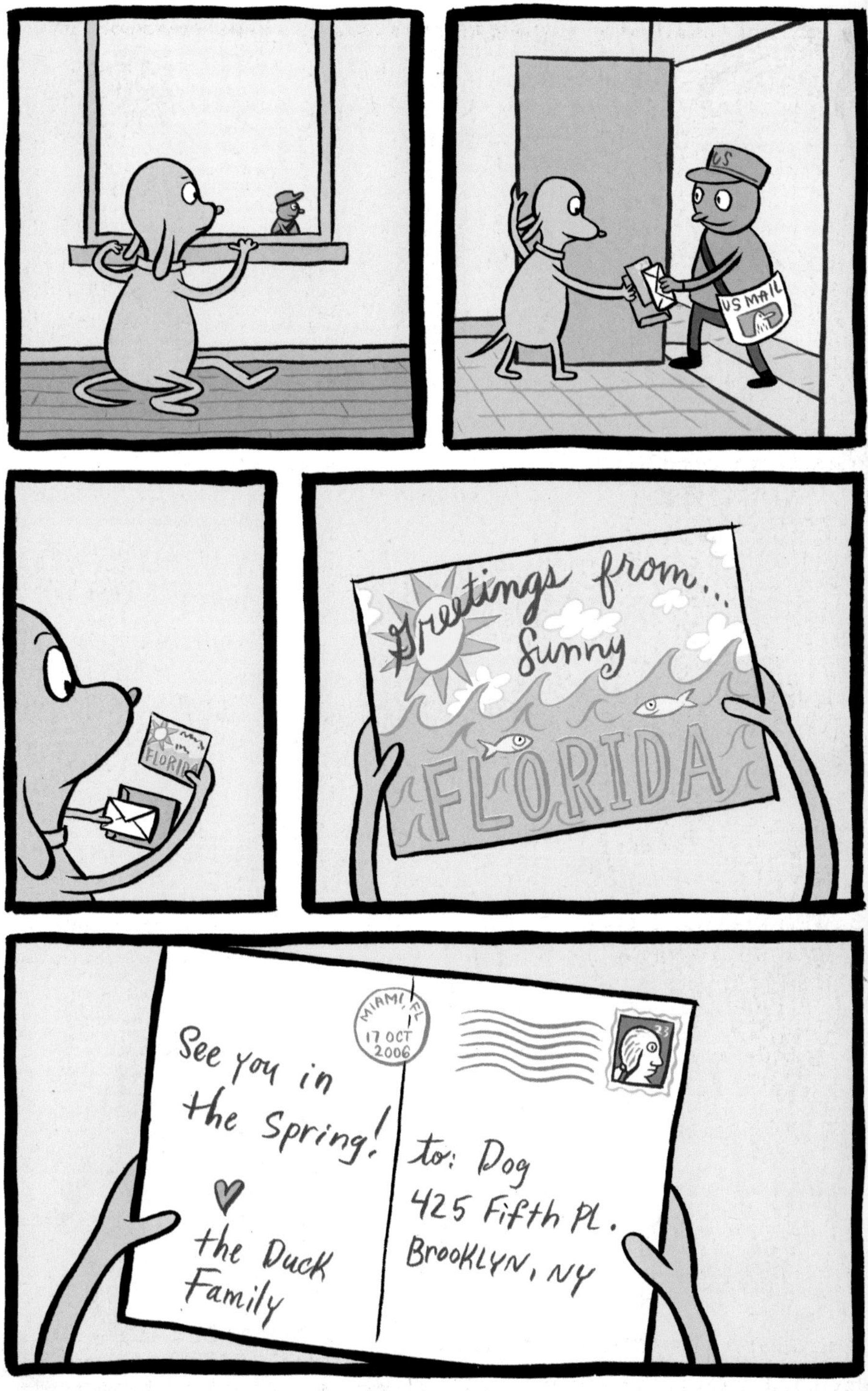

US
US MAIL
Greetings from...
Sunny
FLORIDA
MIAMI, FL
17 OCT 2006
See you in the Spring!
the Duck Family
to: Dog
425 Fifth PL.
BROOKLYN, NY

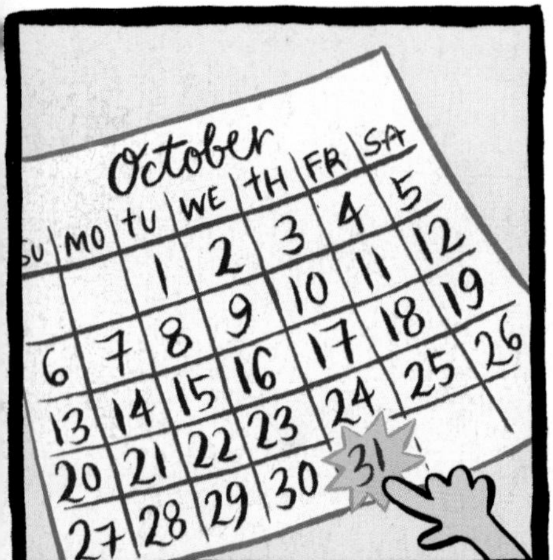
October
SU MO TU WE TH FR SA
1 2 3 4 5
6 7 8 9 10 11 12
13 14 15 16 17 18 19
20 21 22 23 24 25 26
27 28 29 30 31

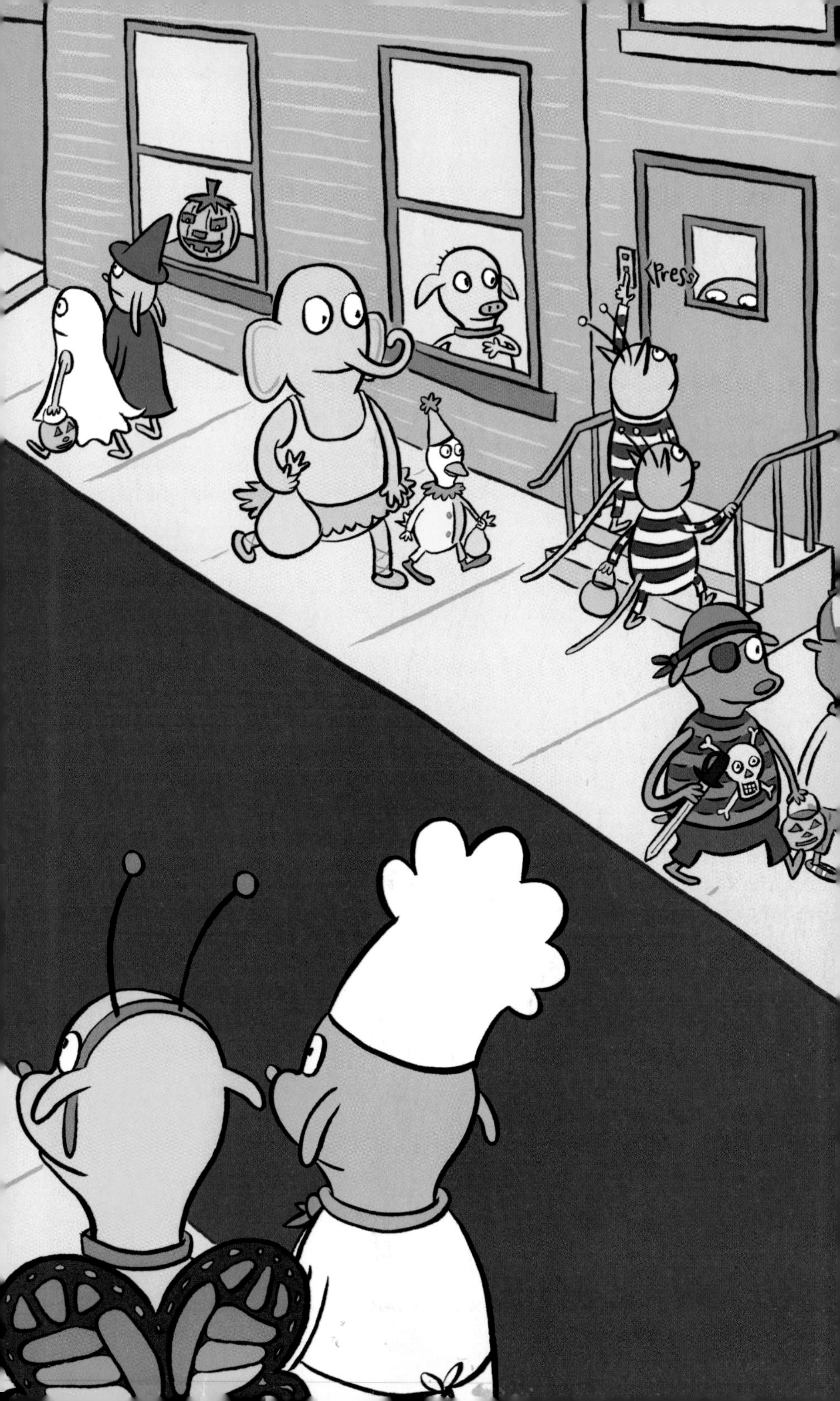
Press

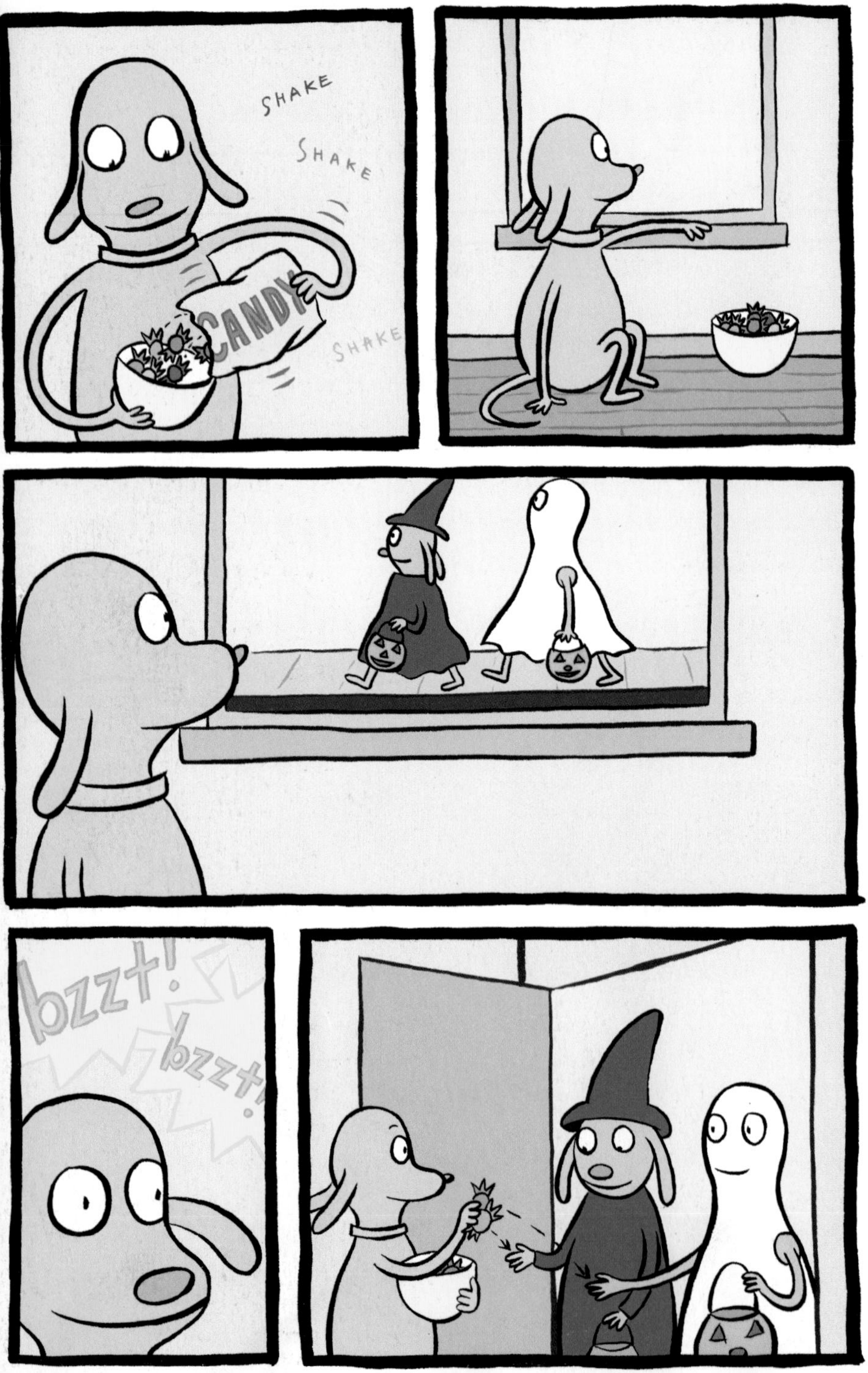
SHAKE
SHAKE
CANDY
SHAKE
bzzt!
bzzt!

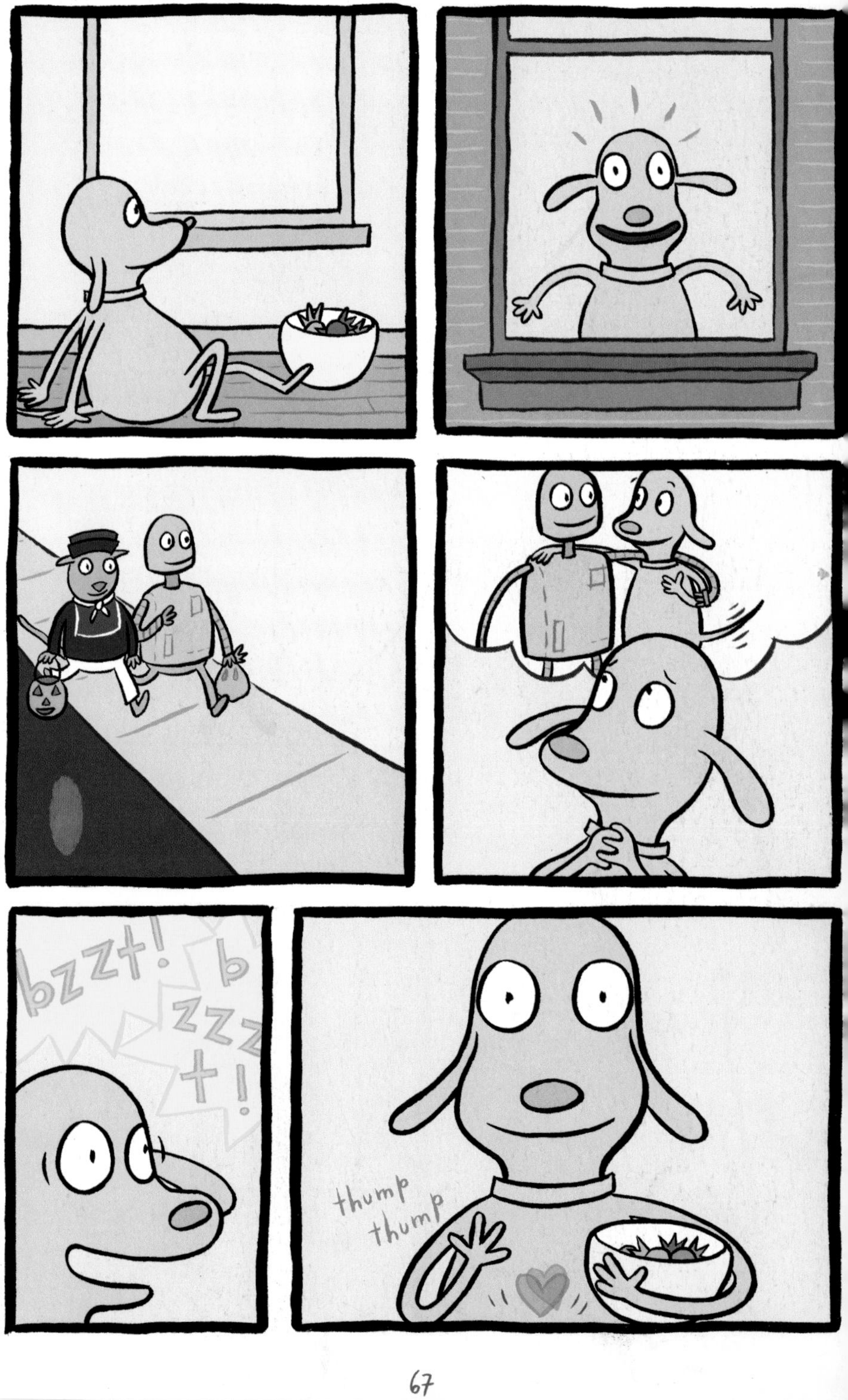
bzzt!
bzzzt!
thump
thump

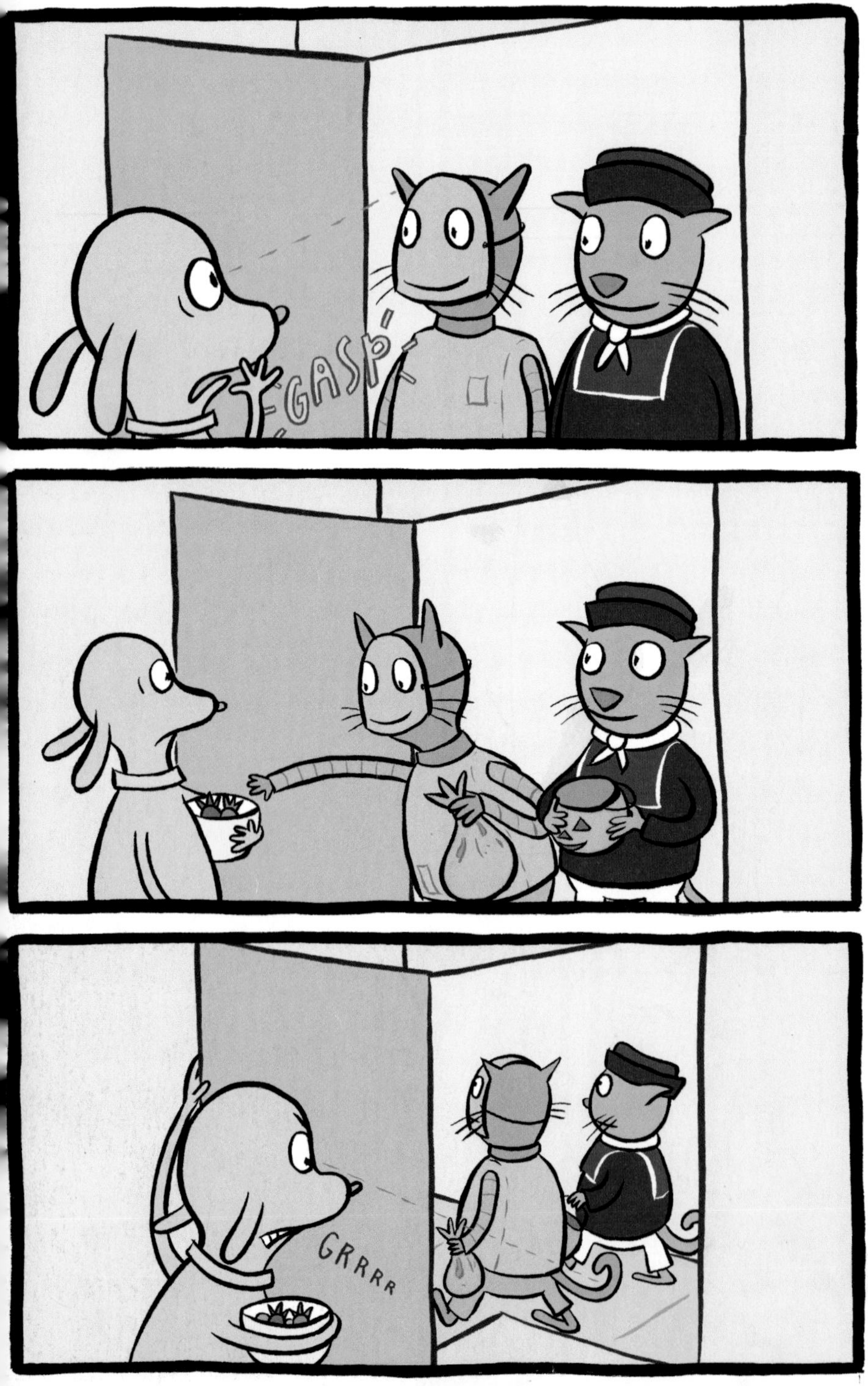
GASP
GRRRRR

November

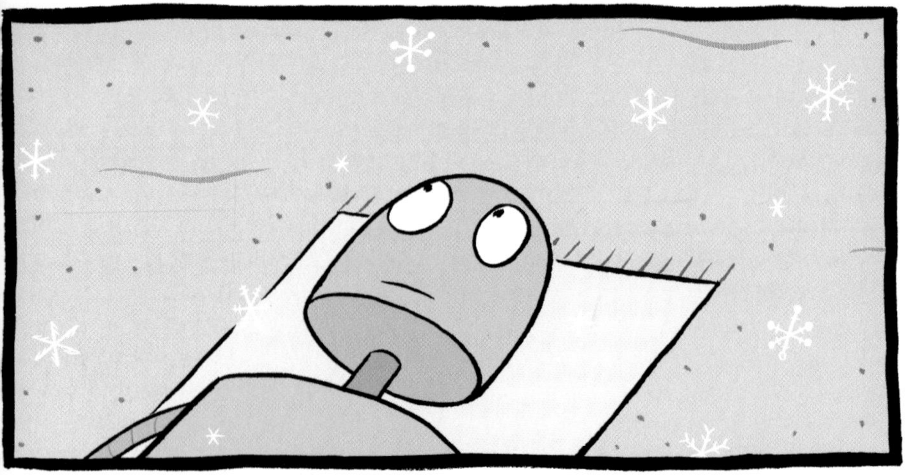

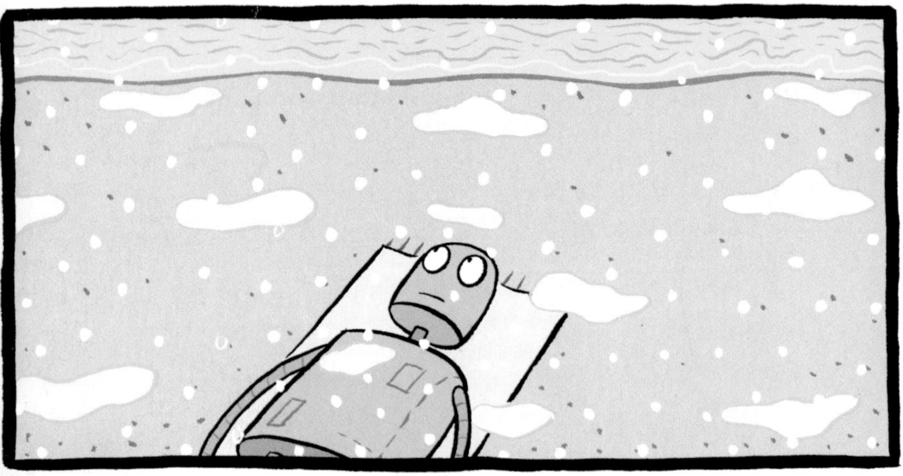

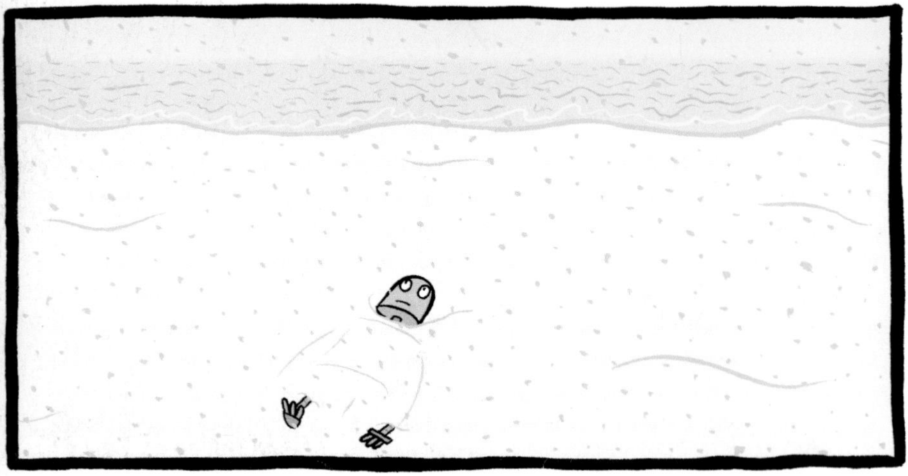

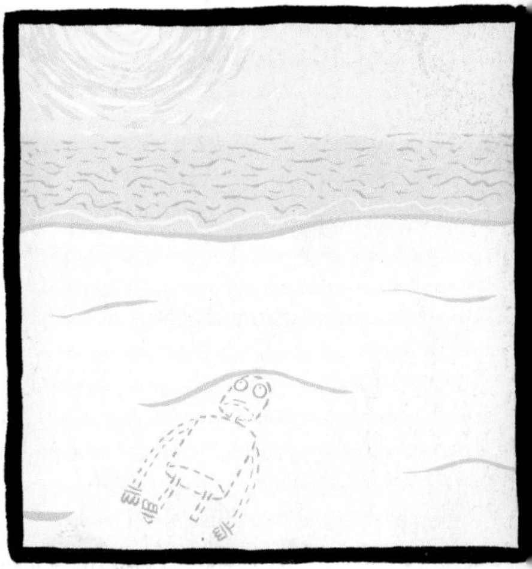

December

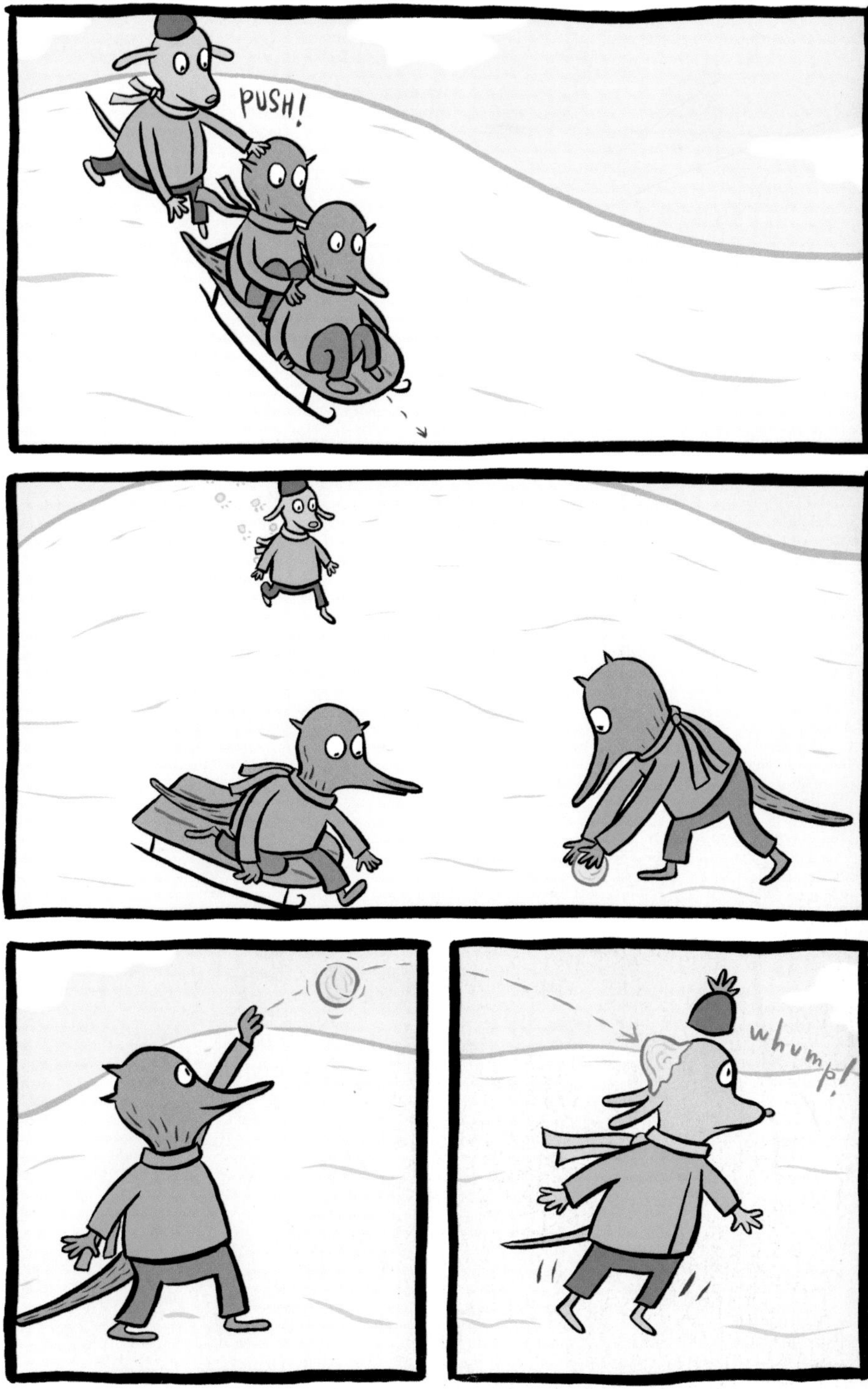
PUSH!
whump!

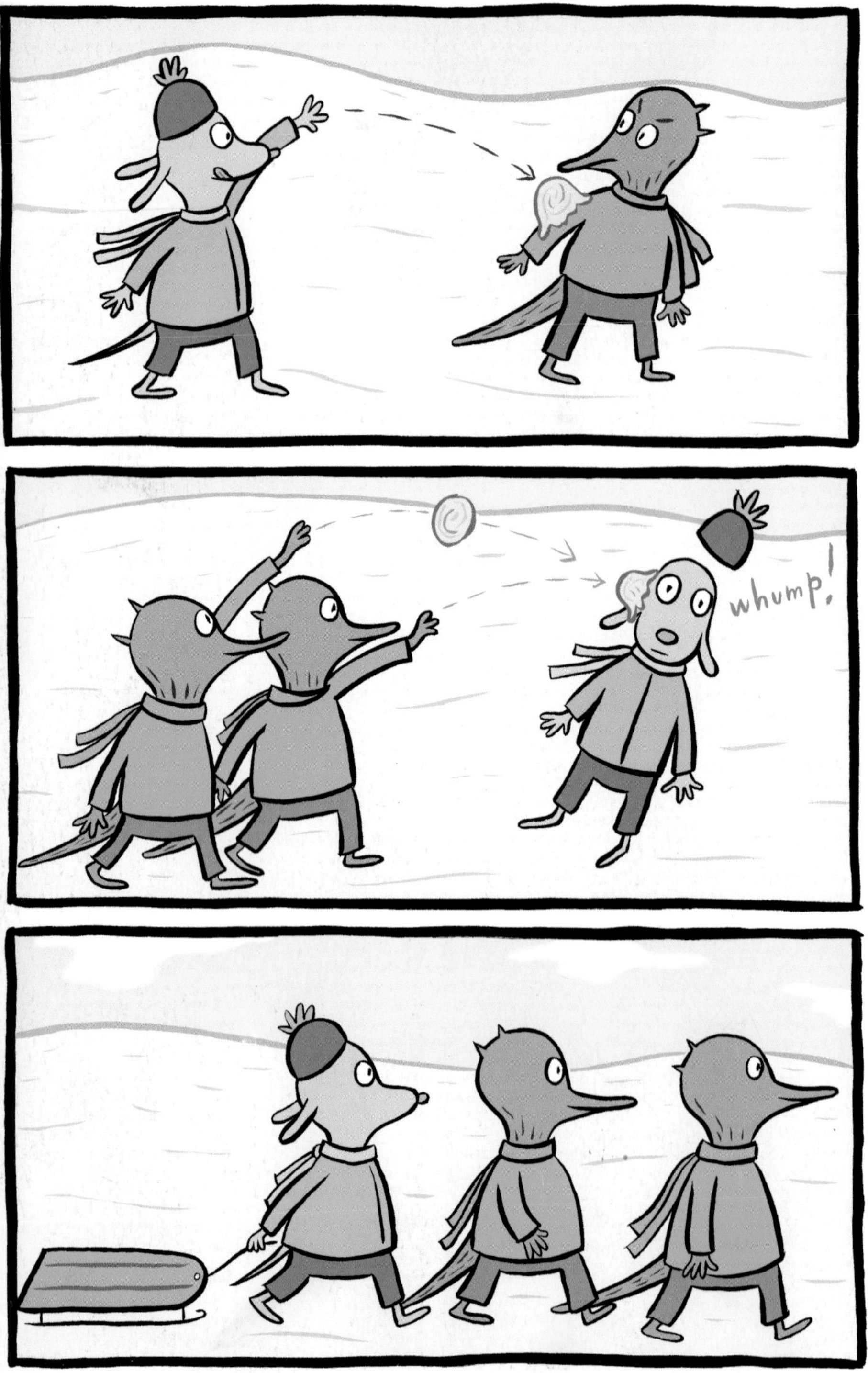
whump!

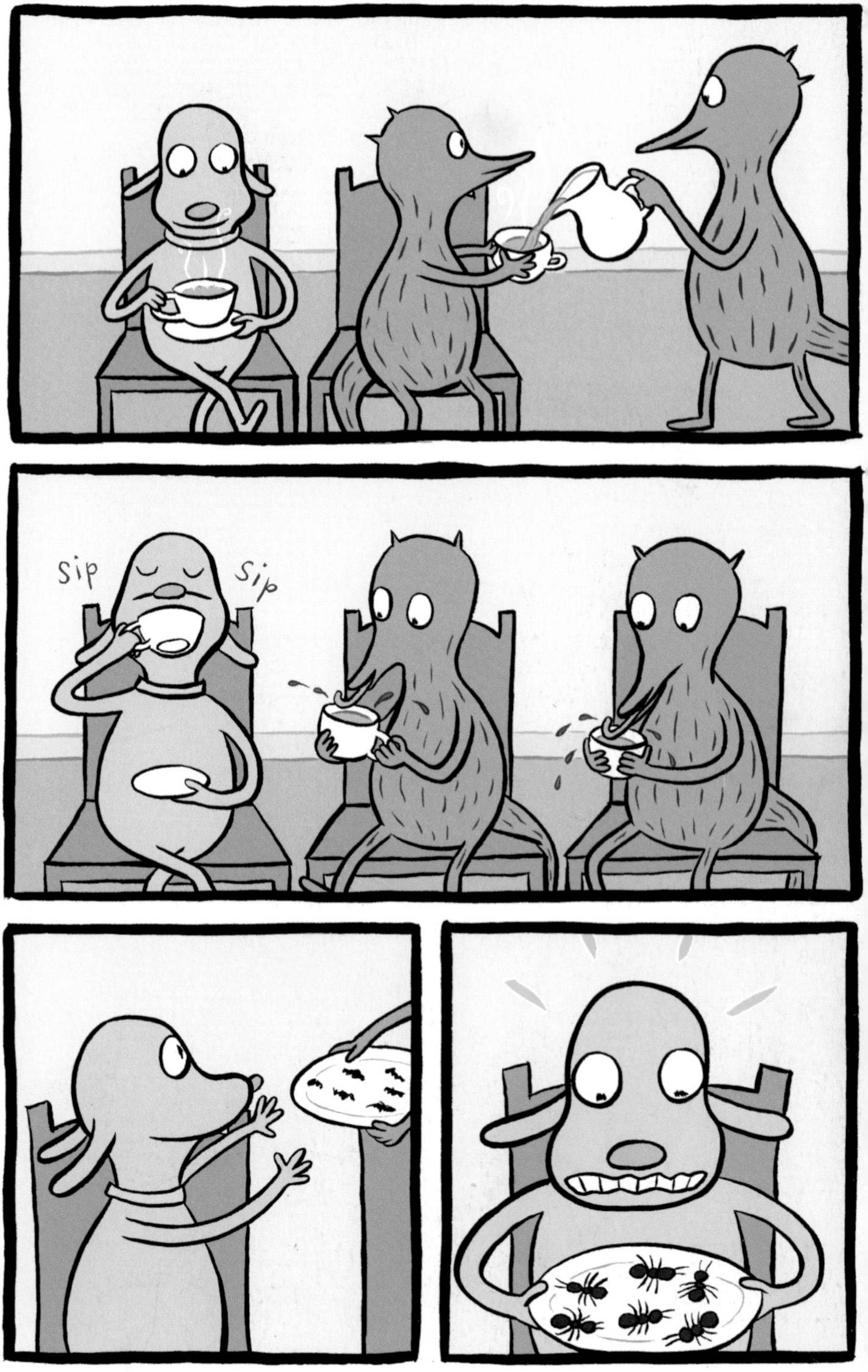
sip
sip

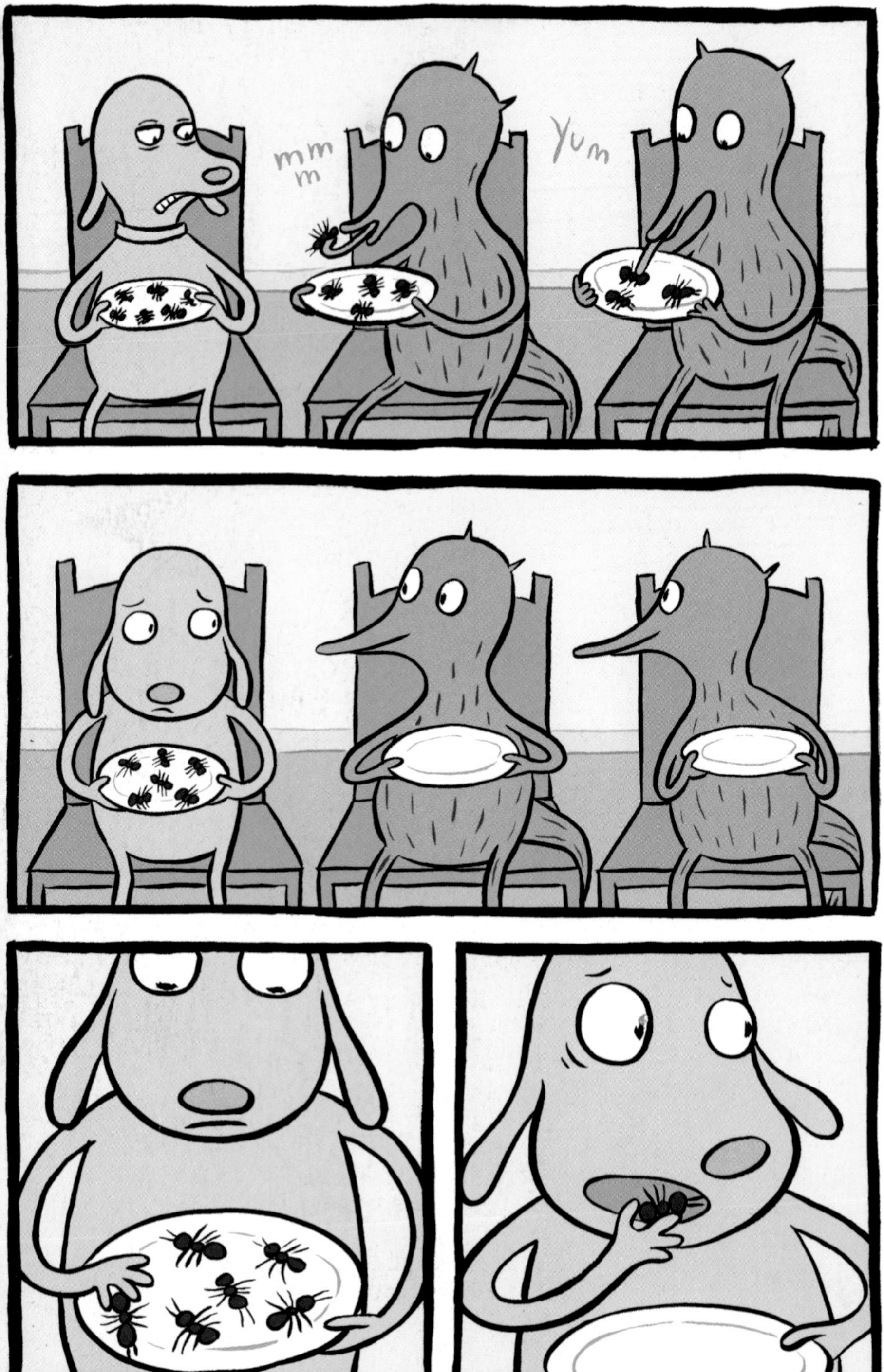
mmm
Yum

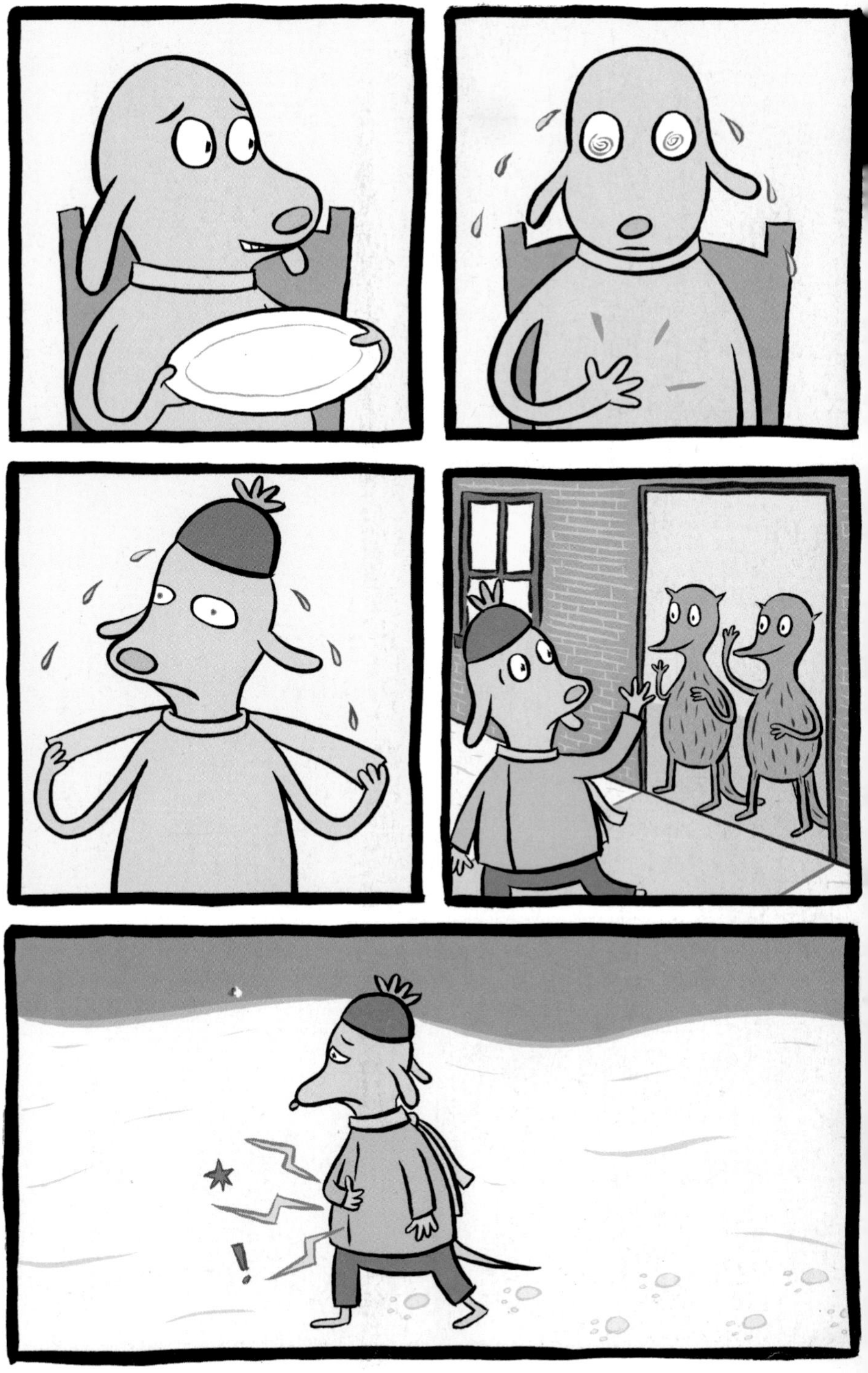
!

January

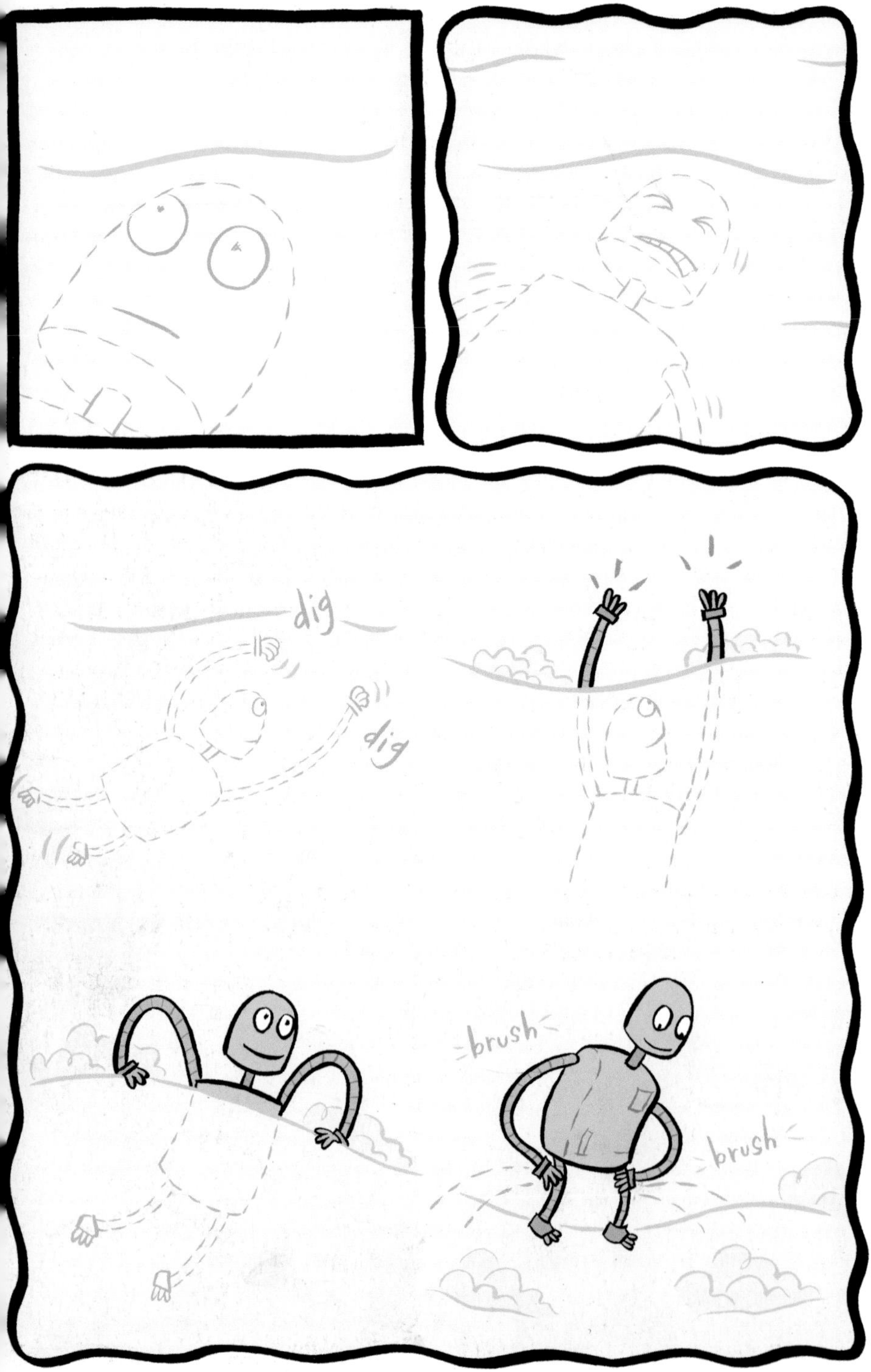
dig
dig
brush
brush

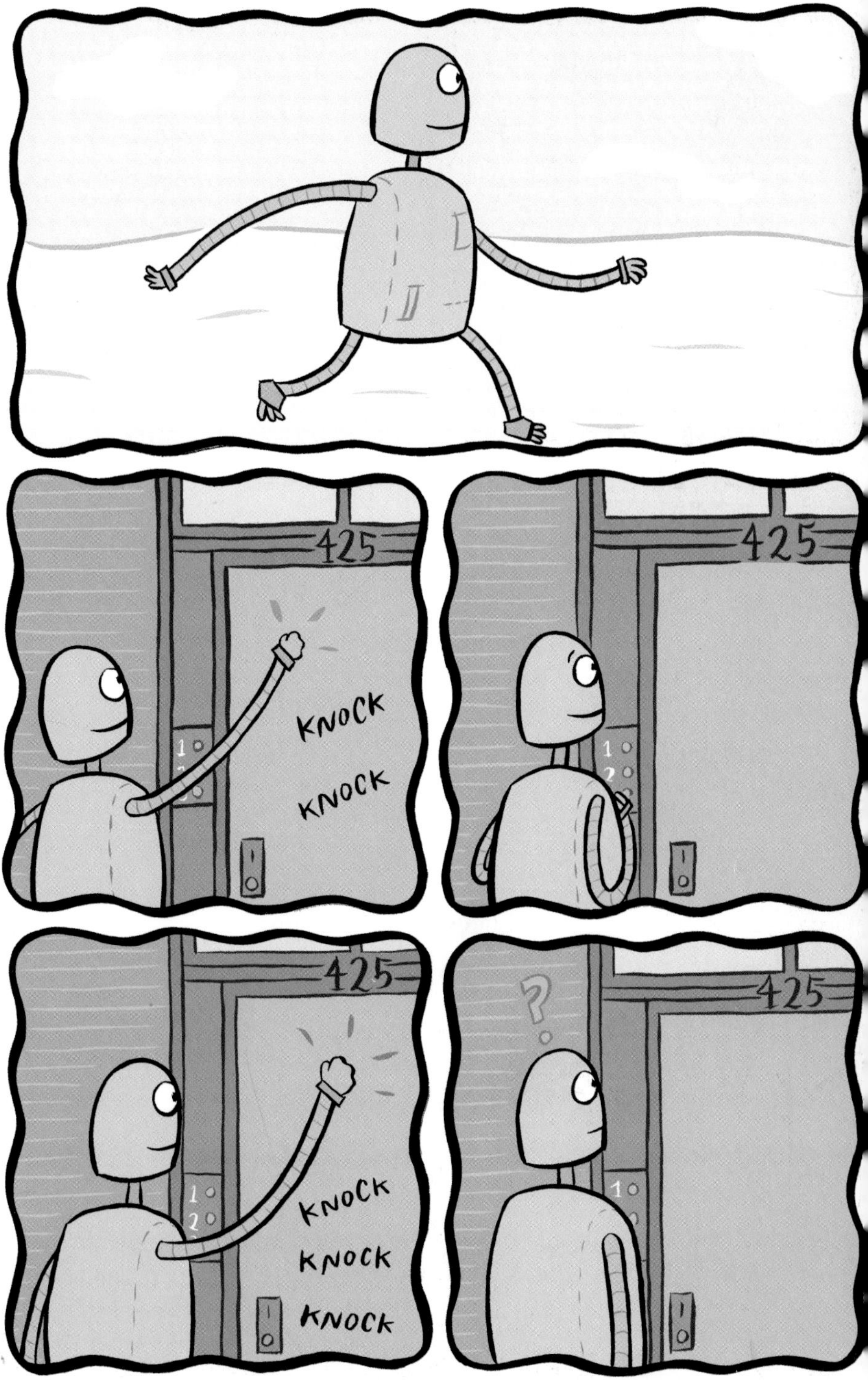
425
KNOCK
KNOCK
425
425
KNOCK
KNOCK
KNOCK
?
425

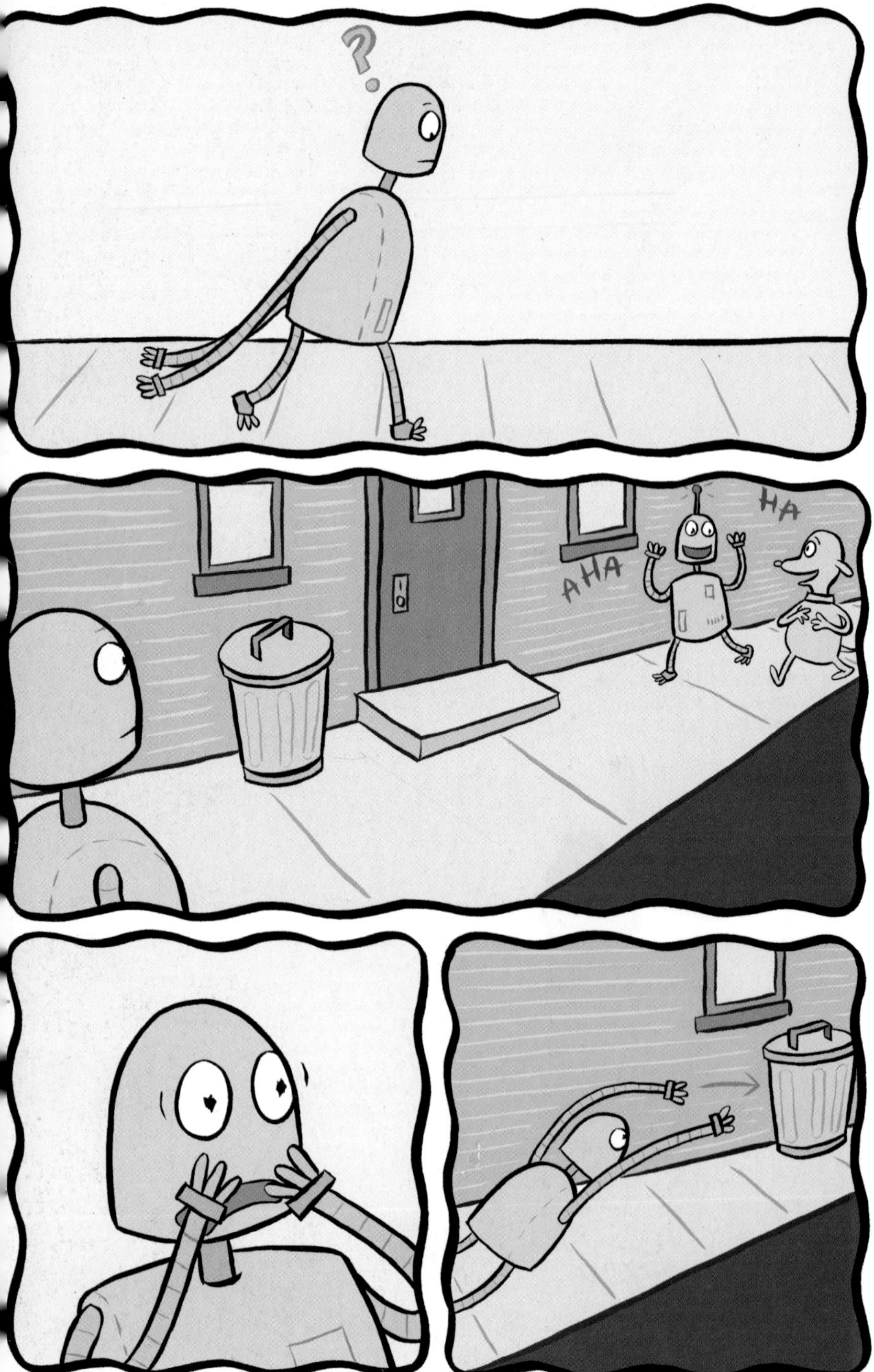
?
HA
AHA

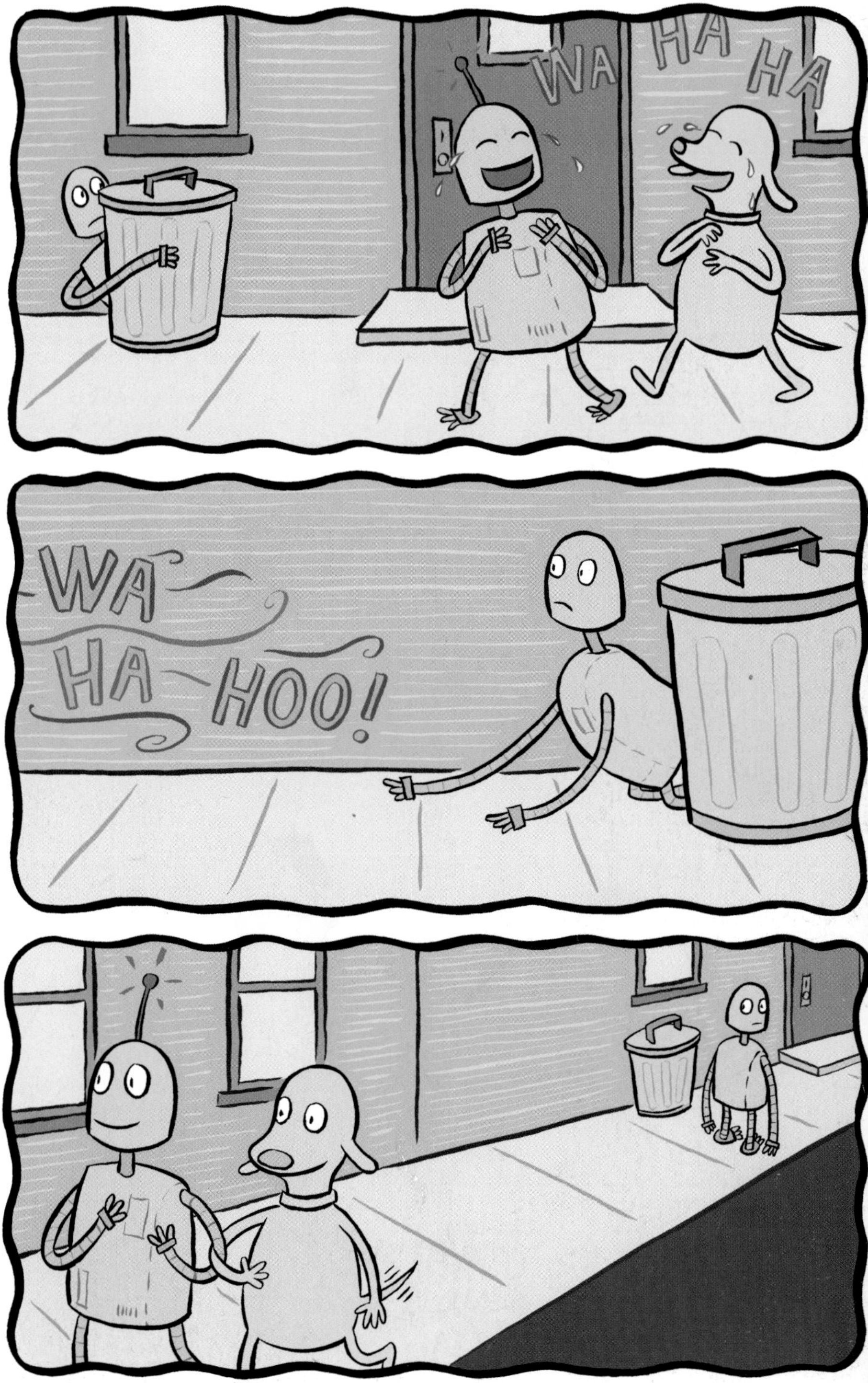
WA HA HA
WA HA HOO!

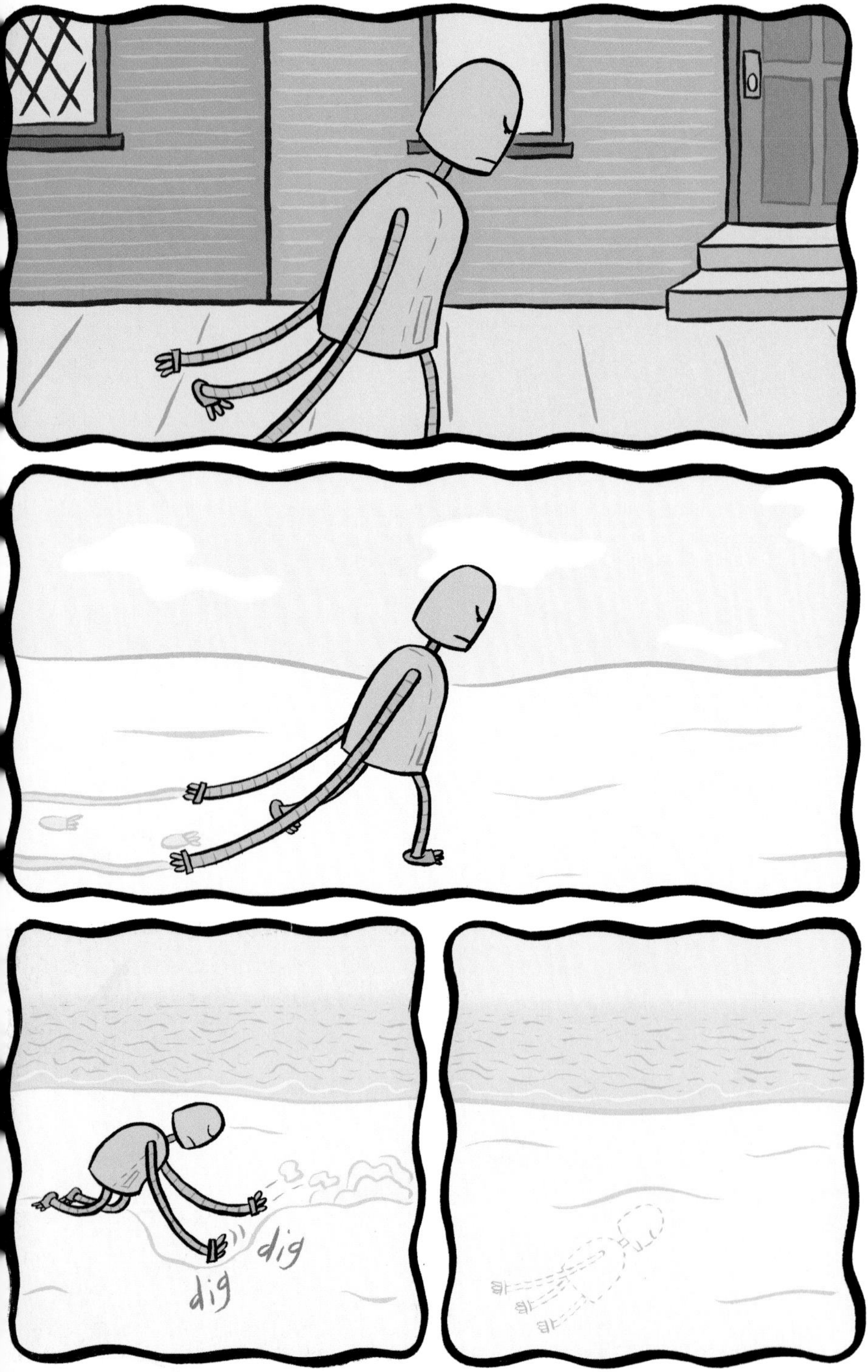
dig
dig

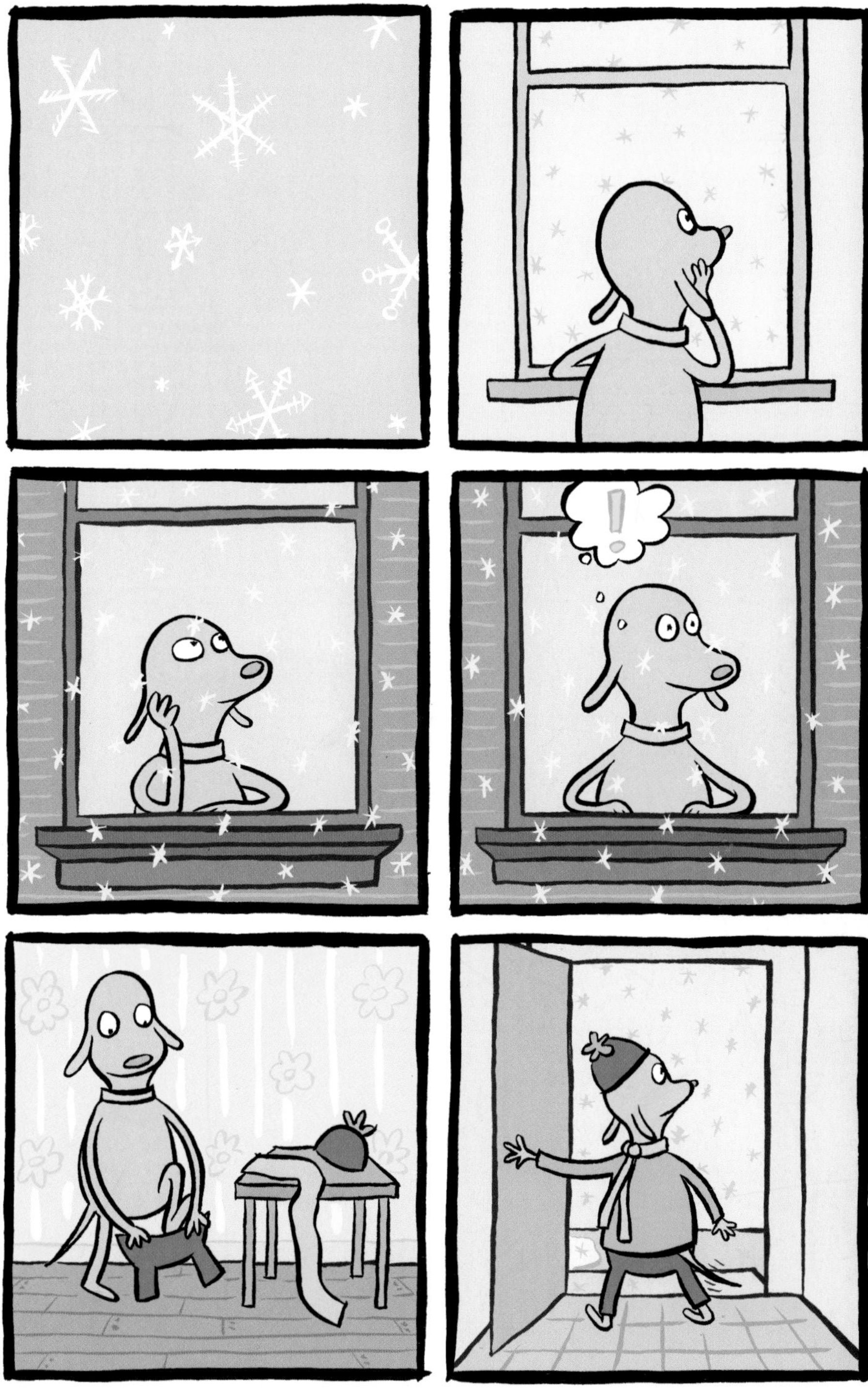
!

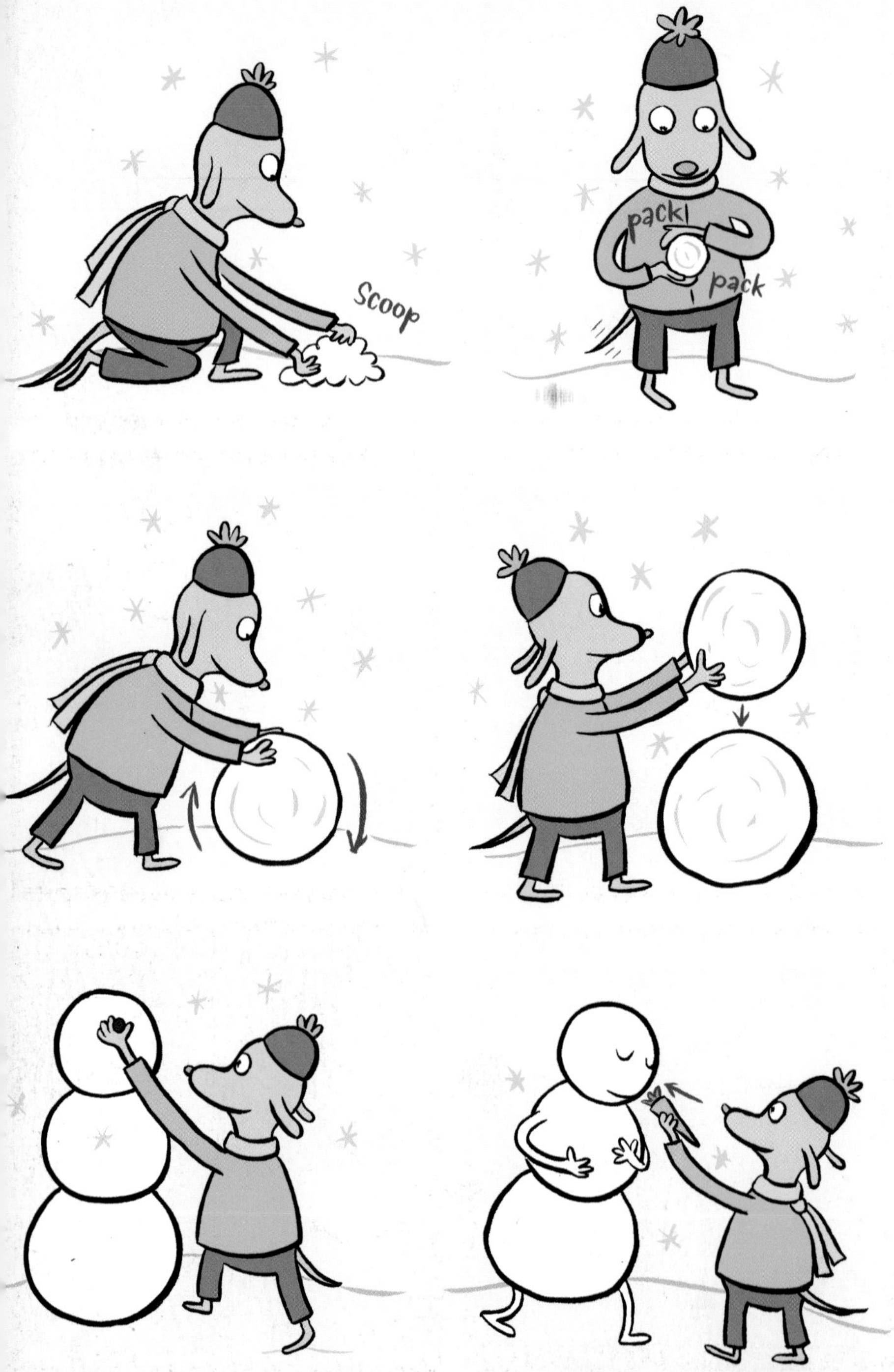
Scoop
pack!
pack

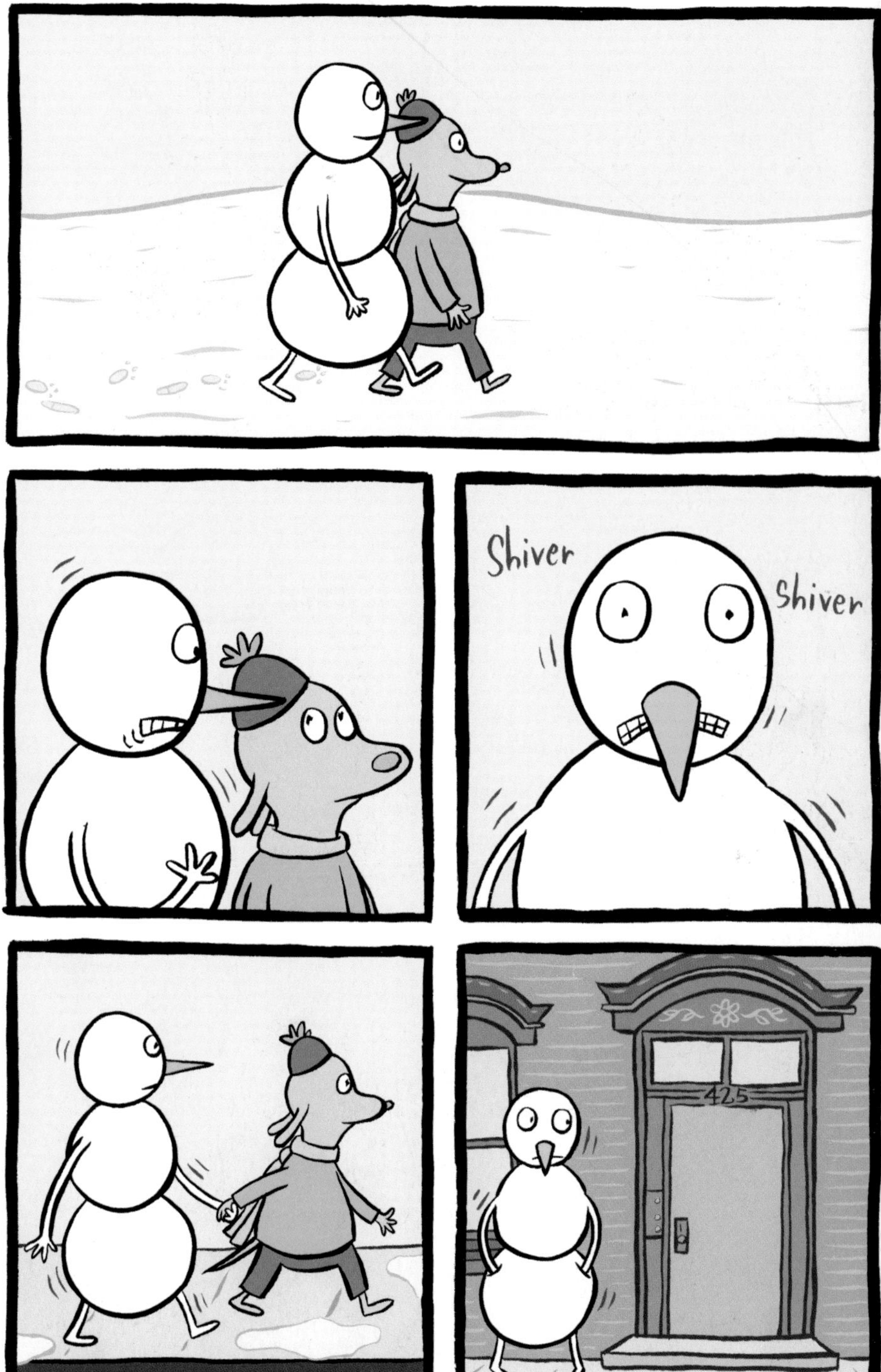
Shiver
Shiver
425

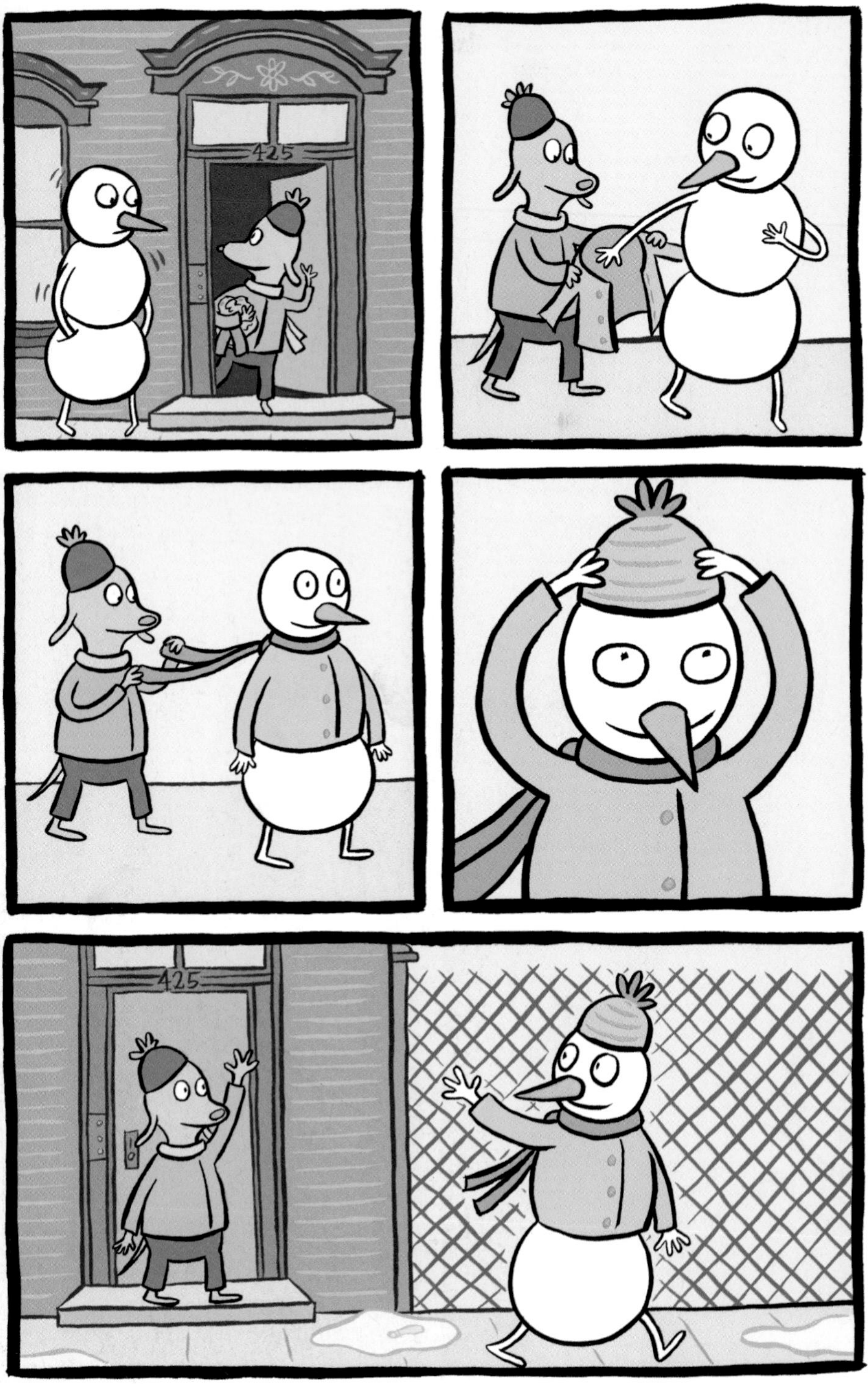
425
425

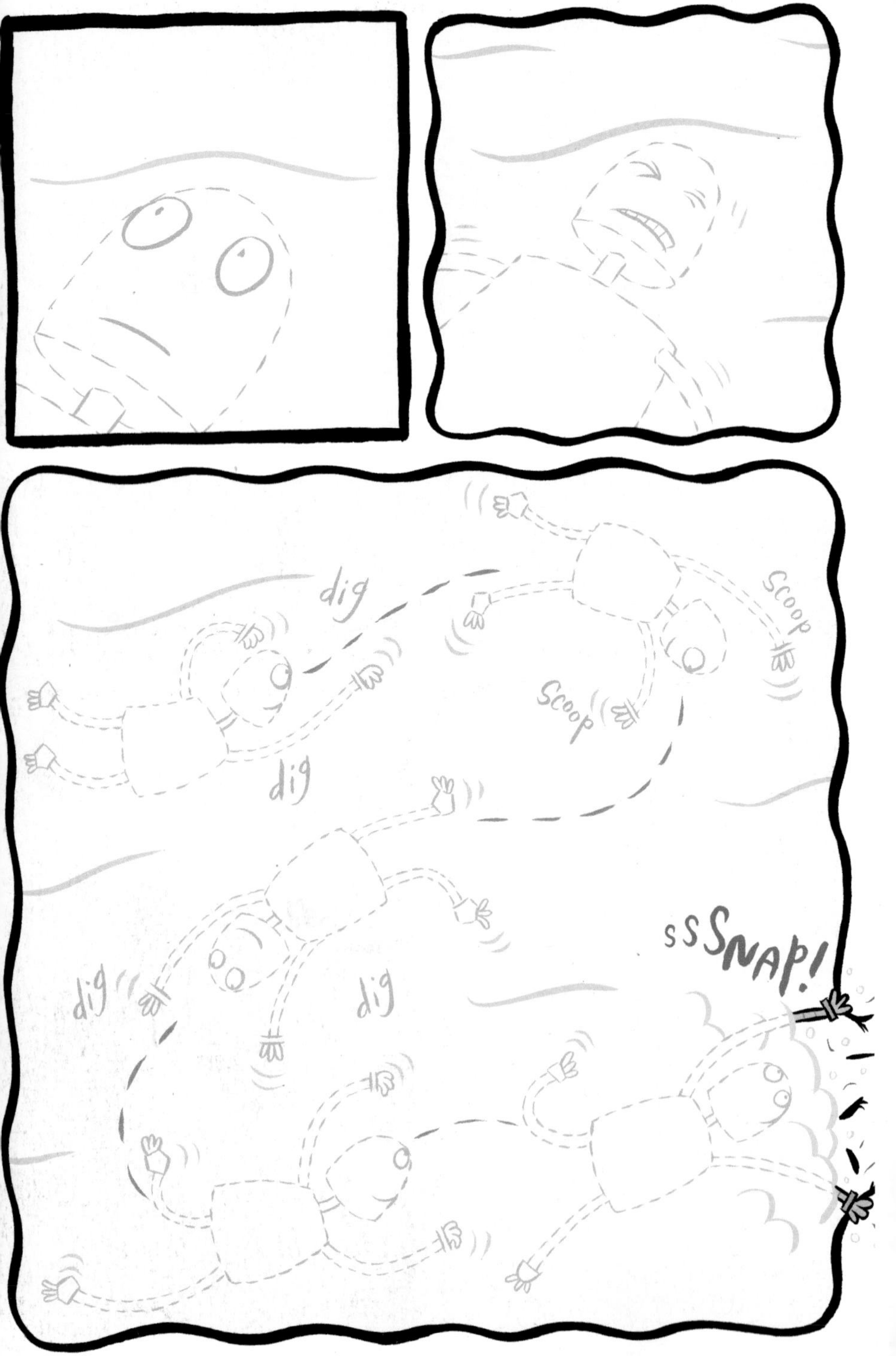

dig
Scoop
Scoop
dig
dig
dig
sSSNAP!

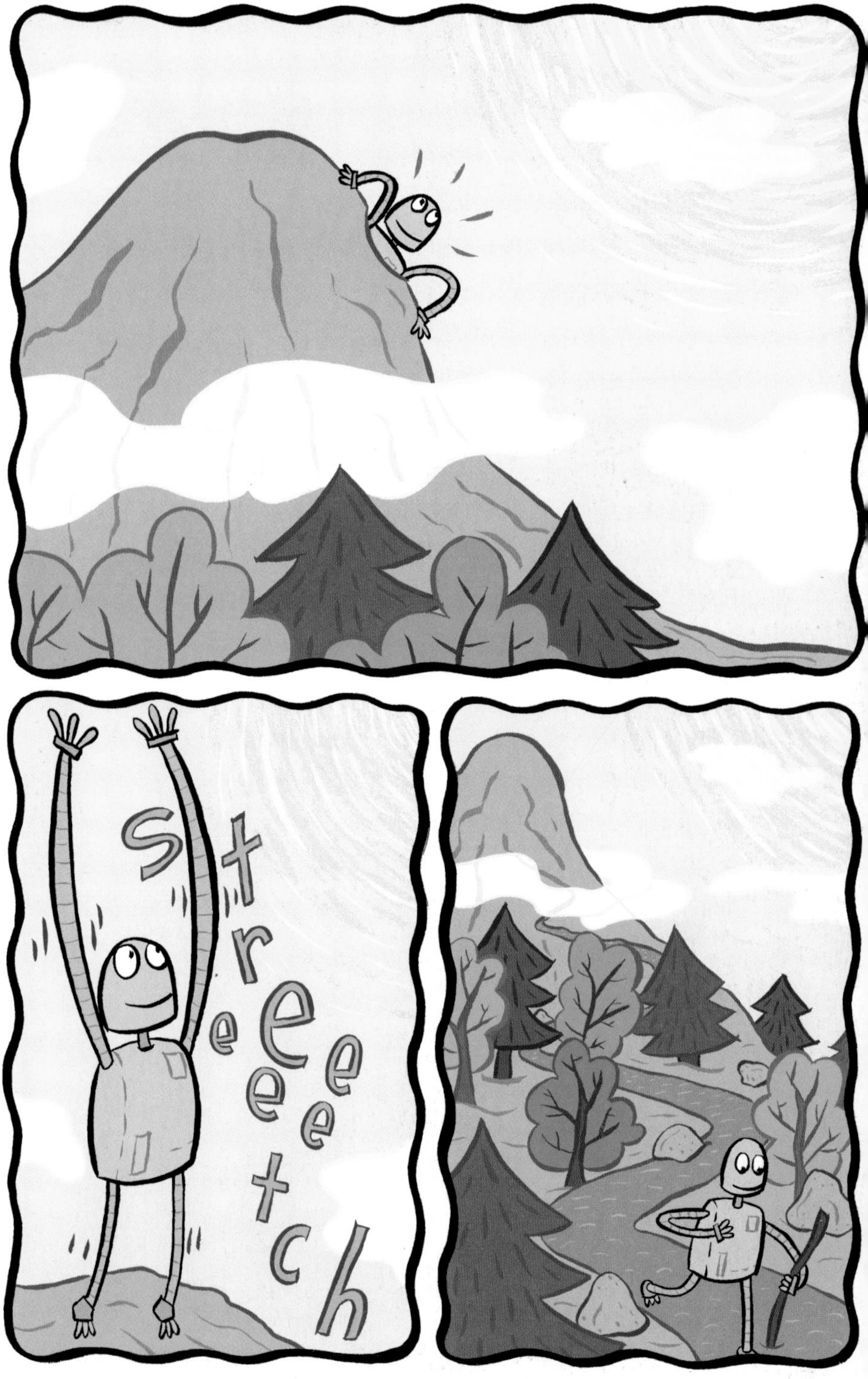
streeeeeeetch

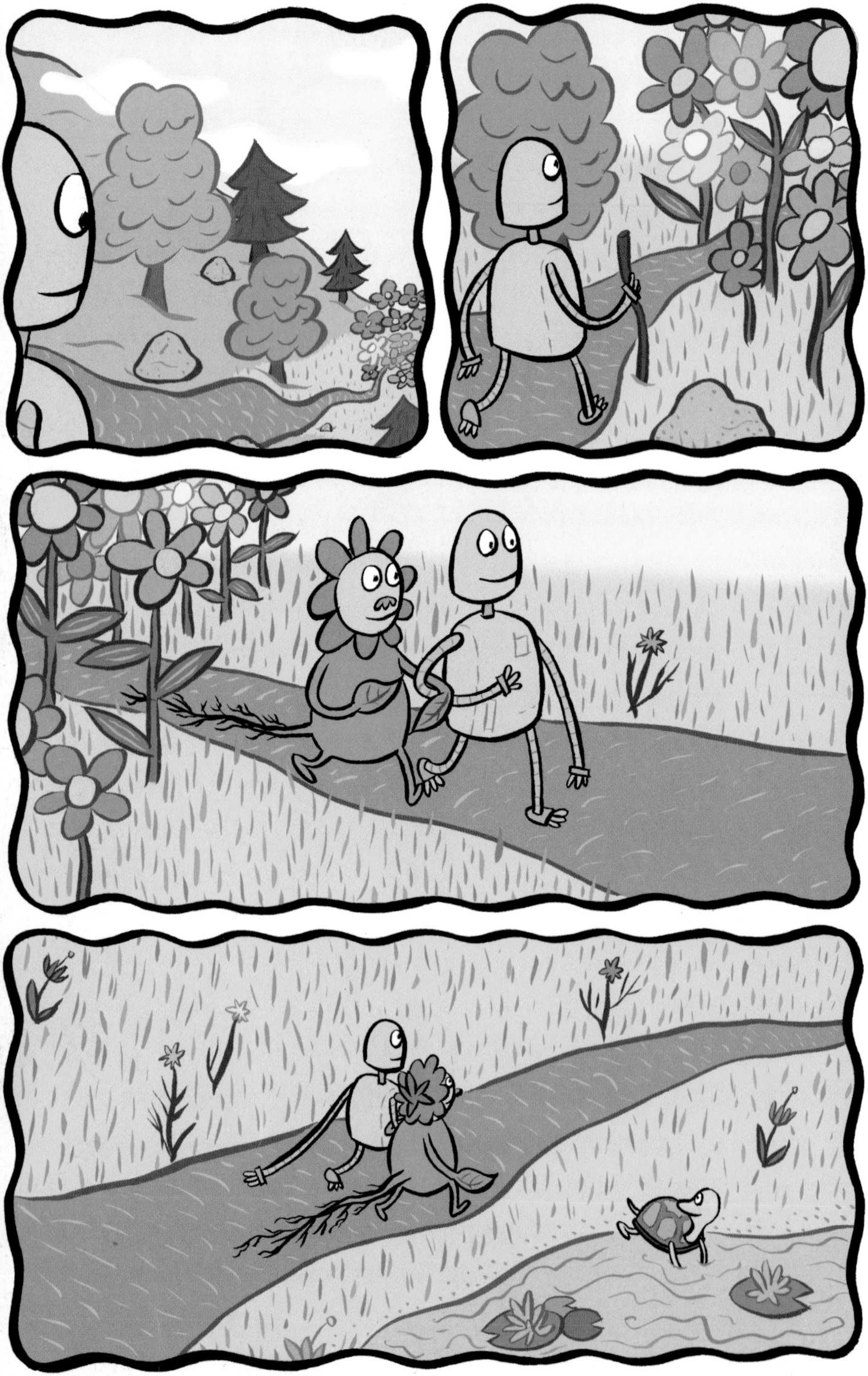

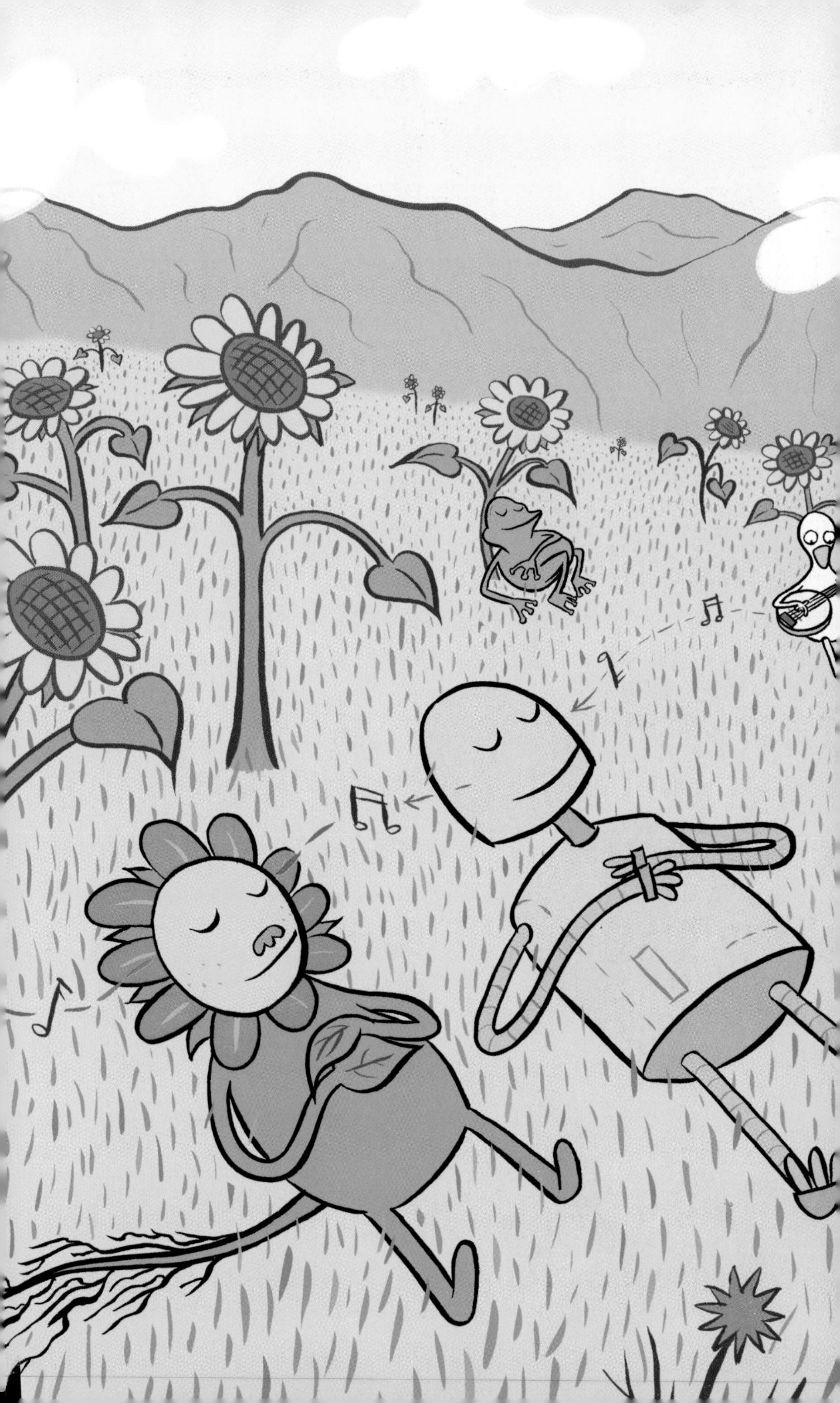

February

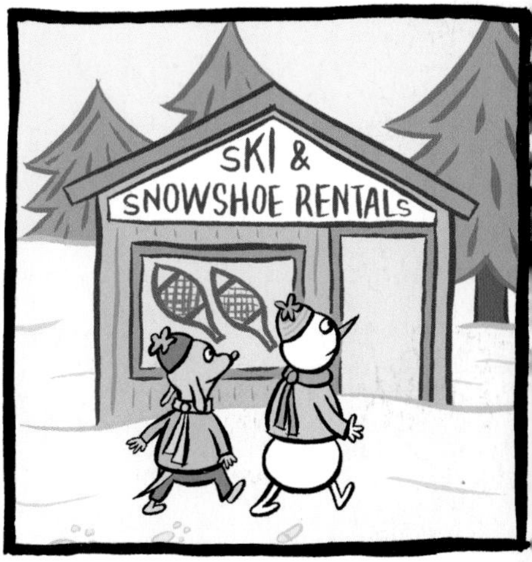

SKI &
SNOWSHOE RENTALS

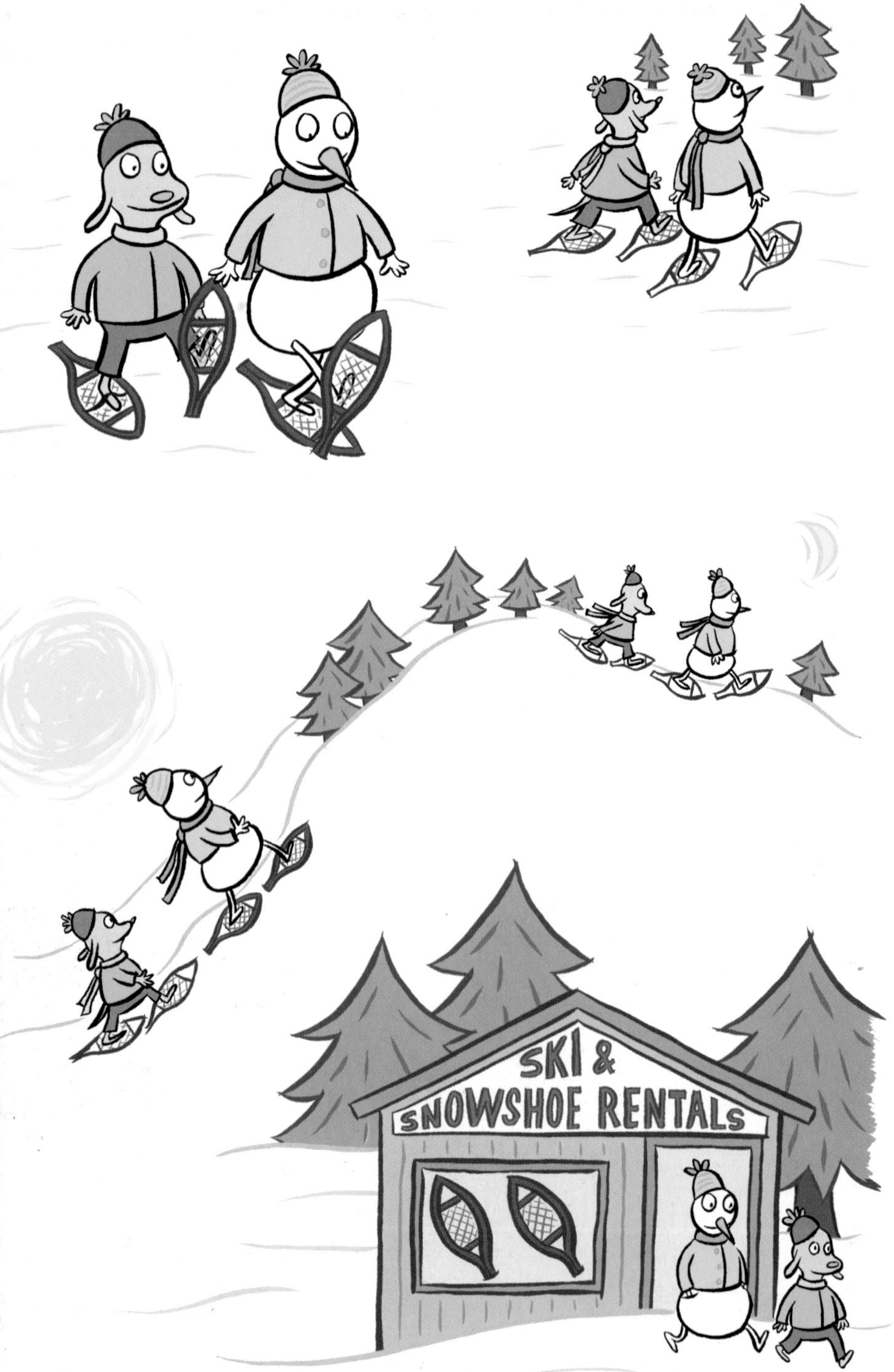
SKI &
SNOWSHOE RENTALS

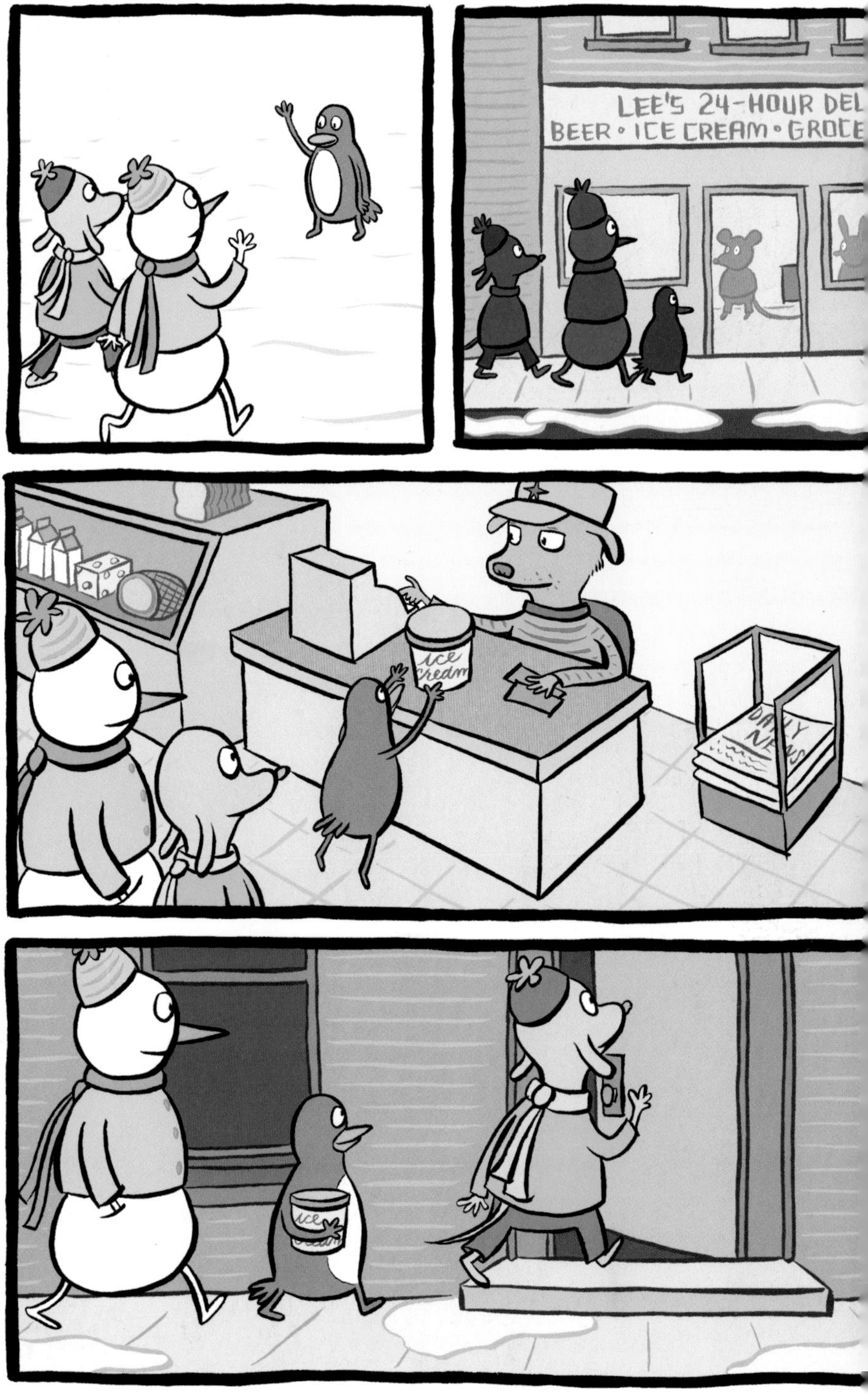
LEE'S 24-HOUR DEL
BEER • ICE CREAM • GROCE
ice cream
DAILY NEWS

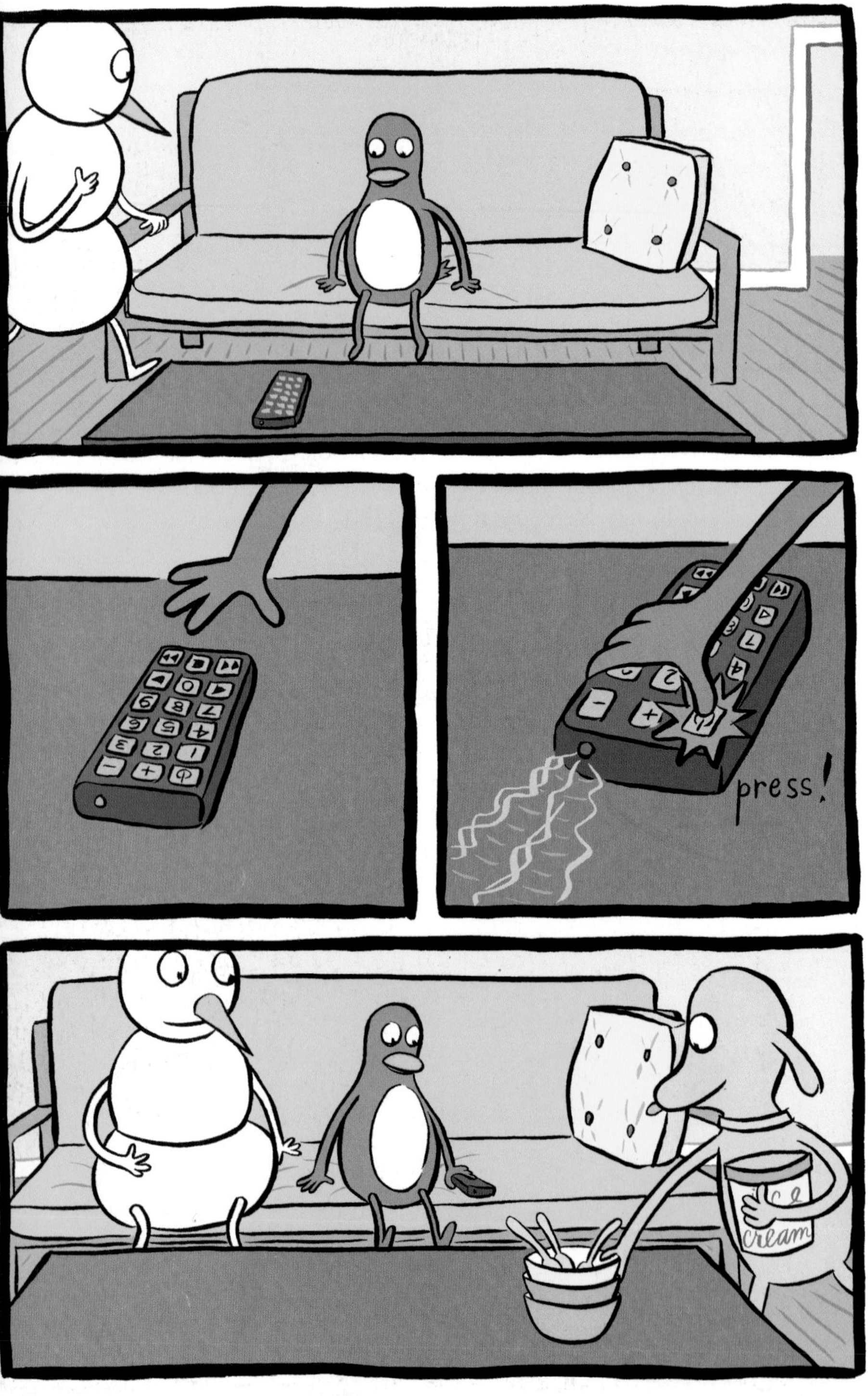
press!
cream

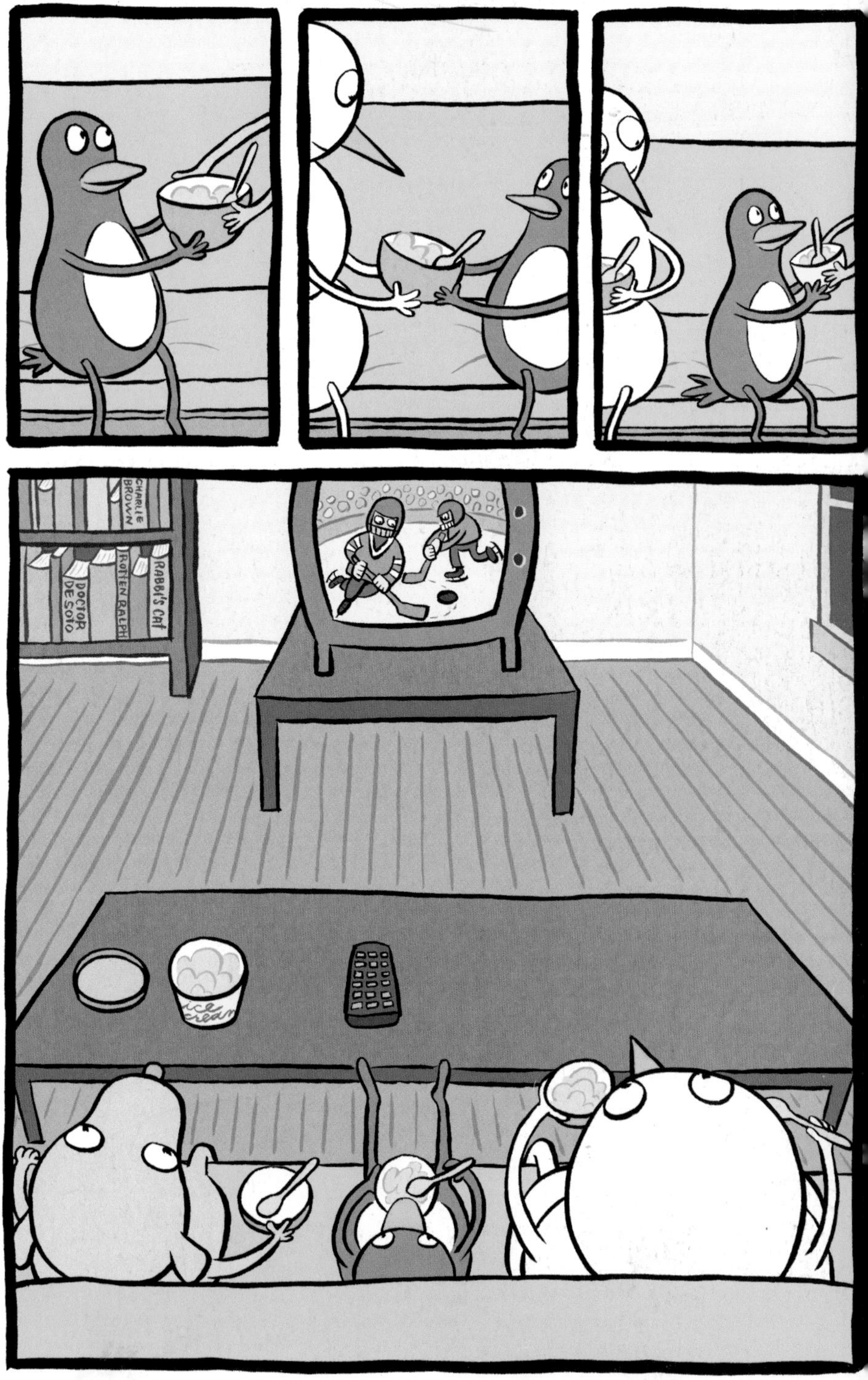
CHARLIE BROWN
DOCTOR DE SOTO
ROTTEN RALPH
RABBI'S CAT
ice cream

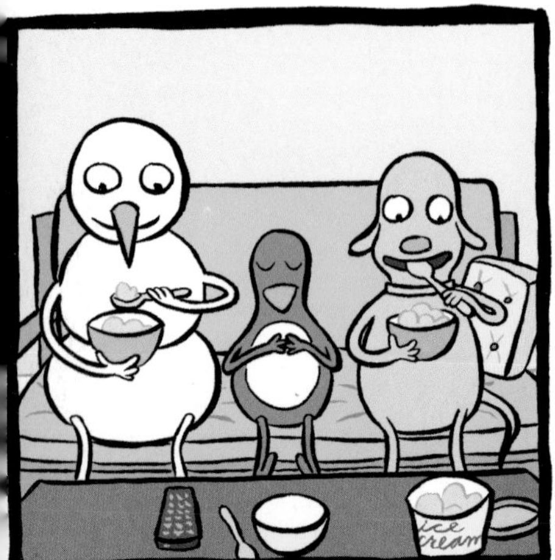
ice cream

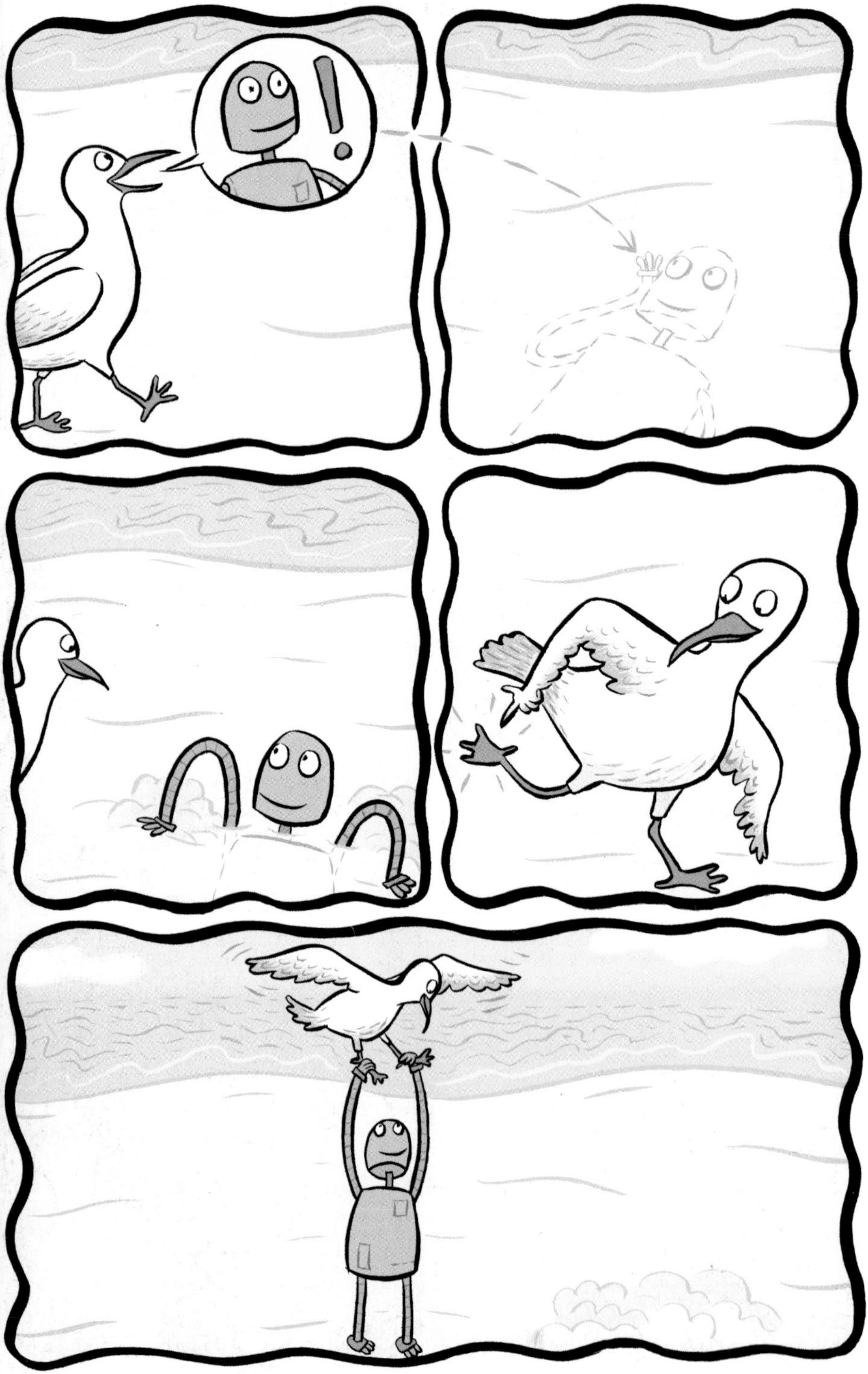
!

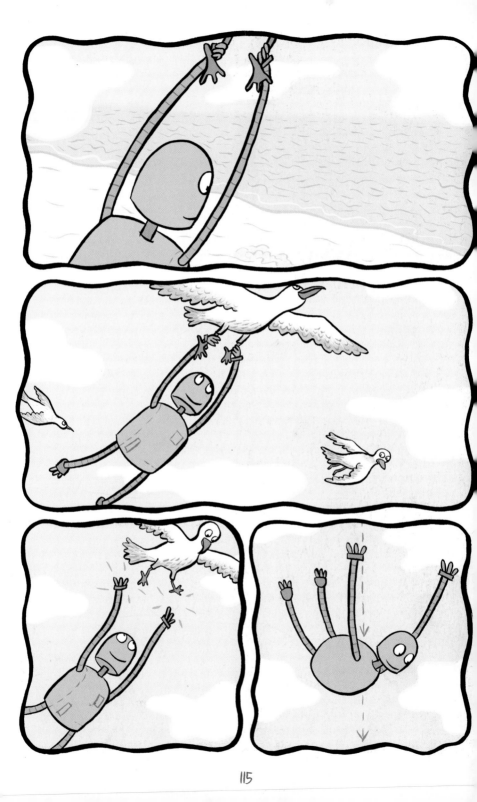

115

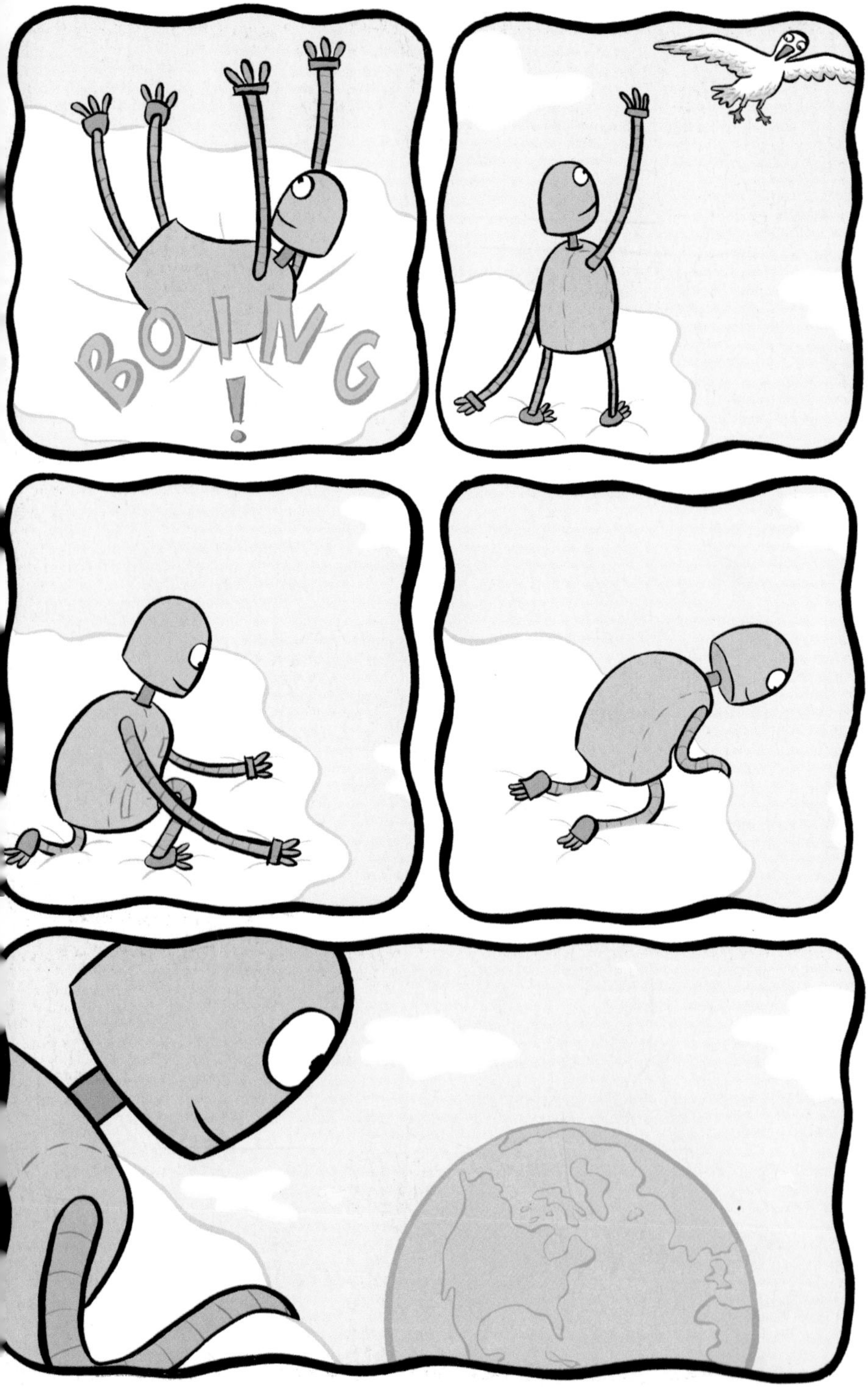
BOING!

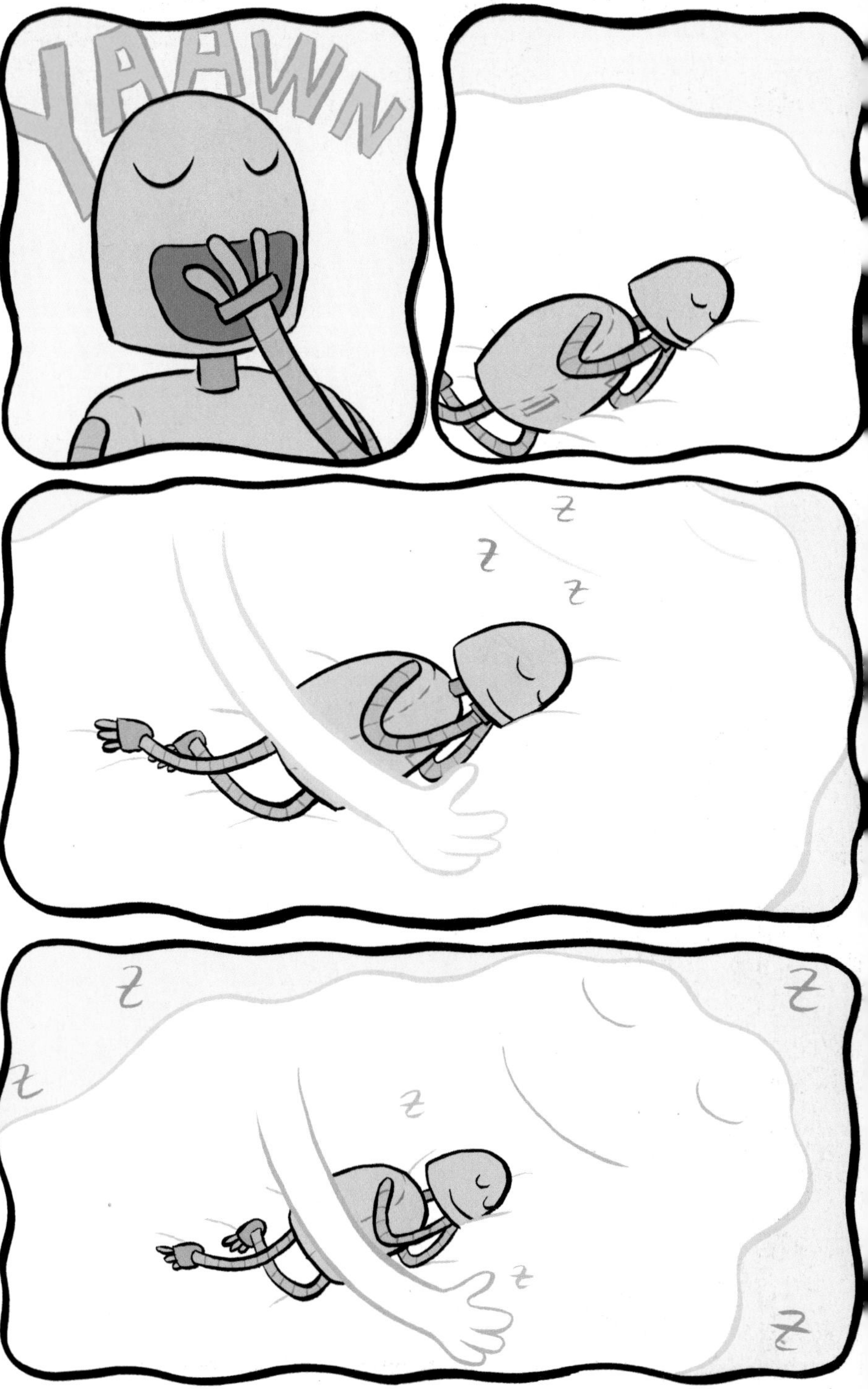
YAAWN
Z Z Z
Z Z Z Z Z

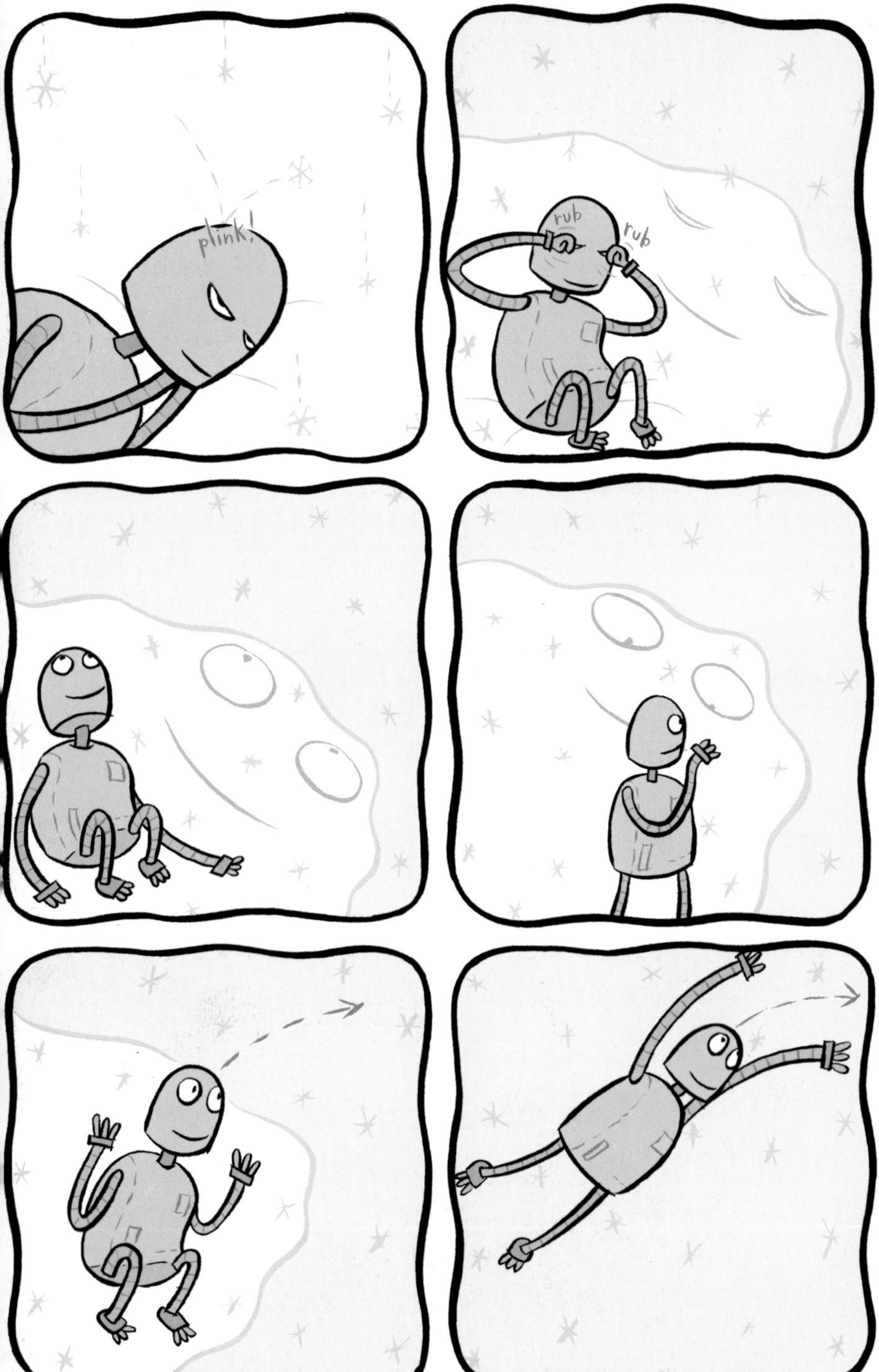
plink!
rub
rub

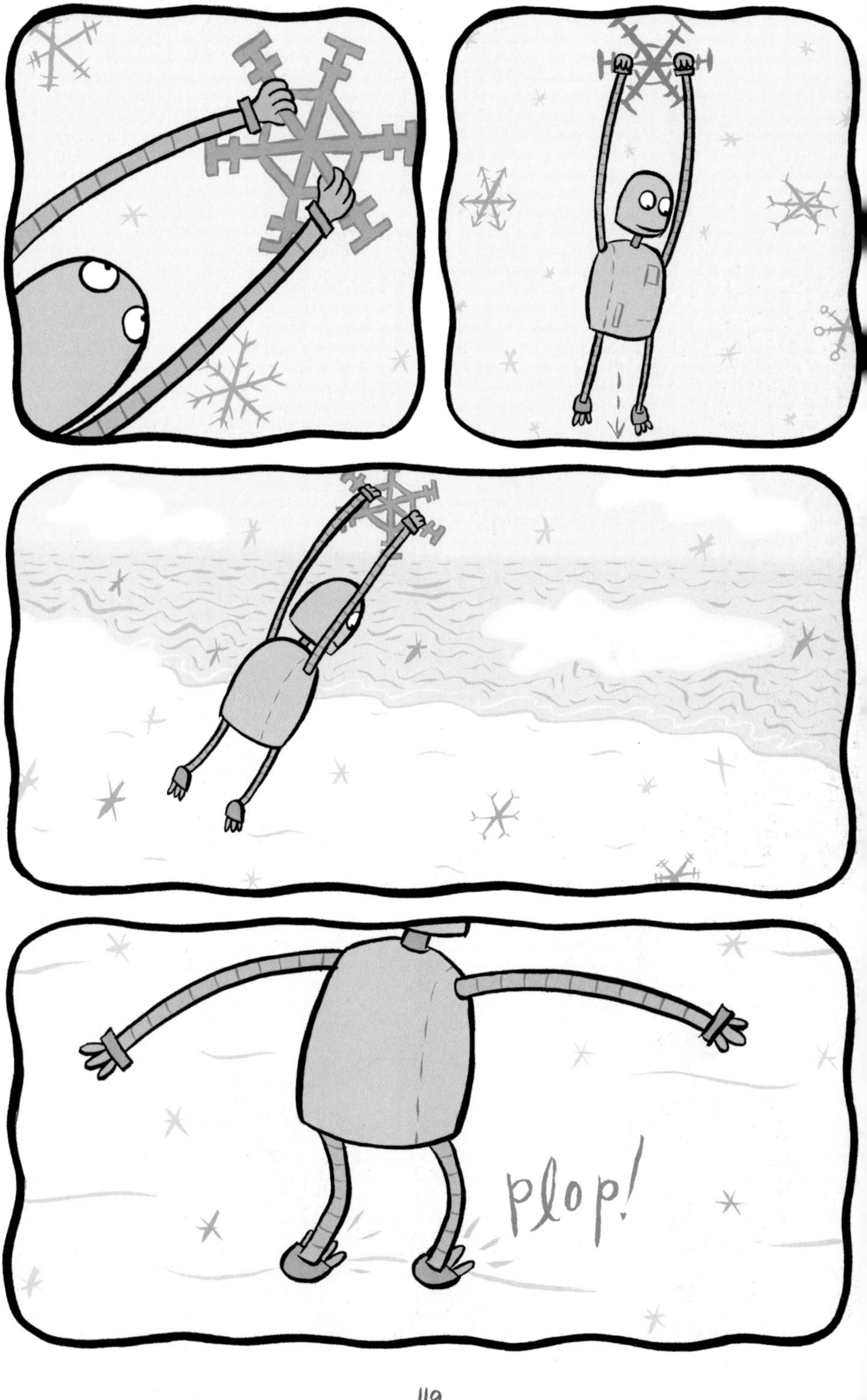
plop!

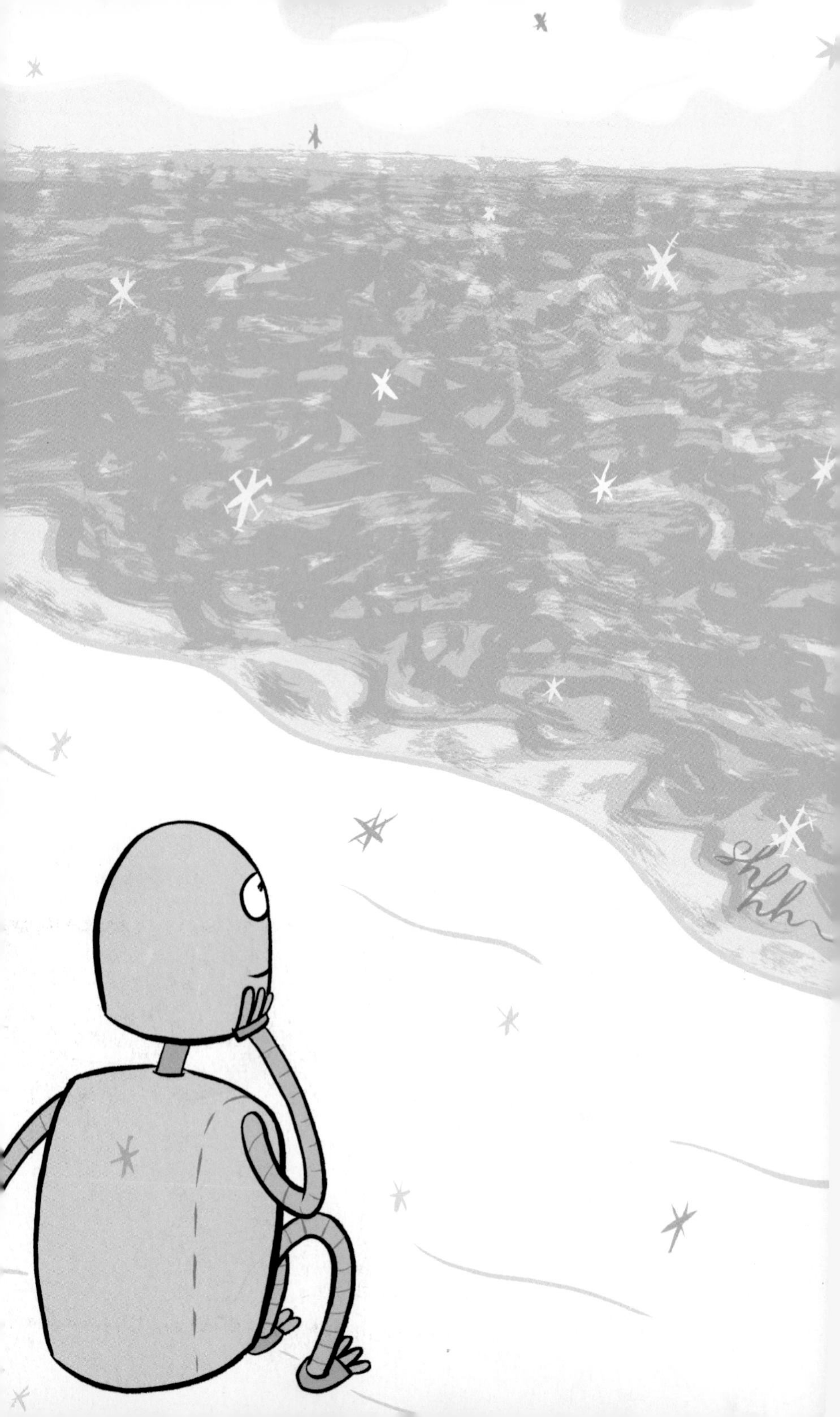
shhh

March

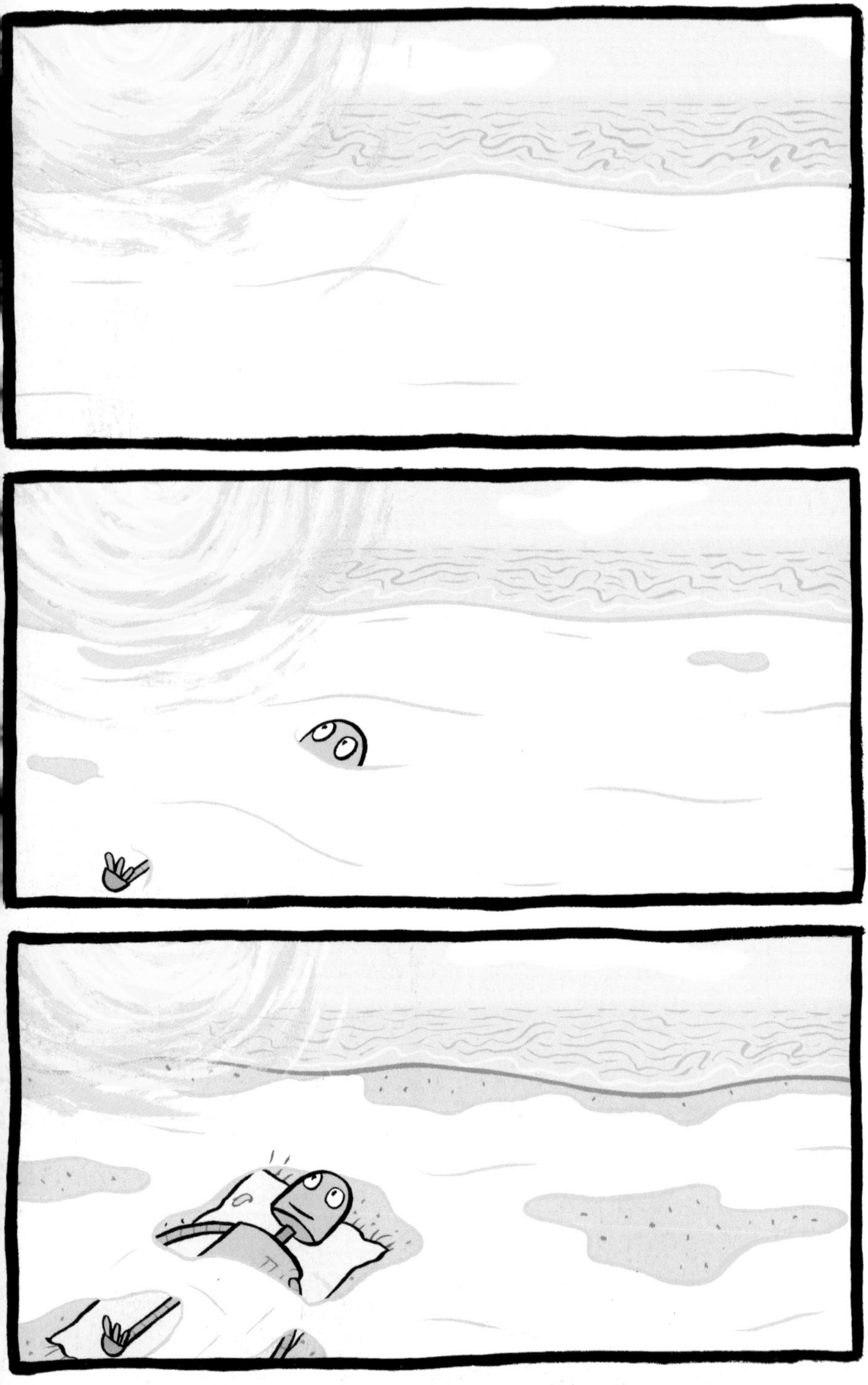

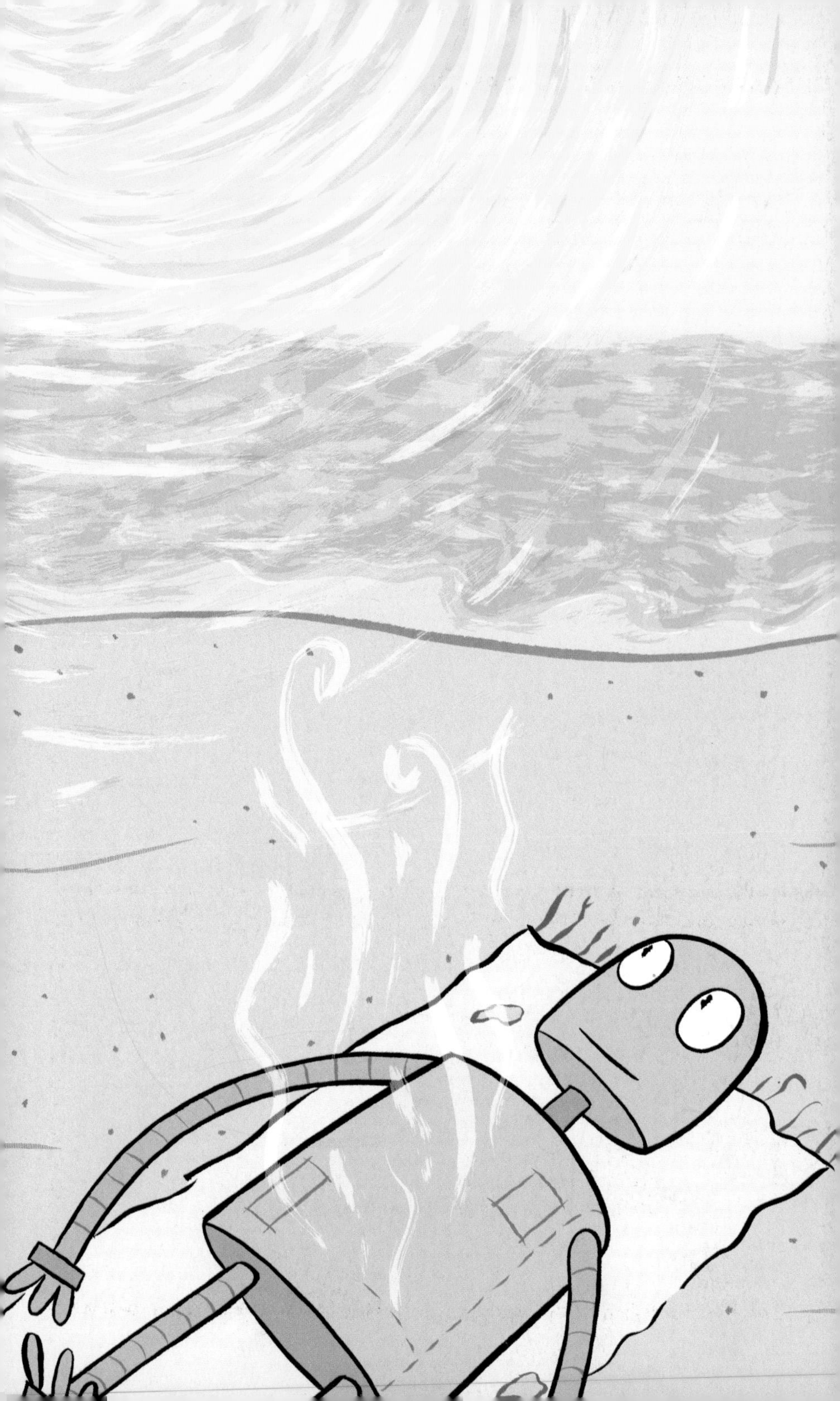

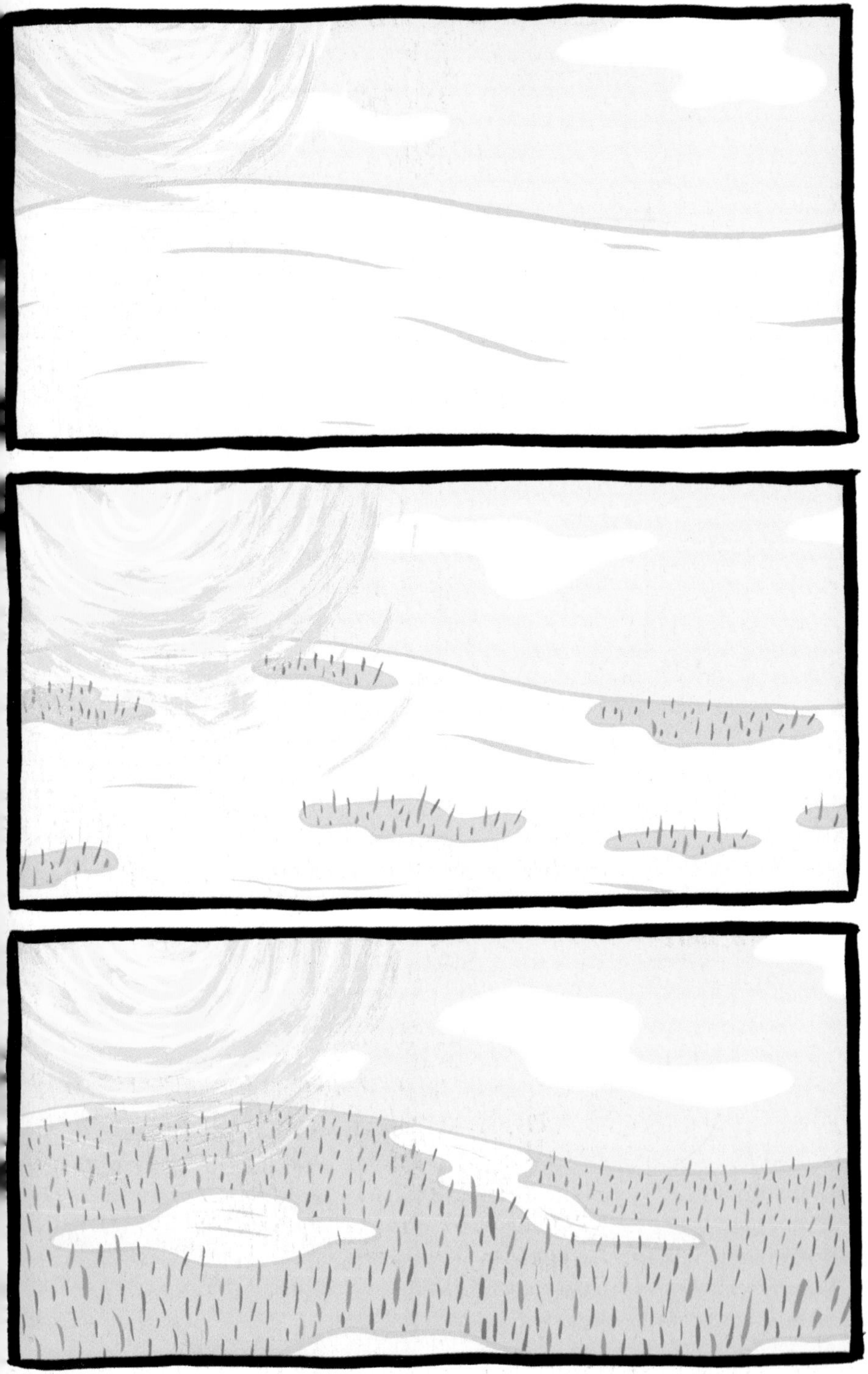

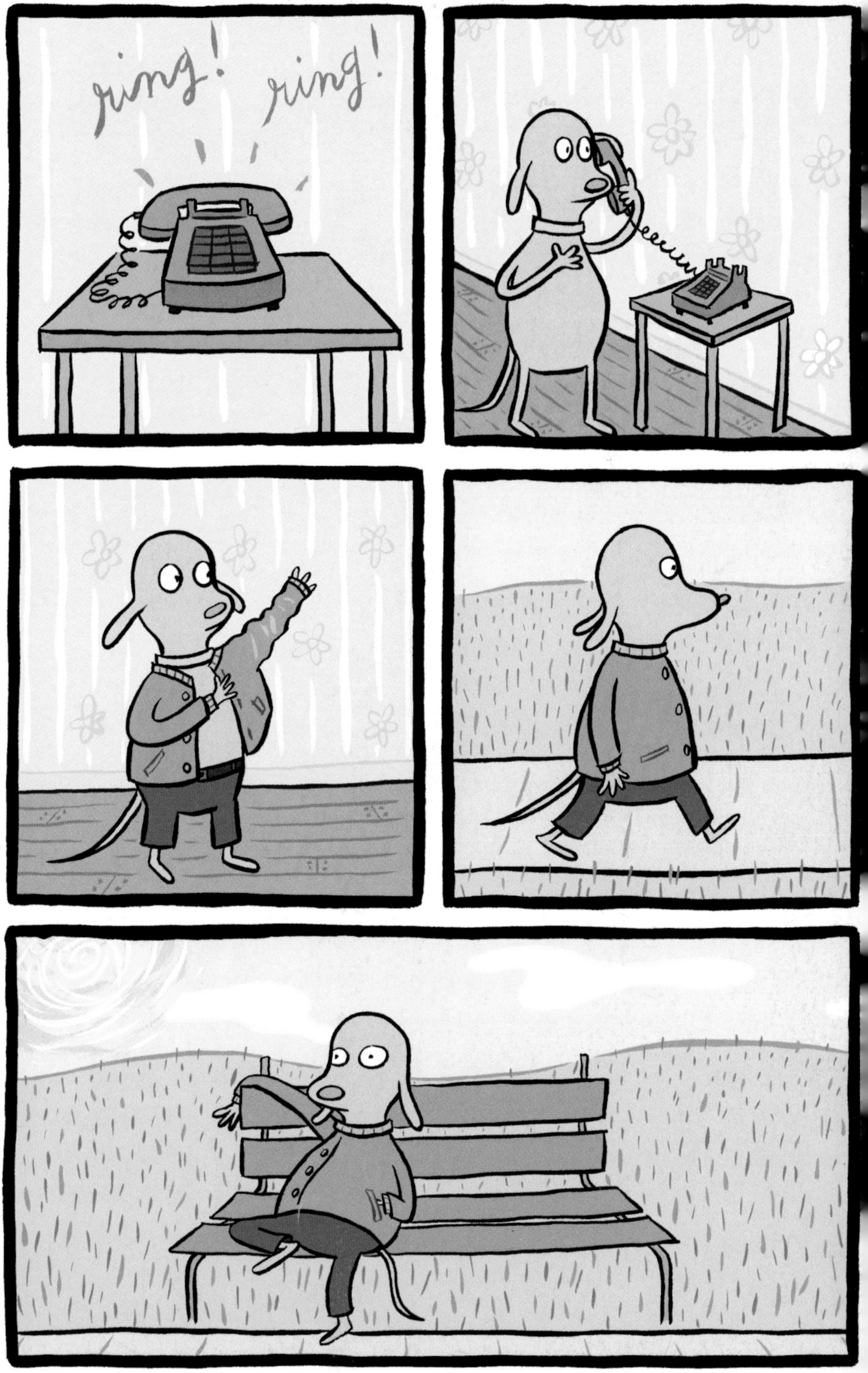
ring! ring!

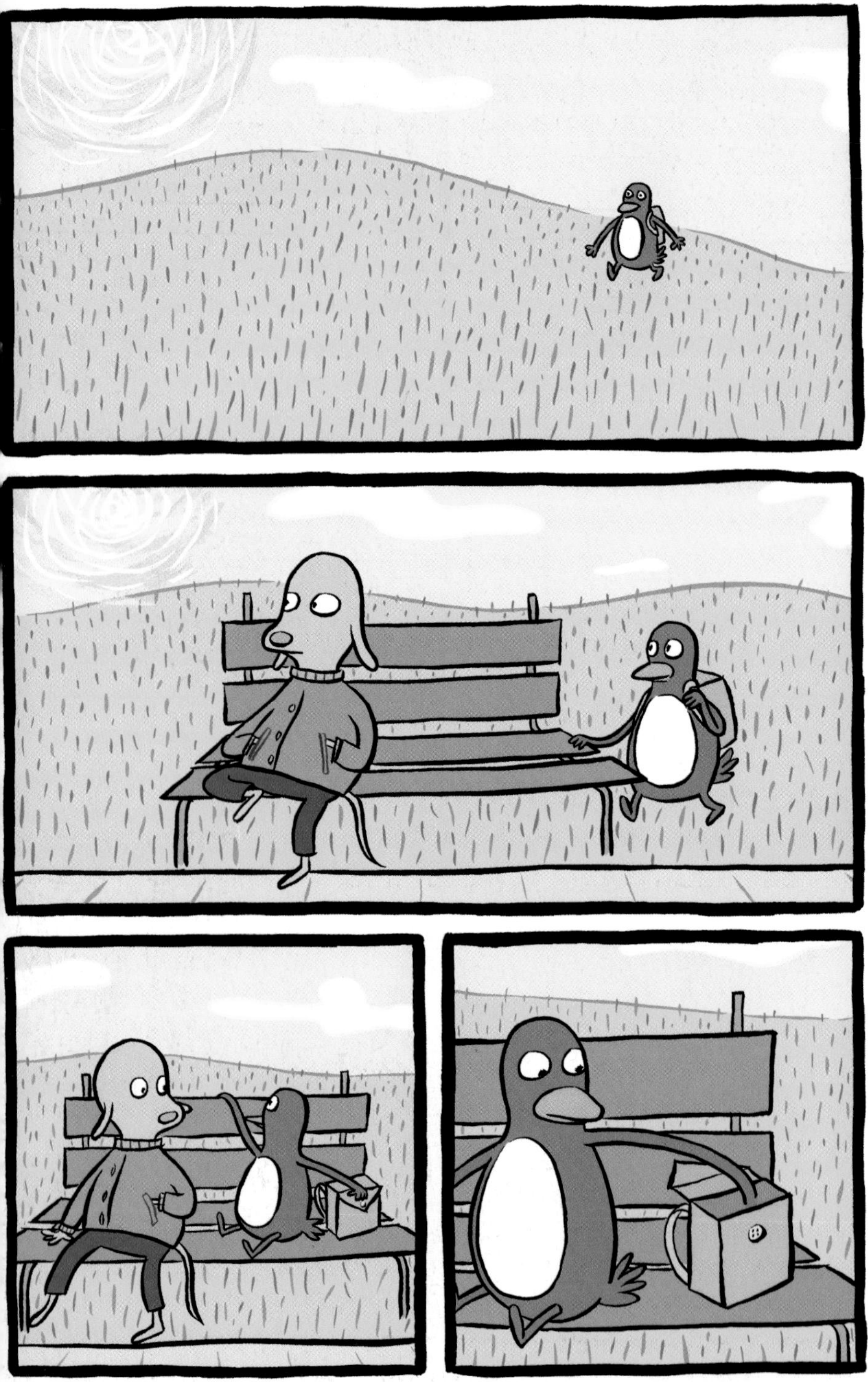

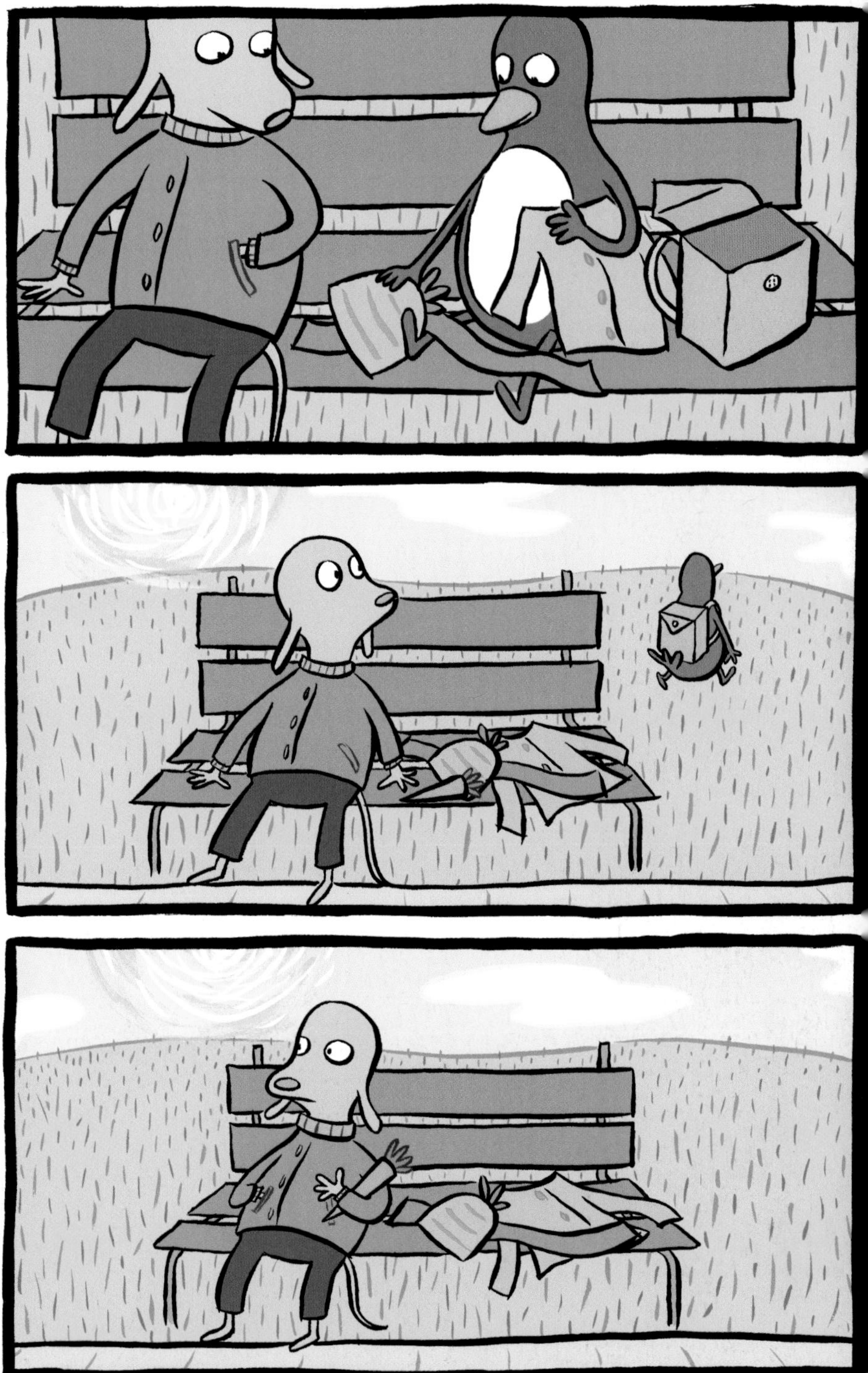

April

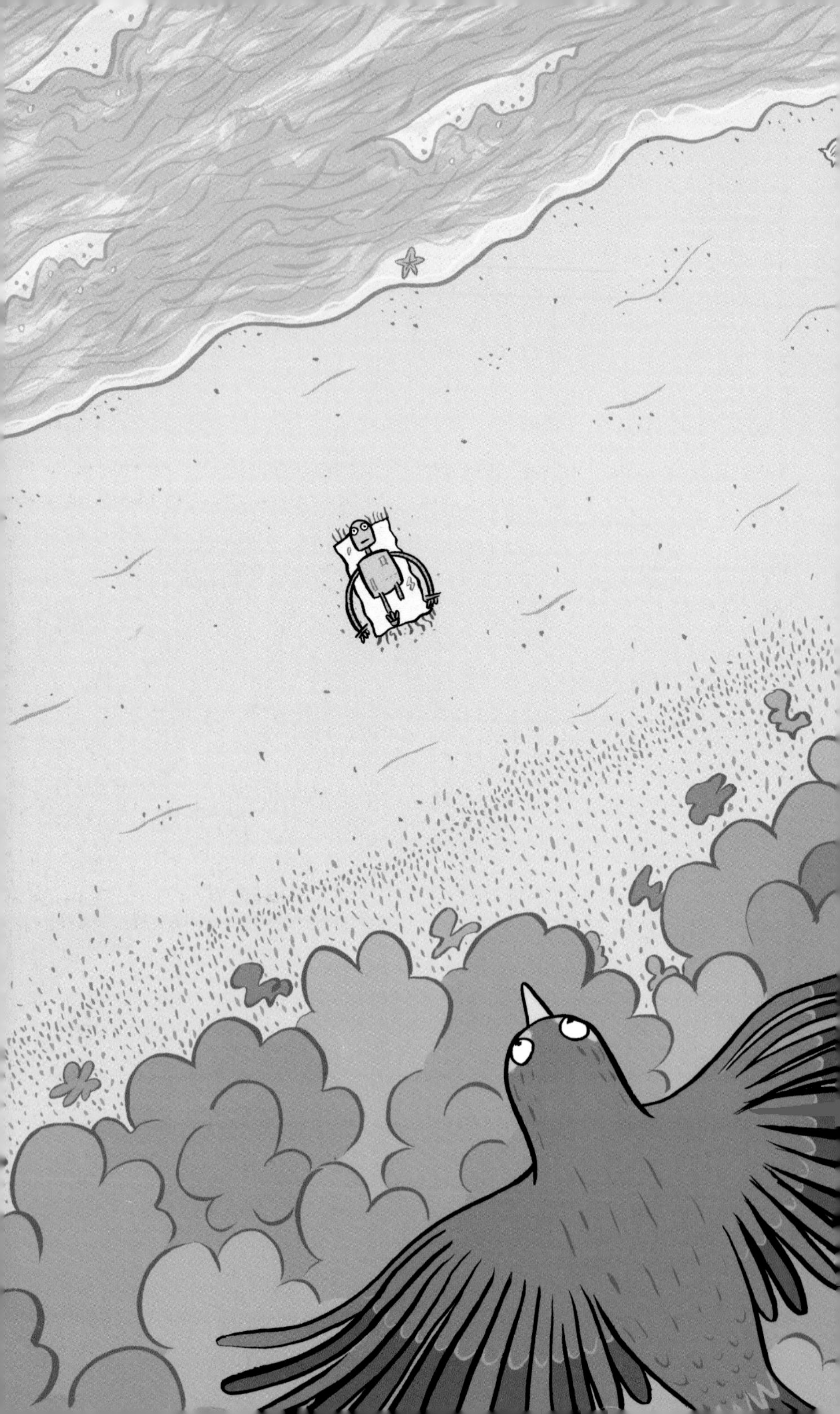

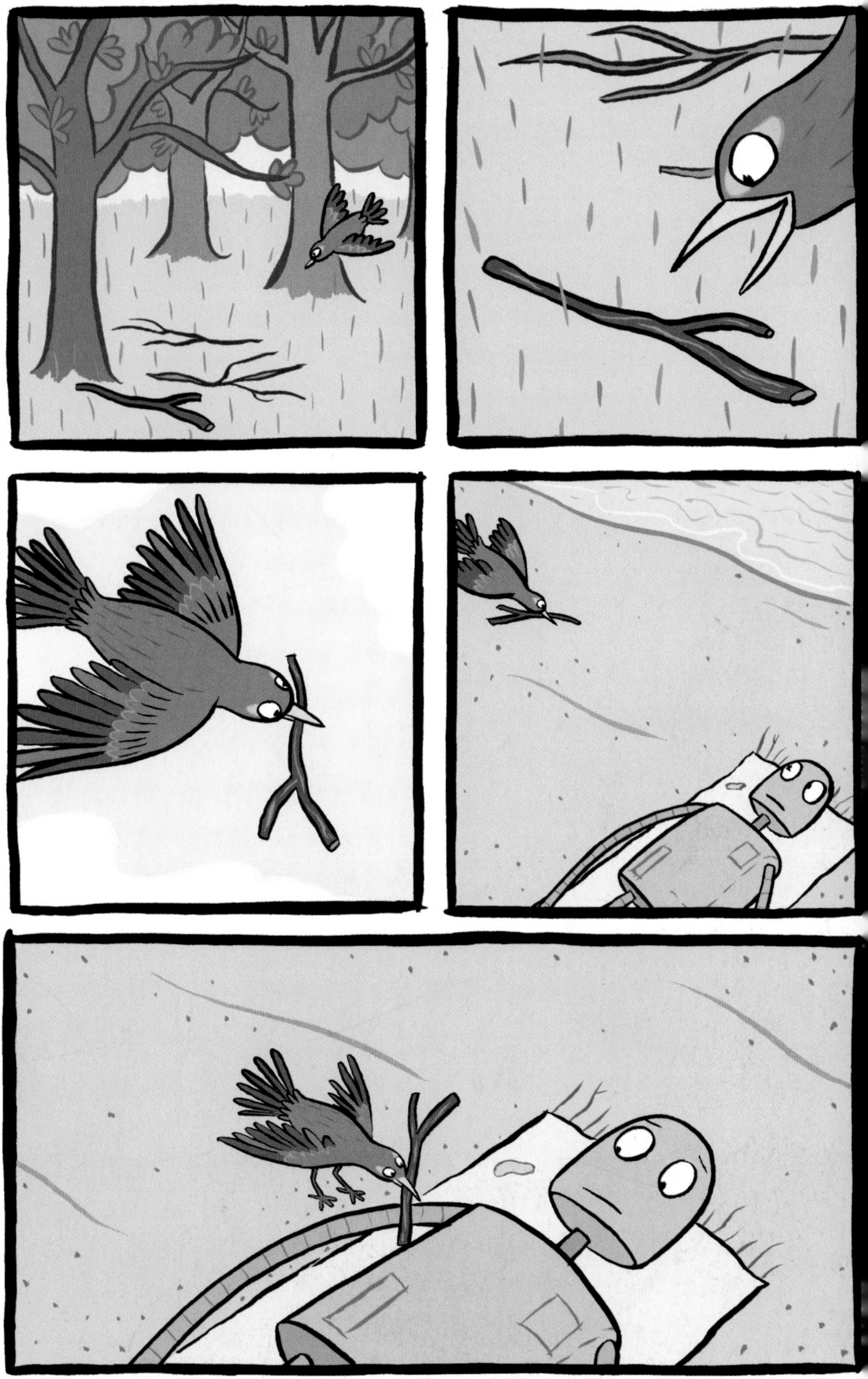

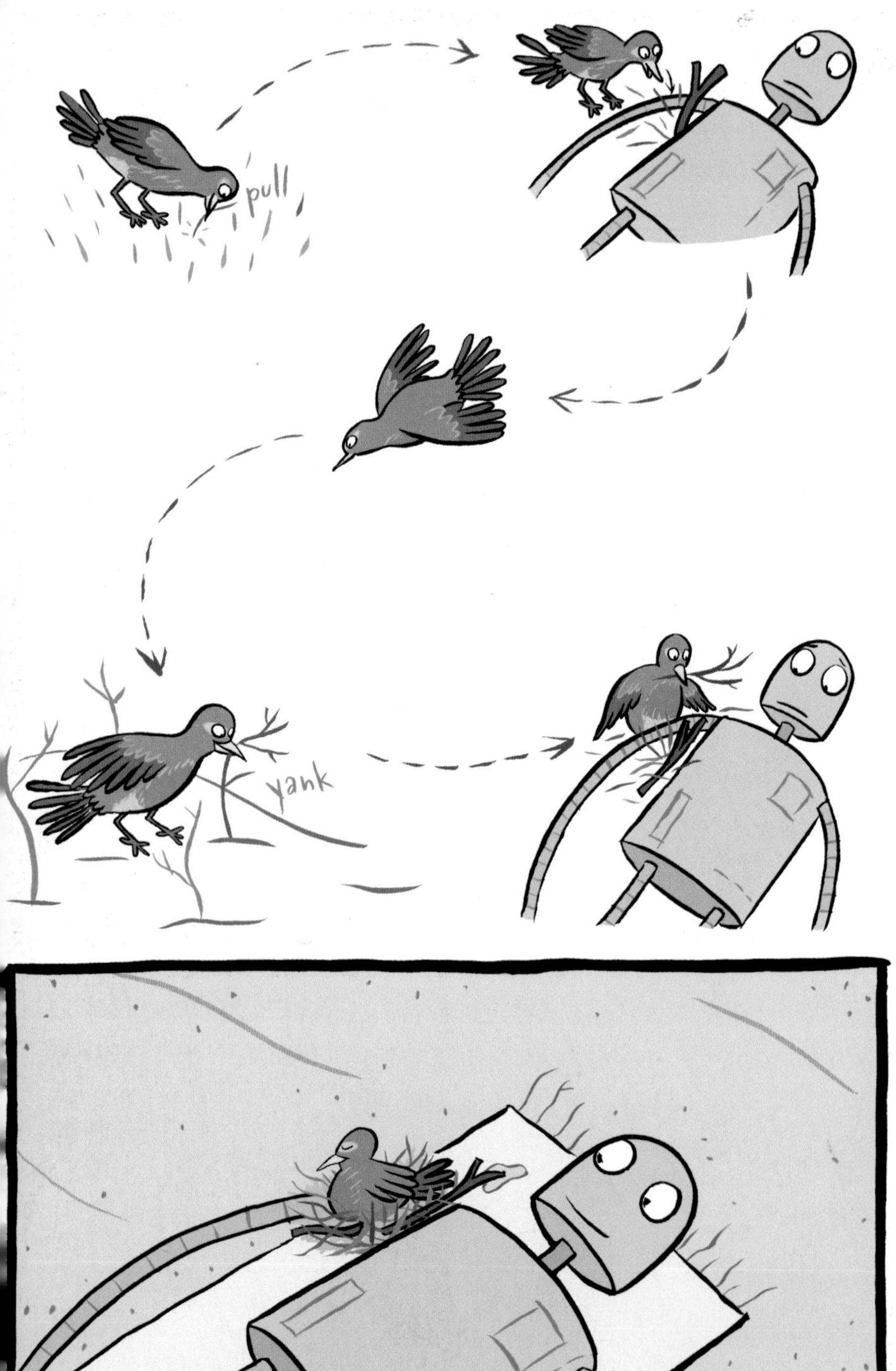
pull
yank

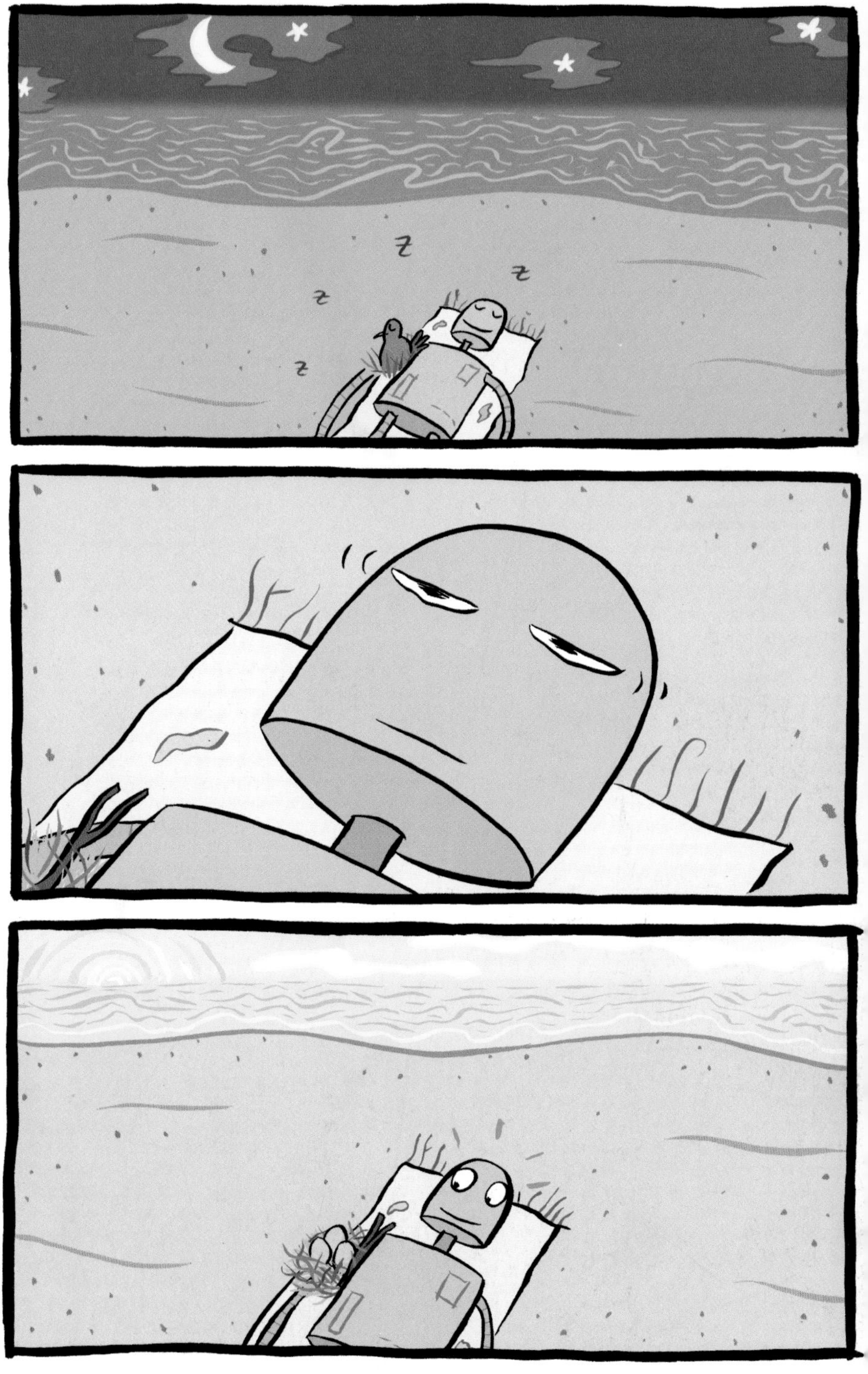
z
z
z
z

peck!

peck!

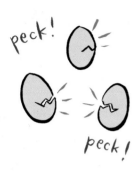

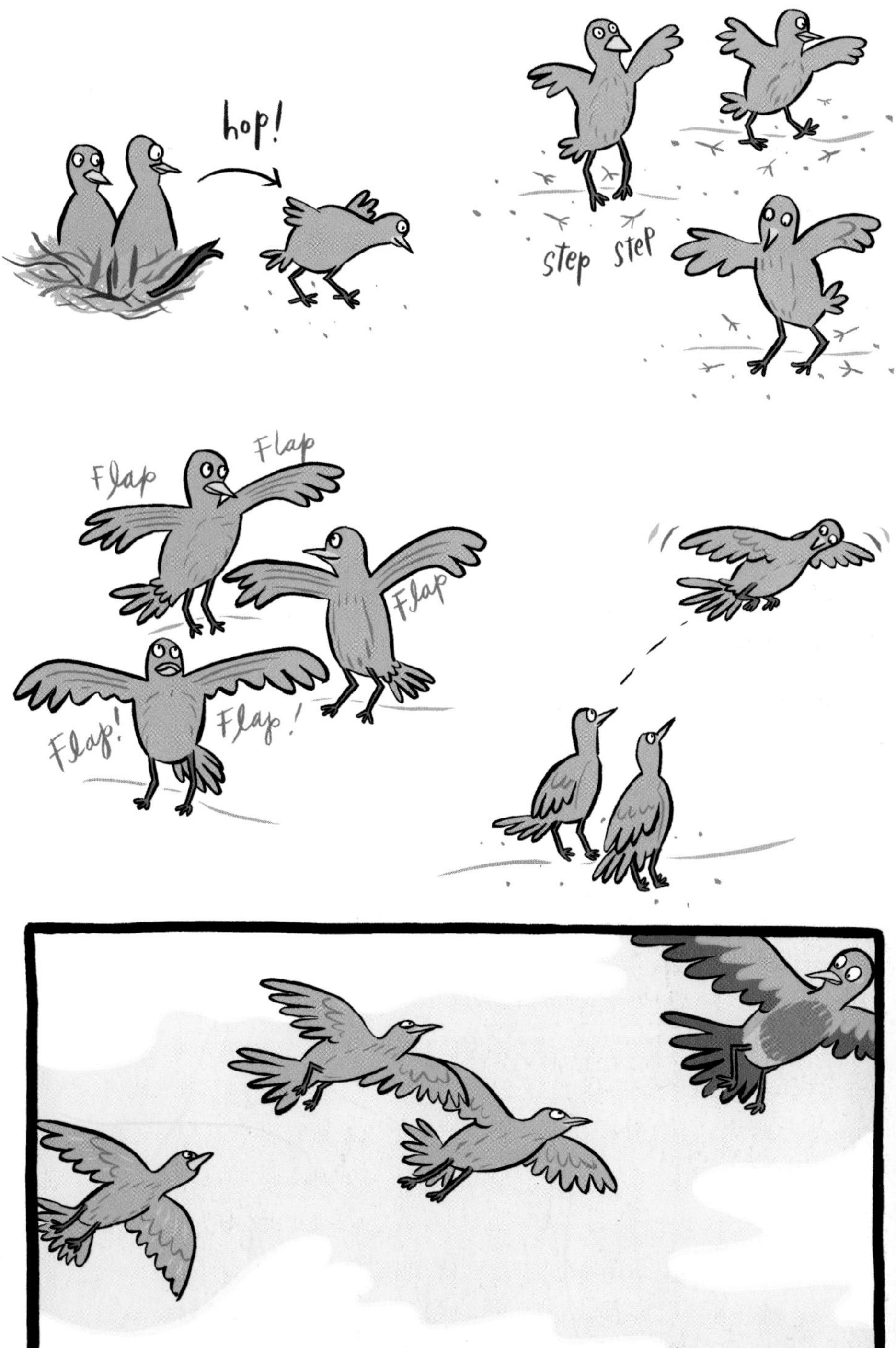
hop!
step step
Flap
Flap
Flap
Flap!
Flap!

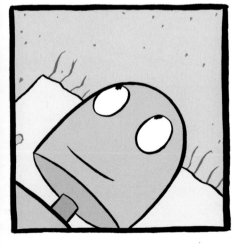

May

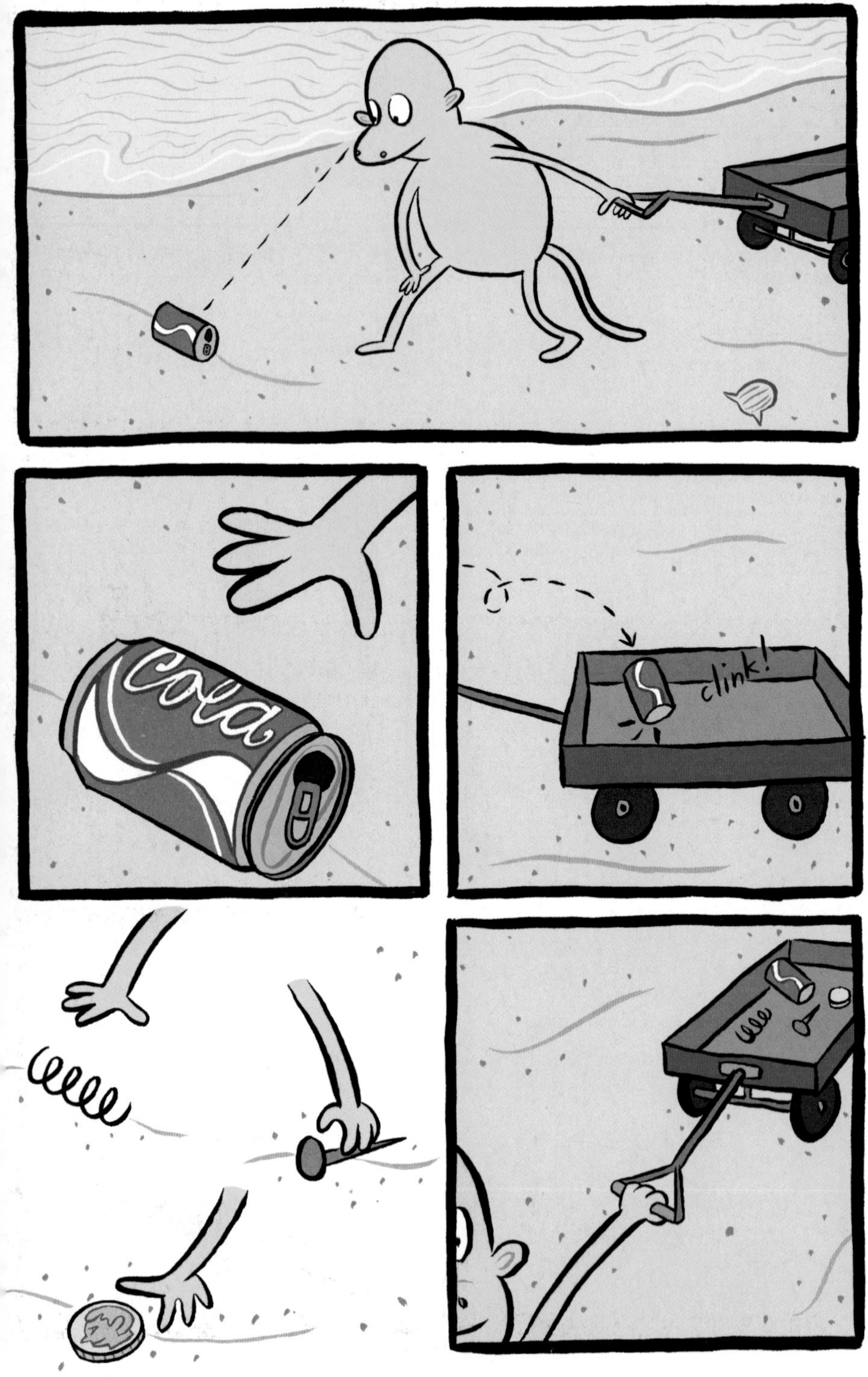
Cola
clink!

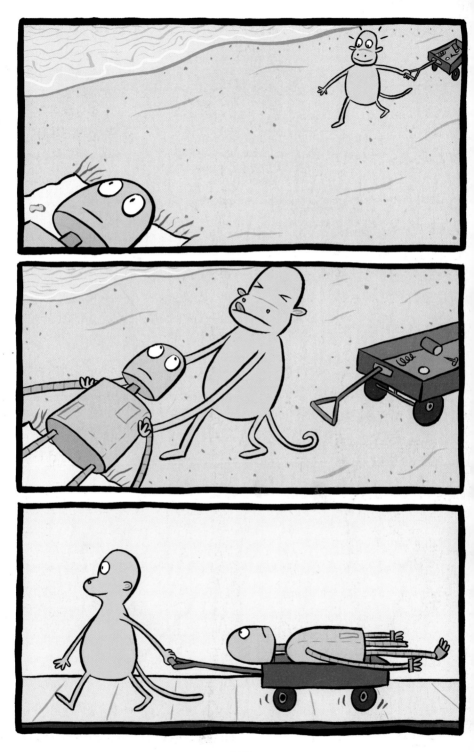

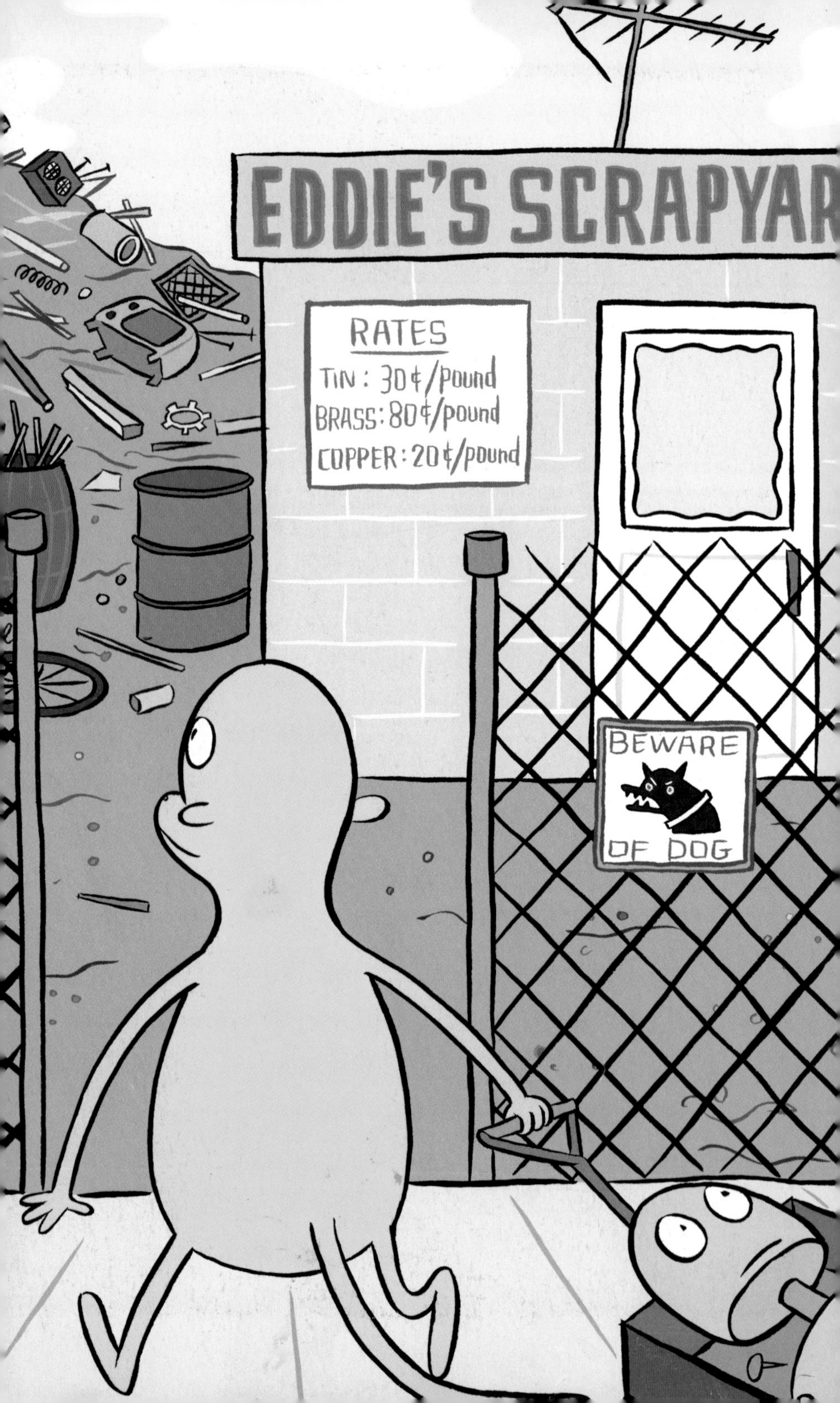

EDDIE'S SCRAPYAR
RATES
TIN : 30¢/pound
BRASS: 80¢/pound
COPPER: 20¢/pound
BEWARE
OF DOG

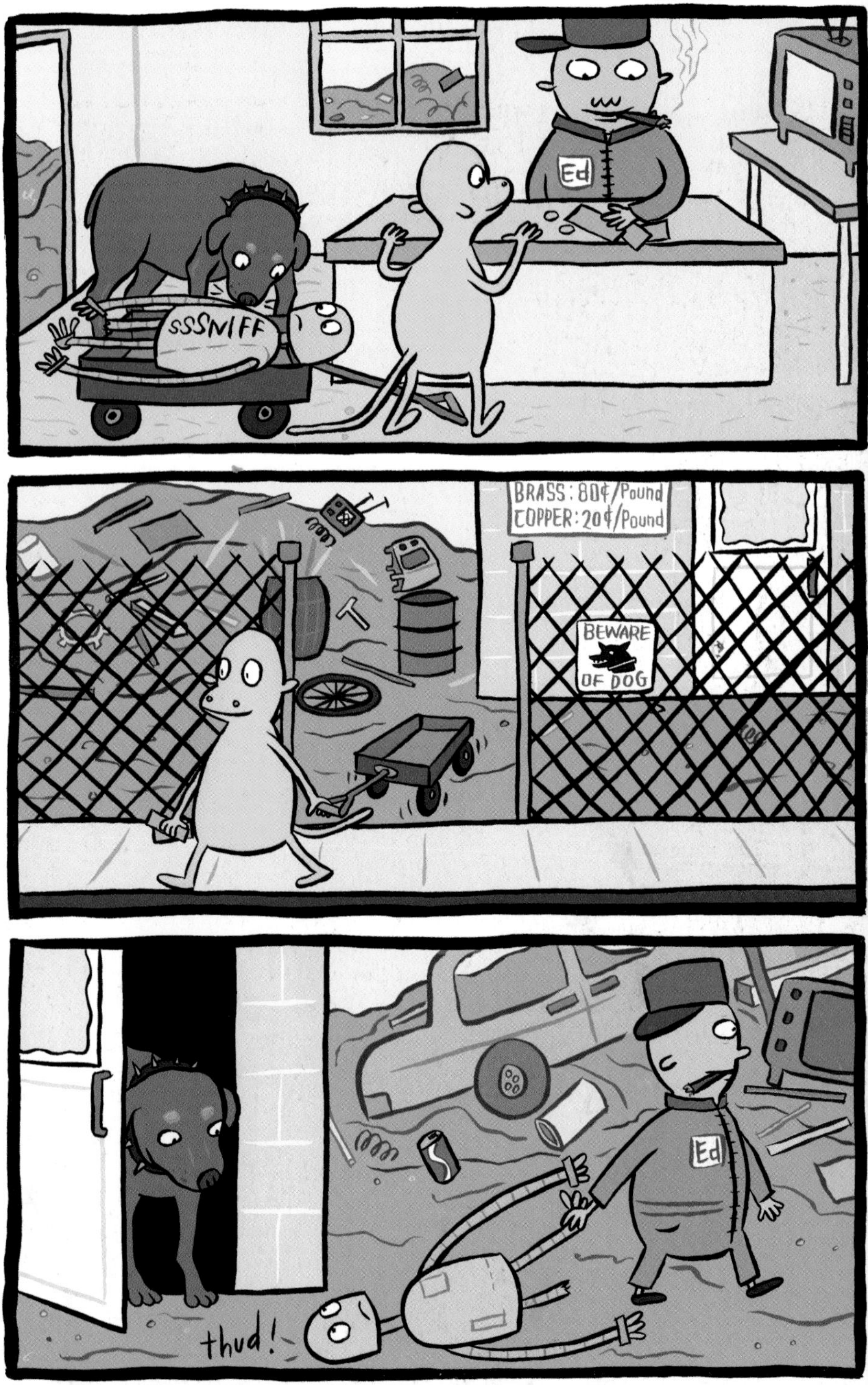

Ed
SSSNIFF
BRASS: 80¢/Pound
COPPER: 20¢/Pound
BEWARE OF DOG
Ed
thud!

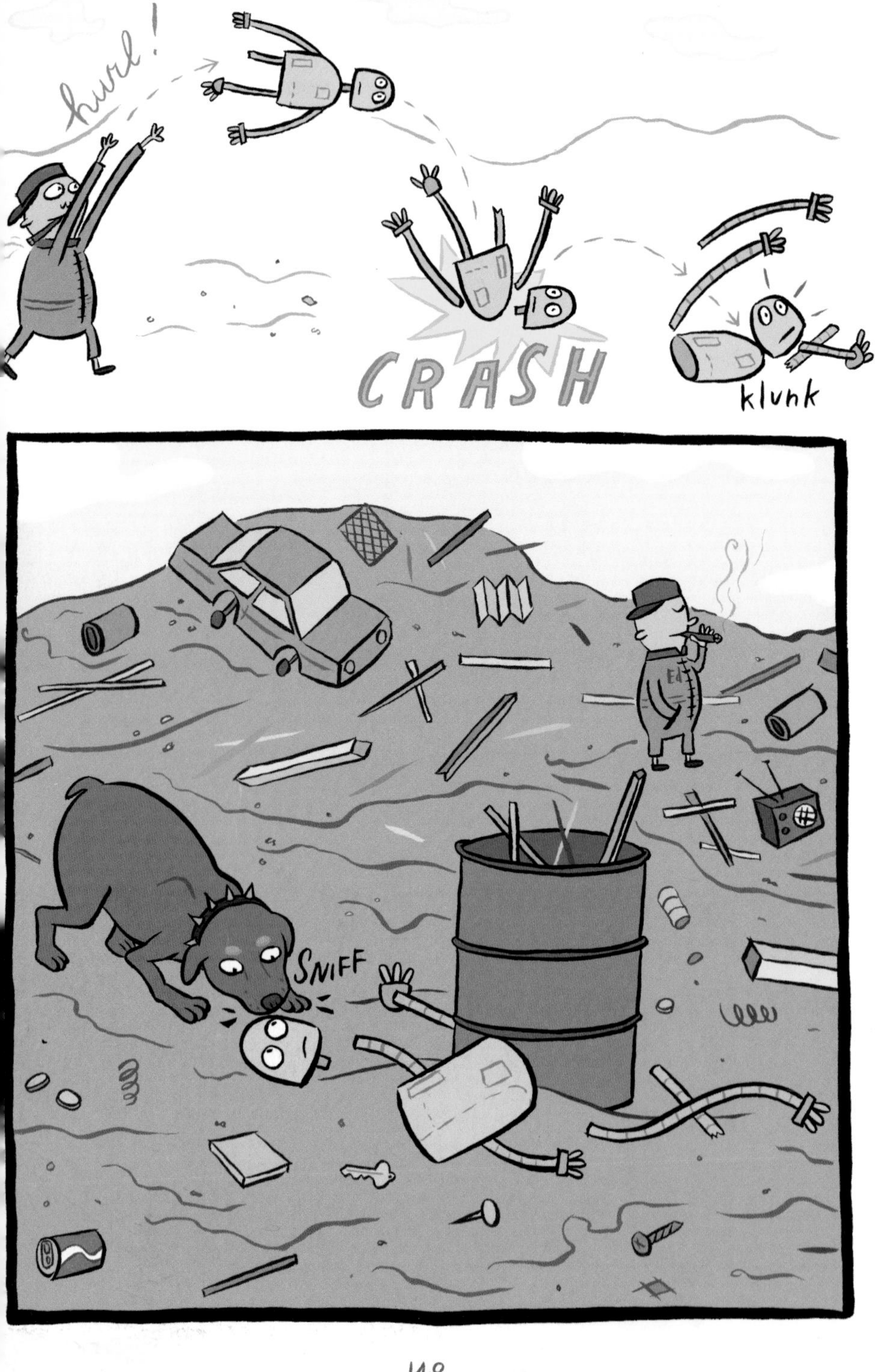
hurl!
CRASH
klunk
SNIFF

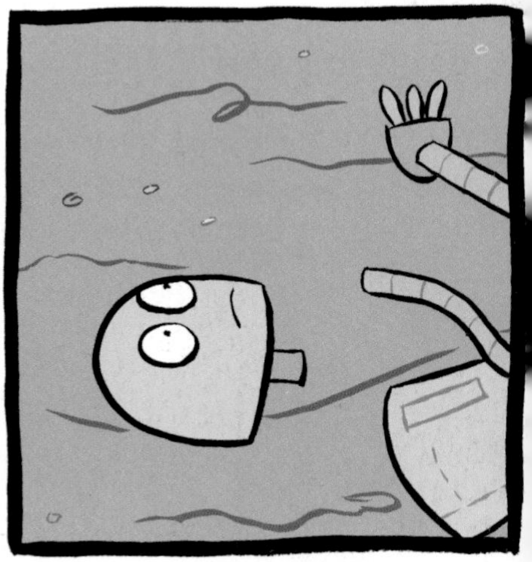

June

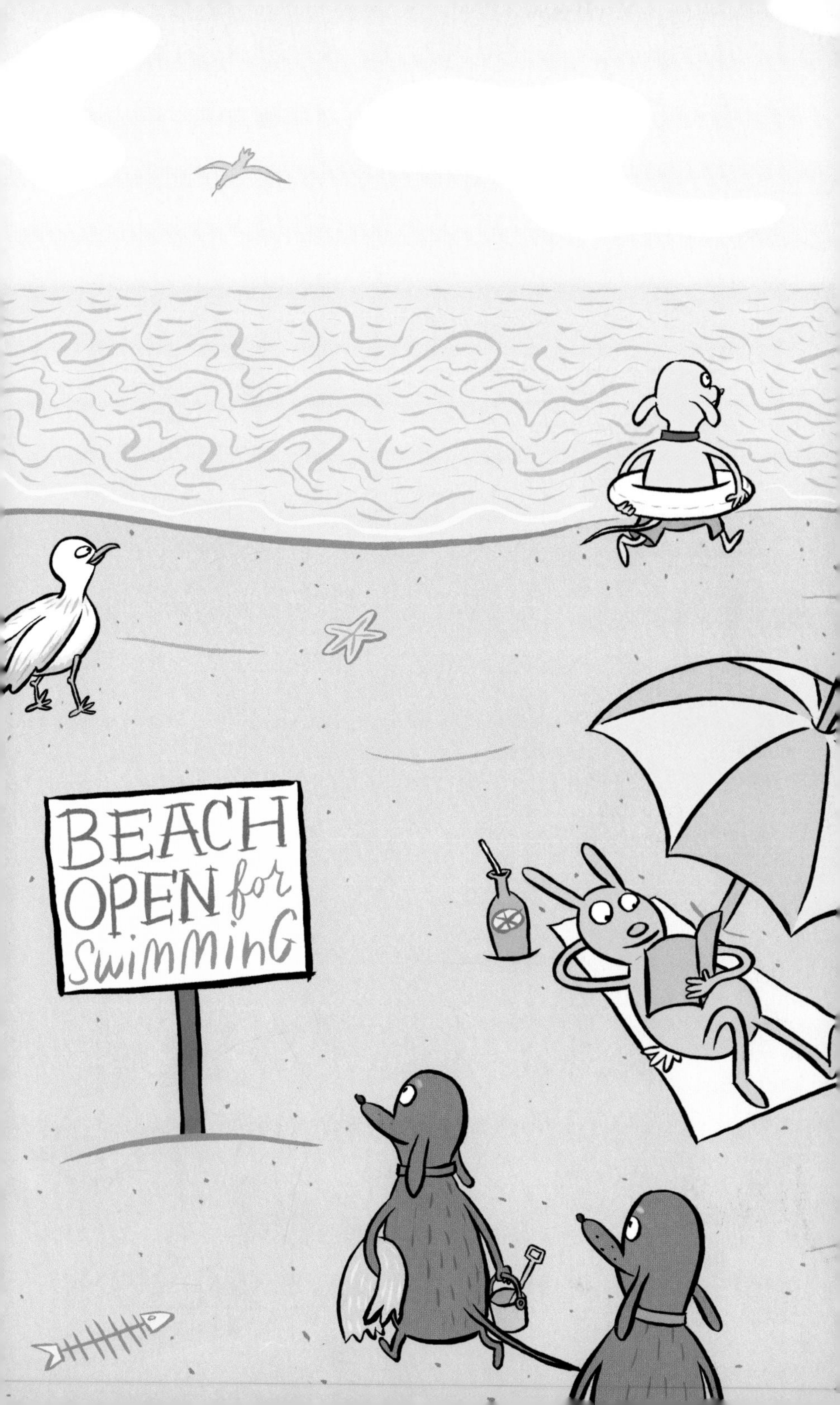
BEACH
OPEN for
swimming

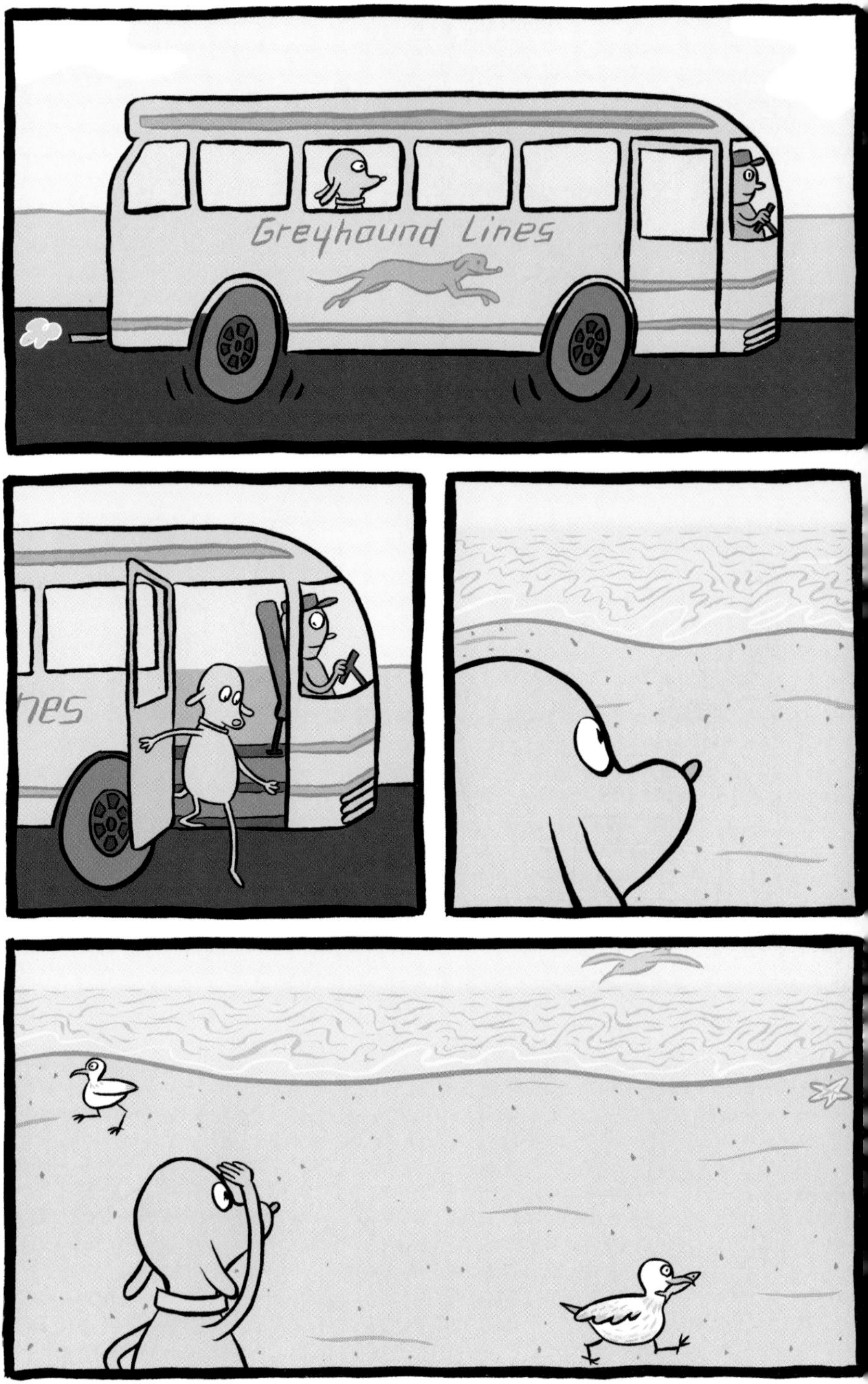

Greyhound Lines
nes

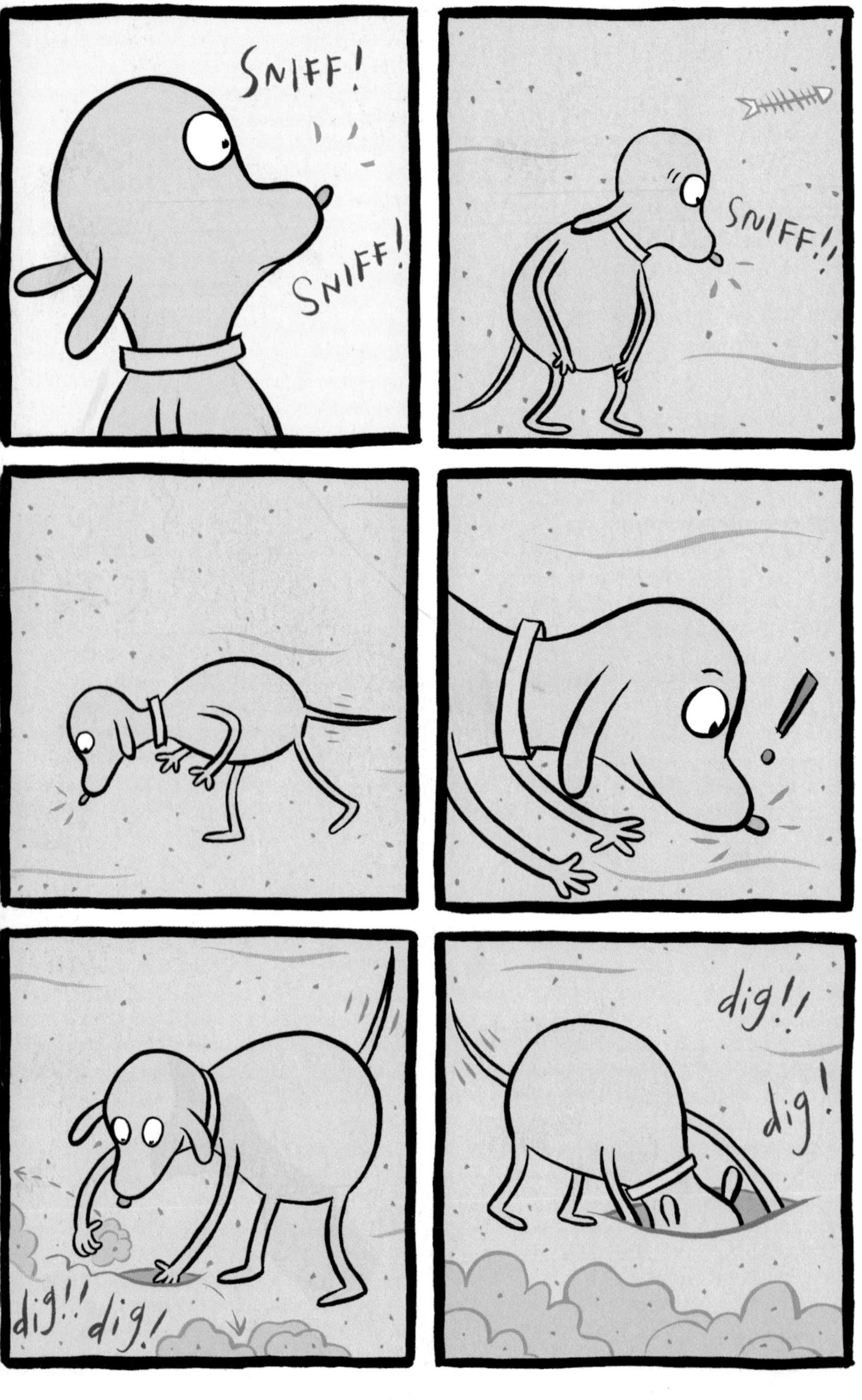
SNIFF!
SNIFF!
SNIFF!!
!
dig!! dig!
dig!!
dig!

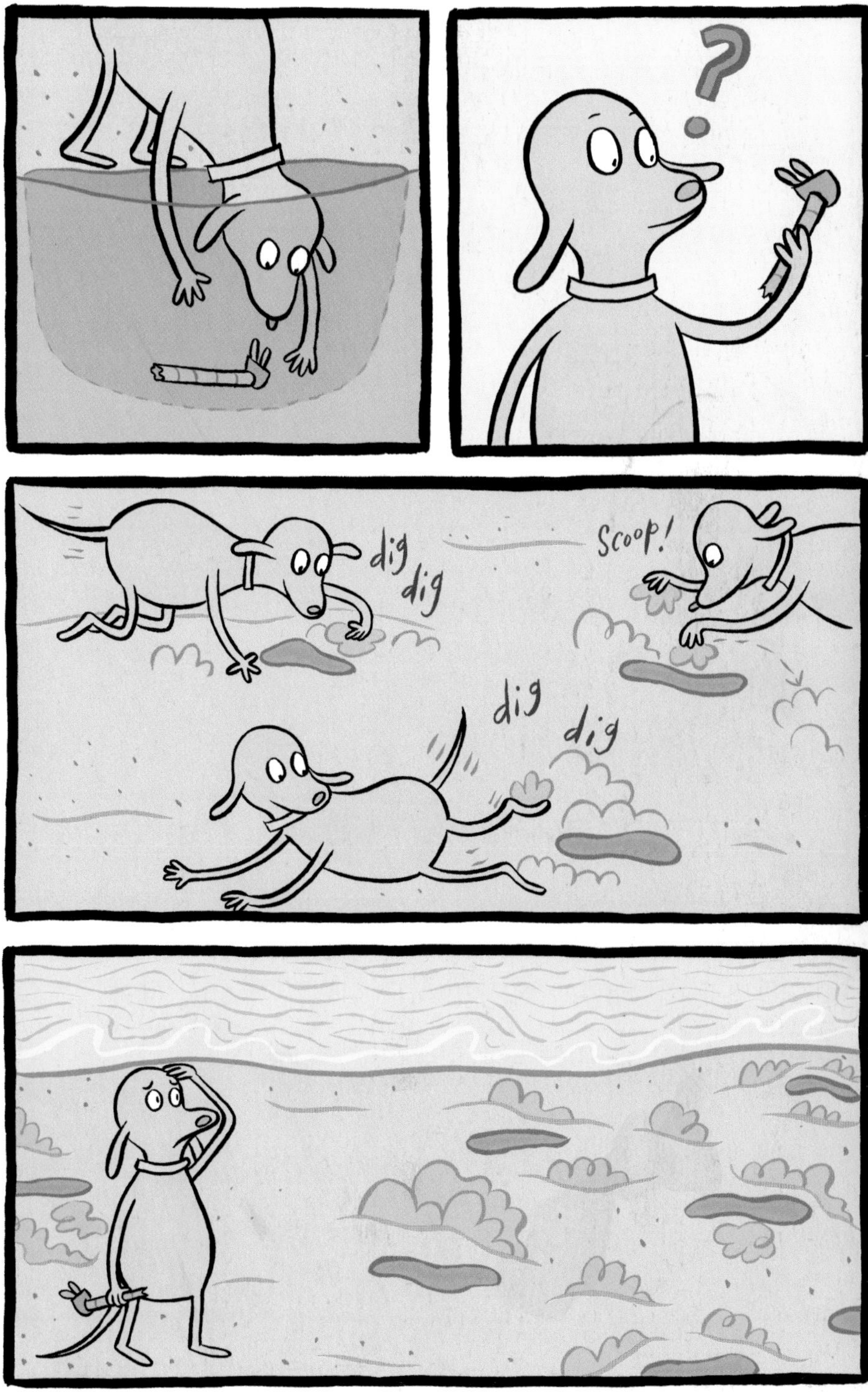
?
dig
dig
Scoop!
dig
dig

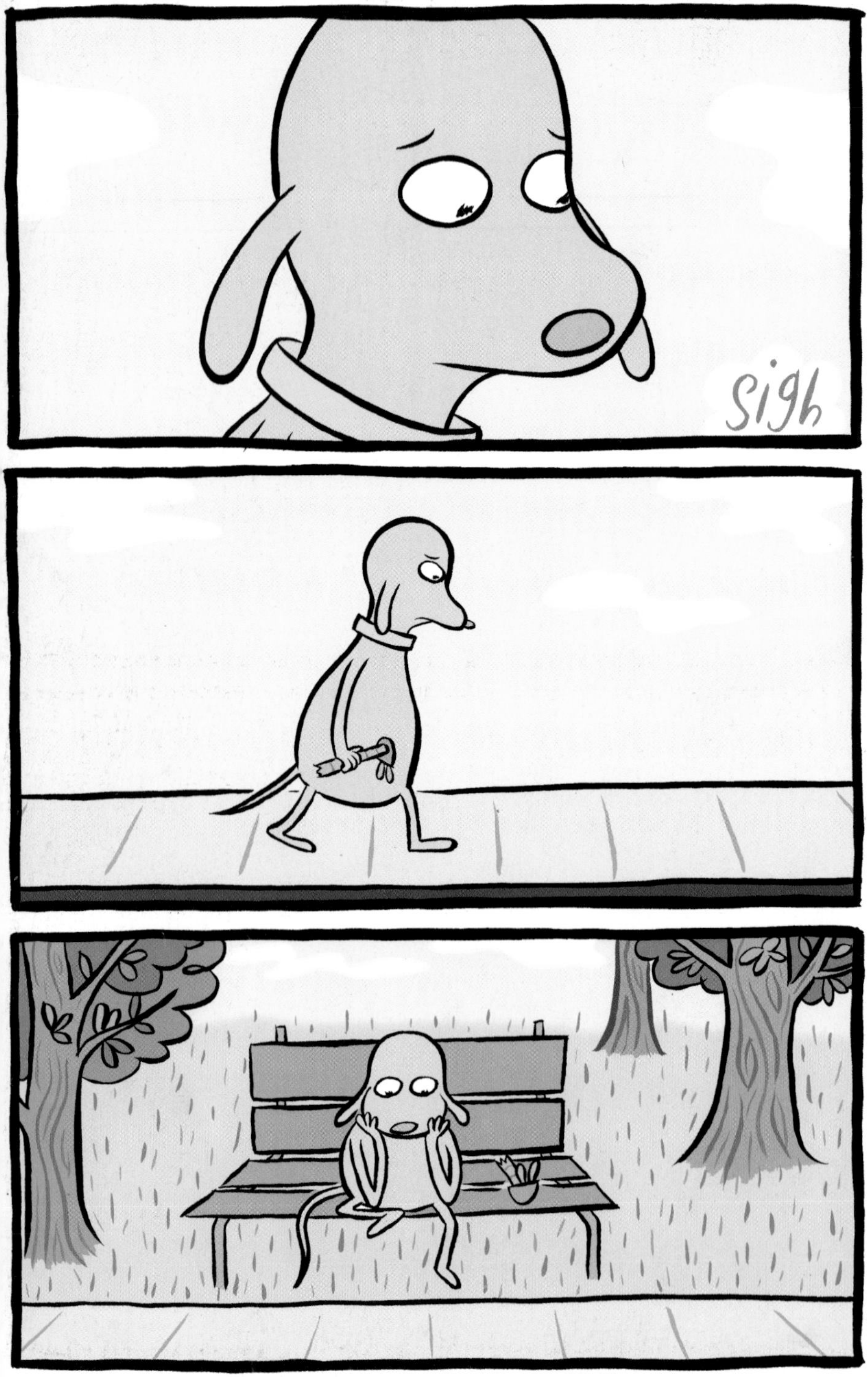
sigh

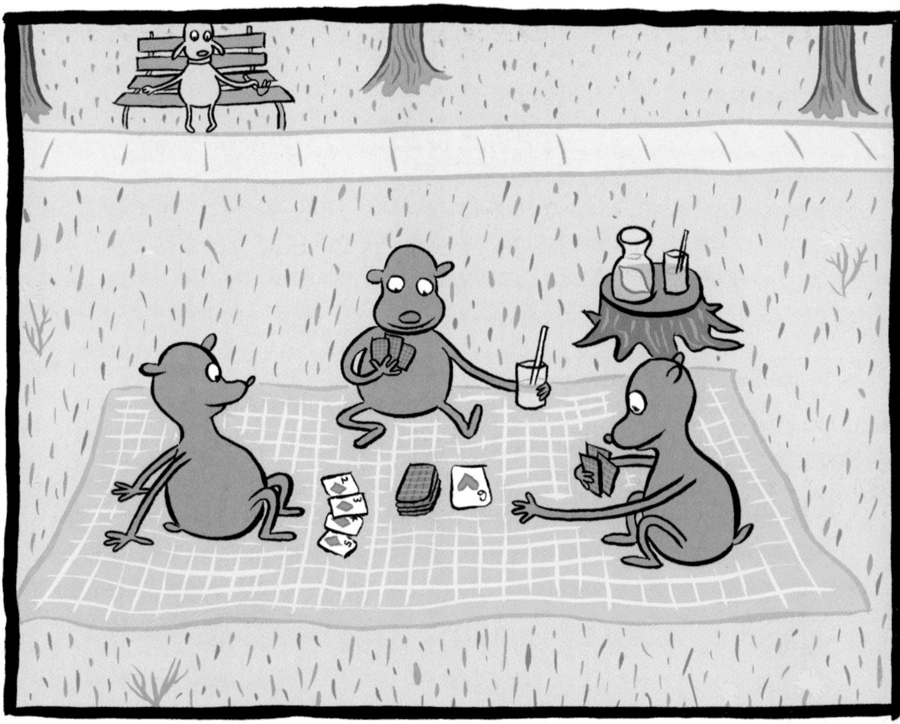

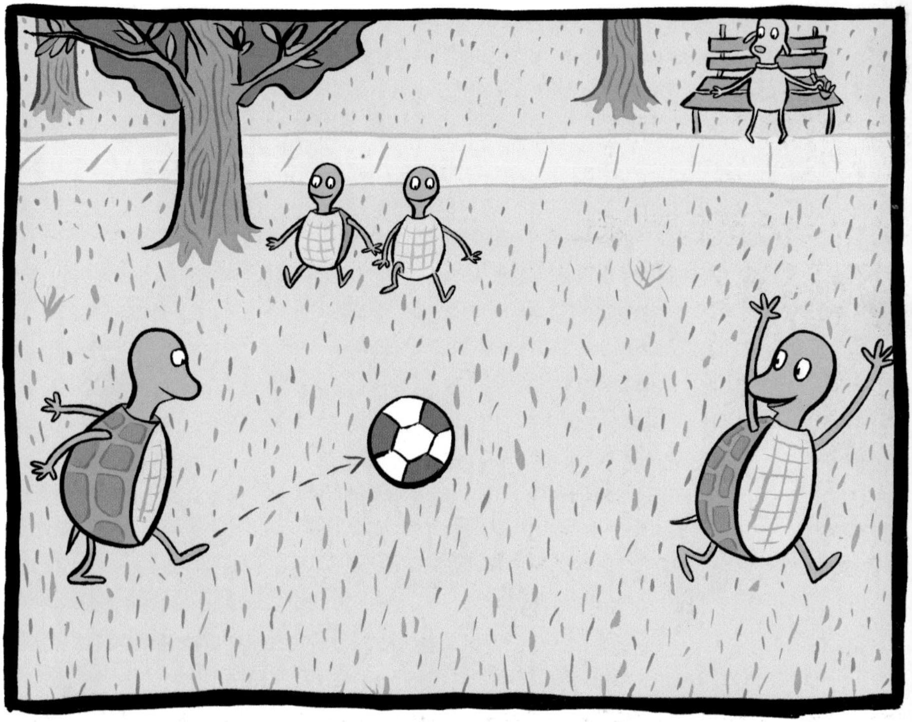

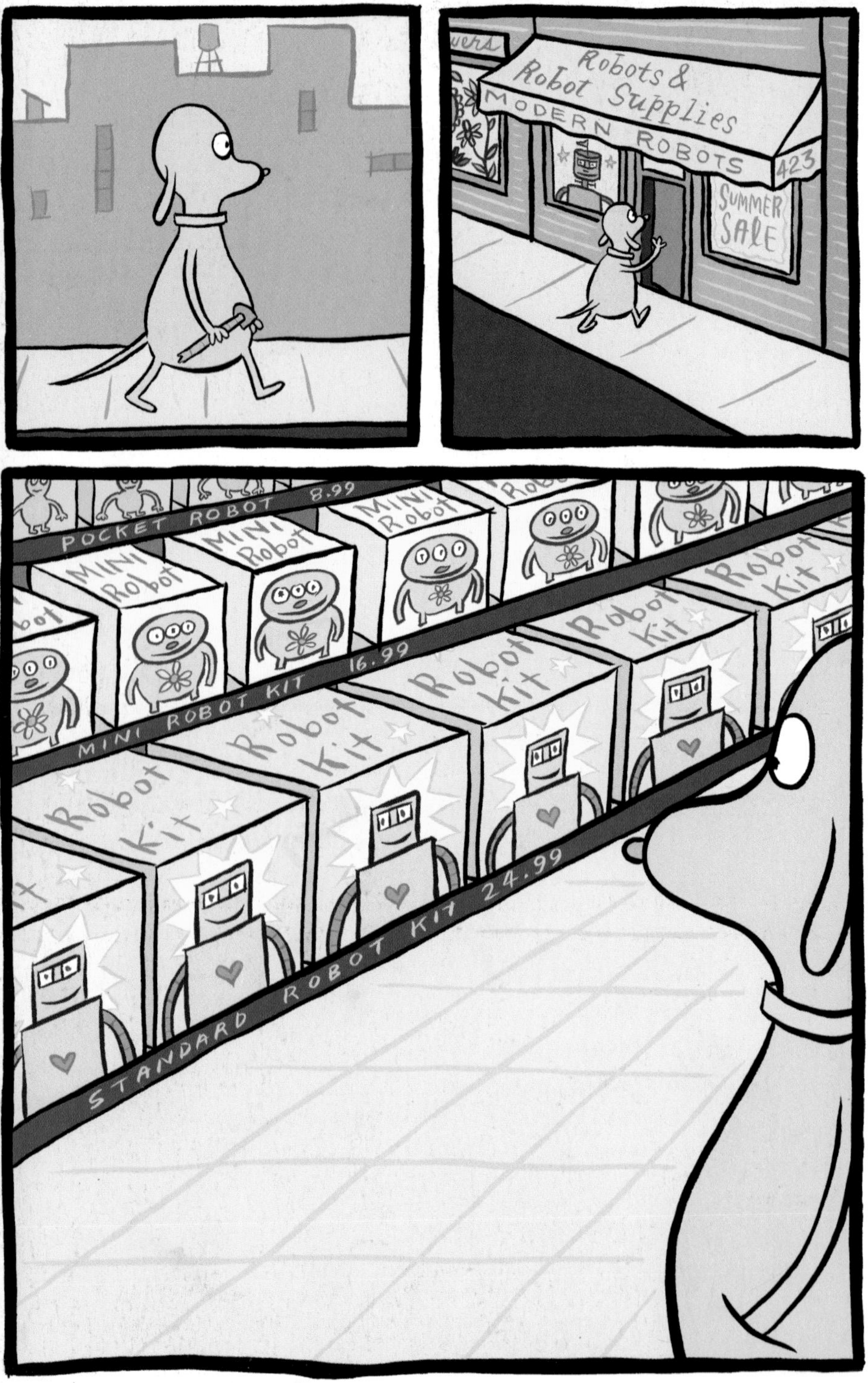
Robots & Robot Supplies
MODERN ROBOTS
423
SUMMER SALE
POCKET ROBOT 8.99
MINI Robot
MINI ROBOT KIT 16.99
Robot Kit
STANDARD ROBOT KIT 24.99

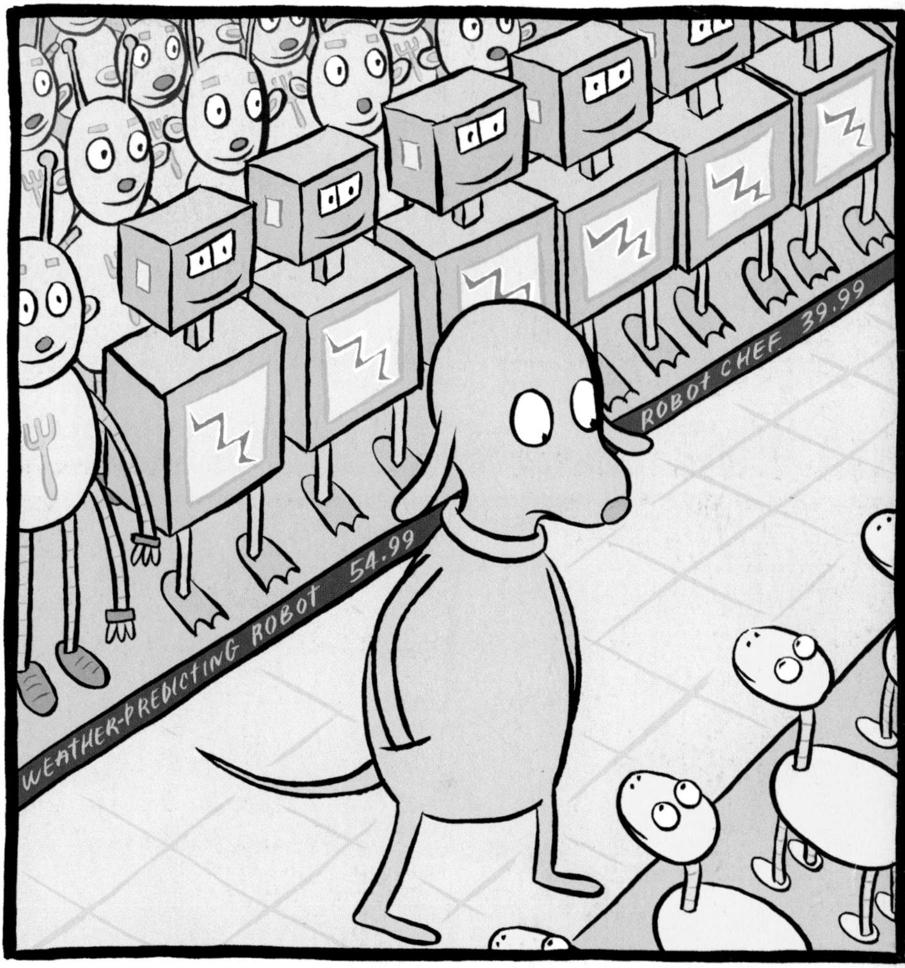
ROBOT CHEF 39.99
WEATHER-PREDICTING ROBOT 54.99

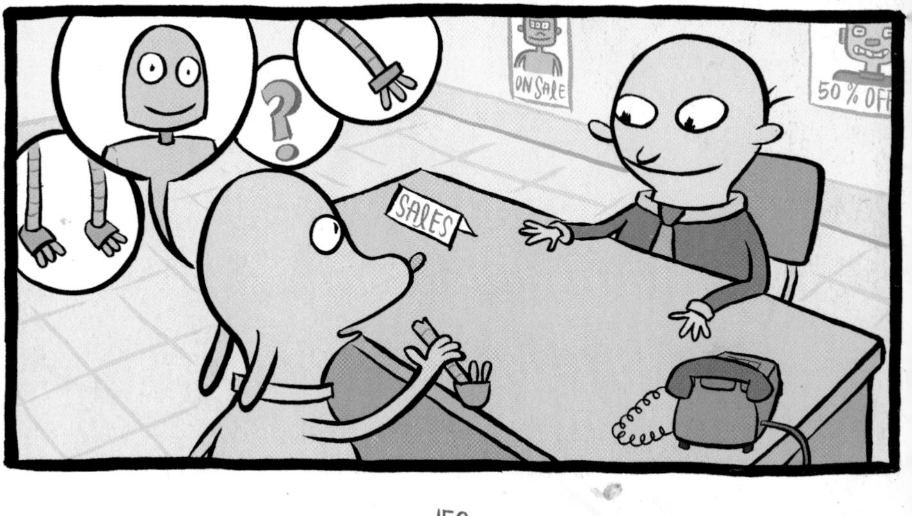
?
SALES
ON SALE
50% OFF

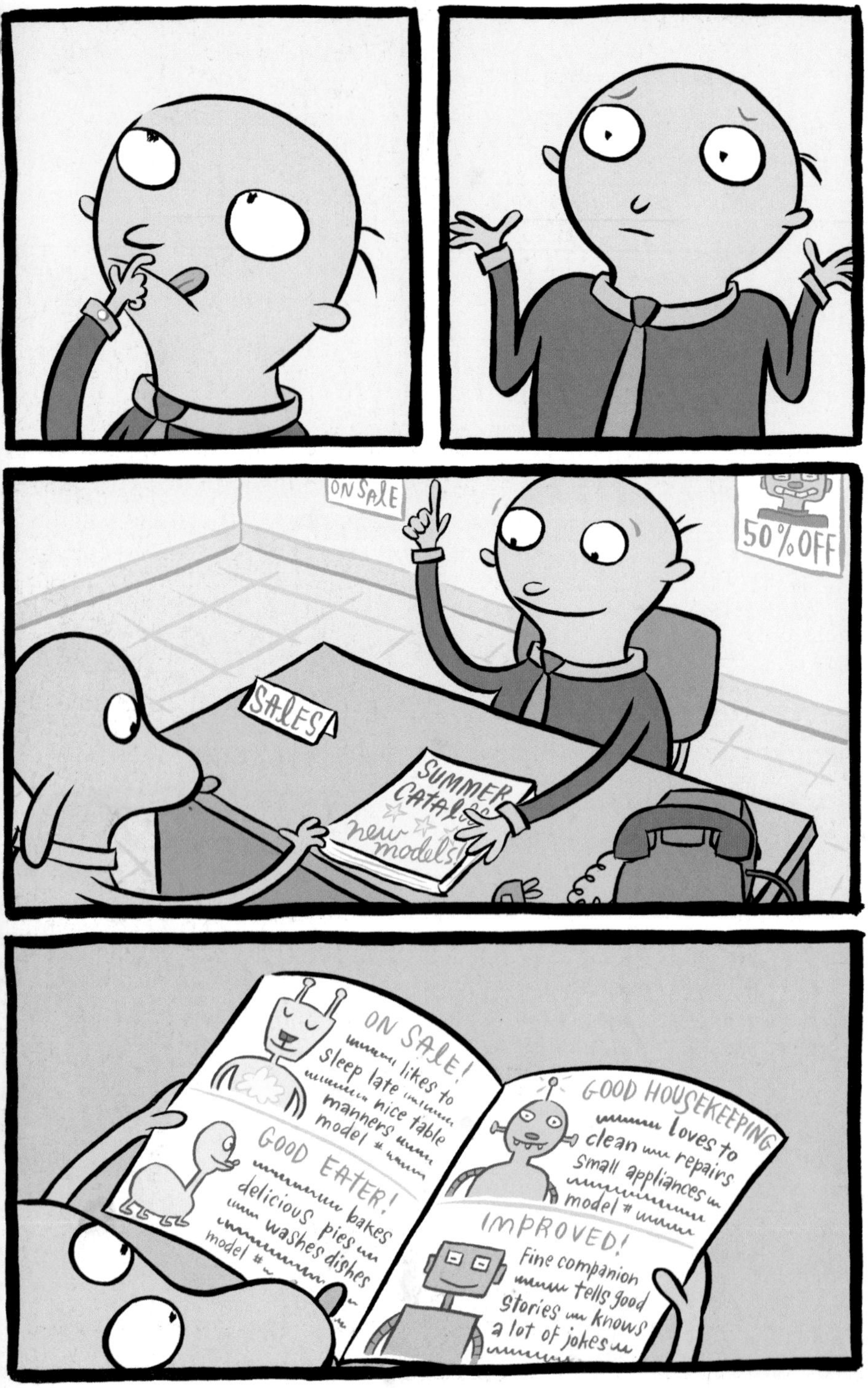
ON SALE
50% OFF
SALES
SUMMER CATALOG
new models!
ON SALE!
likes to sleep late
nice table manners
model #
GOOD EATER!
bakes delicious pies
washes dishes
model #
GOOD HOUSEKEEPING
loves to clean
repairs small appliances
model #
IMPROVED!
Fine companion
tells good stories
knows a lot of jokes

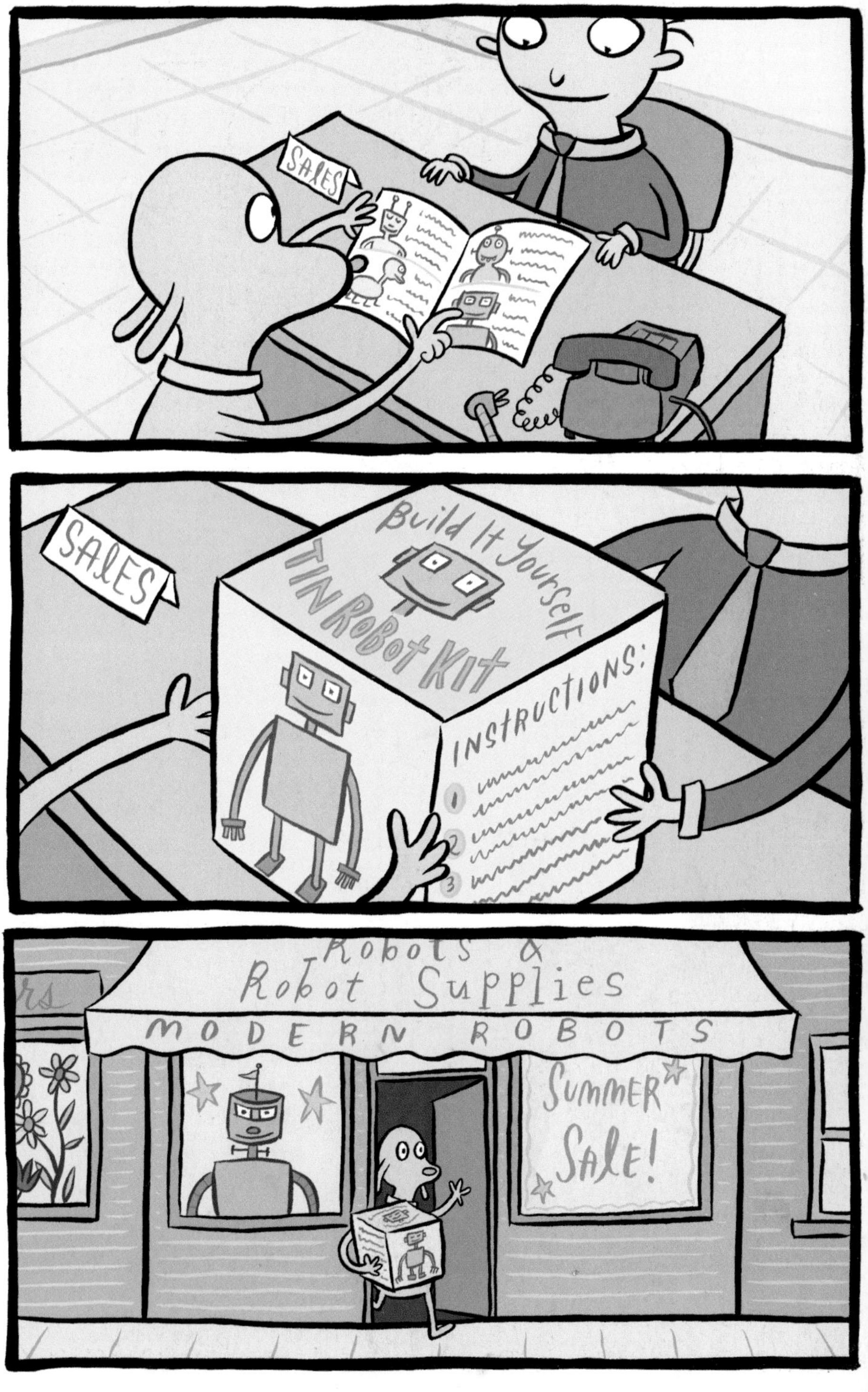
SALES
SALES
Build It Yourself
TIN RoBot Kit
INSTRUCTIONS:
1
2
3
Robots &
Robot Supplies
MODERN ROBOTS
Summer Sale!

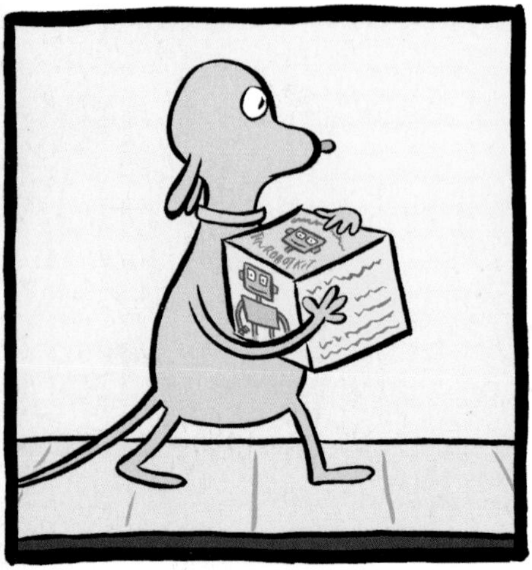
Robot Kit

July

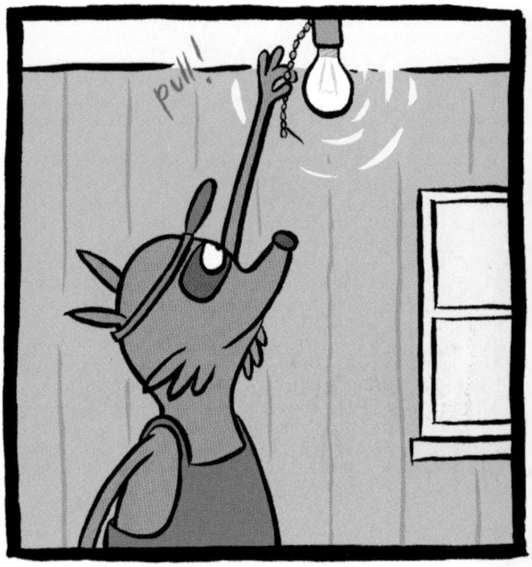
pull!

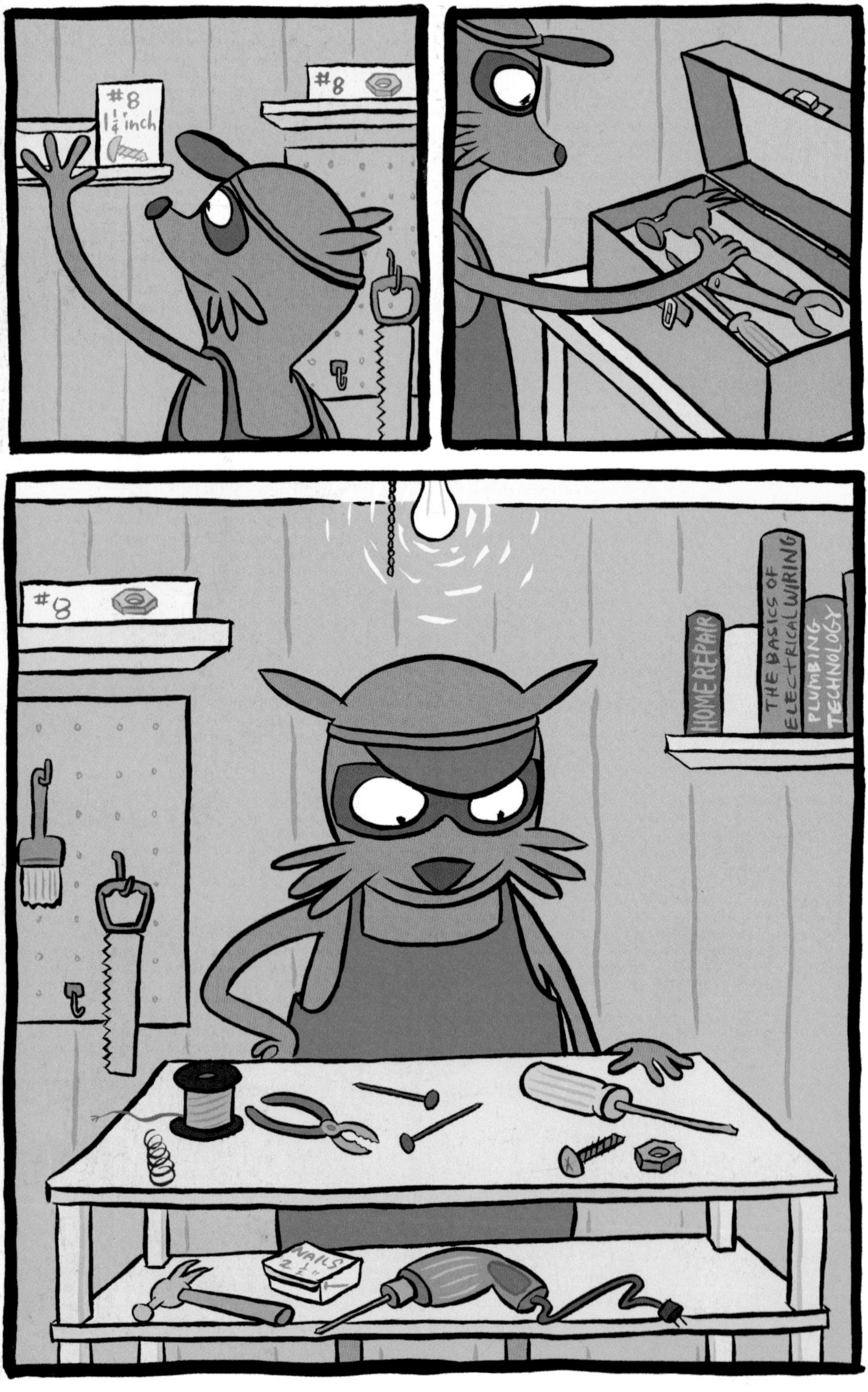
#8
1 1/4 inch
#8
#8
HOME REPAIR
THE BASICS OF ELECTRICAL WIRING
PLUMBING TECHNOLOGY
NAILS

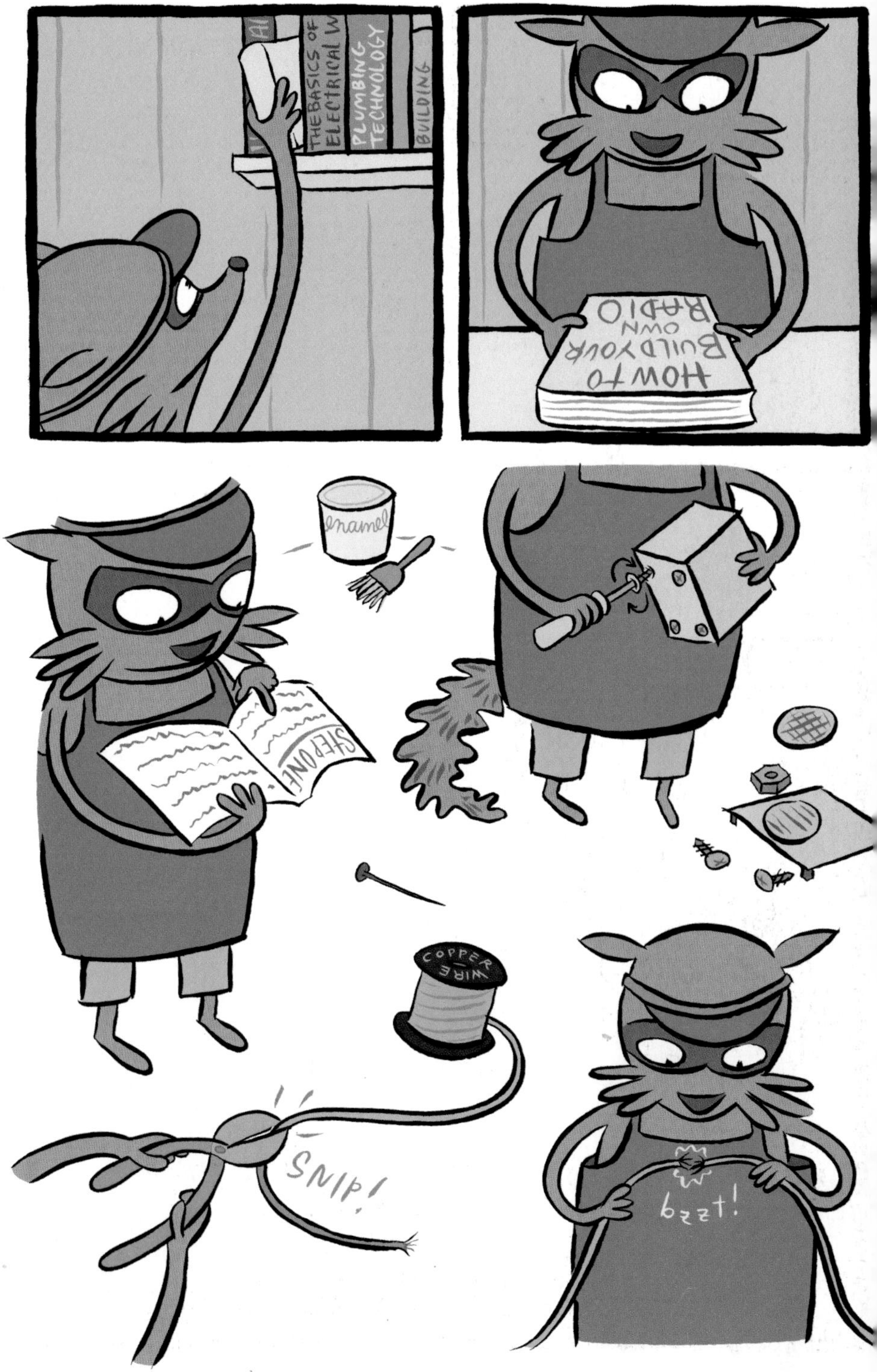
THE BASICS OF ELECTRICAL W
PLUMBING TECHNOLOGY
BUILDING
HOW TO BUILD YOUR OWN RADIO
enamel
STEP ONE
COPPER WIRE
SNIP!
bzzt!

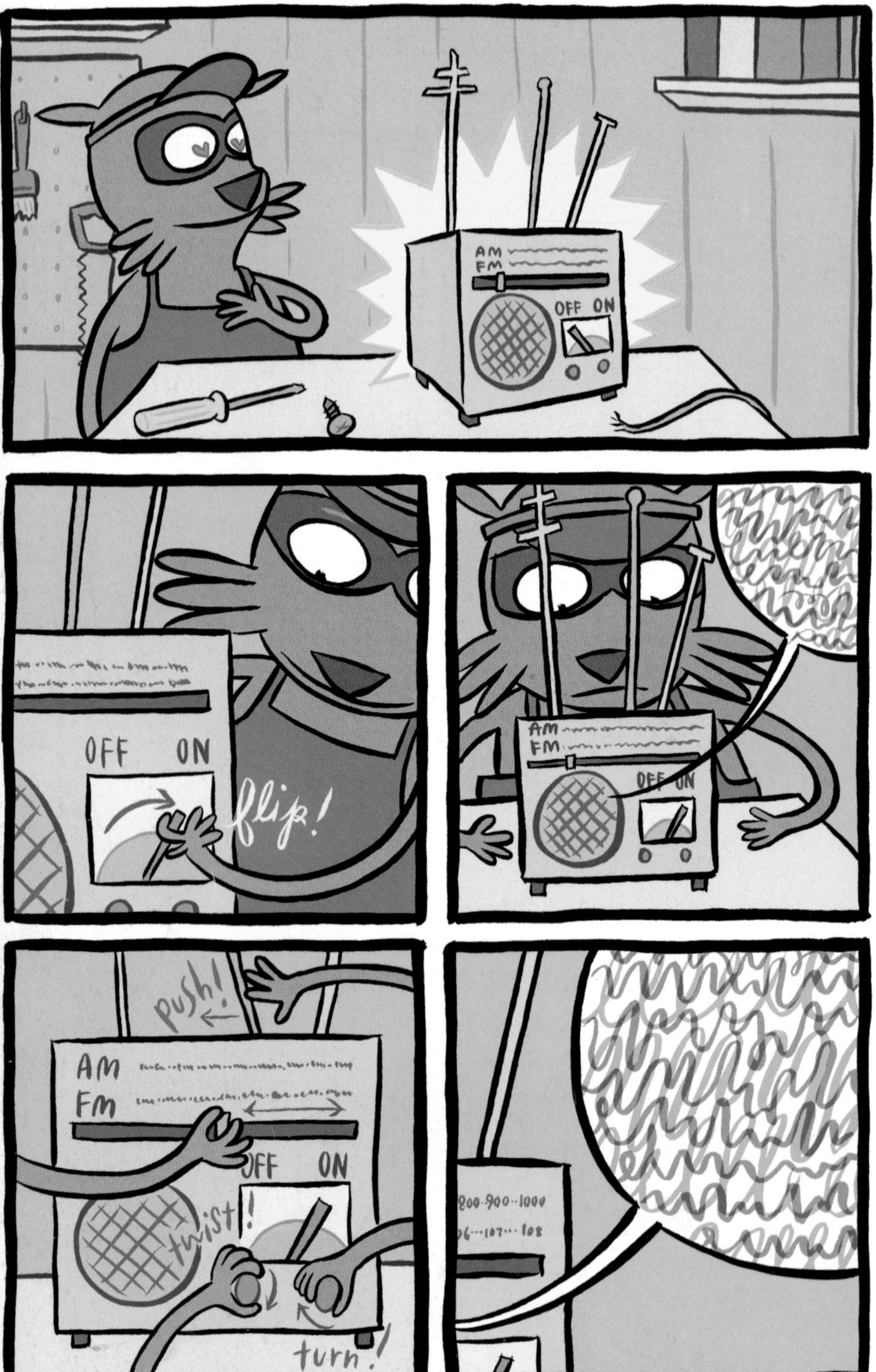
AM
FM
OFF ON
flip!
push!
twist!
turn!
200·900··1000
06···107··· 108

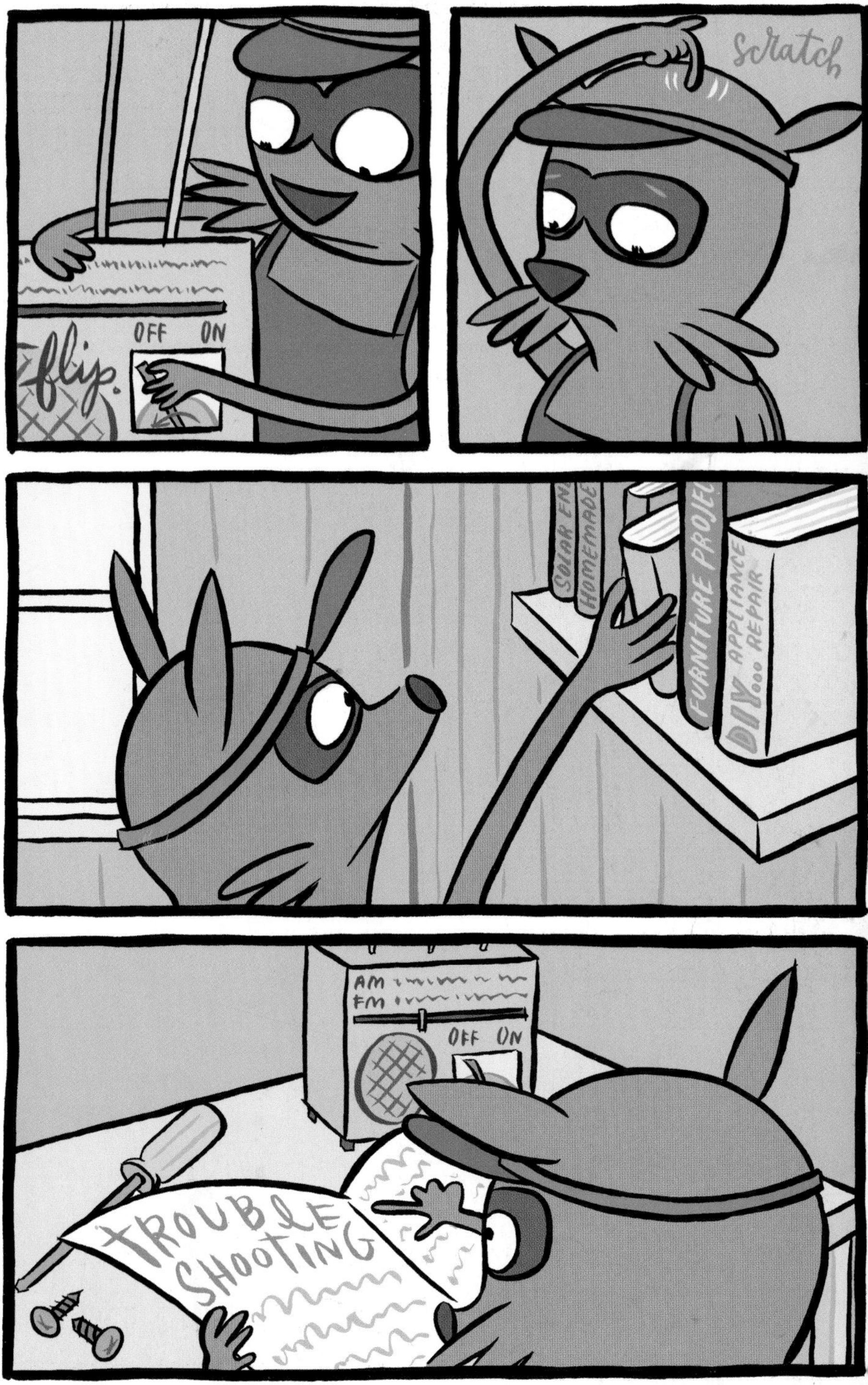
OFF ON
flip.
Scratch
SOLAR EN
HOMEMADE
FURNITURE PROJE
DIY... APPLIANCE REPAIR
AM
FM
OFF ON
TROUBLE SHOOTING

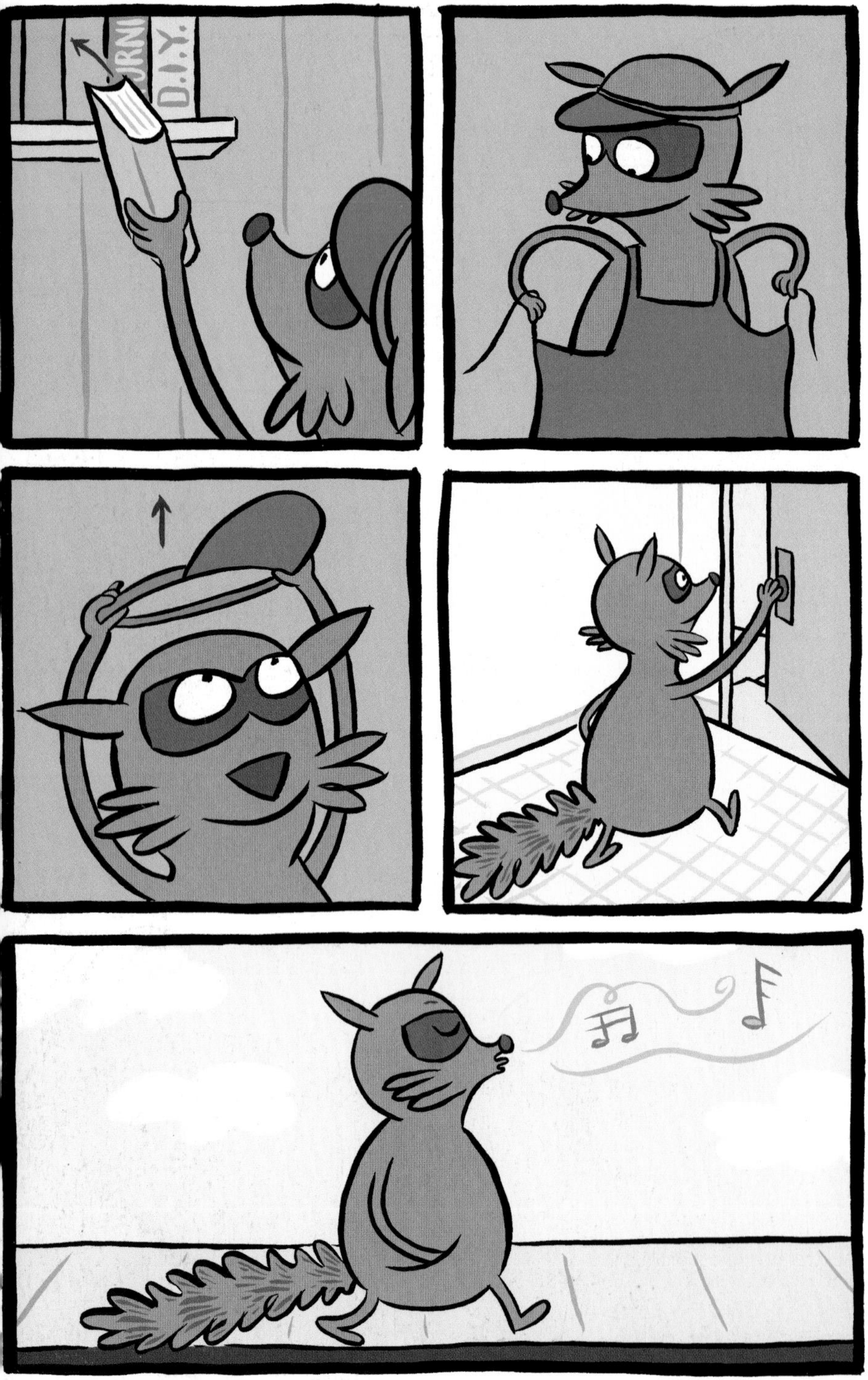

URN
D.I.Y.

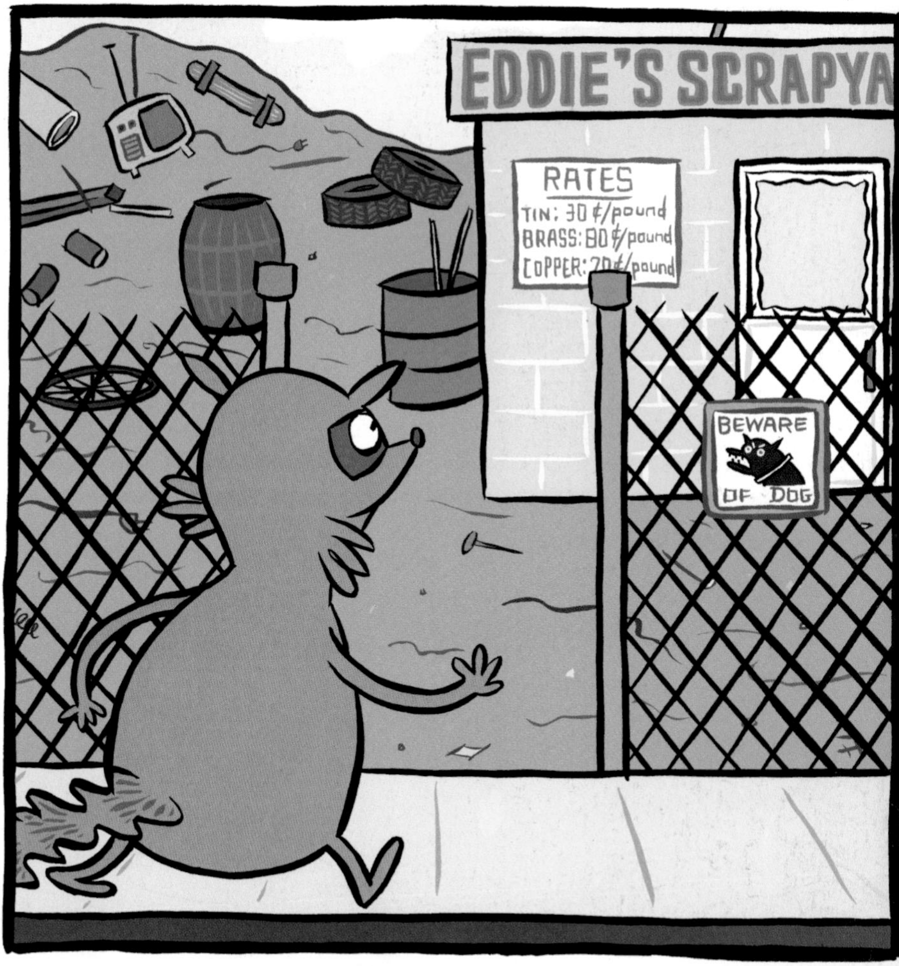
EDDIE'S SCRAPYA
RATES
TIN: 30¢/pound
BRASS: 80¢/pound
COPPER: 70¢/pound
BEWARE OF DOG

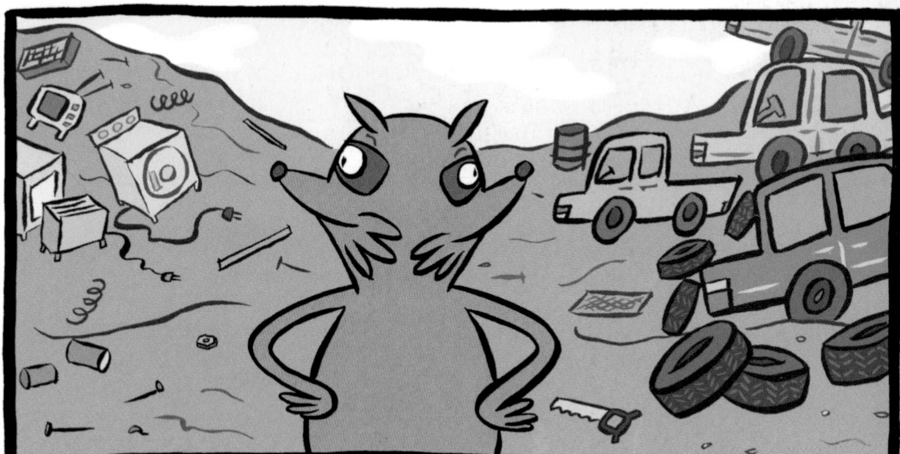

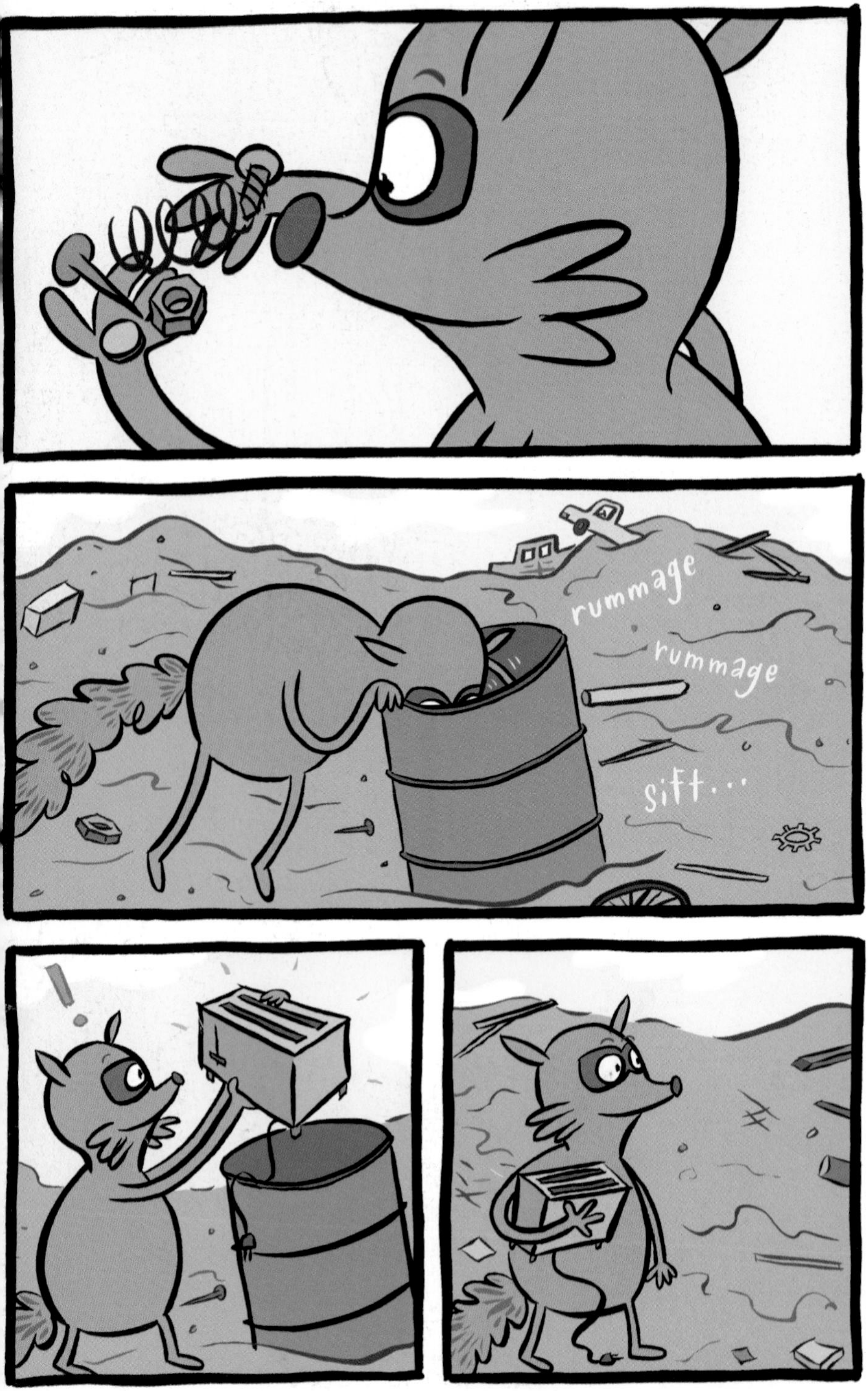
rummage
rummage
sift...

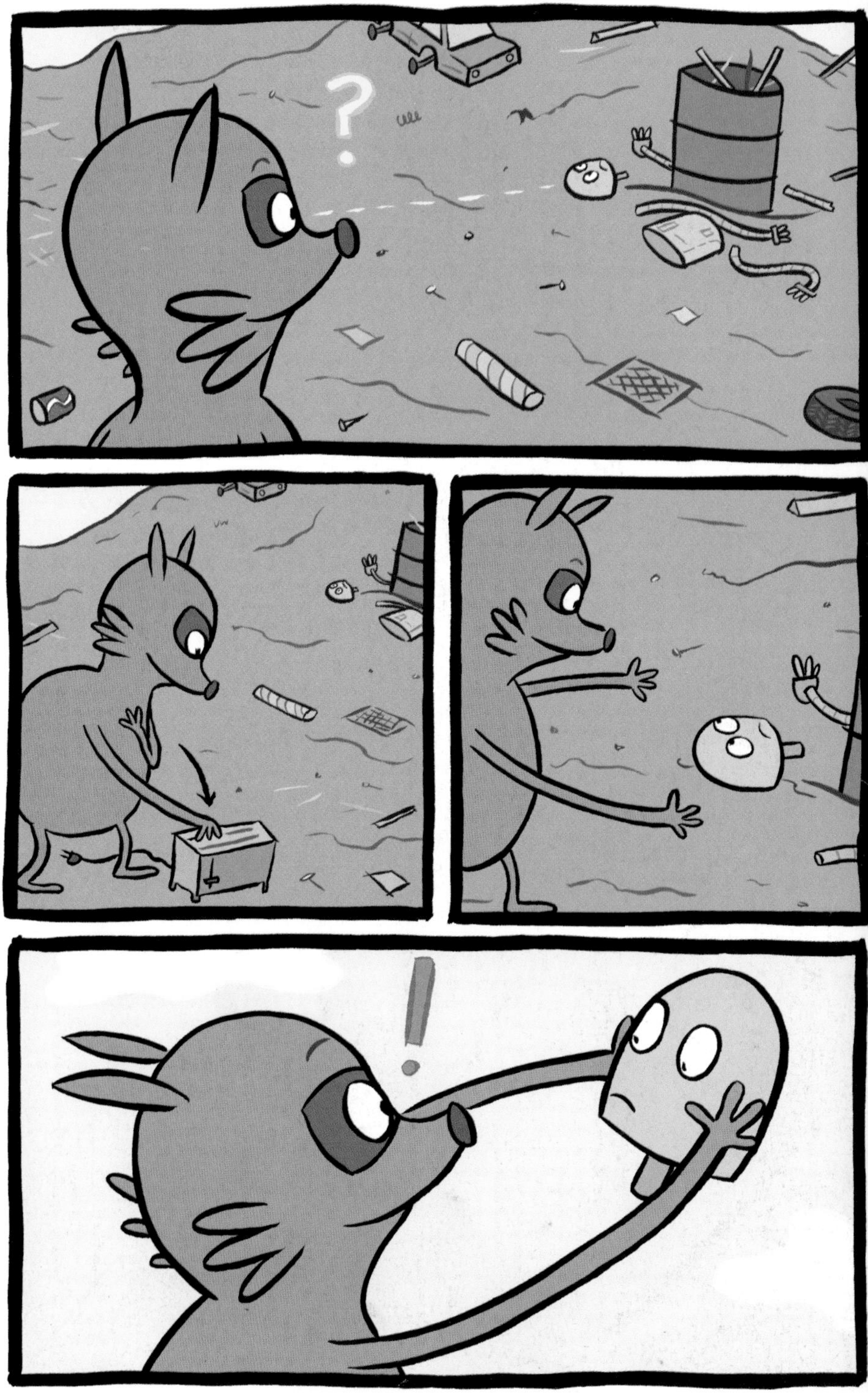
?
!

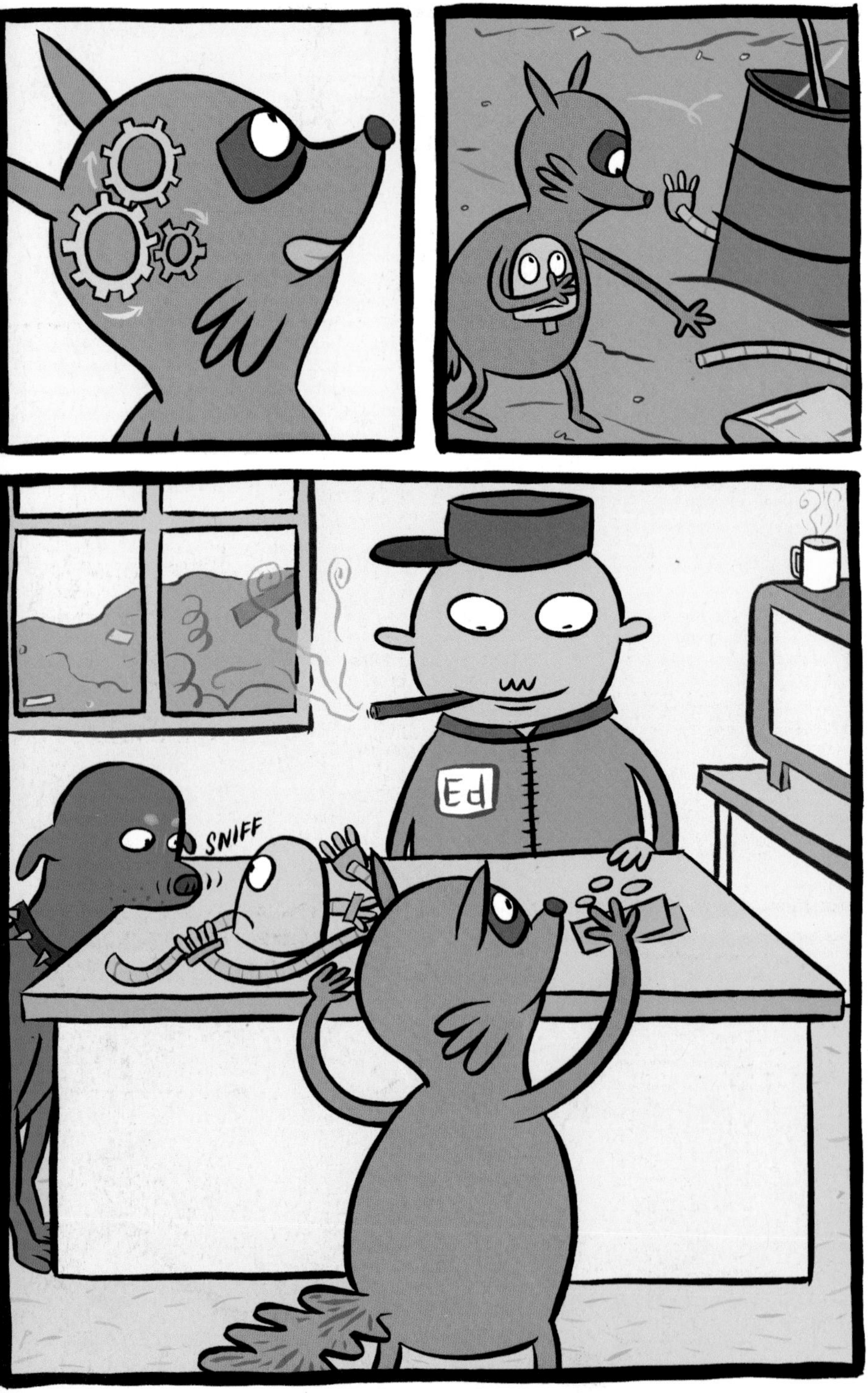

Ed
SNIFF

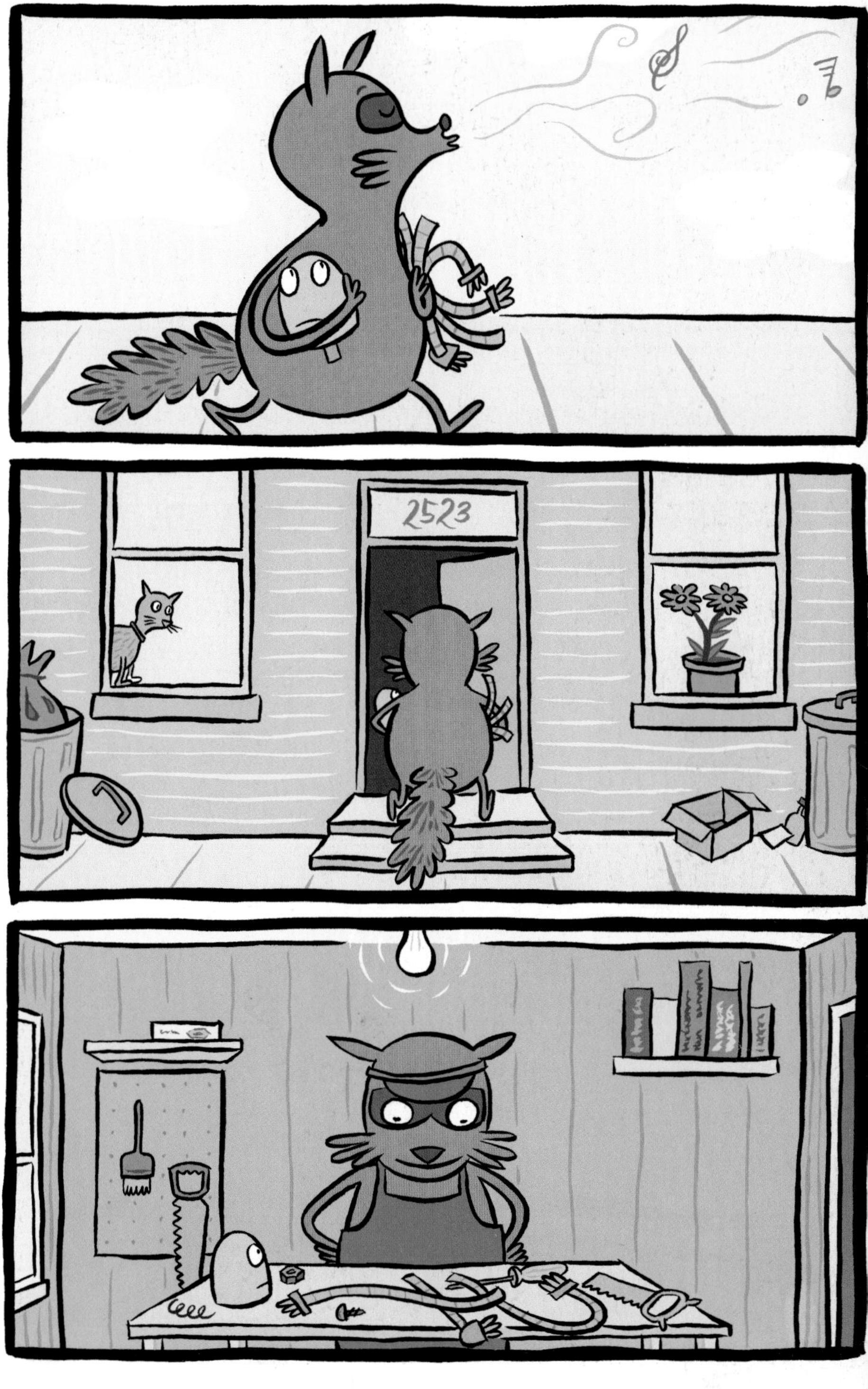
2523

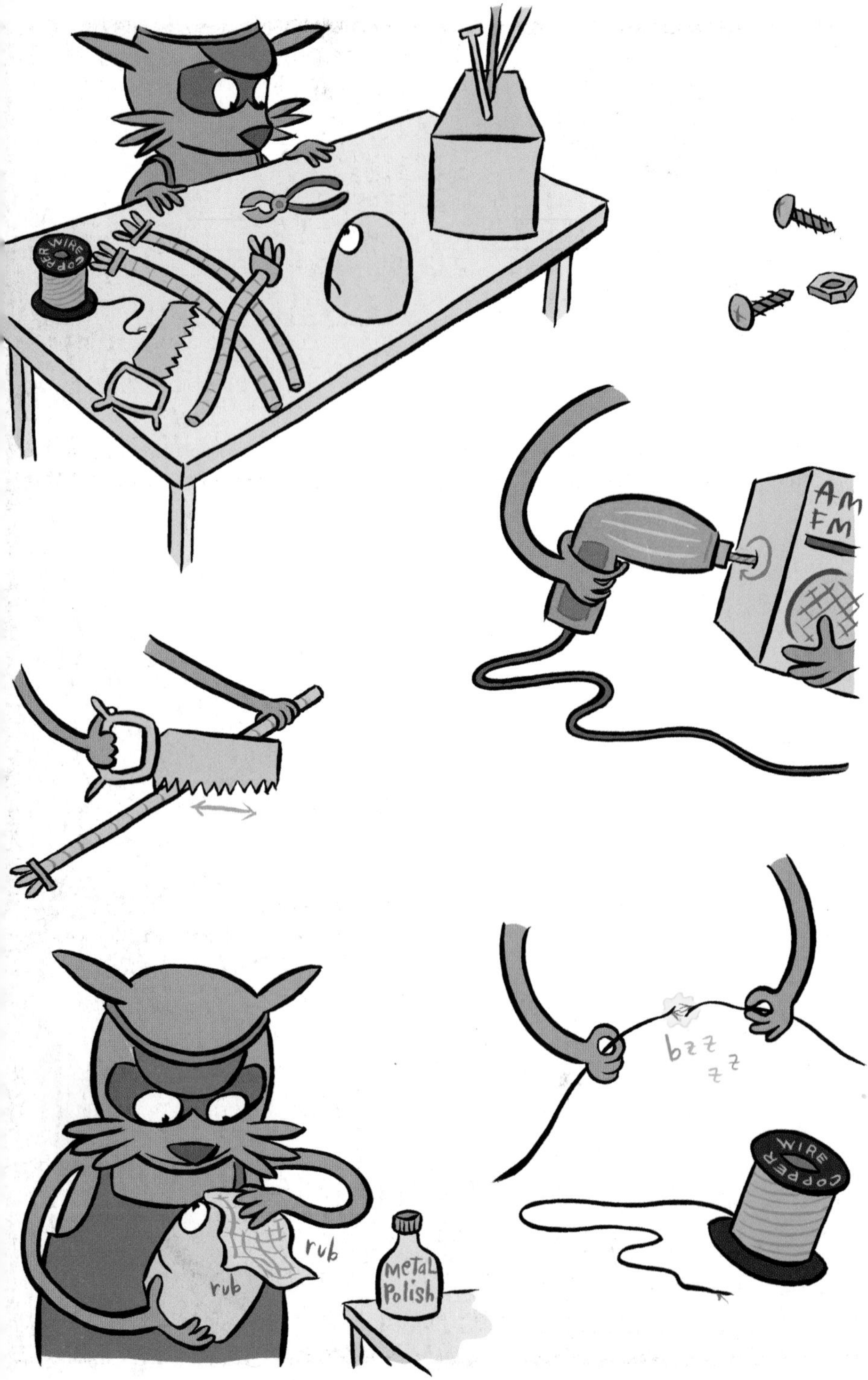

COPPER WIRE
AM FM
rub
rub
Metal Polish
bzz z z
WIRE COPPER

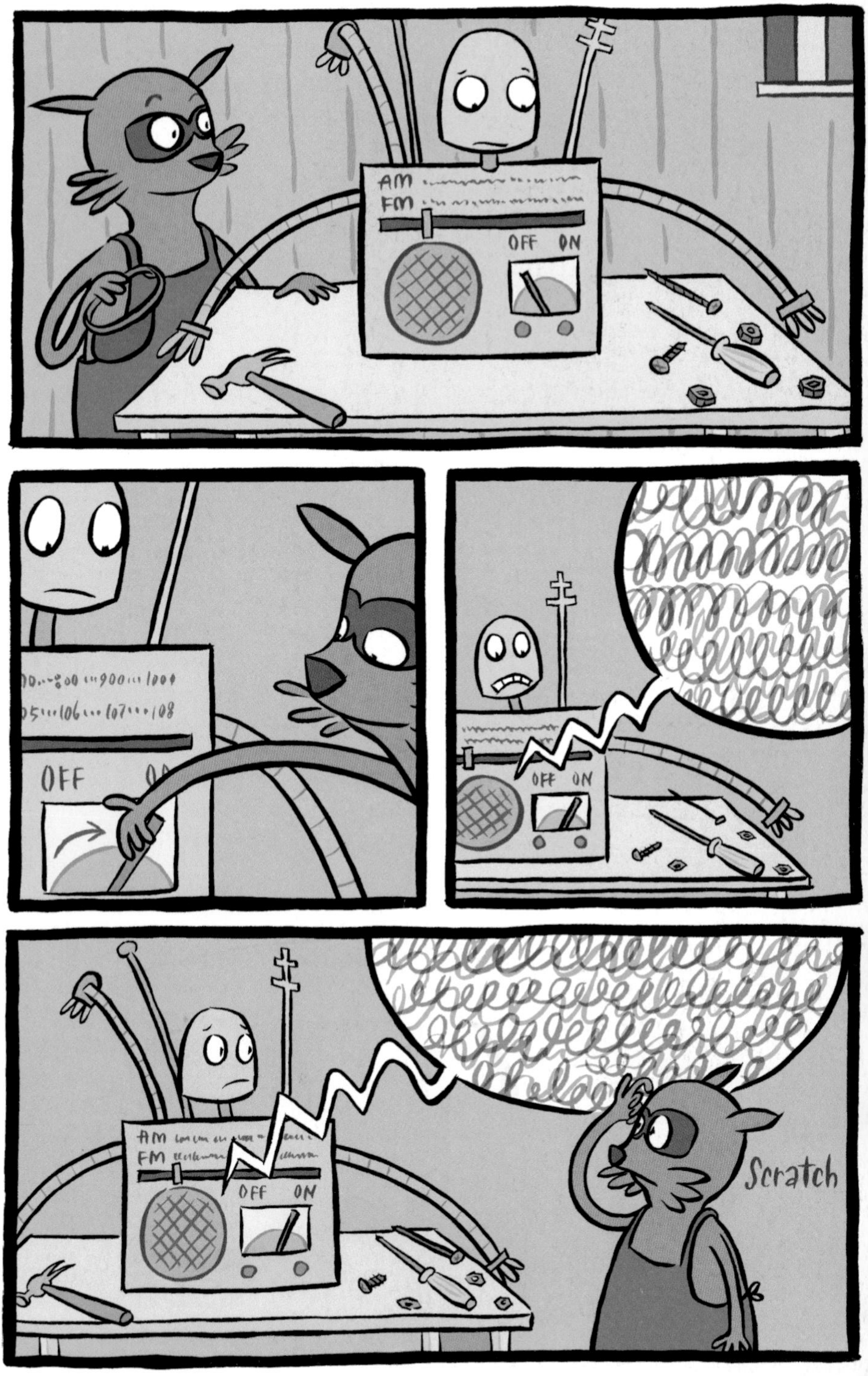

AM
FM
OFF ON
OFF
Scratch

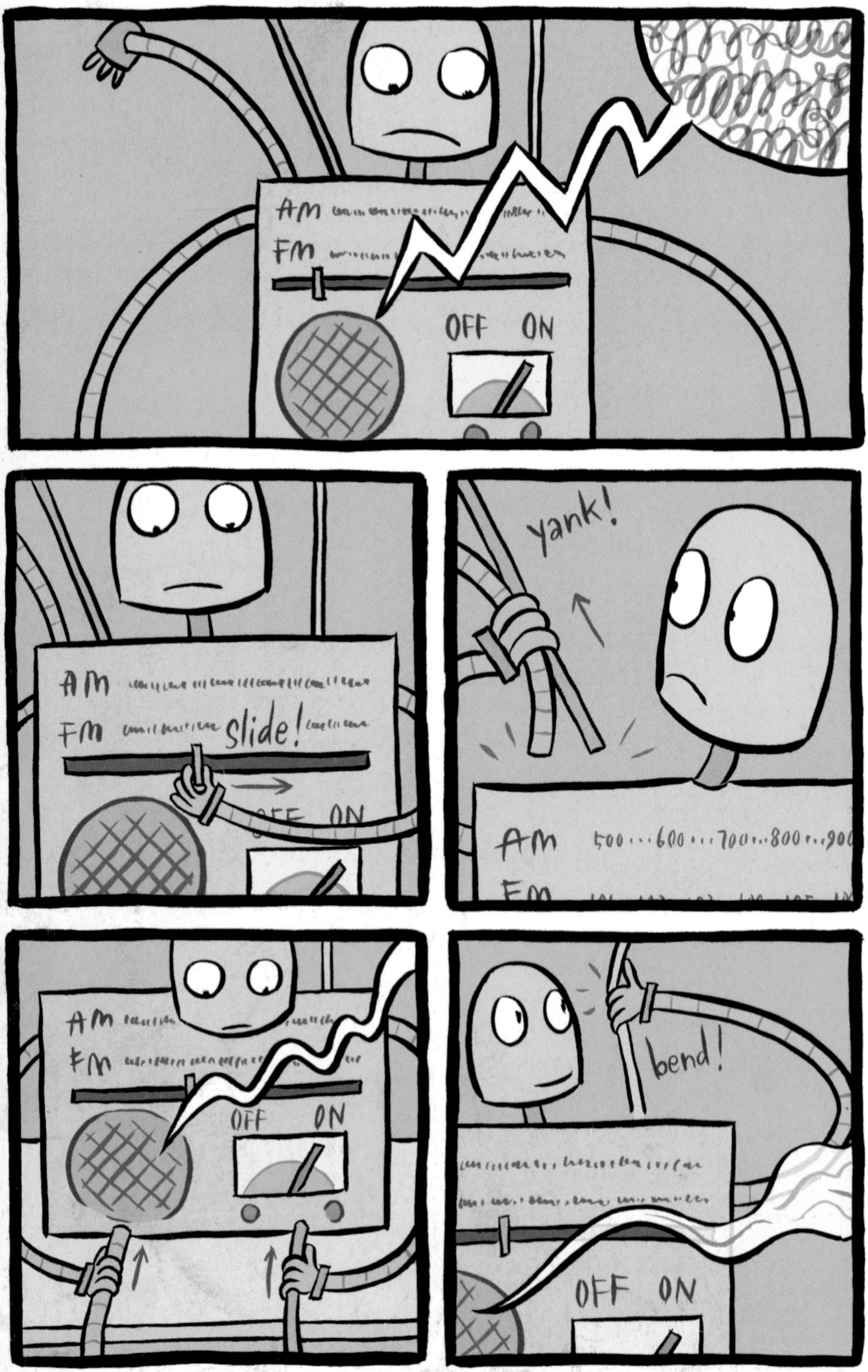
AM
FM
OFF ON
slide!
yank!
AM 500...600...700...800...900
bend!

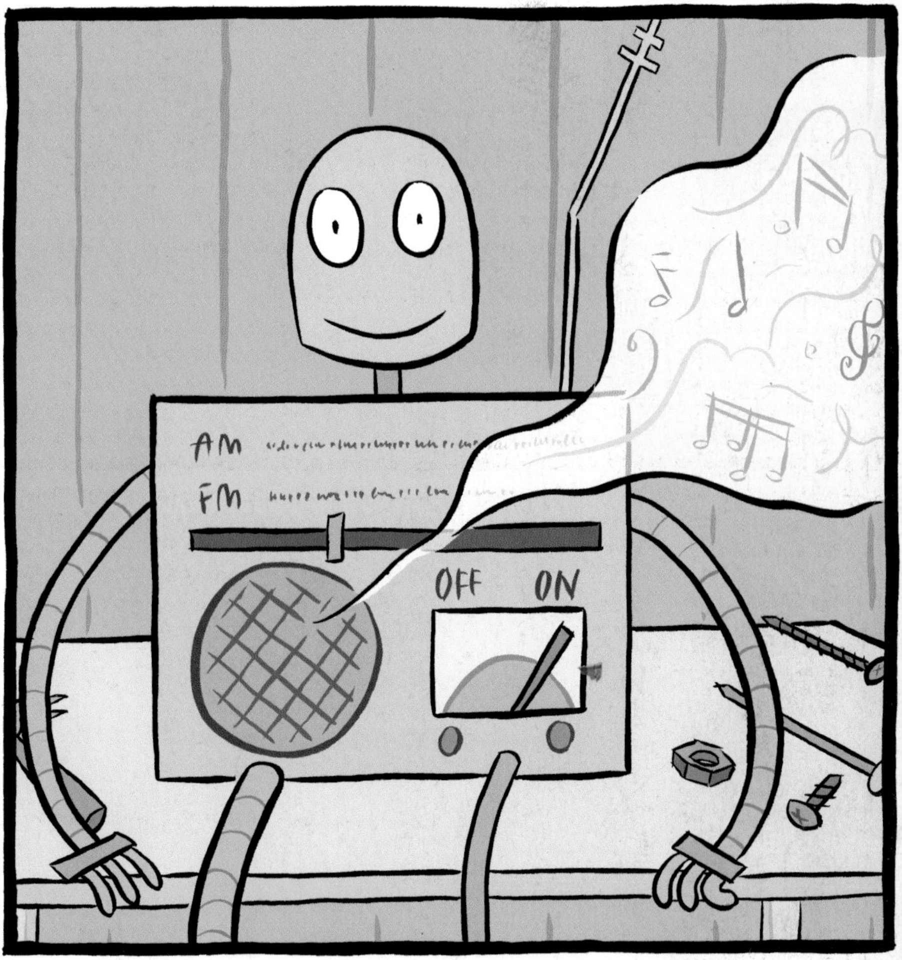
AM
FM
OFF
ON

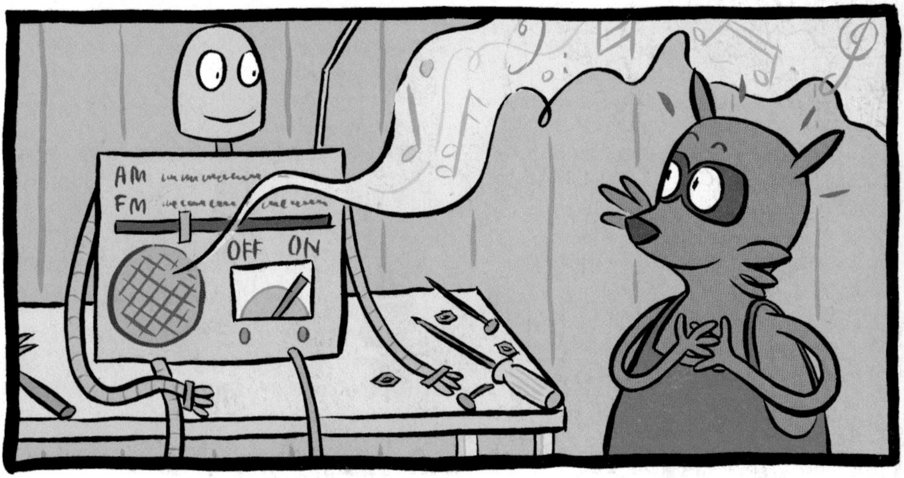
AM
FM
OFF
ON

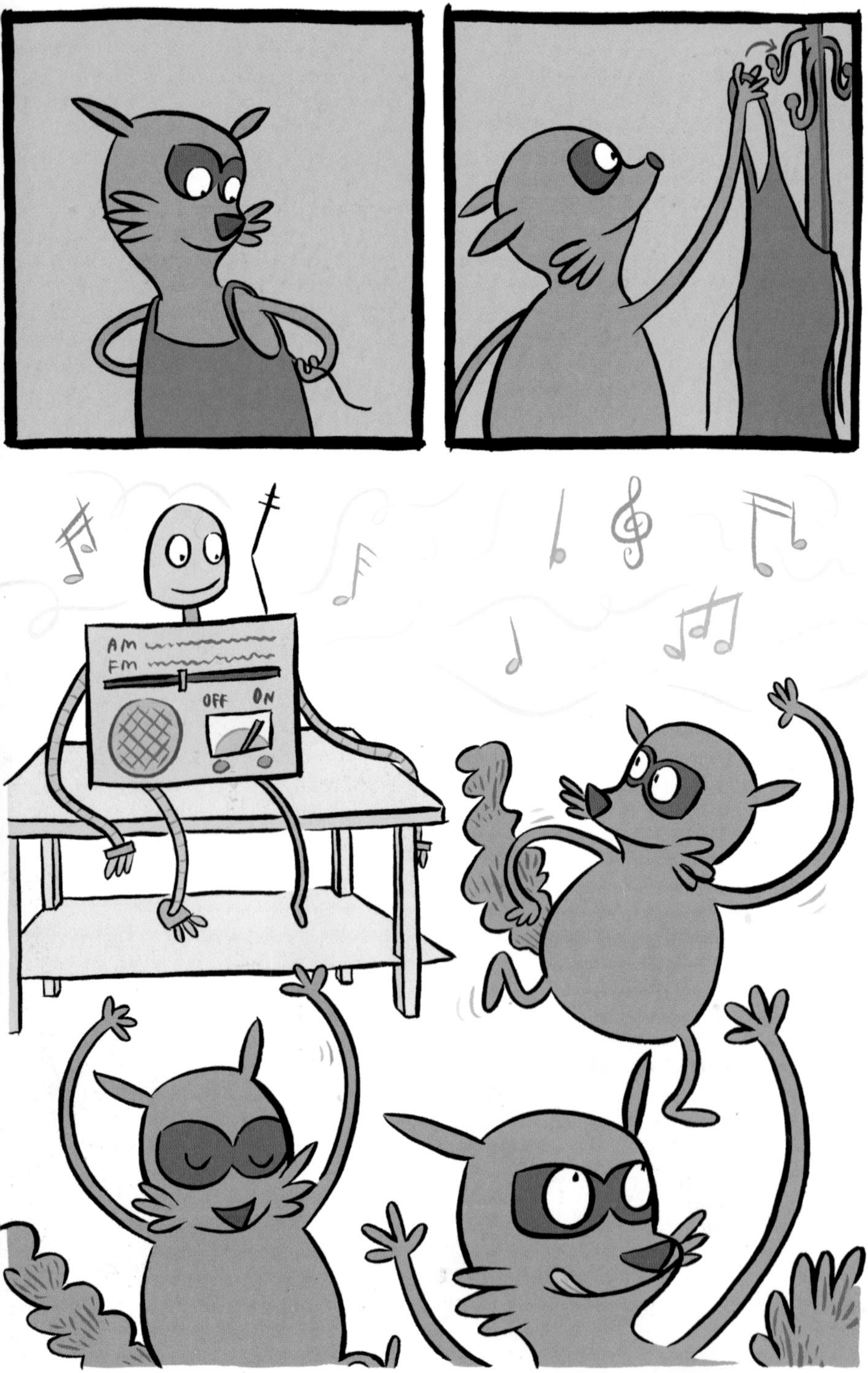
AM
FM
OFF
ON

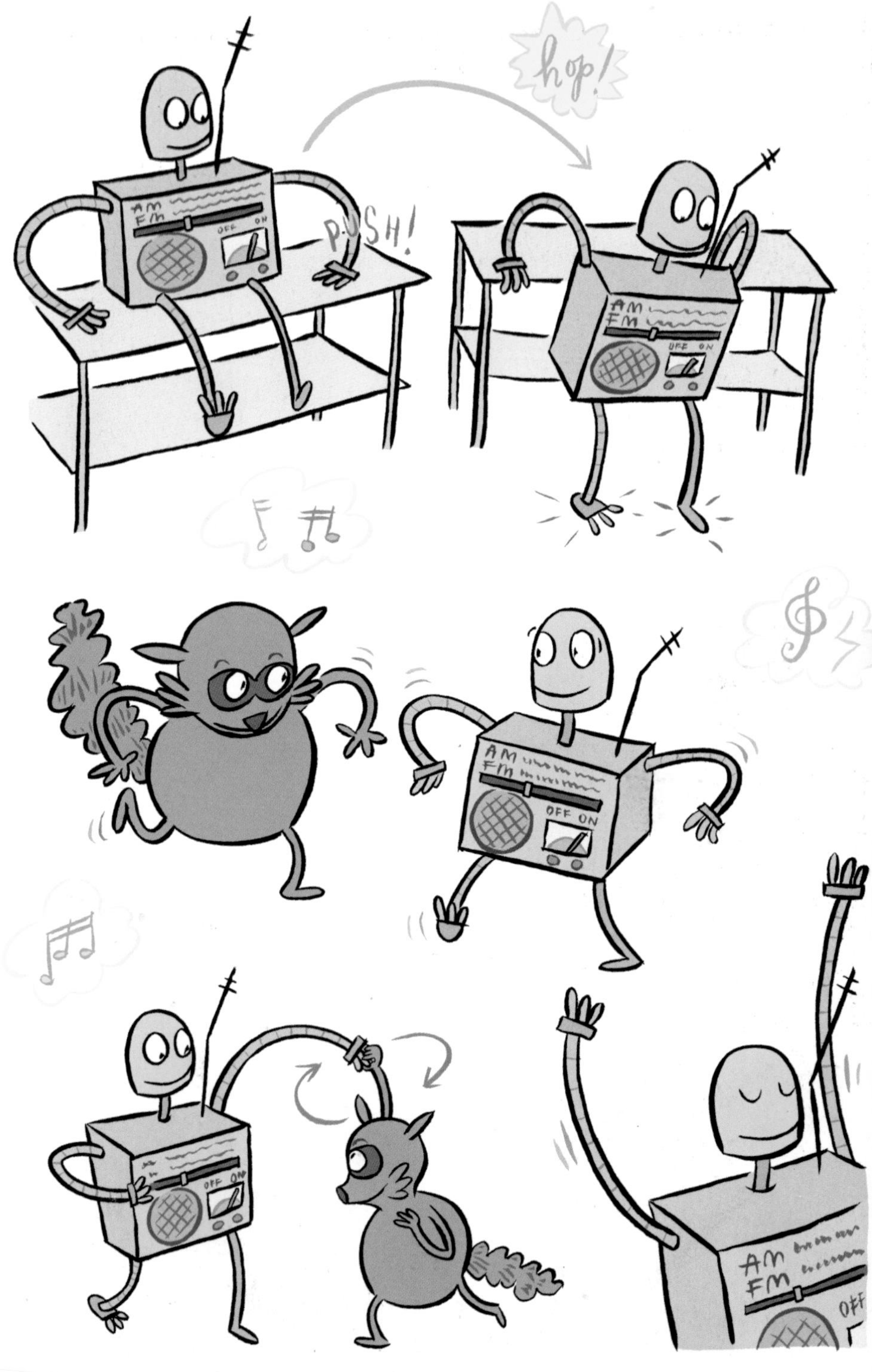

hop!
PUSH!
AM
FM
OFF ON

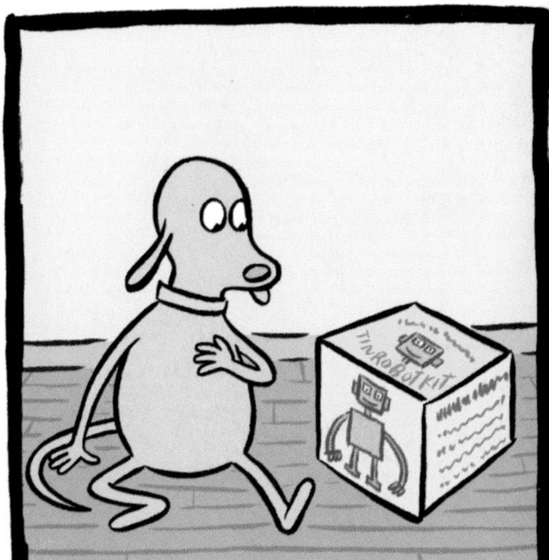
TINROBOTKIT

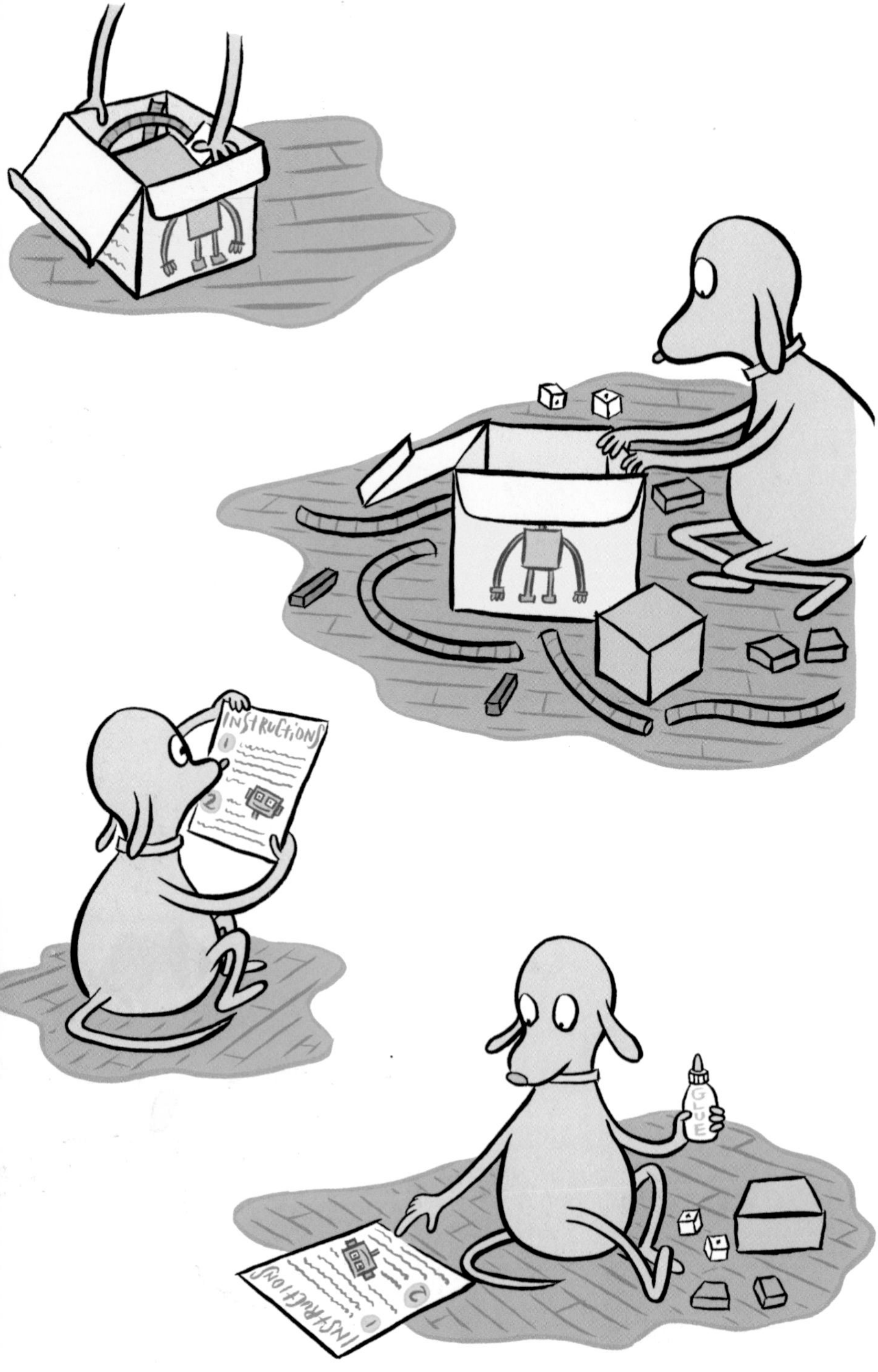
INSTRUCTIONS
GLUE
INSTRUCTIONS

GLUE
100% COTTON

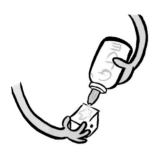

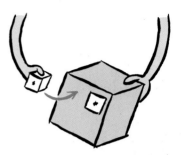

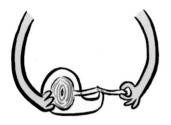

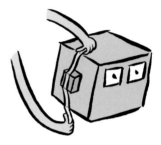

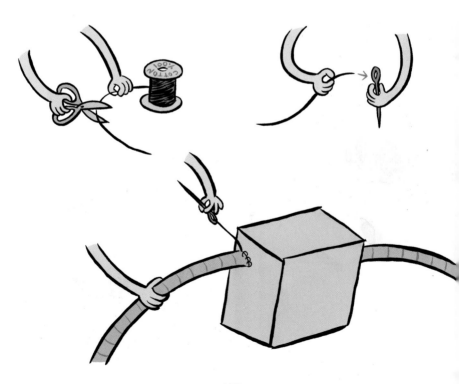

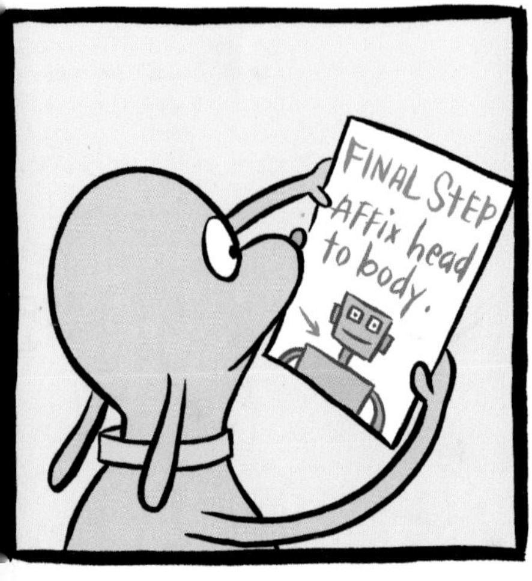
FINAL STEP
AFFix head to body.

August

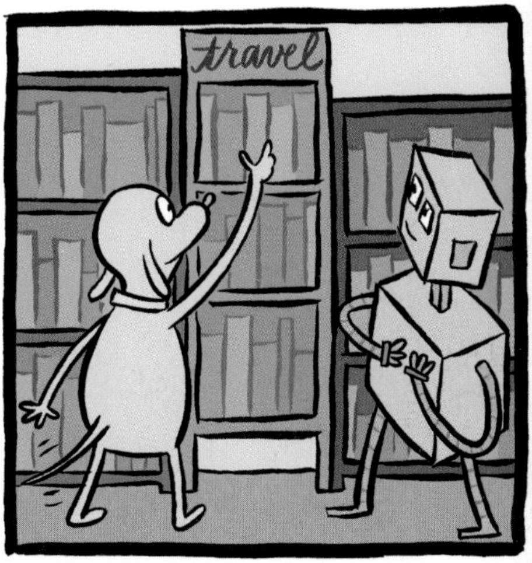
travel

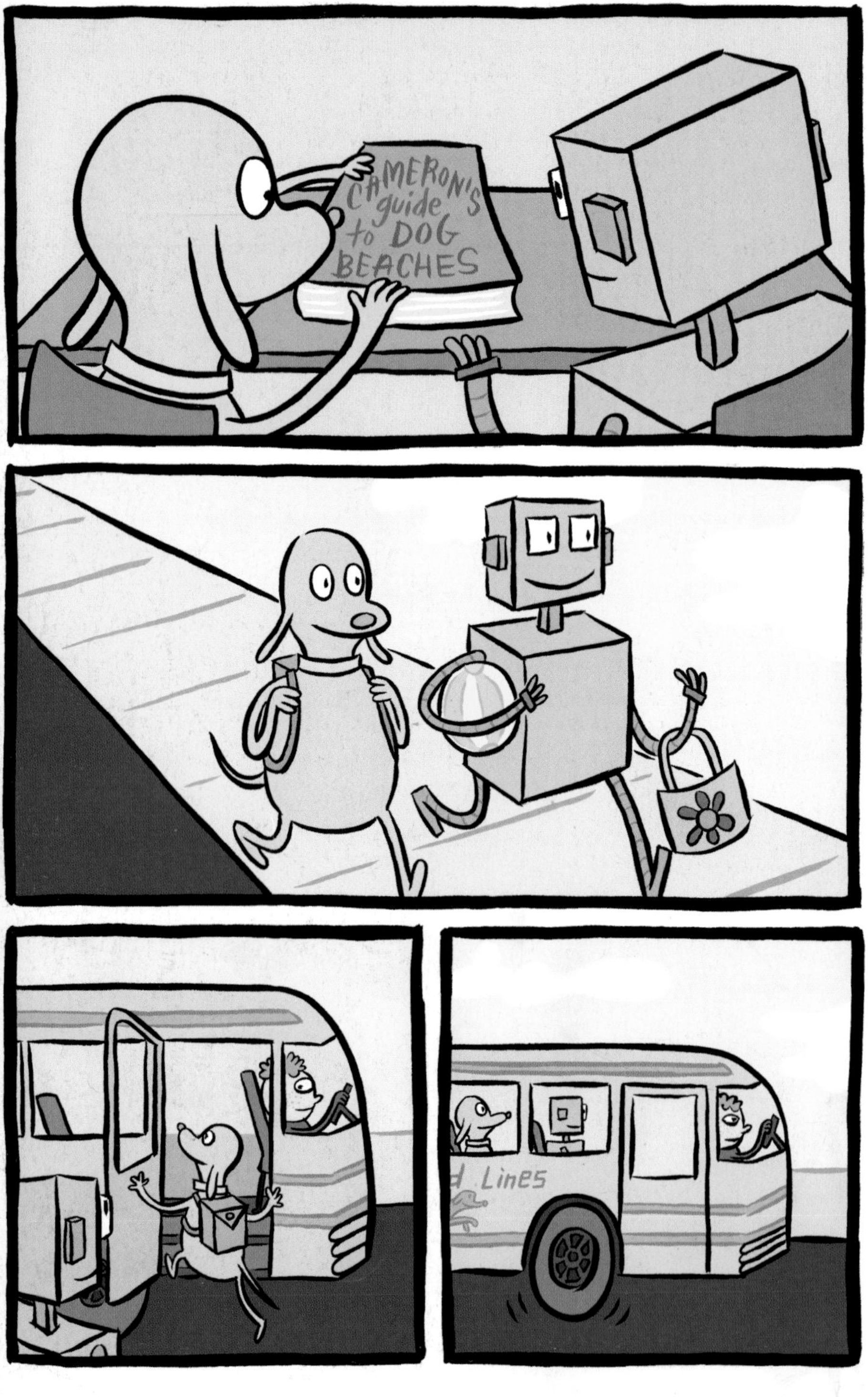
CAMERON'S guide to DOG BEACHES
d Lines

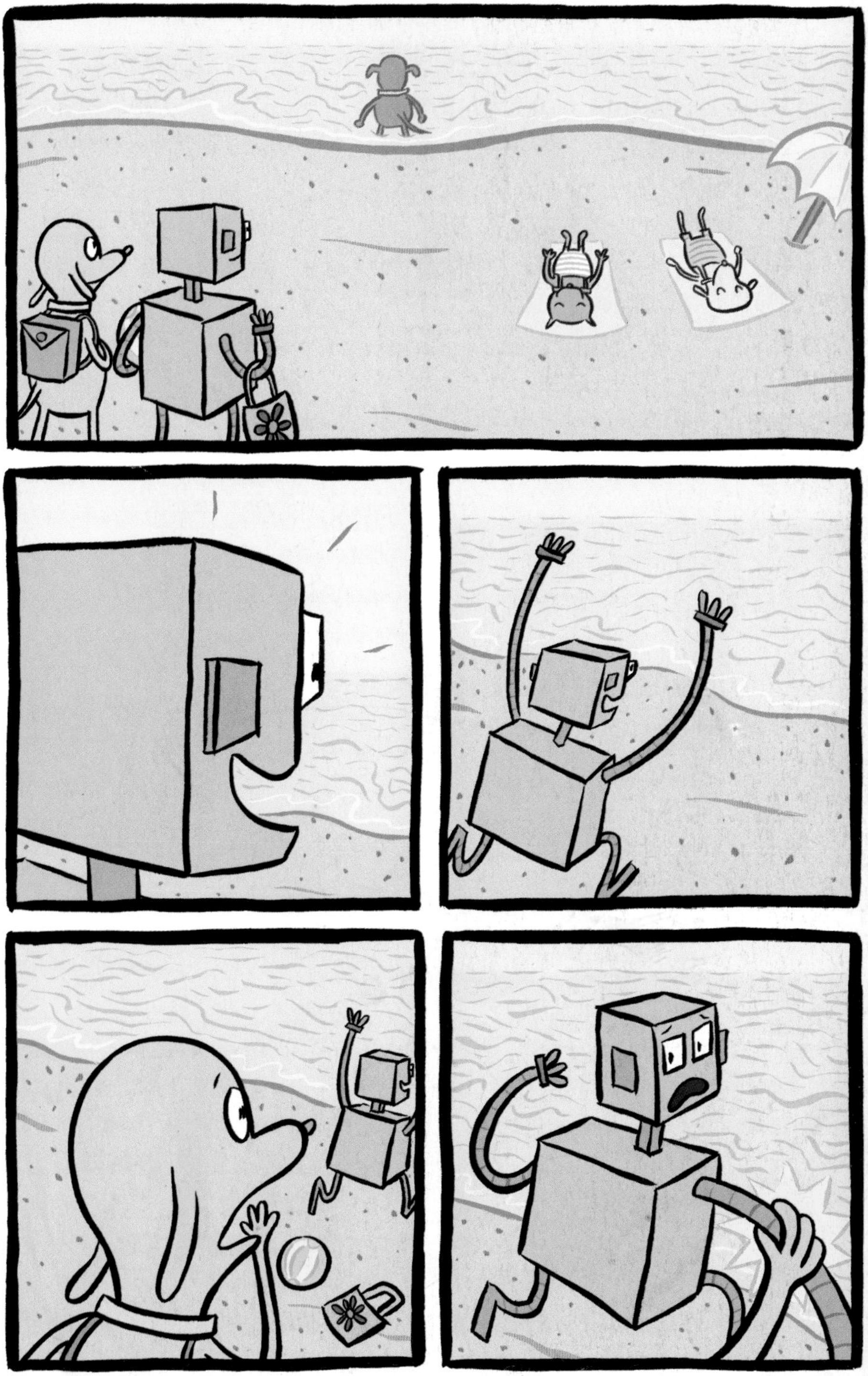

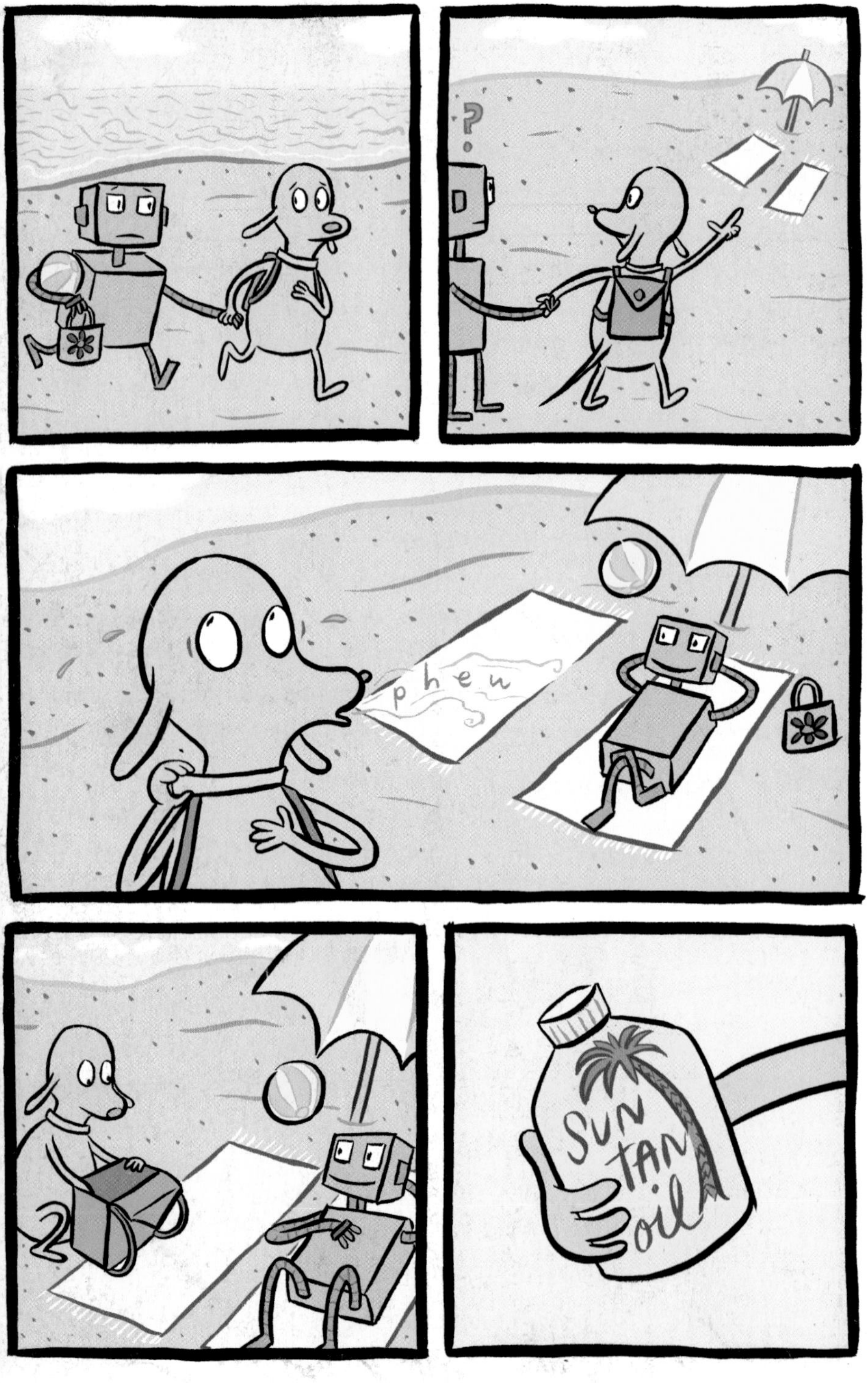
?
phew
SUN TAN oil

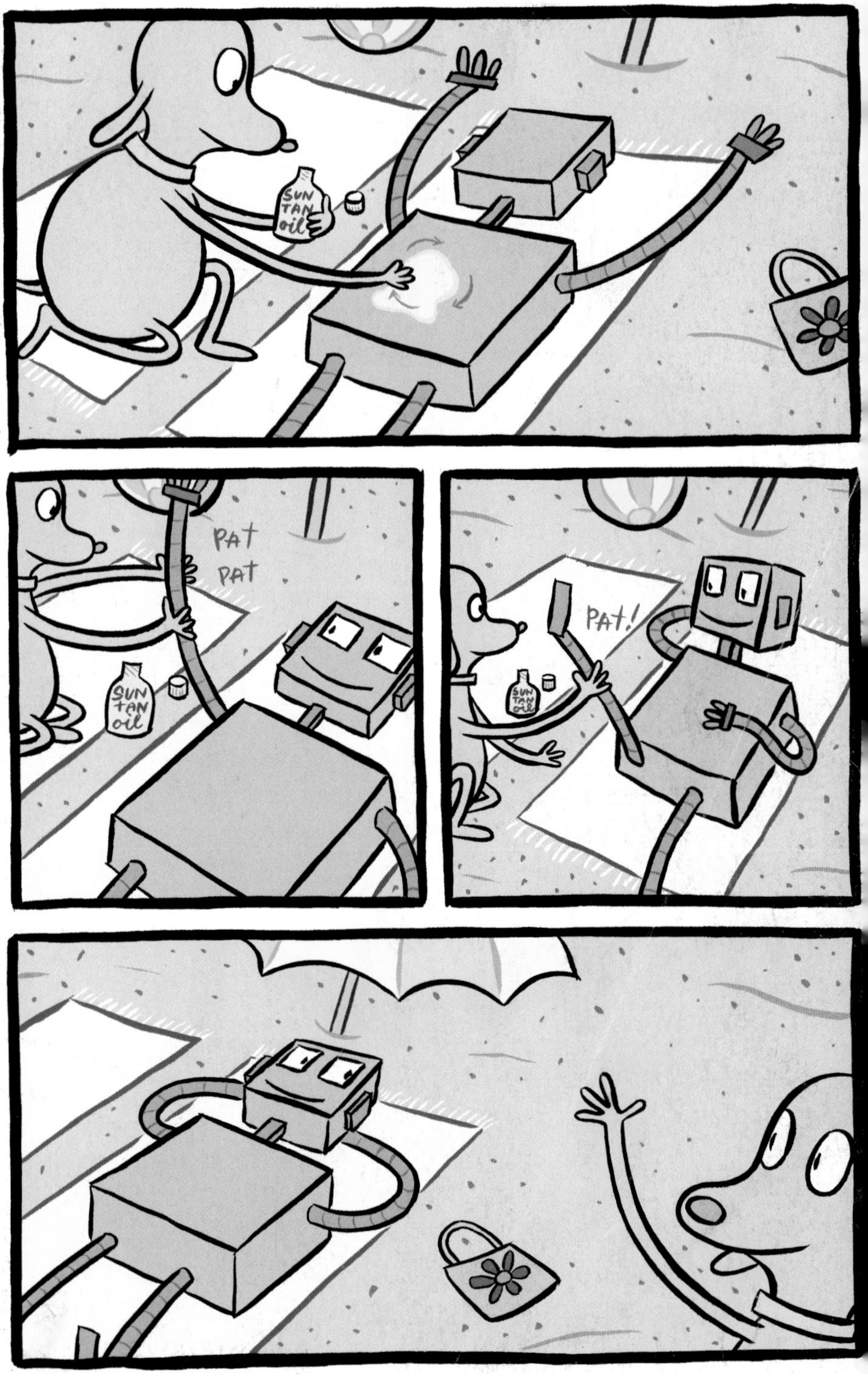
SUN TAN oil
PAT
PAT
SUN TAN oil
PAT!
SUN TAN oil

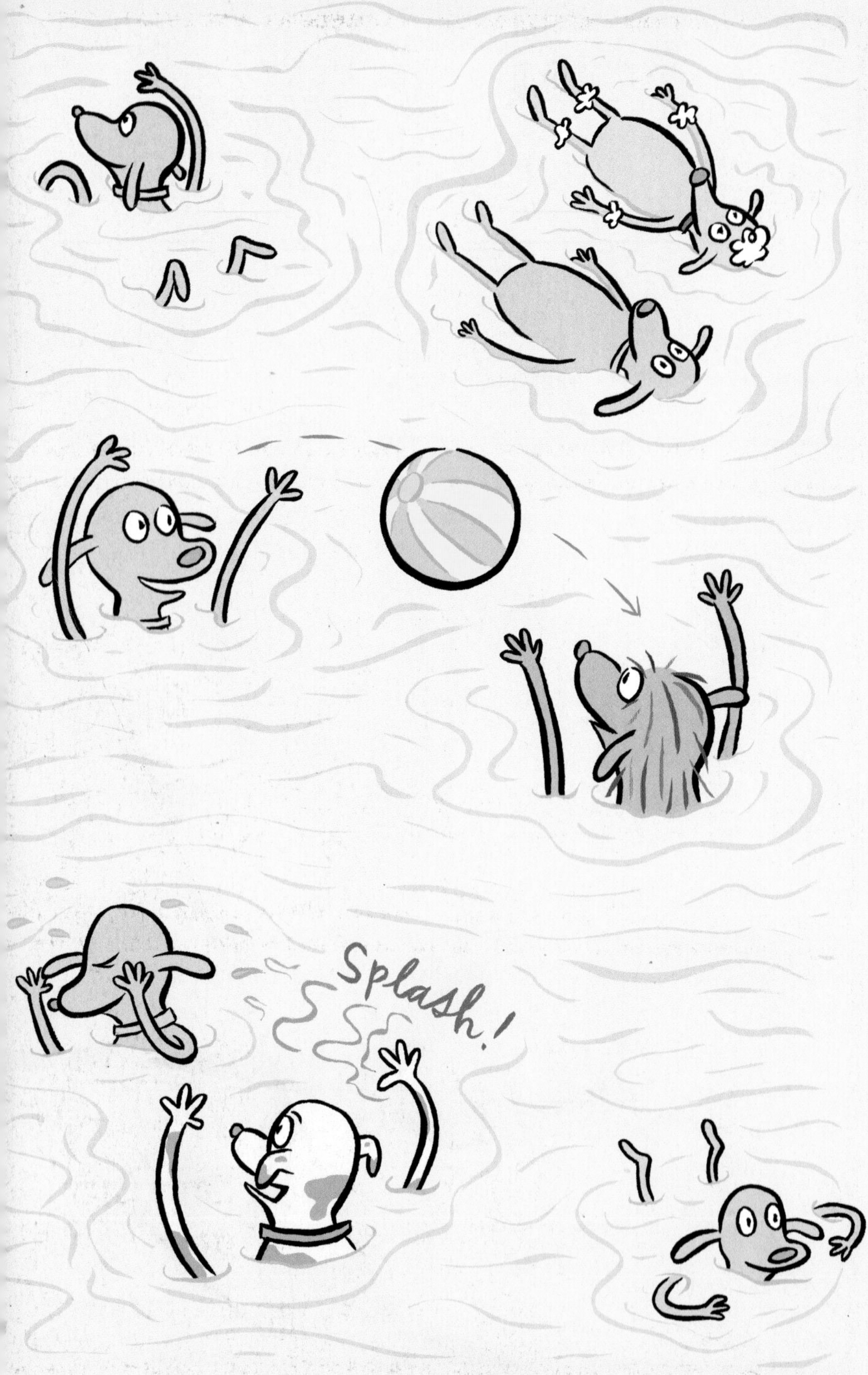
Splash!

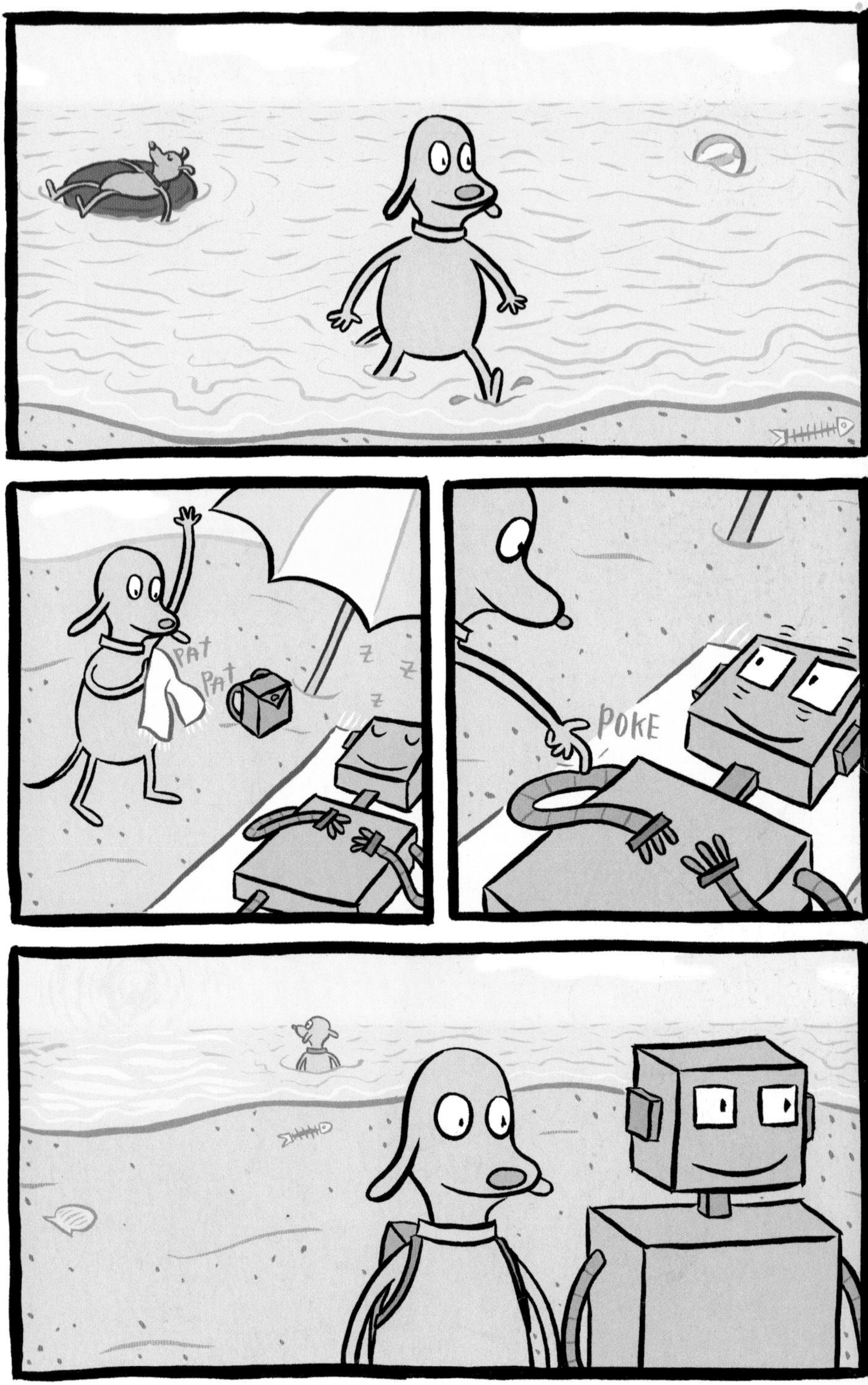
PAT
PAT
Z
Z
Z
POKE

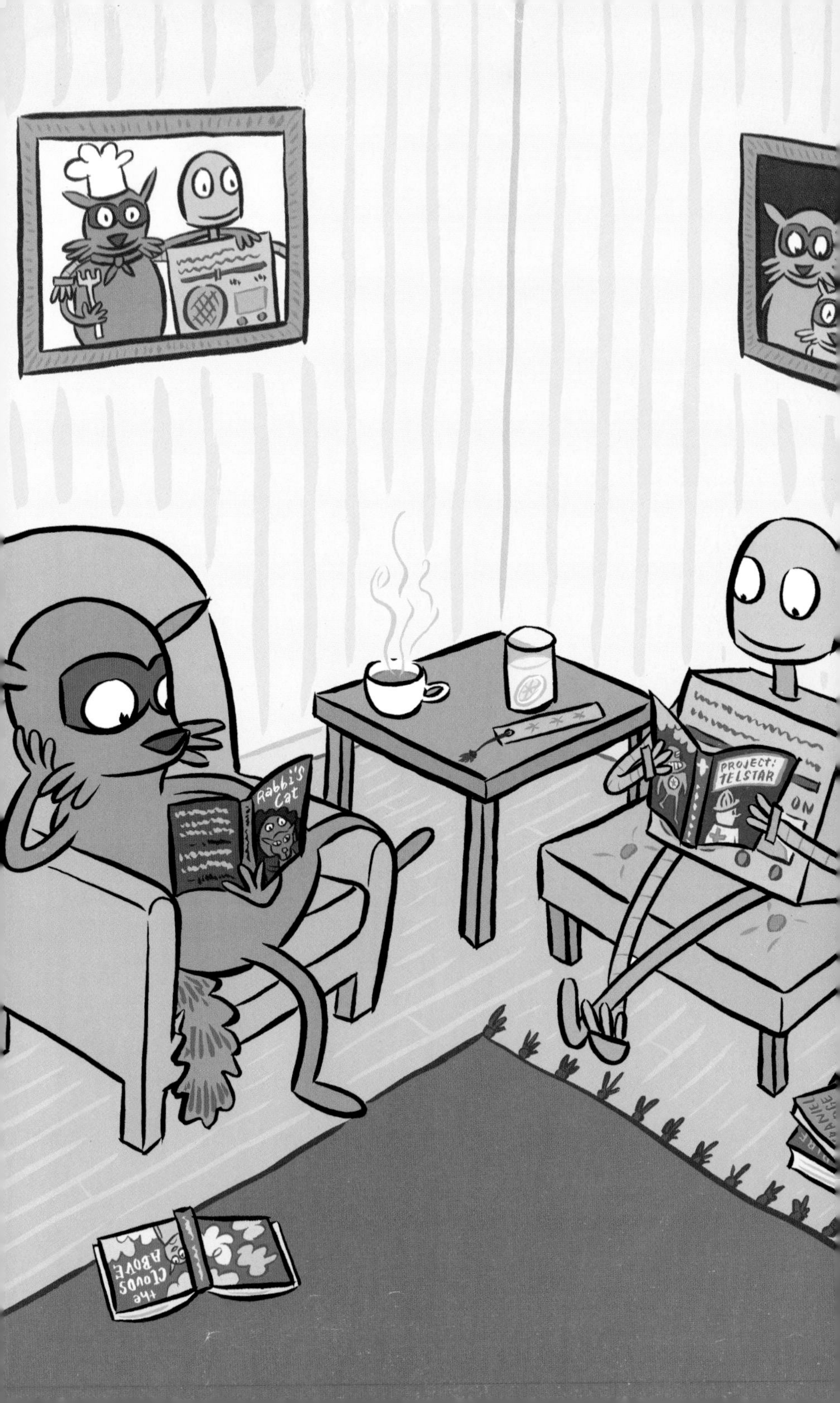

Rabbi's Cat
PROJECT: TELSTAR
ON
the CLOUDS ABOVE

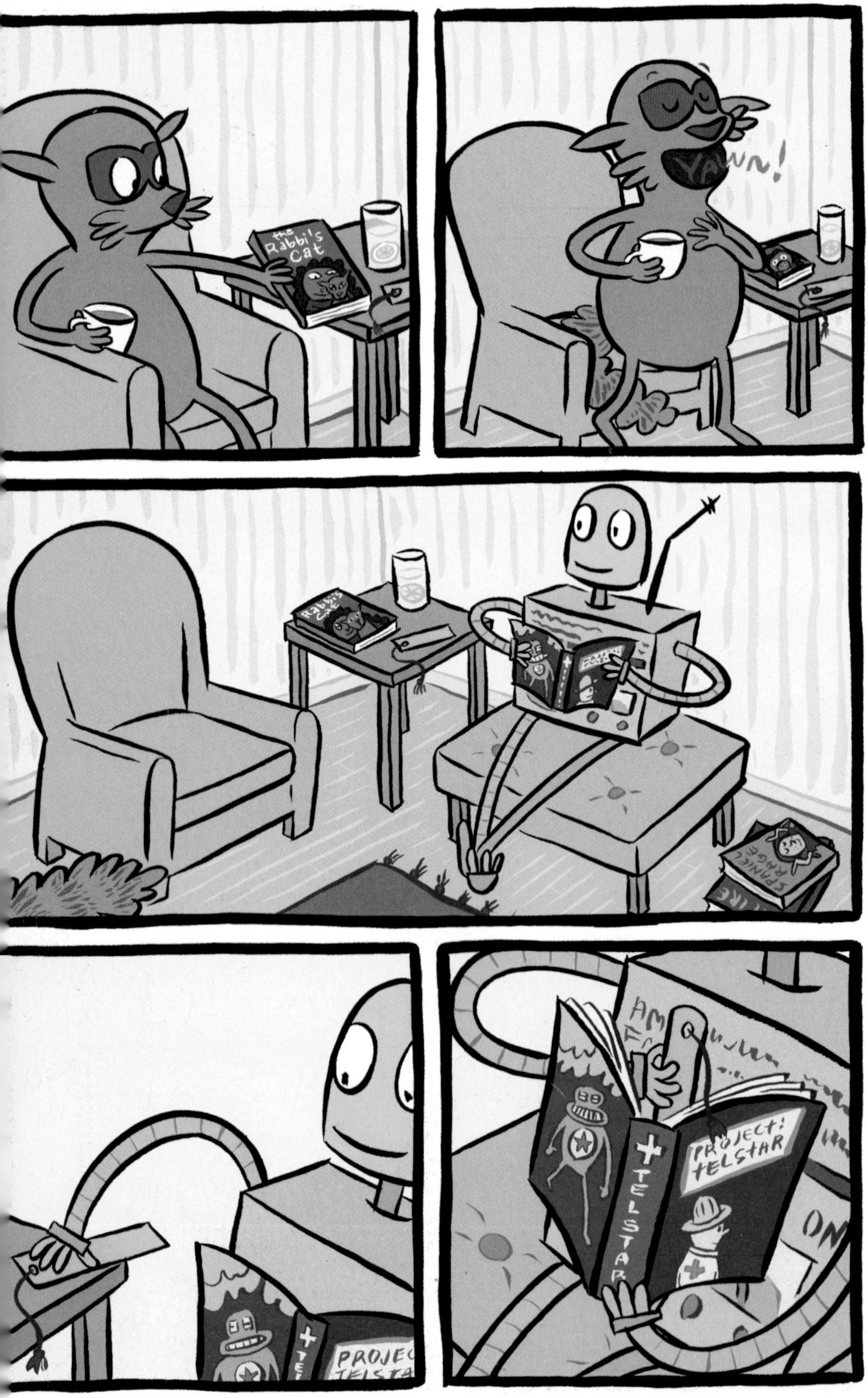
the Rabbi's Cat
YAWN!
Rabbi's Cat
SPANIEL RAGE
PROJEC
PROJECT! TELSTAR
TELSTAR

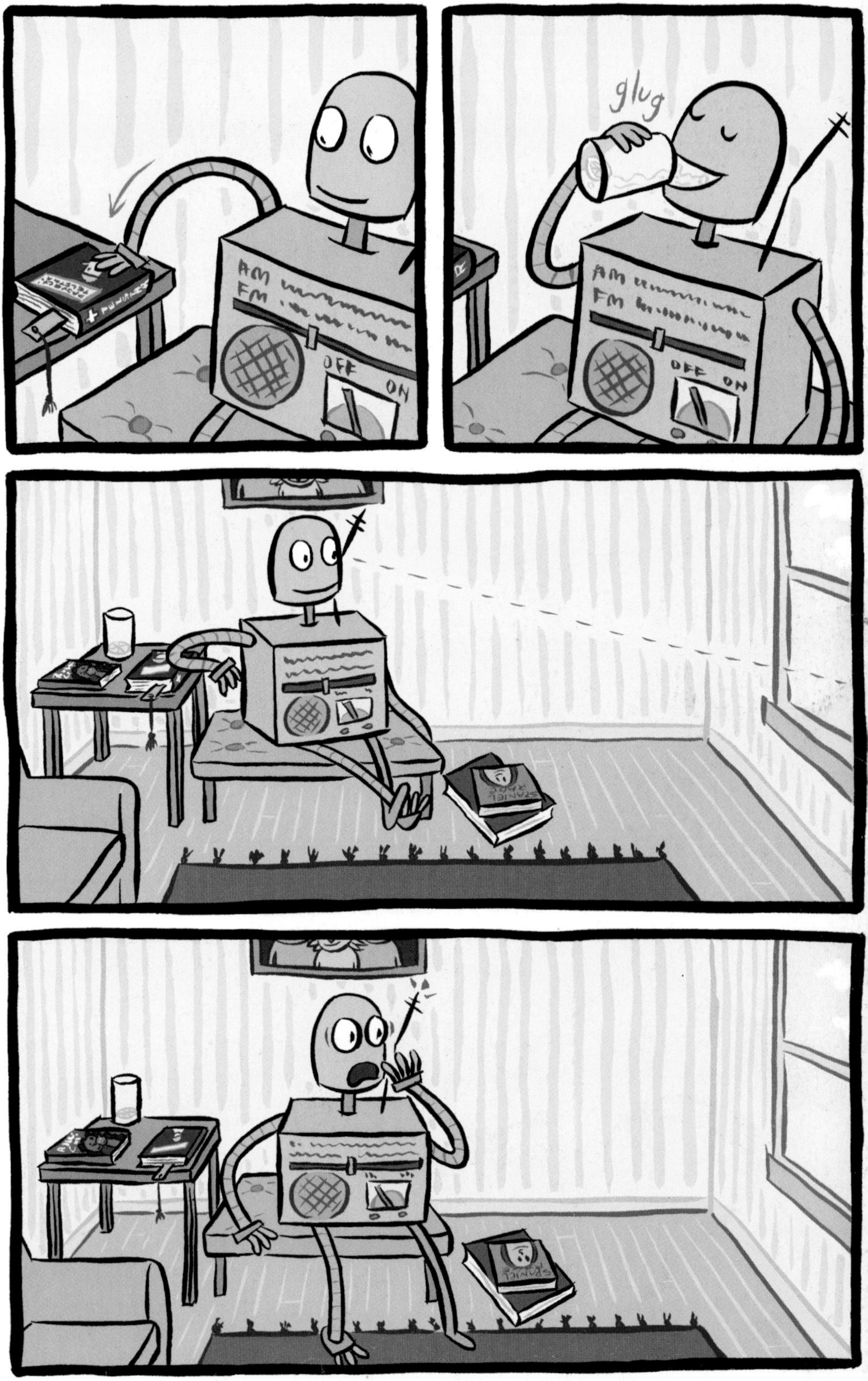
AM
FM
OFF
ON
glug
AM
FM
OFF
ON

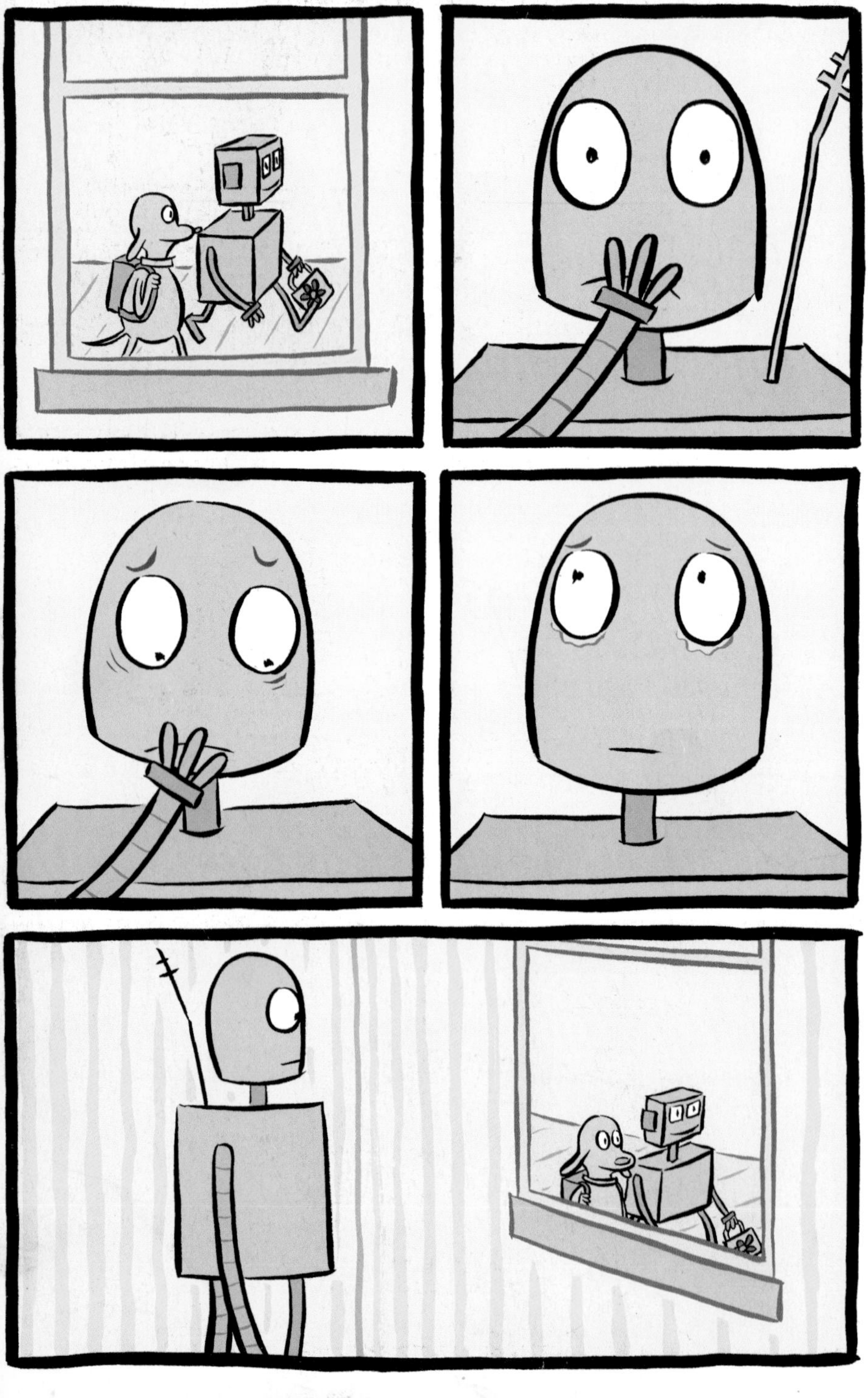

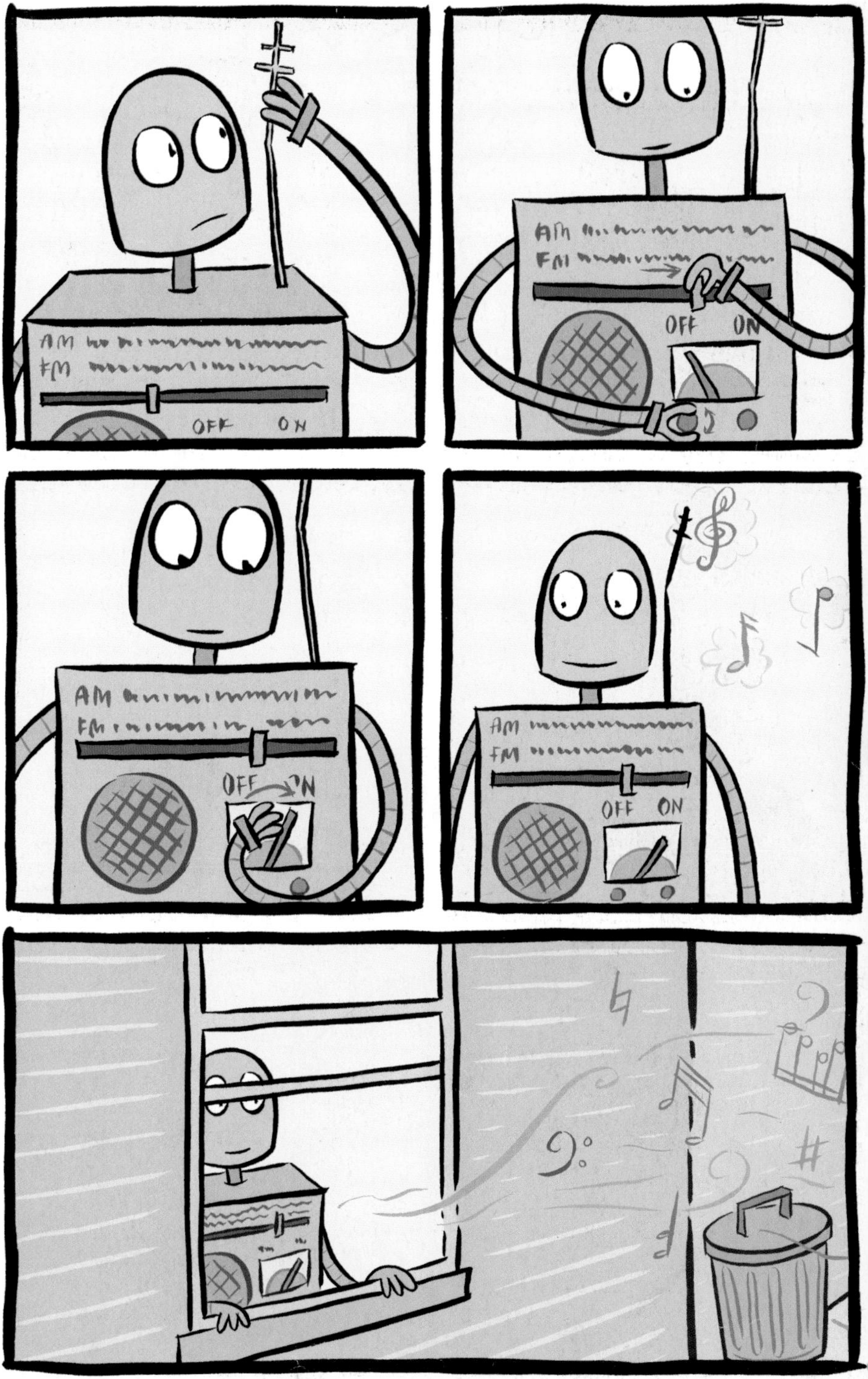
AM
FM
OFF
ON
AM
FM
OFF
ON
AM
FM
OFF
ON
AM
FM
OFF
ON